D0752149

Pursuit

To: Maura & Rob

The Truth will set us free!

David Soares (signature)

Jn 8:32

Other books by
Ward Tanneberg

September Strike
October's Child

Pursuit

WARD TANNEBERG

VICTOR BOOKS

A DIVISION OF SCRIPTURE PRESS PUBLICATIONS INC.
USA CANADA ENGLAND

Editing: Carole Streeter, Barbara Williams
Cover Design: Scott Rattray

Library of Congress Cataloging-in-Publication Data

Tanneberg, Ward M.
    Pursuit / Ward Tanneberg
      p. cm.
    ISBN 1-56476-584-9
    I. Title.
    PS3570.A535P87 1996
    813'.54—dc20   96-20289
                                    CIP

© 1996 by Ward Tanneberg. All rights reserved. Printed in the United States of America.

1 2 3 4 5 6 7 8 9 10 Printing/Year 00 99 98 97 96

This book is a work of fiction. Names, characters, places, and incidents are either the product of the author's imagination or are used fictitiously. Any resemblance to actual events, locales, or persons living or dead, is coincidental.

No part of this book may be reproduced without written permission, except for brief quotations in books and critical reviews. For information, write Victor Books, 1825 College Avenue, Wheaton, Illinois 60187.

This One
Is Dedicated to
Four Special Children
Michele and Tony
Stephen and Nancy

Acknowledgments

There are many people who contribute to a book. I'm always amazed and grateful for their ready contributions and assistance in research and resource materials. My unqualified thanks goes to:

Mehlika Seval, who served as guide and educator through my journeys in the wonderful land of Turkey. She brought me greater understanding of customs, history, and religion in the land of her birth, helping me see that country and its people in a way that has forever enriched my life.

Ken Moore, for his help in providing useful resource materials.

Jan Kinzel, Gretchen Kinzel, and Linda Lenz, who volunteered their time as manuscript readers.

Lisa Wooldridge Norton who, with her brothers and twin sister, grew up in our church. She has added her expertise to this story as a graphic artist to help us better see the truth in fiction.

Carole Streeter, whose copy editing skills make the rough places smooth and bless both writer and reader in the process.

Greg Clouse, Editorial Director at Victor, who has once again disproved the thesis that editors are heartless assassins of the soul of a book. Thanks, Greg, and everyone at Victor Books, for all that you do.

My special thanks to Dixie, who sent me off to Turkey in the first place. And not just to get rid of me. She knew I was in pursuit of a story there. Her insights, suggestions, criticisms, and constant encouragement are more than anyone could ask. Her advocacy of this minister/writer/husband's fascination with the "power of story" to teach and inspire is her greatest gift of all. She has taught me to let words become the artist's colors, applying them carefully until the picture appears.

Last, but certainly not least, my thanks to a small but intrepid band of hardy souls who, along with me somewhere deep in the Taurus Mountains, had nothing better to do one day than listen to me tell this story for the first time.

WT

Cast of Key Characters

In California

Kristian Lauring, television personality and son of Pedar and Sarah

Katrina Lauring, teacher and daughter of Pedar and Sarah

Rev. Pedar Lauring, pastor of a small church in Baytown

Sarah Lauring, Pedar's wife

Tom Knight, director, television talk show

Carole Upton, assistant director, television talk show

In Turkey

Dr. Ibrahim Mustapha Sevali, archaeologist and professor, University of Istanbul

Dr. Bülent Üzünal, archaeologist and assistant director, Anatolian Civilizations Museum in Ankara

Rocco Valetti, foreman at *Kilçilar*

Benjamin Hurstein (Ben Hur), foreman at *Kilçilar*

Çali, driver and gofer at *Kilçilar*

Tahsin Cem, architect at *Kilçilar*

Dr. Gürer El, epigraphist at *Kilçilar*

Ian and Dorothy Hedley, missionary educators

Michelle de Mené, a teacher

İlhan, a shepherd

Rabbi Mordechai Nowitsky, chairman, Interfaith Commission on the *Kilçilar Letters*

Kilçilar, a mysterious underground city in Cappadocia

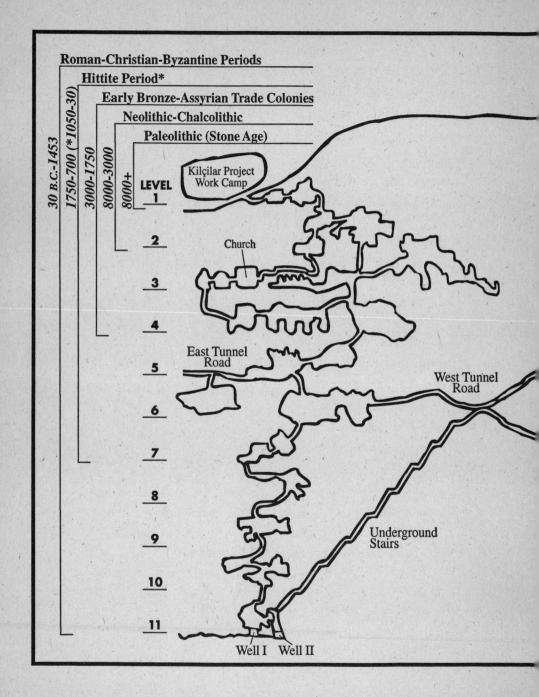

Roman-Christian-Byzantine Periods

Hittite Period*

Early Bronze-Assyrian Trade Colonies

Neolithic-Chalcolithic

Paleolithic (Stone Age)

30 B.C.-1453

*1750-700 (*1050-30)*

3000-1750

8000-3000

8000+

Kilçilar Project Work Camp

LEVEL
1

2

Church

3

4

East Tunnel Road

5

West Tunnel Road

6

7

8

9

Underground Stairs

10

11

Well I   Well II

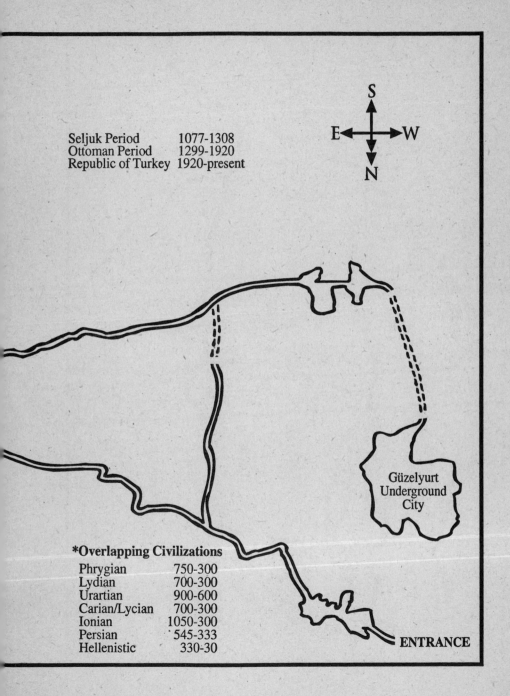

Seljuk Period   1077-1308
Ottoman Period   1299-1920
Republic of Turkey   1920-present

S
E — W
N

Güzelyurt
Underground
City

*Overlapping Civilizations
Phrygian   750-300
Lydian   700-300
Urartian   900-600
Carian/Lycian   700-300
Ionian   1050-300
Persian   545-333
Hellenistic   330-30

ENTRANCE

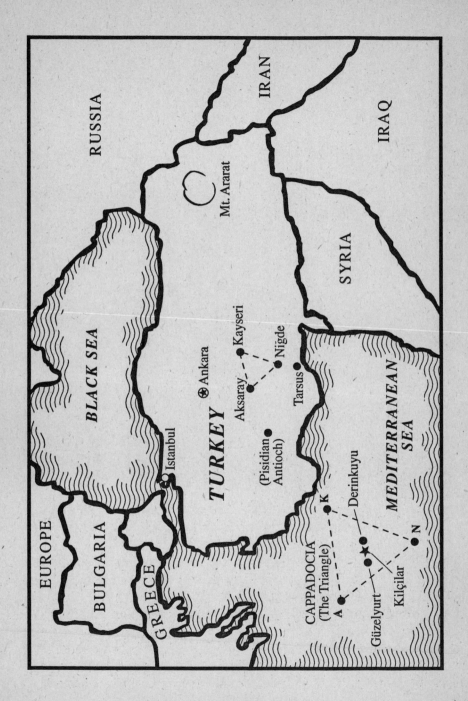

Prologue

There are so many things that I'm still at a loss to figure.

The restlessness.

The need to succeed.

The endless chasing after.

What keeps fueling my engines anyway? Am I every baby-boomer's nightmare? Or am I the only one who's really losing sleep over the Questions?

For a long while, I kept telling myself, "Kris, life will work itself out if you just get clear of the Lauring family upbringing." That's been my big priority for a long time. Easier said than done, though. Trust me on that.

God? I try not to think about Him too much. The problem is that ignoring the subject runs counter to my concept of intellectual integrity, so it just adds more discontent to the overload I'm already carrying in that department. My memories of church aren't very happy either. Add to that the fact that my father was the pastor and well . . . enough said!

Mom's okay, bless her heart. I've always been proud of the way she looks. Her clothes are plain and inexpensive, but still, she's an attractive woman. Maybe that says something about how shallow I am, but the way people look has always been important to me. She was firm with both of us kids, too. Firm, but fair. And tender. Mom's always been the "humanizer" in the family, the one who can make a total stranger feel right at home.

Dad? Well, I try to keep him on the shelf next to God and not think much about him either. I know he's a big part of the negative energy that stokes my emotional life, but I'm not really sure why. I've come to terms with most of his quirks, but it's more than that. There's something deeper in there somewhere that I don't understand at all.

Kat, my little sister, is the bright spot in our family. How she and I ever got to be so close, I'll never understand. We're so different. I guess we needed each other. I don't know. Maybe in some ways we still do. I get kind of crazy when I think about my growing-up years. All I know is she's the one person in my life that I can honestly say I love. Kind of sad, isn't it?

Especially since I'm doing so well in so many other ways. My career is coming together. A couple of good breaks and who knows what may happen? I could reach the dream before I'm thirty. At least, that's what I keep telling myself. And I play the success role well enough. It's not that hard, really. I've always thought I could do anything. A lack of confidence has never been my problem. So, what is it? What is my problem?

Haven't you ever wished you could just climb a hill somewhere and look around and find the answers to all your questions waiting there? Wouldn't that be great?

One. The Hill

Some hills are hardly noticeable, their slopes are so gentle. Others are steep enough to take our breath away as we struggle to reach their crest. We approach them for many different reasons. One person climbs to reach the workplace. For another, merely seeing what lies beyond is reward enough.

Hills are so commonplace that it takes a very special hill indeed to change a person's life. Like the one in Turkey's Cappadocian region, near the village of Kilçilar.

The ancient province of Cappadocia extends from the Taurus Mountains in the south to Galatia in the north, and forms the most striking portion of Turkey's central plateau. It was here that Erciyas and Hasan Dagi erupted, covering the land with a thick layer of mud and ash. Wind erosion then chiseled out an incredible fantasy land of "fairy chimneys." Gradual geologic changes produced the Ihlara, Göreme and Soganli valleys, through which rivers flowed to provide human beings with water and refuge.

Each succeeding century dutifully observed the rhythmic tattoo of time until an altogether different eruption burst upon the land, this one covering the region with word of a Virgin's son, a Wonder-Worker sent from God to the earth. Amazing stories were told by local merchants of what they had seen and heard while on business trips to far-off Jerusalem.

Pursuit

The Wonder-Worker had been killed by His enemies, they said, only to rise from the dead three days later!

One of His followers, a man called Peter, stood on the steps of the Great Temple in that city and told them these things. They even heard some of the Jewish locals praising this God in languages they had never before learned or spoken, including their own native tongue.

A few years after this initial pronouncement, strangers appeared in the region preaching a "gospel" that confirmed the earlier witness of the merchants and resulted in Cappadocia becoming a hotbed of Christian faith and practice, the residue of which remains especially visible in modern times throughout the region between Kayseri, Aksaray, and Niğde, known simply as The Triangle.

At the western edge of The Triangle, halfway between Nevsehir and Niğde, is the smaller town of Derinkuyu. From there, in order to reach the tiny village of Kilçilar (Kil-che-lar'), one takes the highway a short distance south before turning west, the last few kilometers passable only by a gravel road.

Winding down from higher ground, the road meanders past a number of squatty wood and block dwellings constructed against a hillside embankment overlooking a small stream. The young women who live here carry water from the stream to their houses, and mothers wash clothes on river rocks, as mothers have done for generations. Above the village, boys lead flocks of sheep and goats back from the day's grazing. Life looks much the same as it always has.

Except for the men. These days, very few men of working age are to be seen in the village. Most have taken jobs in other places, some as far away as Russia, in order to provide for their families who remain behind. There is nothing for them here that will provide a living wage. Not now. But, all that is about to change. And when it does, life in Kilçilar will never be the same again.

The transforming center of this change lies two kilometers beyond the tiny village. A solitary hill, shaped like a large, inverted bowl, surpasses the surrounding terrain by nearly twelve meters. Sheep and goats occasionally wander off to graze the wild grass of its gentle, treeless slopes, but villagers usually stay away.

To the unknowing eye, the hill is nothing more than one of the earth's countless extrusions.

But there are stories . . . frightening stories, handed down from grandparents and parents to their children . . . stories shaped into myths and legends, told over and over until they carry the cabalistic stamp of authenticity demanded of local village folklore around the world . . . lurid chronicles of villagers vanishing from that hill never to be seen again.

Anthropologists who've studied these tales have declared them mere figments of imagination, rooted in the superstitions of uneducated villagers.

No matter . . . those who live here know.

People have walked to that hill never to return. Vanished without so much as a bone or a tooth left behind. It is accursed. A place of darkness, of sickness and death.

A place to be feared!

Those who live here *know.*

Yet, in spite of this, strangers have come to the hill from faraway Istanbul and Ankara, city dwellers whose curiosity will not be satisfied by the warnings of simple village folk.

This mound of earth was once the central focus of a tribal society. Its mysteries and myths hide in undisturbed darkness beneath the hill.

And now, the truth is about to be found out.

When that happens, there can be no turning back. The world's fascination will focus on this hill and its secrets.

Especially one secret!

November, A.D. 324
Near the village of Derinkuyu

ZIYAETTIN CAST A TROUBLED GLANCE at the ghostly silhouettes in front of him, the only distinguishable night sound that of rhythmic hoofbeats of camels muffled in ancient layers of trail dirt and sand.

What was that?

His eye caught something off to the right. Peering into the darkness, he strained to make it out. There were only dark shadows on the flat desert plain stretching into the night, beyond his line of vision.

Pursuit

This had been the longest day so far. His shoulders hunched forward and a weary sigh slipped from his chapped lips. The sun and wind had been harsh and dry. Now the chill made Ziyaettin wish they had stopped at the caravansary they passed while the sun was still high, instead of trying to reach the next one before dark. He could be beside a fire right now, his stomach full, listening to the music of the desert. Instead, his weary eyes were playing tricks, discerning imaginary dangers. His nerves were as raw as meat hanging from a hook in the open market.

For what must have been the hundredth time since morning, he glanced down at the leather pouch that brushed against his leg, swaying in hypnotic rhythm to the awkward cadence of his mount. His fingers moved across the pouch to a single thong and felt the knot that secured it to the saddle. It remained tight. He knew that, but couldn't resist checking again. And with it came the familiar feeling of relief mixed with disappointment that had haunted him since this journey began.

He wished the pouch were not there. He had prayed for a miracle that would cause it to vanish. In the beginning he had been tempted to destroy it, but integrity would not permit him to break his pledge to see the assignment through to the end. But, to what end? Sadly, he reflected that it might be the beginning of the end of all that had become most precious in his life.

Six days before, he had been casually curious when in his master's house he saw it openly displayed on a low table. By the time his master and the two other men present had explained its importance, Ziyaettin's curiosity had given way first to confusion and then to an unremitting sadness. He watched as they wrapped it carefully in linen cloth and sealed it in a small clay jar which, in turn, was carefully placed in the leather pouch.

His instructions were to deliver the contents of the jar to Eusebius, Bishop of Nicomedia, prior to the forthcoming Council in Nicea. It was a gathering crucial to the Church and the world, set for the following May by order of Emperor Constantine. Ziyaettin's master insisted that an early delivery was essential, giving Eusebius time to assimilate the pouch's contents into what would surely be a passionate debate.

The plan called for Ziyaettin to join the last caravan of the season, leaving the city the next morning on a journey north and west that, with good fortune, would mark his arrival in Constantinople soon after the first of the year.

The importance of Ziyaettin's assignment was stressed one final time, as his master reminded him that he had been specially selected for the task because of his proven trustworthiness and courage. He must guard the pouch and its contents with his very life. Ziyaettin had placed his hand upon his master's shoulder and sworn that such would be the case.

How I wish I had not done so, Ziyaettin muttered to himself. *I'm trapped by my own pledge.*

Suddenly, several beasts of burden forward, a camel's discordant warning cut through the night, jarring Ziyaettin from his rhythmic reverie. His own mount bellowed out a response, piercing his nerves further still. Then, he saw them . . . phantom figures rising up from the desert floor, rushing to surround the caravan on all sides!

Most were on foot, a few rode camels. Those on mounts dashed directly into the advancing caravan. The ones on foot chopped and hacked at legs, animals, anything. Fear twisted like a demon in Ziyaettin's throat as he struggled to draw his sword. Shouts and curses and the bellowing of frightened animals could be heard in the darkness, punctuating the fierce and deadly ambush.

A cry of pain! Seconds passed before Ziyaettin realized it was his own voice. He felt nothing and yet blood streamed down his leg.

Screams!

He saw the rider in front of him yanked from his mount and driven to the ground by two strangers.

More shouting!

Sword in hand, Ziyaettin sliced the air in a desperate attempt to fight off the determined night marauders. Then his mount stumbled sideways and, without warning, a crushing blow came from behind him.

The sword flew from his hand.

Desperately, he grasped for something to hold onto, but there was only the coarseness of camel's hair as he fell face first onto the hard ground. Sickened and stunned, he tried pushing over onto his side.

A simple maneuver. Why couldn't he do it?

His strength ebbed rapidly.

"O Jesus," he whispered as a deeper darkness than the night settled over him. "Jesus . . . help me!"

The pain of his mortal wound was suddenly unleashed with agonizing fury, ripping and tearing its way along each nerve fiber, insulting every fleshly tissue. Ziyaettin pushed his face against the hard ground, fingers clutching at stones and dust as a despairing groan further distanced the remaining sounds of battle around him.

With one last Herculean effort, his mind encompassed the reason for his being here in the first place.

The leather pouch! What will happen to it now?

THEIR SAVAGE ASSAULT COMPLETED, the band of thieves herded together all the uninjured animals, retrieved their booty of grain and fine silks, and excitedly examined the unexpected prize of handmade jewelry found inside the folds of one victim's garments.

Three of the murderers walked through the human carnage thrusting their bloodstained blades here, cutting viciously there, making certain the victims were dead. Others tied the bodies onto beasts of burden, calmly preparing for their retreat. As the order was given, they mounted their camels and pushed off in an easterly direction.

Hours later as innocent wisps of pink and gold clouds traced across the sky, the last of the marauders stole through a hidden entrance and disappeared beneath a hill shaped like a large, upside-down bowl. The small herd of camels had been left to range in the distance, foraging for food among the rocks and scrub brush.

Well below the earth's surface, in a rocky chamber some fifteen by thirty meters in width and length, a meal was quickly prepared and devoured with few manners and much gusto. The marauders talked of the night's adventure, laughing at their prowess in surprising the caravan.

It had been so very easy. Only a few minor wounds to tend, and more than enough spoils to make up for the pain. It had proven to be one of their most profitable escapades. Life was always harder at this time of the year, with few travelers rich enough to rob. But as they looked about their hideaway, it appeared that they were ready to survive the cold, silent winter.

Their leader was a man with a sinister face, a dark beard and a hard, wiry physique. He leaned against the cave wall and pawed through some of the treasures scattered in front of him on the cavern floor. Spying a leather pouch, he picked it up and opened it, taking out a jar and peeling away its seal. Shaking it upside down, he caught the object that fell out.

"What is it?" asked the one nearest him.

"I don't know," he replied, loosening the linen wrap and unrolling two parchment pieces. He stared at the writing. "It's not a bill of lading. It looks to be a letter, but written in a language different from ours."

He looked at the writer's signature, but it meant nothing. He started to throw it into the fire, then hesitated, his attention drawn away by two bandits whose voices had suddenly raised above the others in loud disagreement.

While watching to see if he would have to intervene, he rolled the parchment pieces in their linen wrap and stuffed them back in the jar. Then, his eyes still on the two who argued, he pressed the cover tightly and returned it to the pouch. Motioning for the men to give him their attention, all voices became quiet. He stood to his feet and glanced around for a place to put the jar. There was much to be done before the day ended.

The dark outline of a small crevice caught his eye. He reached over and pushed the pouch into it. Maybe he would look at it again later. . . .

But the pouch was quickly forgotten . . . until centuries later when three unlikely and very different people were drawn together because of the jar and its contents. Three people compelled by its mystery, shaken by its danger, shocked by its power!

Two. Kristian

My sister and I grew up in a parsonage.

Make that plural, because Dad never stayed in any one place for long. He believed his mission in life was to help problem churches "straighten out" and get on with the business of "serving the Lord." In the corporate world, he would have been dubbed an "alligator killer."

There is a good deal of personal sacrifice tied to this sort of Christian service. No matter. Dad was up to it. Always. The rest of us were offered up on the sacrificial stone of parsonage life. It was just part of bearing the Lauring name.

I guess it wasn't so bad during my childhood years. The truth is, I didn't know any better. Every Sunday, I sat on hard wooden pews and listened to my father strike another blow against sin and spiritual darkness. It wasn't until I reached high school that my twisted veneration gradually changed to resentment and, finally, to contempt. Every boy wants to be proud of his dad. The older I got, the harder that became.

After a two-year stint in the army, I attended California State University in Hayward, before transferring to the University of California at Berkeley. During my college days, I worked at Burger King, as a summer janitor in a public school, even had a go at being a bicycle messenger in San Francisco's downtown district. I lasted a month! But, I kept doing whatever it took to make it through. That, together with the help Uncle Sam provided for being a good little soldier, was enough to let me walk away with a degree in communications.

My apartment looks across the tops of some other buildings that stair-step their way down the hill toward San Francisco Bay. It is less than an hour's drive to the parsonage where I spent my high school years. My parents still live there, but Dad and I hardly see each other now. Mom generally stops by on her way home from her rare shopping trips to the city, but it is hard for her. The conversation is always pretty stilted. When Dad and I finally "severed the cord," it was not pleasant. We've hardly spoken since, and I guess Mom feels caught between her two men.

When I think of Dad, I always see him standing on the platform, grasping at the sides of the pulpit with his bony hands, and wearing his usual "dark suit and starched shirt" uniform. It drapes across his angular physique like a funeral pall. His chin is firm, his lips are thin, and his pale flintlike nose flares out whenever he gets excited.

His face is rawboned, a lot like Doc Holiday in the movie *Tombstone,* though I'm sure he would much prefer being likened to Jeremiah or Malachi—two of Israel's fire-spitting prophets. No matter. He's not seen their likenesses by way of comparison, and I'm sure he hasn't seen Doc Holiday because he doesn't believe in going to movies!

But it's the man's eyes that are so striking. They're like windows into his soul. Most of the time they give off this mysterious, haunted look, as though behind their shroud are dark, prophetic thoughts. Heavy end-of-the-world stuff.

Just mention that you think God has chosen him to preach the Word, however, and they light up the way I wished for as a kid, when I wanted to play catch and spend some time hanging out with my old man. Why is it that when you're "called by God" everyone else has to live with the echo?

Dad elected to follow "the Voice" years ago. The rest of us had no vote. We just suffered the consequences, one of which was growing up in the parsonages.

Different church groups have various names for the pastor's house—the presbytery, the rectory, the vicarage, the manse, the parsonage. I finally concluded that rectory sounded the nicest. More transcendental than the definition Deacon Neillson gave when, as a kid, I overheard him talking with a new family in the tiny foyer of one of Dad's churches.

Foyer. See, there's another one of those "words." Foyer, narthex, entry, aula, lounge, vestibule, hall, lobby, anteroom. Whatever you call it depends a lot on whether you are high church or low church, or somewhere-in-between church. No matter. It's still the place where people stand around talking to each other as long as they can, so that they never have to sing the first verse of the opening hymn. In my dad's churches, that verse was always reserved to herald certain saints' grand entries; and, depending on how they felt about keeping God waiting, the second verse might serve the same function.

Anyway, back to Deacon Neillson. In his conversation with the newcomers, I overheard him label our home as "the house across the parking lot that the church owns where the current pastor's family lives rent free." Then he chuckled and said something else that I didn't catch, but it was probably just as well. I was too young to really understand. I just knew that when those visitors looked over at me, I felt terribly embarrassed. They must have been embarrassed too. At least they never returned. I was glad.

Then came the day I discovered that some preachers' families actually own their own homes. Like John Cain* across Baytown, at the big Calvary Church. At first, I was just jealous. Then, I got downright mad! It wasn't fair. Living in a parsonage is not like regular people who rent their homes instead of buying them. Most houses belong to someone. Not many belong to everyone! Maybe the White House, but there are few others. The parsonage, however, belongs to *all* the people in the church. Except the ones who live in it!

Why this sparked such resentment in me as a teenager I'm still not sure. As I grew older, part of it had to do with my increasing awareness that we were poor by comparison to other families in the church. Our parents owned nothing. Well, almost nothing.

It seemed like Dad was always making payments on the few

---

*John Cain is a major character in *September Strike* by Ward Tanneberg. Victor Books, 1994.

things we did have, like our old Ford Falcon. Not enough money to buy a secondhand car outright, much less purchase a house! How could he put up with this kind of life? And why did he have to drag the rest of us into it?

Ultimately, I not only hated the church, but I also grew bitter toward my father for permitting it all to happen to us. By whatever word you called our home, it still meant the same thing—that none of the houses Kat and I grew up in would ever really be our own.

Can you believe that before my room could be made over, the board of deacons expected to be consulted? Especially old Deacon Harden.

"Is new paint or wallpaper really necessary?" he would ask, running his fat, stubby finger over the surface of my wall, while the other deacons looked on. "What color do you propose to use if we approve this expenditure? Do you know yet what it will cost? After all, we can never be too careful with the Lord's money."

To me, it all seemed ridiculous. If the world really was going to hell around them like they seemed to think, shouldn't they be strategizing to do something about it? That is, if they really cared?

To me, "parsonage" was a whole lot worse than a swear word. It meant cleaning out clutter left by Dad's predecessors. Then there were the stale musty odors and the mildew. Every time. The inevitability gave new meaning to the doctrine of predestination!

We all pitched in, scrubbing and scouring and wiping. Then, once the house was squeaky clean, it was room selection time. I knew how this would turn out, even before the ritual began. All it took was a quick look around the new place. Even though Mom and Dad went through the charade of waiting until it was suitably clean before making room assignments, I knew already which one was mine.

Our parents always took the biggest room, and called it the "master bedroom." I've never been sure about that designation. It was probably the reward for being parents. But if seniority worked for grownups, it had nothing to do with the siblings.

Even though I was older, my kid sister always ranked next when it came to room selection. She got the second largest room. The logic surrounding this decision was a little fuzzy to me. It had something to do with the fact that girls, just by the very nature of things, need more space than boys, in order to do whatever it is that they do.

At any rate, if there was a smallest bedroom, I knew it would be mine. Guaranteed. You know, *predestined?* But that wasn't the worst part. A teenager's room is supposedly his own turf, right? Something that reflects his personality? In the parsonage that's also problematic.

"Don't do anything to the walls that will leave permanent markings or holes when we leave," Mother would warn. In her mind, it was only a matter of time. Never *if* we leave, just *when.*

For some reason, the lack of permanence was always more of a problem for me than for any other family member. Mom and Dad accepted it as an occupational reality. Kat seemed able to turn a move into more of an adventure than an inconvenience. She always liked new and different places. But not me. I saw the inevitable social hazard as friends were left behind. Starting over frustrated and angered me.

When I was fifteen, I pocketed some money I had earned working part-time for a local gardener, and went with my best friend and his parents to San Francisco, about fifty miles away. At an art store off Union Square, on my friend's dare, I purchased a life-sized photo poster of Genny Frasier, the same one who had graced *Sports Life* swimsuit edition. A smaller version had already been voted the favorite of the guys at school and had instilled new enthusiasm for keeping track of the school year on the inside of locker doors up and down the hall.

She was beautiful, with the kind of figure that makes hormones race around half-grown bodies at breakneck speed. Most of it was visibly on display, except for a tiny bikini never intended to cover much territory. Of course, that was part of the plan. I knew it by the way she smiled knowingly across the room at me.

She looked really great on the back of my bedroom door. And as long as it was open, no one had a clue about Genny Frasier's abundant presence. Only with it closed did she become visible.

Mom was quite impressed with the way I suddenly took to heart her many admonitions about the usual condition of my room.

"A pig could not sleep here," she would often say, standing in the doorway, hands on hips. "Clean up your room, Kristian!"

Today I realize all I really needed was motivation. And Genny Frasier gave it to me. By keeping things picked up, dusted, and vacuumed, I hoped to keep Mom and Dad in the hallway, with no need to come in and close the door. It worked well for nearly three weeks. Then, one Thursday after school, Kat walked in unannounced.

"Kris?"

"Get out of here."

"I need to talk."

"Go on, sis. Scram!"

"Please? It won't take very long. I need to ask you something."

She stepped inside and closed the door behind her.

"I need to ask you something about boys."

Kat was standing with her back to Genny. The prospect of what my kid sister would say when she turned back to open the door flashed through my mind like lightning, causing me to cast a furtive glance over her shoulder. Unfortunately, she detected the movement in my eyes and turned her head to see if someone was behind her.

And, of course, there was!

For an instant, Kat forgot what had brought her into my room in the first place and turned all the way around to stare at the poster.

"Kris Lauring!" she exclaimed, eyes wide with disbelief. "Do Mom and Dad know you have this?"

"Are you serious?" I growled with as menacing a tone as I could muster up. "Of course not! And if you say a word, so help me, I'll . . ."

My voice faded. I was ticked at having been discovered. And, after all, what can you really do to a little sister that won't get you into more trouble than you're already in?

Kat stared at the poster again in silence.

"I can see why you like her," she said at last, an admiring tone in her voice as she turned back to me. "She's beautiful. Boy, would I like to have a figure like that someday!"

I swallowed my surprise. Kat didn't taunt or scold me. She didn't run out of the room yelling for Mom. It was one of those poignant happenings between siblings that comes when you least expect it. A link forged into the bonding chain. Luckily for Kat, she did grow up to have a poster-girl figure. She's beautiful.

Unfortunately, Genny did not receive the same response the following week while I was at school and Mother entered my room, loaded with socks, shorts, and freshly washed jeans. It was fate! A pair of socks dropped to the floor and rolled to a stop against the edge of the door. Bending to pick them up, her eye caught the fact that something was not as it should be. Pulling the door away from the wall she came face to . . . well, you know. Then, she went to find Dad.

Unfortunately, Genny Frasier received neither a decent funeral nor a proper burial. Her nubile form had been summarily torn from her hiding place and cremated by the time I arrived home. A modern-day Joan of Arc. Ashes to ashes.

All that remained were the tacks and tiny pieces of torn poster paper embedded in the door. For me, however, there was a slower, deeper, and much more lasting burn than the one suffered by Genny. One I had plenty of time to stir and stoke during the thirty-day grounding period that followed.

The attitude of my parents, and what I perceived then as an invasion of privacy, added to my secret well of embittered feelings. I know it's a loathsome thought, but my lasting regret is that old Deacon Harden didn't make the discovery. That would certainly have set a tone in Dad's next board meeting!

I said little. Repented even less. I stuffed it, for by now I had learned that questioning why things were the way they were, and sharing honest feelings, was not at all a safe thing in our parsonage. I dreamed of a new day. A day of escape when I could be free to do "my own thing."

I looked forward to college, but a tour of military duty was first on my agenda. It looked like the best way to put together the necessary tuition money. I graduated in the top twenty percent of my high school class, but that wasn't strong enough for academic scholarships. I competed athletically, but wasn't scholarship material there either.

Why did I want to go to college? Not from any insatiable desire for learning. I just wanted out. Out where I could be free from the stifling role I'd arbitrarily been elected to play.

I hated being a preacher's kid.

But that's history now. It's over. The break is complete.

At twenty-eight, life looks good. Better than good. Great even. I think I've finally made it.

Except for the Questions . . .

Three. Katrina

Certain days are framed in a young girl's memory as sobering reminders or simply for pure enjoyment. This day was one of the latter. A standout day for fluffy white clouds to serve as platforms from which breezes could launch their aromatic bouquet and announce to the world the fragrances of spring.

Walking through the school's front gate, Katrina felt like shouting "thank you" to the sky, doing cartwheels in the grass, skipping through the park, anything as a fitting response to the magic of the season.

She loved spring with a childlike passion. But there was one thing she had learned well in her first twelve years. She knew how to suppress emotions, especially those patterned with color and beauty, music and dance. So, instead, she calmly strolled along the sidewalk with her friend and convinced herself again that controlling emotions was good. After all, she was not a little girl anymore. In eight more days Katrina Lauring was going to be a teenager!

Her parents invariably used her full name when speaking of or to Katrina and disapproved of anything less. Especially her father. Her classmates and close friends shortened it to Katy, except when they were within earshot of the Reverend Pedar Lauring. It was her brother, Kris, who cut it down to a single syllable. To him she would forever be Kat, whether their parents liked it or not.

When she needed the formality and safety of emotional distance, she answered to Katrina. With roommates and treasured friends, she was Katy. And though they often disagreed over matters of politics, lifestyle, religion, almost anything, she was always Kat to the one person with whom she felt the most freedom to be herself.

There was something irresistible that drew Katrina to her brother, freeing her to reveal the ebb and flow of her deepest feelings. He had grown up to be funny, garrulous, opinionated, argumentative, perversely confrontive and, at times, rude without apology. All the things that Kat was not.

Handsome in high school, he had been sought after and sighed over by more than a few of the girls with flowing hair, short skirts, and stars in their eyes. It amused Katrina to observe how much he enjoyed this excessive attention, even manipulating it to his own liking, all the while mindful of its inherent shallowness. Was it inborn discretion? Or was this the way he maintained control over his hidden fears and feelings?

In college he dated often but not seriously, skipped a fair number of classes, was a regular guest at frat parties and, conversely, graduated in the top five percent of his class. He was an enigma, all right, but there was something else that drew Katrina to him. She thought it was loneliness, though Kris laughed that idea off when she mentioned it. Katrina recognized a touch of melancholy too, kept well hidden beneath the surface of his sanguine, outgoing personality. But the thing that set her brother apart, and at the same time drew her closer to him, was his never-ending quest for ultimate answers.

Kris' favorite word was "Why?" His favorite question, "How do you know that it's really true?" In high school he competed, but not in the "big three" team sports. He preferred the more individualistic contests of track and field and was good enough to make the team in his sophomore year. But it was in verbal competitions that he truly shone. He played a lead role on the school debate team, and won Rotary and Lions Club speech contests two years in a row.

Katrina went to all his home track meets, and she sat through the "Great Debates," as he called them. But their parents hardly ever attended. She knew this hurt Kris, but he shook it off with a shrug, saying, "Hey, sis, that's just the way they are. They won't change, so don't sweat the small stuff." The painful bitterness voiced in this assessment caused Katrina to feel a deep sadness.

She loved her parents dearly, even though their lifestyle did seem overly restrictive. She had to be home before dark on school nights unless permission had been granted, usually for a church event. Softball and soccer were okay, so long as she didn't engage in these or any other recreation on Sundays. As Kris wryly put it, "Sunday is the Lord's Day, so one shouldn't be having too good a time."

Television was a relative latecomer in their home, arriving just before her eleventh birthday. Katrina was so grateful to access this window on the world that she didn't argue with the imposed limit that permitted viewing only on Friday and Saturday evenings, a rule that was relaxed whenever school was not in session. Program viewing required the approval of their father. This censorious practice held true even during high school years.

The Reverend Lauring decided certain programming like "The Lucy Show" reruns were acceptable, as were educational features, news telecasts, and selected offerings on PBS. Soaps were absolutely forbidden and, of course, no movies or serial shows containing violence or sexual innuendo were allowed. That meant Katrina missed a lot of television movies and sitcoms regularly watched by her friends; but, considering the alternative, she left well enough alone.

Attendance at movie theaters was prohibited as well, and school dances were out of the question. Table games in which regular playing cards or dice were used were unacceptable. Katrina was informed repeatedly by her father that to let down this standard of conduct could very well lead to a penchant for gambling, and then who knows where after that? The exception to this rule was Monopoly, though she was never able to determine why.

While by California standards their family lifestyle seemed severe, Katrina felt truly loved and protected by her parents. They were good people, even if it seemed like they came from another planet. There were days when she longed for the freedom to enjoy a movie or attend a high school dance with her friends, but she knew that would never be. Not in her lifetime. Anyway, it was a small price to pay for what she had in return. A loving family. Strong Christian values. A healthy body and a keen mind. Certainly more than some of her schoolmates could boast about.

Katrina's escape valve was a good book. She loved to read and she excelled in school. By the time she reached her twelfth birthday, her mind was rapier sharp. The difference between her and Kris was motivation. She always finished homework assignments in plenty of time to read books of her own choice in an ever-widening variety of subjects. She could well have been dubbed "the brain" or "the bookworm" by her classmates, were it not for her outgoing personality and natural athletic ability.

Katrina was not the most popular girl at school, but she had enough friends. And by age twelve, her potential for physical beauty was beginning to be noticed, as she started that desperately awkward, highly emotional journey from gangly girl to grown woman.

Through it all, she remained resolute in her obedience and respect to her parents; but it was her dashing and charismatic older brother to whom she gave an almost worshipful deference. Whereas Katrina chose to conform in order to get along with her parents, Kris seemed ever ready to live on the edge, break the rules, challenge authority. Katrina watched his antics with amusement and a secret envy.

Beyond school, church was Katrina's primary social outlet. And unlike her brother, she actually enjoyed it. Oh, it was boring at times, especially when her father droned on from some unintelligible Old Testament passage. The music was lively but simple, lacking any artistry or grandeur. The churches her father pastored were always too small for a music minister, even part-time. It was mostly congregational singing, performed sometimes sitting, at other times standing, occasionally on key.

Prayer at church was generally offered up with a loud voice, almost a shout. This was a necessity for the person leading out, if he was to be heard over the chorus of other voices united in the audible, passionate exercise of calling on God. Katrina often wished people would remain silent during this time and unite their thoughts with those of the one trying to lead in prayer. Still, there were moments when she felt a kind of electricity flowing through the crowd as public prayers were punctuated with "Amen!" or "Hallelujah."

It wasn't until college, and especially her postgraduate years in seminary, that Katrina experienced a much deeper taste from the Church's common cup of faith and worship. That taste would bring her a whole new world and with it more questions.

It was the "questioning" that her father, Pedar Lauring, seemed to struggle with the most. His disappointment in the direction that Kristian's life had taken was not assuaged in the least by Katrina's announcement that she intended to go into some form of Christian ministry. His dreams of a son who would one day be a preacher had been dashed, while his views on women in the clergy were outspokenly combative.

The Apostle Paul had been very clear on that. Women were not permitted to teach when men were present. They were to keep silent in the church. In the end she surprised all the family and most of the little congregation by tearfully, and somewhat apprehensively, taking control of her life and matriculating at Tower Seminary in San Bernardino. . . .

Katrina thought again of Fluffy White Cloud Day, when she was twelve. Until then, she had not given much thought to boys or even to her own physical appearance. On that morning, however, after showering she closed the door to her room and examined herself carefully in front of the full-length mirror.

Frowning, she groaned, "I look like a stick! I'm ugly and I'm going to be ugly for the rest of my life. Yuk!"

Turning away she threw herself down on the bed and burst into tears. She wanted to yell. Scream, even. But she didn't. She did not want to go to school, but she did. There were new, strange, powerful things going on inside her girl-woman body. Her mother said this was a wonderful time in her life, a time of change. Katrina didn't know about that. This was one change she was not at all happy about.

That is, not until Tommy Burton ran up to her on the way to school and slipped her books under his arm.

"You look real pretty today, Katy," he said admiringly.

"Thanks," she replied, as an oddly warm feeling began spreading throughout her body. She smiled. So did Tommy. And the rest of the day had been beautiful!

That afternoon, walking home from school, Tommy was at her side again, carrying her books as he had done that morning. He lived two blocks beyond her house, and they had been friends ever since the Laurings had moved to town. Tommy's father was a sales representative for a candy company. His parents were nice and she felt comfortable with Tommy. Besides, he was kind of cute.

"Katy," Tommy asked, a tiny line of perspiration beading across his forehead as he gathered up his nerve, "would you like to go to the movies with me on Saturday?"

A flutter of tension stirred in Katrina's stomach. An answer jumped to the tip of her tongue, but she knew it was not the one she would give him.

"Thanks, Tommy. I wish I could, but I can't."

"Why not?"

"Nothing special. I just can't."

They walked on together, the silence dangling between them like an empty swing. Then Tommy spoke up again.

"Is it because your dad's a preacher? Don't you go to movies?"

"No."

"No, it's because of your dad? Or, no, you don't go to movies?"

"I don't go to movies."

"Never?"

"I've never been to one."

Katrina watched out of the corner of her eye as Tommy tried to assimilate this astonishing bit of information.

"But, why? I love going to movies."

She pondered her answer carefully, embarrassed by being placed in this position. She wanted to be loyal to her parents. Yet, it didn't seem fair to have to assume total responsibility for their convictions. Finally, she chose the middle ground.

"We don't go to movies."

"No one in your family goes? Not even your brother?"

Katrina suspected that Kris might be the exception. She had a hard time imagining him as a total abstainer in this or most other things, for that matter. But she had no way of really knowing.

"No one," she repeated finally.

"Why not?" Tommy pressed.

"We don't believe in it," Katrina answered lamely.

"Are you serious? What's not to believe? Like movies are movies, Katy. They're here forever. And they're great, man. Mom and Dad took me to see the new *Star Trek* movie last week. Wow. It's a total blast!"

Katrina didn't respond. Instead, she focused her eyes along the sidewalk, wishing they would hurry and get to her house so that this conversation could end.

"Wow!" exclaimed Tommy, still trying to grasp what life without Captain Kirk and the starship *Enterprise* must be like. "I just can't believe that you've never been to a movie. Do you guys watch television at your house?"

"Sure. All the time," Katrina responded quickly, stretching reality somewhat in a vain effort to regain some acceptable ground.

"What's the difference?"

Katrina thought a moment more before answering.

"I guess maybe it's because it's dark inside a theater."

"So?"

"Things can happen there. In the dark."

"Like what?"

"Besides, your parents aren't always there to make sure that what you're watching is okay," Katrina continued, ignoring his question. But Tommy would not be ignored.

"What things?"

Their steps slowed a bit.

"People kissing and stuff, I guess."

They were nearing her house now. Only one more block to go.

Tommy stopped.

"Have you ever kissed anybody?"

Katrina's heart suddenly began pounding. Unconsciously she licked her lips while searching for the right answer to this latest twist in their conversation.

"Sure," she said finally. "Lots of times."

"Who?"

"My mom and dad, you ninny. And my brother too."

"Oh, sure, everybody does that," Tommy snorted. "Wait a minute. You've kissed your brother?"

"Sure."

"On the lips?"

"Of course not! Nobody kisses their brother on the lips!"

"Then you've never kissed anybody on the lips, except maybe your mother or father?"

Katrina was silent.

"Well?"

"No."

With his free hand, Tommy took her arm and turned her until she faced him. He was staring at her, a curious look in his eyes that increased the tension Katrina felt swelling like a balloon inside of her.

"Would you like to try it?"

"Are you serious?"

"Yes."

"No."

"Why not?"

"I . . . well, I . . . it wouldn't be right."

"What's wrong with kissing someone?"

"Aren't you supposed to be married or in love or something?"

"I guess. But how will you ever know you're in love if you don't kiss someone first?"

That was a thought too profound for a quick answer. Unfamiliar feelings were converging from all directions on an emotion-jammed intersection far too crowded for logical reasoning.

"I . . . I don't know," she stammered apprehensively.

"Katy, I think I love you."

Katrina's mouth went dry. At first she felt bewildered. Then she wanted to laugh. One look at Tommy's eyes, however, and she resisted. He was serious. Even Tommy's voice sounded strange, a little on the hoarse side. He cleared his throat nervously as he waited for a response to his grand declaration.

"Would you like to try a kiss?" he asked again, breaking the awkwardness of the moment. "Just to see what it's like?"

"Have you ever done it before?"

"Sure, lots of times."

Tommy is thirteen, going on fourteen, Katrina thought. *He could be telling the truth.*

She remained still, unable to move or even think of anything to say. Tommy took a step toward her.

She closed her eyes as his lips touched hers.

At first, the sensation was electric.

Then, it was wet. And slippery!

Her eyes opened wide while Tommy's mouth pressed hard against hers. Then he drew back, a triumphant grin on his face.

"There. How was it?"

"It was . . . okay."

"Okay? Just okay?"

"It's my first time, Tommy, so I'm not much of a critic." Katrina wiped the moistness from around her mouth with the sleeve of her jacket.

"Want to do it again?"

"No thanks, not now. I need to get home."

They resumed their walk in silence. In front of her house, Tommy handed over her books.

"Bye, Katy. See you tomorrow, okay?"

"Sure. See you."

Katrina turned and walked slowly along the sidewalk from the gate to the porch, resisting a sudden impulse to dash up the steps and into the house. She knew Tommy was watching her. At the front door, she paused to look back. Sure enough, there he was, still standing in the same exact spot. He gave her a half wave. She tossed her head and flashed a quick smile in his direction. Then she opened the door and stepped inside.

With a sigh of relief, Katrina dropped her books on the hall table, knowing full well if her mother found them there, she would get a scolding. Well, whatever. She suddenly had something very important to ask, and there was only one person who would give her a straight answer. She needed to talk to him before anyone else knew she was home.

In the hall, she hesitated for a moment, gathering her thoughts.

"Kris?"

She knocked on the half-open door and walked in, closing it behind her.

"Get out of here."

"I need to talk."

"Go on, sis. Scram!"

"Please? It won't take very long. I need to ask you something."

. . . Katrina smiled at the memory of that afternoon. It had been thirteen years since Fluffy White Cloud Day. Yet, in some ways, it was only yesterday.

Now, Katrina knew the time had come again. She needed to talk to Kris, to garner his support. To feed on the resistant strength that enabled him to go his own way.

Before she broke the news to her parents.

Four. Ibrahim

Lisla, Turkey

Not far from Lisla's dusty village square, where the narrow potholed road curves gradually to the south, Ibrahim Mustapha Sevali, the youngest of ten brothers and sisters, lived with his father and mother.

Their home was a modest single-story building of white-washed concrete. There were three rooms in all, four if you included the large, unattached verandah in front. A second floor had been added to the original structure, following the Turkish custom of investing family resources in the expansion of an existing structure, or beginning an entirely new one for married children setting up their own families. All of the Sevali children had grown up under the watchful eyes of their parents in this house that had been lovingly built with their own hands.

Ibrahim's childhood was simple but happy. Barefoot and bright-eyed, he literally followed in his brothers' footsteps as they worked in the cotton, corn, and poppy fields near the village. Later, two kilometers further along the same road, his two older brothers built their own houses. They were close enough that Ibrahim could visit. In fact, he did so often, occasionally staying overnight with them.

Pursuit

The road leading south from the village square was mostly paved, except for one long stretch about six kilometers from town. The paved portion, directly in front of the Sevali home, was in a perpetual state of disrepair. During much of the year, there was little traffic. Farm machinery, the occasional automobile, and a truck now and then would disturb the calm and send young Ibrahim running out to the verandah to wave to passersby.

But during harvest season, the road became an exciting window on the world. This was Ibrahim's favorite time. The road didn't simply flow with traffic—it jerked. A steady, stop-and-go stream of autos, trucks, tractors, donkeys and carts, and people on foot moved in each direction, drivers honking, waving, shouting.

It was a scene that intrigued and aroused Ibrahim's boyish senses as he watched from the verandah. This was the season during which his mother repeatedly cautioned him each time he walked to the village or to one of his brothers' houses. His main goal was to avoid being run over.

Being on the road at harvesttime was a great adventure! It spoke of a world beyond his own modest dwelling, nourishing a boy's dreams of people . . . places . . . adventure . . . the unknown. He loved the blustering activity. When it was not there, he experienced a profound sense of loneliness and waited impatiently for the next harvest season.

Most of the Sevali children had scattered by the time Ibrahim was five. Gürer, the eldest son, was only a name to his youngest brother. He had been killed in a construction accident while working on a high-rise hotel in Antalya, two years before Ibrahim was born. Ahmet and Cemil lived down the road and worked in the fields, like their father.

Seyda, Nazan, and Eda lived on nearby farms with their husbands. Having scored at the very top of her training program, Ibrahim's sister Selva, the one closest to him in age, landed a receptionist's job at a resort hotel in Kusadasi and resided in that distant Mediterranean community with an aunt. Only two unmarried sisters, Asli and Ozden, remained at home with him and his parents.

Ibrahim's father, Mustapha Sevali, was well known throughout the village and the surrounding area. Living near the roadway assured him of daily visitors, almost all of whom were long-time acquaintances. Since retiring from the fields at fifty-five, he spent most of his days on the verandah or walking into town to sit in the square and swap stories with old friends.

At his modest home, he sprawled in an ancient armchair that his wife, Sevei, regularly threatened to chop up, burn up, or simply throw away, with or without him in it, depending on how she felt at the moment. His short, barrel-chested form stretched out from the chair and his bare feet were almost always propped on a small wooden stool. He wore the same clothes he had worked in during his days in the fields. Though he now had time to shave, he rarely did so. His friends were not the kind to be offended by a little scruffy informality.

When Ibrahim was seven, he was told that he could sit on the verandah with his father and the other men, if he promised to be quiet. If he had been told to stand on his head all afternoon, he would have done so in order to be able to listen to the men as they talked. It was the place to be!

Voraciously, he gathered into his memory the stories he overheard. Stories of days gone by, of family, of wars and adventures that were perhaps partly true. In the process, Ibrahim acquired a huge appetite for history. He was filled with a desire to know more about the people and the land. About the world beyond his valley. About everything!

By the time he was ten, he could tell the stories better than his father. These patriarchal tales were now vivid pictures in his mind.

Unusual scenes . . . happy occasions . . . familiar episodes . . . his father learning to swim in a wadi where there was a stream of deep water. Playing ball games with a stick and a rock because there was no bat and ball. Visiting his sister's husband's brother who was a fisherman in a small Mediterranean coastal village near Adana. Selling most of the day's catch to his regular customers. Broiling the rest over charcoals and eating them. When his father recounted that story, though Ibrahim had never been to the sea himself, he could almost smell the fish, his mouth watering at the very thought.

A deep well had been the main water source when his father was a boy. It was located about a kilometer outside the village. The women would go there two or three times a day to bring back water in jars carried on their heads or in goatskins strapped onto the backs of donkeys. In those days, it was the women who also went out to gather wood for the family fires.

Similar events to those of his own childhood. Similar and yet vastly different. Times were changing throughout the world. And Turkey was no exception.

The amazing thing to Ibrahim was that he could *see* these stories. They were like works of art brushed with an artist's hand onto the canvas of his mind. By the time he was twelve, he could vividly recreate each narrative, embellishing details with the ever-expanding universe of his imagination.

"When do I get to go to school, papa?"

It had been a recurring question from the time he was five. Everyone had chores and the older children were expected to help work in the fields. A decade or two before, formal education had not seemed terribly important. But this was a new day, and Ibrahim's papa was wise enough to realize it.

Though the old man rarely said so, Ibrahim knew that Papa was pleased with his quickness at learning. His older siblings had either not attended formal school or had completed only a few grades. Ibrahim, however, was destined to attend *ilkokul* (primary school) for five years, *ortaokul* (middle school) for three, and three more years of *lisé* (high school), always at the head of his class.

After school and during vacations, he helped out at home and also worked with his brothers in the fields, plowing and sowing and harvesting. Depending on the season and the crop, harvest normally took place between May and October. For the Sevali family, life was hard, yet productive. Steady, yet pleasant. Ordinary, yet hopeful. There were always golden stories from the past and glorious dreams about the future.

Somewhere during this ordinary, rural life, Ibrahim made an exciting discovery. There were hidden treasures yet to be found in the soil of his native land, but not from plowing and sowing and harvesting.

By the time he entered high school in Saraykoy, his mind was dancing with stories of the past. With antiquities, the unimaginable heritage of the ages, revealing the souls of the human families who had lived and died here. Their legends. Their hopes. Their faith.

Their loves. As a student, he devoured every history lesson like a fine meal.

Then came the fateful day . . . the glorious day when Ibrahim realized Allah was guiding him toward the calling that would someday become his lifework.

It was not the consequence of an extraordinary event or a spiritual visitation. Like so many revelations, it came to him out of the ordinary affairs of his life. He simply picked up his books at school one day and prepared to exit from the classroom. As he did, the teacher called him over to his desk.

"I want to loan you this book, Ibrahim. I think you'll enjoy it. Take it home with you. Bring it back when you're finished."

In a hurry to catch his ride, Ibrahim thanked the teacher and stuffed the book in his pack without looking at it.

That night, beneath the light at his bedside, he removed the book from the pack, opened it, and began to read.

That was it. He was hooked.

By the time his mother called to him for the third time, telling him to turn out his light, Ibrahim knew exactly what he wanted to be!

Five. Katrina

Katrina sat in the last of the nine rows that sloped gradually toward a small stage equipped with a black leather swivel chair and three smaller stationary chairs. Banks of stage lights and three large television cameras surrounded the set. She noted a fourth camera, mounted higher on the steel grid and pointed in the direction of the audience.

Unlike big network shows, no band hovered in the wings. From her two previous visits, she knew that all the music, including the upbeat jazz theme, was prerecorded, and the cameras were operated by remote control from a distant room. Jazz was not Katrina's favorite sound, but it fit the carefully crafted image of San Francisco's very popular "KL Show." The last of today's audience was through the door now, rapidly occupying the upholstered audience chairs.

On her way inside, Katrina had walked past a line of at least a hundred persons waiting for tickets to tomorrow's telecast. She showed her letter and special pass to the security guard who smiled, opened the door, and waved her through. "Welcome, Ms. Lauring. I guess you know he's in Studio 2B." She ducked under his outstretched arm, as a buzz of conversation trailed after her.

"Who's she?"

"The guy at the door said her name was Lauring."

"Is that Kris' wife?"

"No, stupid, he's not married."

"Must be a relative, then. Has he got a sister?"

"Don't know."

The voices faded to a general din as she hurried into the elevator. Moments later, she stepped out onto the second level, crossed the worn gray carpet of the mezzanine, and waited for security to check through her small handbag before perfunctorily opening the door marked Studio 2B.

Once inside, a flurry of voices erupted again. She was one of the last to be seated, fifteen minutes before the show began. From four to four-thirty, it would be "live to tape" with the studio audience and at six-thirty in homes wherever KFOR could be viewed.

During summer months, while the competition pulled up reruns or guest hosts or both, she knew that Kris had determined to keep up the quality and freshness of the "KL Show" for his growing number of Bay Area fans.

Kris delivered a unique combination of journalistic humor, his forté, and melded it mostly with interviews of well-known political and sports figures. His easy humor and natural interviewing instincts, combined with his willingness to tackle controversial issues, had resulted in a strong market share of San Francisco's early evening viewing audience.

The disparity between humor and interviews on substantive matters had initially been impossible for KFOR's executives to grasp, and so they had deep-sixed the idea as the precocious whim of a starry-eyed news writer barely out of college. But that was "history" now, at least as the word is abused in the precarious and unpredictable world of television. The "KL Show's" meteoric rise in ratings had, in the short span of two seasons, made it the most talked about television show in suburban coffee klatches and lunchrooms in Bay Area office buildings.

Last month during dinner in her small apartment on the north edge of San Bernardino's Tower Seminary campus, Katrina had shown her roommates a full-page article in *People* magazine, complete with Kris' picture and the header, "KLS: Contagious and Spreading Rapidly from San Francisco." "Can you believe that's my big brother?" she asked laughingly, shaking her head in amazement.

Kris' break had come unexpectedly, two and a half years earlier, while Katrina was finishing up her first year at Tower. Stephanie Wolfe had arrived on the set of her nightly half-hour show, "Lights Across the Bay," literally too stoned to go on. As the show's director wrung her hands over what to do, Kris volunteered to fill in with less than ten minutes lead time. Sally Grayton, the "Lights" producer-director, knew Kris from his exposure as the station's summer booth announcer and fill-in for the weekend weather crew. Desperate and out of options, she waited while he ran to get his jacket and tie and then gave him a three-minute briefing about the guest of the evening.

What promised to be a total disaster had Sally and the camera crew smiling and high-fiving each other thirty minutes later. Kris had stepped from the ranks into the lineup at the worst possible time and had scored a big win.

Jerry Menting was working as an assistant in the third-floor control room that night and later told Kris what he had overheard. After the show, Jerry's boss, Vern McNair, was wiping perspiration from his forehead when he glanced over at Claude Jardin, KFOR's vice president in charge of local news and special features. Jardin's hands were stuffed into his pockets. He chewed his lip as he gazed at the electronically projected pictures of the crew milling about in Studio 2B.

"The kid didn't do too badly, I'd say," McNair grunted, heaving his bulk out of the chair and stretching in front of the control console.

Jardin continued watching the screens. Slowly he turned toward McNair. "That's an understatement, Vern. But you know that, don't you? The kid did a great job! Did you see the way he handled Ed Sanders? That old codger has been through more interviews than a presidential candidate. I thought he'd chew Lauring up the way he does the few opposition members in the State Legislature that are still crazy enough to take him on, but the kid didn't give him a chance. Looked a little like a sword fight for the last five minutes, didn't it? Parry. Retreat. Thrust. And the audience was with him all the way. They loved it!"

"So what're you going to do now, Claude?"

"I'm going downstairs to congratulate him. Then I'm taking another look at that idea of his we tossed a few months ago. You were there, remember? I don't believe it, but he was like a young Letterman out there tonight, sprinkled with a generous dose of Tim Russert and Mark Russell. Now that's a combination worth taking a second look at!

"I'll need to watch him some more. But he's fresh meat, Vern, something the public can chew on for a while before they get tired enough to spit him out. And as far as I'm concerned, Stephanie just wrote her epitaph. I've put up long enough with her sucking the life out of this show and right up her nose! She's earned a long vacation at Betty Ford's."

Jardin paused at the door and turned to McNair. "Ten bucks says we've got the makings of a new talk show host. And if we shape him right, he could be big time."

"No argument on the first premise, Claude. I've seen some of his clips. He's pretty good. Big time? I don't know."

"In two years they'll want to pick him up on the network."

"I can risk ten on that."

"You're on."

Katrina had heard the story from Kris as they talked on the telephone after his impromptu debut. He'd been so excited.

Well, small wonder. And look how he's done since.

Her wandering thoughts were interrupted by a man in an open-collared shirt and jeans who walked onto the stage, signaling the audience with hands held high.

"One minute to air time, everybody. Thanks for coming. You met Kris a few minutes ago when he was out here. Now give the guy a big welcome when he comes on stage. Remember, you're an important part of the show. So, be enthusiastic! Cheer. Yell. Clap. Okay?"

The crowd needed little encouragement. They had already stomped feet and yelled in a practice run led earlier by this same fellow.

All eyes were turned to right center stage where they knew Kris would make his entry.

Music.

The director's hand was up as she took her place just to the right of the middle camera's large lens. Her fingers were counting down. Three . . . two . . . one. The hand dropped, pointing to center stage right. The curtain opened and a smiling Kris Lauring, hands stuffed casually in his pockets, strolled onto the stage. The crowd, mostly people in their twenties and early thirties, stood and cheered, clapping madly, some even stomping their feet.

For the next thirty minutes, their icon was front and center!

TWO HOURS LATER, KRIS AND KATRINA were handing their menus back to the waitress, having just placed orders for fresh scallops and baked salmon, respectively, with small Caesar salads on the side. The aroma of fresh San Francisco sourdough bread rose from the basket between them.

"Cheers." Their glasses clinked and Katrina sipped her lemon-flavored tea while Kris lifted a glass of fumé blanc, bottled on the north coast near Mendocino. "Wouldn't a glass of wine go well with your salmon, sis?"

"I'm sure that it would, but I'm still a teetotaler," she laughed softly, holding up her glass. "Get it? *Tea*-totaler?"

"I got it, Kat, but what do I do with it? Your jokes are still off the wall and bad as always."

"You're right. I give up. I'm in the presence of the most quick-witted mouth in San Francisco. By the way, my roommates want your phone number, brother dear. What do you say?"

"I say show me their pictures."

"They're really great people."

"Forget the pictures. They could look like Eve and Bathsheba and still not get my phone number. Can't you see me hooked up with somebody who stands in the pulpit every Sunday in her long flowing robe, presenting me with the 'Ten Commandments for Making Our Home a Happier Place'? And my not getting a word in edgewise? We'd live in a *parsonage* and raise little 'preacherettes.' Our marriage would be like the anteroom of hell!"

"Whoa. How did we get from phone numbers to a marriage made in hell?" laughed Katrina, touching the corners of her mouth with her napkin.

"You know, Kat, you're the only person I know who can make wiping her mouth look like a work of art!"

Katrina dropped the napkin onto her lap. Her slender fingers pointed toward Kris and, with the natural grace of a ballerina, she made a gentle flowing motion with her hands. "And you are as full of it as you always were. Tell me, is there anyone special in my dashing brother's life these days?"

They paused momentarily as the waitress placed their salads on the table. Kris grinned, reached for his fork, and speared some lettuce. "Nope, not a soul. I'm married to my work right now, and serious female relationships will have to wait. Now, not so serious ones? Well, that's another story."

At the precise moment he filled his mouth, Katrina spoke up. "Would you like to say a blessing on the food, Kris?"

They looked at each other, eyes dancing mischievously, until the smirk on Katrina's face broke up into a girlish giggle.

"It's been a while, Kat," he said, managing a sheepish look as he swallowed. "I wouldn't want God to die of a heart attack, and He just might if He heard me praying. Why don't you do the honors?"

They bowed their heads.

"Thanks, Lord, for letting Kris and me be together tonight. You know how much I love my brother, and miss him too, even though he is a bit of a rapscallion. Keep Your eyes on us both as we look to the future. And bless this wonderful meal. In Jesus' name, Amen."

Kris gave Katrina a long look.

"Rapscallion? You sit there talking to God Almighty and call me a 'rapscallion'? What is that? A seminary word reserved for the theologically elite?"

Katrina burst into laughter and soon they were regaling each other with "memory stories" from childhood days. The main entree was served, devoured, and then replaced with cups of freshly ground coffee. Outside, it was dark and few lights could be seen from their window view of the Bay. A piano began playing in the background. Katrina glanced at her watch.

"It's nine-thirty," she said, her voice taking on a more serious tone. "I'm staying with the folks tonight and I'm still a forty-five-minute drive from home, so let's talk."

Six. Kristian

"All right, Kat, let me have it. I know it must be important to drag you all the way up here to talk to Dad and Mom. Are you pregnant?"

"Kris!"

"Okay. Just kidding. How long has it been since you've seen them?"

"Last Easter. And you?"

"When we were home together on Christmas Day. I've seen Mom a couple of times since then, but only for short visits."

"It must be hard."

I said nothing. My hand had begun to ache again, as it always does whenever the subject of our father comes up. I rubbed it with a napkin, flashing back to the pain in his eyes as he "sealed my fate forever" with words crushed in his teeth like grain beneath a grinding wheel.

"You could have been somebody, Kristian. You could have done something worthwhile with your life. But a TV talk show? What is that? A waste, nothing more! You'll have to answer to God for such squandering of your gifts and talents!"

The pain was increasing. It always does when I think how I extended my hand to him as a kind of peace offering before I left. He refused it. We've not spoken since, except to say "hello" and grunt a few innocuous words to each other during the few hours I was at home last Christmas.

"Maybe if you tried again . . . " Katrina's voice broke the silence that hung between us, then trailed off.

I grimaced and pushed back from the table. "Been there. Done that. Dad thinks I'm headed straight for hell in a handbasket. Maybe I am. Mom doesn't want to upset the man, so she stays in the background. I understand that. She's got to live with him. I don't."

"Dad is really not that bad, Kris."

"Dad is Dad! He's opinionated, stubborn, bigoted, and totally unwilling to compromise on any point. It's his way or the highway. He harangues from the pulpit every Sunday with his narrow-minded, simplistic interpretations of Scripture, giving the impression that he knows everything about everything."

"And you don't?" asked Katrina sweetly, with an innocent look. "Remember, big brother, I saw your show today."

"Touché."

"You two are actually more alike than either of you will admit."

"That's really gross, Kat," I retorted, feeling a sudden flash of angry resentment. "Did you come all the way up here just to insult me, or is there something else?"

Her eyes became moist. I could see the tears taking shape. I always hate it when someone I care for looks as though they're about to cry, so I pretended to search for a clean napkin.

"You're right. I'm sorry. There is something else. Do you remember back three years ago? You were new at KFOR, still on probation, I think. I was really proud of you and, in some way, I think it was you who gave me the courage to speak to Dad regarding seminary and the feeling that I have about being called to ministry."

"I heard about it from Mom," Kris answered. "She cried when she told me. I guess she was feeling pretty vulnerable at the time, what with us going our separate ways and all. Maybe she was just coming to the realization of being stuck with him for the rest of her life and we were out the door. I don't know.

"She told me about him giving you his 'women should keep silent in the church' shtick. I have to hand it to you, Kat. You did what you had to do. You stood up for yourself. In some ways, I think you disappointed him as much as I did. Two rebellious brats. Although, going to seminary doesn't seem to be terribly mutinous for a crew member of the Good Old Gospel Ship."

"I know," Katrina responded. "I'm sure Dad felt that seminary would expose me to all sorts of doctrinal liberalism and cause me to stumble over questions that have no adequate answers. I think he was afraid I would lose my faith, or worse, become one of 'them.' And, of course, there is the 'male only in church leadership' thing. Dad really feels strongly about it. I have to say that it was the hardest thing I ever did, going with such finality against his convictions. Until now, that is. He's so strong and forceful. Yet, down underneath, he's a good man. He just doesn't know how to cope with matters of disagreement."

"I'll go along with the 'strong and forceful' part. So what's this 'until now' all about?"

"Okay. This is why I'm up here. I needed to talk to my big brother before going home to the folks. I'm at another crossroads, Kris. In a few weeks, I'll be graduating."

"I've got it marked on my calendar. Count on my being there. Wait a minute. Does this mean I have to meet your roommates?"

Katrina nodded with a knowing smile.

"Gimme those pictures. Forewarned is forearmed."

"Be serious, big brother. I'm about to throw myself into the lion's den and you're the one person with whom I've always felt close enough to share my feelings."

"Okay, here I am being serious."

"I've accepted a job."

"Since you'll be graduating shortly, it sounds like the thing to do. Where?"

"I'm going to be teaching high school students in a Christian school."

"Great! Congratulations. Teaching ought to sit better with dear old Dad than having his daughter pastor the First Church of the Rude Awakening. So what's the kicker?"

"The kicker, as you so picturesquely put it, is that I'll be teaching in Antalya, Turkey and helping in a mission there."

That one caught me so off guard my mouth dropped open in surprise.

"Turkey?"

"Yep."

"My little sister is going to Turkey? Like to live?"

"And to teach."

I let out a low whistle, just as the waitress brought the check. "Shades of Genghis Khan!"

"Will there be anything else?"

I looked up. "Will there ever! Fortunately for you, it won't be happening here. But thanks for your service. The change is yours."

"Thank you, sir," she replied with a puzzled smile. "And both of you have a pleasant evening."

We walked at a leisurely pace toward the exit. As we passed by the table host's desk, Katrina put her hand on my arm and gave me an imploring look, one that bordered on sheer desperation. "Will you come with me?"

"You mean home? Tonight?" I stammered, taken even more by surprise at this invitation than at her announcement. "Get a life, girl. Our father hasn't talked to me about anything except the weather in over two years. Besides, they're probably in bed by now."

"I know. But, you could stay over, and we could all have breakfast together."

"Like old times?"

"Kind of."

"Come on, Kat. It will be 'old times' until you drop your plans on two unsuspecting, middle-aged people who've never been east of the Mississippi River, north more than a hundred miles into British Columbia, south past San Diego, or west of the Golden Gate Bridge."

"This *is* crazy, isn't it?"

"Crazy is for people who've lost the ability to think rationally for themselves. You don't qualify for crazy. You're totally out to lunch, sis! Bonkers!"

"So does this mean you'll come with me?" she asked in her sweetest voice. She took my hand, flashing her blue eyes with that most "helpless female" look. "I'll drive you back after breakfast in the morning."

I squeezed her hand and put my arm around her shoulders. "Kat, I wouldn't miss this for the world!"

Seven. Katrina

2350 local time
Baytown, California

It was midnight by the time Katrina turned into the drive and came to a stop in front of the carport.

"There's the old Falcon," Kris muttered under his breath, their lights illuminating its dated profile. "I wonder if it's paid for yet."

"What?"

"Nothing. Just talking to myself."

"It really bugs you, doesn't it? I mean the fact that Dad has struggled his whole life in small, difficult churches, earning barely enough to make ends meet."

Katrina's words were soft, without a hint of accusation. She turned off the lights and the motor. The stillness brought with it the feeling of being in a time warp, suspended between the past and the present as they stared through the windshield at the familiar outlines of the old car, the sidewalk, the house where they had last lived together as a family.

"Yeah. I have to admit that it does." Kris sighed heavily, ending the peaceful, halcyon minute. "I like nice things. Hey, that dress you're wearing says you do too. I hated having to live the way we did, and I hated the church because it seemed to take great joy in making 'pauperism' possible for us. As long as we're being gut-level vulnerable tonight, I'd have to admit resenting Dad because he let himself settle for pennies all his life and dragged the rest of us through near poverty as well."

"He didn't have to, you know," Katrina responded quietly.

"Say what?"

"He could've made good money if he had wanted to."

"How so?"

"He has a degree in accounting."

"A what?" Kris turned to her, his eyes wide with surprise. "When? You're kidding, of course."

"No. He earned a degree in accounting from Washington State University before he and Mom were married."

"I don't believe it. I've never heard that. How did you find that out?"

"Mom told me. When I was home last Easter."

A long silence.

"If that's true, then why didn't he use it? Why didn't he get a job as an accountant or something and make some real money?" Kris asked wonderingly. "Why didn't he just go out and do it?"

"I asked Mom the same question."

"What did she say?"

"She said that Dad became a Christian in his senior year at WSU. He was living in a men's dorm and had been partying the night before."

"Get out, Kat! Our dad partying? That's impossible! He doesn't know how to spell the word, much less act on it!"

"Believe it, big brother. From Mom's lips to your ears. The next morning, a guy that Mom doesn't know, someone down the hall from Dad's room, came in and I guess really talked to him. He challenged Dad to get his life together. Told him about the difference Jesus Christ had made in his life and said the same thing could happen to Dad. I guess they even prayed together right there."

"I've never heard a word about this. In fact, now that I think about it, Dad's been vocal about everything *except* how he became a Christian."

"Mom says he's so ashamed of some of the things he did

before becoming a committed Christian that he refuses to talk about them. Even with her."

"Dad? Ashamed?" Kris repeated incredulously as he stared at Katrina.

"We all carry shadows from the past. Forgiveness comes from Jesus, from loved ones, from friends that we've hurt. But we still remember. Anyway, when his faith took hold, Mom says he felt so strongly that God was calling him into ministry that he gave up everything he had worked for, including a job promised him by a prestigious accounting firm in Seattle. Just chucked it all and went to Bible school for two more years. That's where they met."

"Yeah, I've heard that part. But I can't believe that I never knew about WSU. I just assumed the two years in Bible school was all the education he had."

"Mom says that Dad never looked back after that day. He's really not a great preacher, as preachers go. You know that. We all do. But there's not a man more completely sold out to God and to the ministry. He's given God and the church the best he has to give. Maybe that's the reason we felt short-changed at times as kids. He didn't know how to maintain the balance between his zealousness for God and his love for his family. From what Mom says, I think he's aware of that now, but you know Dad. He certainly fits the old saying, 'You can always tell a Dane, but you can't tell him much!'"

They both chuckled, as Katrina continued.

"She says he has his regrets, though. He just doesn't know what to do with them. Think about it, Kris—he's helped several small congregations get through their most difficult and divisive times. That sort of work takes a really strong man. He's led those churches back to their primary reason for being, and today their people are making positive contributions to their communities and to God's kingdom. There are lots of pastors in bigger churches who can't do what Dad's been doing all these years. And, if you ask me, we didn't turn out too badly either, in spite of it all. Of course, that's a purely subjective opinion and may be slightly skewed by my own bias."

"Then why . . . " Kris' voice trailed off as he stared at the rear end of the old Falcon, playing back in his mind what he had just heard.

"Why is he so narrow-minded and hard-nosed?" Katrina finished his question. "Why is he so difficult at times? So hard to reach?"

"Exactly."

"Maybe he's seen the spiritual darkness out there. You know, firsthand? Maybe he understands what a lot of us don't, like the terrible reality of evil and its resulting tragedy in people's lives. His ministry *has* had a kind of prophetic edge to it. And, you know what I think? I think maybe he's not as certain about having all the answers as he would like for us to believe. I grew up thinking Dad had answers for everything, but now I'm not so sure. I get the feeling that he becomes alarmed over some of the important questions for fear there are no answers. I'm positive that was a main reason he didn't want me to attend seminary—or, at least, the one I chose."

"Could be. And then again, maybe he's just a cantankerous old goat who has his horns stuck between the pages of the Old and New Testaments and can't get loose!"

Katrina shrugged with an air of resignation toward her brother's cynicism. "Maybe."

Kris opened the door.

"Come on. Let's catch some Zs. I have the feeling we may both need a good night's rest come tomorrow. Do you have a key or do we have to get in the way I used to when I was out after curfew?"

He stepped onto the gravel driveway.

"Kris Lauring!" Katrina's tone of shocked disbelief was quickly replaced by mischievous laughter as they walked to the door. "You are bad, you know? Maybe that's one of the reasons I love you so much!"

Thursday, 29 May, 0835 local time

PEDAR AND SARAH LAURING WERE SURPRISED to awaken the next morning and discover their children sleeping in their old familiar rooms. Sarah hugged both of them, with exclamations of happy elation. Pedar kissed Katrina on the forehead before walking across the hall to offer a perfunctory handshake to Kristian.

Sarah hurried off to begin breakfast after assurances from

both children that they were totally famished, a borderline fabrication given the size of their dinner on Fisherman's Wharf the night before. Still, they were acting on every grown child's basic instinct when returning home to mother, fulfilling the hallowed requirement to look or at least sound underfed so that she can go to the kitchen and revive a bygone family era, getting on with what mothers do better than anyone else on earth.

Katrina came out of the bathroom, her hair wrapped in a towel, suntanned face freshly washed and free of makeup, wearing blue jeans and a white blouse tucked in at the waist. Her feet were bare. Pedar was just finishing placing four settings around the small breakfast table. Faint sounds of running water indicated that Kris was still in the shower.

"It's good to see you again, Katrina." Pedar smiled as he stepped away from the table, eyes double-checking what he had just done to be sure nothing was forgotten. "What a pleasant surprise to wake up and find both of our children at home. How long can you stay?"

"Actually, I have to take Kris back to the city this morning. I met him yesterday afternoon at the station and we had dinner at DiMaggio's."

"Is everything all right?" asked Sarah, looking up from the stove as she ladled out buttermilk mix onto a hot griddle. The batter formed tiny mushrooms that erupted in small volcaniclike sinkholes across the golden surface. When there were just the right number of these irregularities, she flipped the rounded pancake over on its back. "You usually call before you come. Not that it matters, of course. This is such a wonderful surprise."

"Everything's fine, mom. I just needed to talk over some things with both of you and I asked Kris to come along." Out of the corner of her eye, Katrina caught signs of a sudden tenseness in the lines that crisscrossed her father's thin, pale face. "I plan to stay over tonight, if that's okay. I've an appointment to see someone this afternoon at two. After that, we can spend the rest of the day together, unless you've other plans. I have to head back to school early tomorrow morning."

"Of course it's all right, dear," her mother smiled affectionately. "I just wish you didn't have to go back so soon. We don't get to see you as often anymore. Perhaps after you graduate . . . you are still graduating, aren't you? There's not a problem at school, is there?"

"No, mom. I'm still graduating," she said with a half smile. "The Dean informed me last week that, if I don't mess up during finals, I'll graduate *magna cum laude.*"

"How wonderful! Did you hear that, Pedar? 'With great distinction.' Oh, we're so proud of you, dear! Aren't we, Pedar?"

Katrina glanced at her father. His lips forged a thin line beneath the aquiline nose while his eyes sought to mask his conflict at being drawn into affirming an accomplishment which was repugnant to him. There was no sign of happiness on his face, even though he nodded his head briefly in the affirmative. Katrina looked away in the disappointing knowledge that even her *magna cum laude* achievement would not be enough to gain his approval.

Three years had not been sufficient time to repair her father's feelings of insult and outrage. She had acted over his strong protestations. In so doing, Katrina had effectively removed herself from his protection and authority as both parent and cleric. At least, that was how he perceived it. She had hoped that it would ultimately be nothing more than a discordant interlude in their relationship, but she had been wrong.

Kris strode into the kitchen, making a series of sniffing noises as he came up behind his mother who was busy spooning out more batter onto the griddle. "I do believe . . . yes, it is. Homemade hotcakes just like the ones my mother used to make. In fact, dear lady, you remind me a lot of my saintly old mother who used to slave over a hot stove just like this one, heroically trying to satisfy the pangs of hunger eructing from her husband and their first and second born. Alas, she failed miserably, for if she listens carefully, those same sounds can still be heard rumbling in close proximity today."

"Eructing?" Katrina repeated.

"'Burping,' to you unlearned rapscallion magna-come-latelys."

Katrina and Kris burst out laughing.

"Oh, you silly . . . " laughed Sarah, as Kris hugged his mother, pinning her arms to her sides. Even Pedar smiled as he watched the two of them gently wrestle back and forth. "Now you let me go, Kristian Lauring, or I'll see to it that you go on hearing those hunger pangs of yours for a good long time. You'll be getting no breakfast from me if you don't settle down this minute!"

Kris released her and reached for a peach slice sticking up in the nearby bowl.

"Out, young man," Sarah exclaimed, playfully slapping at his hand. "Pour yourself some coffee and sit down. In fact, come on, everybody. Breakfast will be ready in one minute."

A half hour later, the pile of hotcakes had diminished until, try as she might, Sarah could not entice anyone to eat more. Only juice remained in the bowl that had been heaped with peaches. Clearing away the dishes, she poured one last cup of rich, black coffee for each of them and sat down.

The banter and catching up that had crisscrossed the table during breakfast slowly quieted. Fingers played around the edges of cups. Waiting. Kris reached for the milk and poured until the contents in his cup turned the color of pale ivory. Katrina glanced nervously at him. He winked reassuringly. Their silent connection was not lost on Pedar or Sarah.

"Well," Katrina began, clearing her throat uneasily, "I said earlier that there was something I needed to share with you all, so I guess now's the time."

Pedar's face was expressionless, his eyes steady as he gazed at his daughter. His attentiveness made her even more nervous. She wished he would at least blink or something. Her mother's fingers were intertwined, holding tightly to her inner feelings. Only Kris was smiling as he leaned back in his chair, hands behind his head, waiting to see what would happen next.

"I think what I have to say is really good news, but I'd be less than honest if I didn't have some concerns about how you all will feel about it. I have accepted a teaching position. My term of employment actually begins this summer."

"A summer teaching position? Does that mean you won't get to come home after graduation, dear?" asked Sarah, the disappointment showing in her voice. "You've worked so hard at school and at your job in the evenings. I had hoped you could come home for a few weeks anyway. Don't you think you need time to rest, at least for a little while?"

"I'm afraid not, mom. I'll have just enough time to clear my things from our apartment before I fly out. The girls have a new roomie waiting to come in as soon as I leave."

"What do you mean, 'fly out,' Katrina?" It was Pedar who spoke up now, his steady gaze having never left her. "Where is this new teaching position? What school will you be working in?"

"It's a new Christian girls' school, only a year old, and it's located in Antalya, Turkey. It's sponsored by several evangelical church groups here in America."

There was a long moment of eerie silence, broken only by the sounds of people breathing. Katrina waited. Kris' eyes darted back and forth between their parents. Pedar finally looked away from Katrina and stared wordlessly at Sarah before turning back to her again.

"Let's see if I understand you clearly now." His words came slowly, each one distinct and edged with bridled emotion. "You have accepted a job to teach in a school?"

Katrina nodded.

"And this school . . . is someplace in Turkey?"

"Yes."

"That's a Muslim country."

"Yes."

"But you'll teach at a Christian school in this Muslim country?"

"Yes. And I'll also be helping in the mission there."

"You're going alone?"

"There'll be some other teachers there and a missionary couple; but, yes, I'm going alone. I don't know anyone at the school."

"Katrina . . . " Sarah started to speak, but Pedar held up his hand.

"Why didn't you discuss this with us before? You've already signed a contract?"

Katrina nodded.

"I've committed myself for one year. After that, I'll decide if I want to renew. Of course, they will be deciding at the same time if they want me to continue. If it's not something that I choose to do long term, I'll return to the States and look for a church where I can serve on the pastoral ministries staff. I'm fully qualified to go either way, except for the needed experience.

"As to your question about discussing this with you beforehand, I wanted very much to talk with you. But, in all honesty, I knew what your answer would be. And as much as I love and respect you, that answer would have been unacceptable. I really believe this is God's will for my life right now and I must answer to Him first, even before you, daddy."

Pedar pushed back his chair and rose from the table. He stood erect and still, eyes flashing as he looked down at Katrina.

"You're right about one thing, Katrina," he said finally. "I would have opposed your decision, had you spoken to us earlier, just as I oppose it now. Just as I did when you went against my wishes and enrolled in that seminary three years ago.

"The woman's place in the church is clearly stated by the Apostle Paul. And it's not without good reason that the Scriptures command children to obey their parents. You need the wisdom of our experience to guide you. It's not right that you should be making such important decisions without consulting your mother and father. You have no husband to protect you. You are only twenty-five years old."

"There's a different way to say what you just said," Kris broke in, leaning forward in his chair, hands together, elbows on the table. "Kat's a single, twenty-five-year-old woman. She's voted in two elections for the President, and in a few days she'll have her Master of Divinity degree, *earned with distinction*. For goodness sake, dad, Kat's a grown woman. Why don't you treat her like one?"

"Don't you tell me what I should or shouldn't say or do," Pedar snapped back, glaring across the impassable chasm between them. "You may be able to tell everyone what to do at that television station, but I'm your father. The Scriptures make it very clear that I am to lead my children in the way they should go, but I cannot lead in this house any more than Moses could lead the Israelites through the desert. You don't seek your mother's or my advice. You simply do as you please and then tell us after it's done."

"In this family, it's easier to get forgiveness than it is permission," Kris retorted angrily. "Although I think there's even a shortage of forgiveness around here these days."

"Don't give me your smart tongue, young man! You have a quick mouth and it's gotten you a job in which you daily go about questioning the very things your mother and I spent a lifetime imparting to you. You welcome godless men and women to your program and condone their 'feelings' and their 'rights' when you should condemn their sin and try to lead them to Jesus!"

"Hey, dad, I'm not in the pulpit . . . "

"No, you're not," Pedar confirmed harshly. His thin shoulders slumped and he stared down at the table as though he were suddenly alone in the room. Slowly, deliberately, he repeated the words, "No, you're not."

"Daddy! Kris! Stop it!" Katrina was standing by the table, tears running down her cheeks. "What is this anyway? We were talking about me, remember? Will you two stop arguing and listen for a change?"

"What is there to listen to?" Pedar asked. "You've made your decision. If you've come home for a blessing, I'm sorry. I will pray for you as I do for my children every day. I'll ask God to make of your lives something special. But, I do not see that He will bless either of you on the paths you have chosen. I'm sorry, but that is what I see."

Katrina looked helplessly at her mother. Sarah's face was drawn and tears streamed unchecked along familiar lines, lines now further deepened by the pain that had shattered her brief family moment. Kris shook his head as he pushed back from the table and stalked out of the room.

"I'm sorry, too, daddy," Katrina said finally, looking up at her father. "I'm so very sorry. For all of us."

Eight. Katrina

1350 local time

It was nearly two o'clock when Katrina paused at the receptionist's desk. The young woman smiled as she looked up. "Hi. I'm Joyce. How can I be of help to you?"

"My name is Katrina Lauring. I have a two o'clock appointment with Pastor Cain."

"Let me tell his secretary that you're here," she answered pleasantly as she punched in the extension numbers. "Hi, Grace. Katrina Lauring is here to see Pastor. Yes . . . yes . . . all right. I'll send her down. Thanks."

The receptionist stood and leaned across the desk, pointing to her right. "He's expecting you. His office is straight down this hall, last door on the right. It's a glass door and you'll be able to see Grace when you get there. Okay?"

"Yes, thanks for your help."

"It's quite all right."

Katrina felt a little more relaxed after her encounter with Joyce, a good person in the right spot. At the end of the wide hallway, she found the glass door and, beyond it, a pleasant-looking woman working at a computer. Katrina pushed the door open, causing the woman to look up from her desk.

"Hello," she stood and greeted her warmly. "You must be Katrina Lauring."

"That's me," Katrina responded.

"I know Pastor Cain is looking forward to seeing you. He mentioned it to me this morning while we were going over his schedule. I'll tell him that you're here. By the way, my name is Grace."

"Thank you, Grace."

She walked to a door a few feet from her desk and knocked softly before opening it. "Pastor, Katrina Lauring is here to see you."

A moment later, a familiar-looking man strode through the door, his hand extended. "Hi, Katrina, I'm John Cain. It's a pleasure to see you again. The last time, I believe you couldn't have been more than fourteen or fifteen."

"Fifteen is right, Pastor Cain." Laura smiled as she accepted his firm handshake. "My brother and I attended your church's junior and senior high camps three years running. Our own church youth group was virtually nonexistent, so our father let us go to yours. I think those times were the best part of our summers when we were kids. Here, this is my card. It's so new that you're the first person I've been able to give it to."

"Come on in and sit down," Pastor Cain said, as he motioned her through the door. "Grace, hold my calls unless it's family, okay?"

"Of course, pastor."

"I was with your brother on the 'KL Show' last year," Pastor Cain continued as they seated themselves across from each other. "He was kind enough to give me some media exposure while we were looking for our missing daughter, Jessica."

"He told me about it when he heard that I was coming to see you," Katrina replied. "He mentioned that he'd like to get you, and perhaps a rabbi and a priest, to discuss some of the 'Great Questions of Life,' as he puts it."

"I've seen his show a couple of times since. That might be a rather intimidating experience. He's one of the most direct talk show hosts I've ever seen. He likes to push the envelope, doesn't he?"

"That's my brother."

"How does your father take to all that?"

"Let's just say that he has yet to come to terms with it. I think it's about to become even more difficult this fall. There's a possibility the network may pick Kris up and throw him to the media wolves in September."

"Wow, that's pretty heady stuff for a young man. How old is he?"

"Twenty-eight."

"Impressive. And you, young lady. I understand, from what Grace told me when you called earlier, that congratulations are in order. You're graduating in a few weeks. That's terrific! Do you have plans for the future or are you taking some time out?"

Katrina was feeling more relaxed than at any point since she had awakened early that morning. She liked this man. Like millions of others, she had followed the media's coverage of terrorists taking over Calvary Church late last summer, holding hundreds hostage as they gathered in a worship service. Those events, together with coordinated terrorist attacks in Boston and Israel, had been dubbed the "September Strike" by the media.

An extended part of that terrifying weekend was the kidnap and disappearance of Pastor Cain's daughter while traveling with her father in the Middle East. Agonizing months of searching had followed. This man had been through a lot. That was one of the reasons she wanted to meet with him.

The other was the memory of him from ten years before, when he visited their youth camp. He had spent the afternoon playing volleyball, sitting by the pool talking to the kids, and that evening had been part of the chapel service.

She recalled Pastor Cain asking the "preachers' kids" attending the camp to stand. At first, she had been too embarrassed, thinking that she and Kris were the only ones there. But then, John's son, Jeremy, was standing and eventually six others. Nine all together, out of the one hundred and fifty-plus in attendance that week. Pastor Cain talked briefly about what being a PK was like and how much the other kids meant to them. There was a big applause after he was done, and later on the other campers had been especially friendly. Katrina never forgot the man or the feeling of belonging he had left with her.

"Actually, that's part of my reason for being here today. I've been accepted for a teaching post at the new Christian school in Antalya, Turkey. I'm leaving right after graduation. I'll be working with high school girls for the most part and assisting in the mission."

"And I suppose you're still in need of some financial support?" Pastor Cain asked.

"Well, now that you mention it, yes, but I didn't come to ask for money. I've done pretty well working my way through school. There's one outstanding loan that I'll be chipping away at for some time. Other than that, I've managed a pay-as-you-go approach. I needed to raise funds for my plane ticket until this morning. While my brother and I were driving back to the city, he volunteered to pay for it."

"That's very nice of him," Pastor Cain commented.

"Several friends and a couple of churches are contributing $50 to $100 a month to help me with incidentals. The school provides me with room and board. I know it won't be easy, but the more I trust the Lord, the more He seems to provide."

"I've found that to be true," affirmed Pastor Cain. "So, just what is it that you have on your mind?"

Katrina took a deep breath. "It's about our family, Pastor Cain. I never forgot the night you visited our youth camp and talked about what it meant to be a PK. You seemed to really understand. I'm sorry to say that some of what you said, however, is the exact opposite to what Kris and I have experienced at home. I remember you telling us that being a PK was a great privilege, but that it also afforded big challenges. You said that it was hard being the son or daughter of the person who stands up every week and tells people how they should live.

"Well, in our family, the hardest part of being a PK has come from within, not from outside."

"I need you to help me track, Katrina. Are you saying there are problems at home? Serious ones?"

"Nothing immoral or anything like that, Pastor Cain. Our father is a good man, and our mother's the best. But by nature or by calling, I'm not sure which, Dad is more of a prophet than a papa. Life is very black and white for him. There's no gray, no room for compromise. He's suspicious of everything that doesn't come directly from the Holy Scriptures."

Katrina paused and looked down for a moment, then back at

the pastor. "And right now I'm feeling guilty about bringing any of this up. Like maybe I'm betraying my father by talking about it. Do you understand?"

Pastor Cain nodded and smiled reassuringly. "I've not gone through the same experiences as you, so I'm sure there are elements that I don't understand. But, Jeremy . . . that's my son . . . he and I have been through some very difficult moments. So much so that at one point I wondered if we'd ever have a real relationship as adults."

"That's exactly my concern, pastor," Katrina said as her eyes moistened. "Our family life has never been the greatest, but now I'm afraid that we're losing even the little there is left."

"Katrina, I want you to sit back and relax now. I have no other appointments this afternoon and I want to hear whatever you wish to tell me. God obviously has His hand on your life and has prepared you for a wonderful task. If I can help lighten the load a bit, this day will have been worthwhile."

For the next two hours, Katrina explained her family as best she could, answering all of Pastor Cain's questions, listening as he commented and tried to bring perspective.

"I thought maybe he'd mellow on his views of women who feel called to ministry," she said, as they reached the point of Pedar's hostility toward her direction in life. "I know that it may be out of the ordinary, but still . . . "

"There were several women in leadership roles in the early church, Katrina," Pastor Cain countered. "Priscilla in the Book of Acts and Phoebe, the deaconess in Romans 16, to name a couple. The formality of office was not really in play at the time, but these were influential women who left an indelible mark on the church of their day. I know that some denominations are restrictive in this regard and can call up verses of Scripture that appear to support their position. I respect their right to do so, though it's not the position that I personally take.

"You'll simply have to find a group that is open to women in ministry and go from there. That shouldn't be difficult for one as spiritually and academically qualified as you, and I'll be happy to help in whatever way you may need. I understand the desire to have your father's blessing and perhaps that will come someday. In the meantime, your Heavenly Father's approval is the most important confirmation and it's all you truly need."

They talked further until finally she stood and prepared to leave, thanking the pastor profusely for his time and attention.

"It's been my privilege. Esther and I will be praying for you in this new adventure. And for Kris and your parents, as well. You are loved by God, Katrina Lauring. He has a wonderful plan for you. Pursue it with all your heart!

"There'll be lots of challenges to overcome and many questions that will need answering. Every once in a while we get a glimpse as we walk in His steps. But much of the time, He keeps us in the dark. I've decided it's because He knows everything and is never surprised. So, in order to keep from getting bored, He likes to surprise us!"

They both laughed at that and shook hands as John opened the door. They said good-bye beside Grace's desk.

"God go with you, Katrina."

"Thank you, Pastor Cain."

"Oh, I almost forgot. Grace, I have to run, but would you call Accounting and have them cut a check for $1,000 for Katrina from the undesignated missions fund?" He turned to Katrina. "Can you wait a few minutes until someone brings it in here?"

"Why, I . . . Pastor Cain. I . . . I don't know what to say," Katrina stammered.

"Just say thanks to our church family when you get the opportunity. Write us from Turkey. And consider Calvary Church as one of your sponsors. I'll approach the missions committee at their next meeting about some monthly support as well. You'll be a refreshing new missionary from our own hometown, with God-given gifts and skills and lots of enthusiasm. You're the kind of person our church looks for when it comes to expanding our financial support of home and foreign missions. You'll be hearing from us soon."

"Thank you so much!" Katrina felt her face flush with grateful embarrassment.

"You're most welcome. You are going to one of the most exciting and challenging parts of the world. I expect that God is going to use you in a special way, Katrina. Remember, Jesus is full of surprises. And He always knows where we are! Take care of yourself and God bless."

Pursuit

He disappeared through the doorway, his long strides quickly taking him from view.

Katrina sat down and looked at Grace who gave her a thumbs-up signal. Then they both broke into laughter. Ten minutes later, a check for $1,000 in hand, Katrina walked out of the church and started across the parking lot. She looked at the check, then up at the clear blue sky, as she shook her head in amazement. The last few hours had been an emotional roller coaster.

There's no doubt about it, Lord, she thought, as she reached for her keys to unlock the car door. *You really are full of surprises!*

Nine. Kristian

Thursday, 29 May, 1045 local time
San Francisco

It was hard to put my mind back to work after our little "parsonage scenario." I should never have gone home with Kat, but hindsight is always great, isn't it?

I drove the car back to the city and waited for Kat to pull it together before saying good-bye. I'm not sure what she was hoping for. A miracle, maybe. But, when it comes to the stubbornness of the Always Right Reverend Pedar Lauring, I think God is one miracle short.

After a quick stop at my apartment to change clothes, I headed for the station, hoping that the "KL Show's" producer-director, Sally Grayton, had today's guest bio sketches ready. Ironically, two of them were "men of the cloth," a pastor from a large Charismatic church in San Jose, and the other from a Congregational church here in the city.

The third guest was the organist at a Baptist church in Oakland until recently being fired after "coming out of the closet" with the admission that she was currently living with a lesbian lover. She was suing the church for wrongful termination and had agreed to the interview with the stipulation that her attorney be present. The church had taken the position that her lifestyle ran contrary to their religious beliefs, making her no longer employable.

I was thinking about this and about Kat and life in general when I pushed open the door to the station's Stockton Avenue entrance. To my surprise, red and white balloons had been loosed in the entry area. Sally was standing by the security desk with a huge smile on her face. She insisted that I wait until she could make a call. A couple of minutes later, Claude Jardin stepped out of the elevator, also grinning from ear to ear.

"There you are, my boy," he gushed effusively. "We were about to start without you."

"Start what?" I asked curiously, following them into the elevator. They both wore smug looks on their faces and I was trying to remember if I had read all my in-house memos. "Did I miss somebody's birthday?"

"No," Sally said, her eyes sparkling with excitement.

"Did Disney buy us out along with everything else?"

They laughed and shook their heads.

"Ted Turner then?"

"No, this is good, but not that good," Jardin chuckled, as the elevator doors opened onto the second floor.

"For he's a jolly good fellow, for he's a jolly good fellow . . . " The area in front of the elevator was surrounded by KFOR employees, mostly those who worked in some way with the "KL Show," and most of them singing off-key. A desk had been cleared of its usual debris, in itself something bizarre for a television station. In place of the normal clutter was a cake with a single candle. Wine glasses were set beside bottles of the Napa Valley's finest reds and whites and it looked as though the party was under way.

"Would someone mind telling me what this is all about?" I asked. At that moment, Regina Levine stepped out from behind an office partition, waving a sheaf of papers in her hand.

Regina had visited our show the first time nearly nine months ago, the result of a phone call from Claude. He had earlier encouraged me to get an agent. I would need one, he said, if I were going to really make it in this business. He was right. There were "ropes" that I had not learned yet; in fact, I didn't even know where the rigging was located.

Somehow he had squeezed a promise out of Regina to come by the next time she visited her daughter, who was a freshman at UC Berkeley. The day she came, it turned out that even Claude didn't know she was there. She just filed in with the rest of the crowd. I think she planned to slip out the same way, if she didn't like what she saw. But she stayed for the entire show and afterward introduced herself, inviting me out to dinner.

Regina is a brassy-mouthed tough talker who started out as a secretary and later moved up to an agent's position for WorldWide Creations in the early seventies. It was during this period that she met Asher Levine who, after years with NBC, happened to be forming a new agency. It was her first, his second, when they married. She joined him in the business, they had two children of their own plus one from his first marriage, and the rest was history. Today, International Talent Management represents some of the biggest and brightest stars in show business.

Regina wanted to know about my background, dreams, and goals for the future. While complimenting my "winning personality," she pointed out that my "experience line" was very short. I was, in her own words, a mere "pup" when it came to "star stuff." She asked if I had a Q-score. I said, "Do you mean IQ?" She rolled her eyes as if to say, "Here, let me help you out of the cradle and hold your bottle."

The longer we talked, the more I realized how little I really did know about this business. I had stepped into a major market, virtually by accident. If I still believed the way I had been brought up in church, it was like I had been "divinely led" or something. My natural skills and good coaching from Sally helped knock off some of the rough edges and, before I knew it, I was on my way.

Listening to Regina, however, made me realize that I had been hatched in a cocoon and now I was being asked if I could fly. I said yes as quickly and confidently as I could, but what does a caterpillar really know about flying anyway? "And what is a Q-score?" I asked finally.

It turned out to be a rating produced every spring by a Long Island company called Marketing Evaluations, Inc. Network programmers use it as a casting device. It measures a performer's recognition and popularity within his or her working category as an actor or broadcaster or whatever. I told her that since I hadn't even known what it was, I doubted any Q-score existed with my name on it, and the longer we talked, the more I was beginning to wonder about the existence of my IQ score. She laughed.

No matter, she said. Conan O'Brien came out of nowhere to take over the microphone of "Late Night" at NBC, after Letterman went to CBS. He had been popular even without a Q-rating. Besides, she and Asher had already watched a couple of show tapes sent to them by Jardin without my knowledge. If I was interested, so were they. And that's how I became a client with ITM.

I guess a lot of life's successes are the result of being in the right place at the right time. If that's true, I did have one important advantage. KFOR was one of a half-dozen major market stations owned and operated by the network. As things were going in my relatively brief television career, working at an O and O station gave me an edge that I would not have had working with an independent. That too is hindsight. The truth is, I was so green that I grabbed at the first job offered.

And now, nine months after that initial dinner with Regina, she was back here at KFOR waving some papers and smiling from ear to ear. Claude introduced her to the crew standing around. She greeted everyone effusively and then picked up an empty glass and waved it to the staff as they closed in around me, giggling and laughing.

"Kris, we have a contract! You're going to the network this fall!"

"What? Are you kidding?"

"Yea!" "Attaboy, Kris." "It's the Big Time, buddy!" "Can I have your autograph now before it's worth something?" "Can I have it before it *isn't* worth anything?" People were shaking my hand and slapping me on the back.

"So, what's the deal?" I managed to ask finally, looking at Regina.

"The deal is that the network has decided, in its great and wonderful wisdom, to put your face on every screen in America, Kris. You are about to become a household word . . . a four-letter one at that."

Everybody laughed and then the party really got going.

Sally was busy cutting the cake. People stood around pouring and drinking. And drinking and pouring. It looked as though tonight's commute hour was definitely in jeopardy.

Vern McNair reached into his wallet and pulled out a $10 bill. "You win, Claude." I could hear them laughing as Claude touched the bill to his lips.

"You're on your way, fella, to L.A. or New York. That part hasn't been decided yet."

Three days later I had my contract and my destination. The new show would be based in Los Angeles. Its format would be live-to-tape, Monday through Friday, expanding from our current thirty minutes to one hour, aired in the 6:30 to 7:30 P.M. time slot, right after the network news, and opposite programs like "Extra," "Entertainment Tonight," and "Hard Copy." It was the time slot in which the network had consistently achieved its lowest ratings. Sponsors were being sought. Five already looked fairly committed. Two network people were being assigned to oversee and assist in getting programming off the ground.

If all that wasn't scary enough, I heard more of what the network's Big Boys wanted just twenty-four hours before signing on. In a conference call with Jim Stanton, network President of Entertainment, and Sid Maples, President of Productions, I was told of their desire to combine journalistic humor with news, music, and light interview features, the target audience being parents with kids at home and also the seniors who want something different than a magazine show or television's version of the *National Enquirer.*

My first question was, "Why don't you get somebody older if you're trying to hit that age-group with this show?" The more I thought about their answer, the more excited I became.

"Kris," Stanton answered, "to begin with, we think you look like everybody's son or grandson. Older people have no problem with youth, but they want youth with intelligence. You've got that. If they are sports enthusiasts, they're rooting for people your age and younger, right? They know them by name, admire them, follow their records and achievements and live vicariously in their footsteps. The same is true with musicians who will play stuff this age-group listens to or at least tolerates."

"But a lot of television programming is focused on the inane and the ridiculous during this time slot," Maples interjected. "The emphasis is on Hollywood's "Triple S's. Screen personalities, sexual titillation, and scandal. It's not that we don't want you to handle this sort of thing. Hey, it gets viewer attention. We just don't want the program to dwell on it, or if it does, it's because you're taking the subject or the guest to a deeper level in an effort to answer the Why questions. Besides, Washington is pushing pretty hard on 'media influence on family values.' Our sitcoms are coming off as a total rejection of the White House's call for reform, so we need something to balance that problem."

"They liked Johnny Carson, Kris," added Stanton. "And they still like Leno and Letterman and even Koppel. However, those guys target an audience that doesn't mind staying up till midnight. But a lot of seniors shut it off at nine or ten. The same is true of parents with kids and jobs that make them get up too early to stay up so late.

"We think this new show makes a lot of sense. Good humor, probing interviews with interesting people, done by a guy that every parent wishes they had raised."

I didn't say anything, but I thought, *Every parent, maybe—but my own.*

I was told that Tom Knight, one of the most prestigious names in late night, had agreed to work with us for six months as the executive producer in order to get things off the ground. His involvement was apparently the result of some serious arm-twisting, since he was heavily involved with late night programming and a new movie that his own production company had just started.

A woman named Carole Upton had been his choice to serve as the assistant producer-director. I had never heard of her, but if she worked with Knight she must be good. They were coming to San Francisco for two weeks to study the "KL Show" in its current format. I told them that I was contractually committed through the summer at KFOR and that any changes would have to be worked out through Regina.

The entire conference call took about forty-five minutes. Stanton concluded with, "A lot of thought has gone into this decision. The executives have scratched off their entire list of candidates for the job. You're our man, Kris. Number One! Welcome to the network family."

I called Kat that night to tell her the good news. She had gone back to Baytown to stay with our parents. She was excited for me, of course, but I sensed some melancholy in her tone. I reminded her that she was graduating in one week and this was a high point celebration in her life too, but she downplayed the whole thing.

No, she said when I asked, Mom and Dad would not be there. Yes, she was looking forward to my coming down. We concluded by agreeing that we now had two things to celebrate. My new show and her academic achievement. Still, no matter what, I could tell by her voice that it would not be enough to fill the sad void caused by our parents' absence at her commencement.

When we hung up the phone, I felt like kicking something. Or somebody!

Ten. Pedar

The day following Katrina's graduation, Pedar Lauring paced back and forth over the living room carpet in their modest Baytown parsonage, hands clasped tightly behind his back, face pinched with worry and apprehension. Sarah sat silently in her chair nearest the archway that opened into the kitchen. Head down, she wiped at her eyes with a tear-dampened handkerchief.

"What else did you tell her, Sarah?" he asked finally, towering over his wife, his neck above the white shirt collar turned red from anger.

"Only that. Nothing more." Her face wrinkled with sadness as she looked up at her husband.

"You're certain?"

"Yes," came the soft reply.

"Why?" he asked, the tone of his voice filled with frustration as he turned away to resume his pacing, only more slowly now than before. "Why did you tell her?"

"It was Easter. We were just talking and one thing led to another. But that doesn't matter. She has a right to know. They both do. She wants so much to be loved by you, to know that you are proud of her. And I want her to be proud of you too."

"You had no right," he persisted.

"I'm sorry, my dearest, but you're wrong. You're wrong in all of this, and you are near to losing them as a result. Kristian for sure. I think perhaps Katrina too."

Pedar stopped near the door. His voice sounded hoarse and he was suddenly overcome with an emotion different than anger as he turned to face his wife. "I love her, Sarah. I love them both. More than life I love them!"

"I know, I know. But they don't. Your own children don't understand just how much you love them. How can they when you refuse to tell them the truth?"

"I can't," he murmured.

"You can," countered Sarah, leaning forward in her chair, "and you must! I've gone along with you on this for years, Pedar. But no longer. How can we continue this way when not telling the truth is tearing us apart?"

He started his slow pacing again, then suddenly stopped and stood still. For Pedar, the living room had become a numbing mausoleum of memories, a place filled with might-have-beens. And what came after would remain frozen in Sarah's heart for the rest of her life.

She stared disbelievingly as the Reverend Pedar Lauring clutched suddenly at his chest and with a groan sank to his knees, dropping forward to the floor!

Terror ripped at her insides as she rose from the chair, and wordlessly reached out her hands. *Call 911! That's what I'm supposed to do, isn't it? Time is of the essence!*

Then the room's hush was shattered by a woeful, pitiful moan that grew until its bellowing noise reverberated through the entire house. Sarah thought her own heart would collapse as she dropped to the floor and wrapped her arms around her husband, while his lament beat against the walls in a mournful dirge.

This was no heart attack, at least, not in the ordinary sense. It was instead the long and bitter wail of a proud man's anguish and pain, a man who at last was nearing the end of his trail of deceit. The garb of the cleric had covered his guilty secret for too many years. But no longer.

The Reverend Pedar Lauring had finally broken beneath its weight!

Eleven. Katrina

Two suitcases, a carry-on and two boxes were stacked on top of each other behind her bedroom door. On the opposite side of the bed were the rest of her things, addressed and ready to be shipped to her parents' home in Baytown.

Sorting out what to store and what to take with her had been a deliberative process during the last week. Katrina reread the letter from missionaries Ian and Dorothy Hedley, confirming her expected arrival and including a short list of clothing and miscellaneous items for her to use as a packing guide. She learned that she would be living with another teacher, Michelle de Mené, from Nice, France. Ms. de Mené would be teaching French and German in the *ortaokul* and *lise* (middle and high school) sections of the school.

She stared at the two Turkish words and wondered if she could ever get a handle on the language. She had been number one in her New Testament Greek class for two years and faintly remembered a year of college French, but could bring only some of the simplest phrases to mind. Maybe Michelle would teach her. Hey, that was a good thought. Actually, she needed a few more of those "good thoughts" right now.

Katrina had read what she could about the country, and had even managed to find a small *Turkish for Travelers* guidebook in a Los Angeles bookstore. Still, the literature available left her with many questions and a growing feeling of uneasiness.

She was nervous about what clothes would be suitable to the climate and the culture. What books should she take? What type of shoes would serve her best? Would she find toiletries and makeup there? She wished that she could talk with Mrs. Hedley, but there was no time. She had tried calling them, but they were in another part of the country both times.

These were all mundane matters and yet the questions continued to pile up, as did her anxiety. She was determined not to show her trepidation outwardly to anyone. Still, the fact was that Katrina Sarah Lauring, young adventuress about to set out alone on a trip halfway around the world and live in a foreign country for a whole year, had never been east of Nevada!

Kris had given her a small portable radio with a shortwave band built in, and a tape recorder with mini-cassettes, when he came for her graduation. Her parents had sent a check for $250. The letter said that it was from them both, but the check had been signed by her mother and the letter was in her handwriting as well. Katrina wondered if her father even knew about the gift.

She had converted it, together with a few cash gifts from friends and her small savings account, into a cashier's check for $1,000. Kris had also paid for her one-way ticket, and the $1,000 check from Calvary Church had been used to draw down her student loan, leaving a balance of $3,000 still to be paid back over time. She wondered at the wisdom of traveling so far with so little cash, but she reasoned that this was what the Lord had provided and now was not the time to stop trusting.

There had been moments, though, during these last weeks, when she felt extremely apprehensive about her future. Questions persisted behind the center stage of her "public" faith and trust in God. *Who do I think I am? What can I hope to accomplish anyway? Turkey, of all places! Maybe Dad is right. Maybe this is just a crazy pipe dream. It seemed right when I made the commitment. But now, I'm not sure.*

She reached over and picked up her academic degree from

off the empty dresser, looking at it again for the twentieth time. She had done it! *Magna cum laude.* A 4.0 grade average, in spite of the fact that she had worked part-time while carrying a full-time student load throughout the last three years.

She loved the church world. Her seminary days had afforded her a wealth of new ideas and experiences. The wide range of biblical and theological studies had opened her mind to a deeper understanding of the Scriptures and the Person of God. Christian education and discipleship methodologies had awakened insights into just how she could translate what she was learning into practical ministry within the local church.

She had surprised herself at her interest in hermeneutics and homiletics, uncovering latent skills that were admired by her classmates. And on the Sundays that her roommates occasionally chose to sleep in, she explored the gamut of worship styles from the quiescent and tranquil Episcopalians to the lively and at times unpredictable Charismatic and Pentecostal expressions of the church.

Her last year as a paid intern at High Point Community Church had proven the most rewarding of all. Teaching a young adult class each Sunday had been a challenging discipline. And filling the pulpit for three weekends while Pastor Miller took his summer vacation was a fantasy come true.

At first she had been reluctant to accept the assignment, wondering if her interest in preaching might have more to do with defying her father than glorifying *the* Father. Finally, she offered her concerns to Pastor Miller.

He allowed that in some parts of the church, the interpretation of Scripture as it related to feminine leadership was very restrictive. This was not the mind-set at High Point, however. True, there was a strong male leadership in the church. But, there was also a sincere belief that God gifted people quite apart from gender distinction and that, when these gifts manifested themselves in a person and were affirmed and accepted by the church body, opportunity for their use should be given.

Pastor Miller gently pointed out that her concerns could well be the ghosts of her father's outspoken views on the woman's role in the church and that, based on her own understanding of God, the Scriptures, and her calling, it was something that she was going to have to work out for herself. After prayerfully thinking about it for a few days, and discussing it at length with her two roommates, she had accepted and was ultimately glad that she had done so. The reception she received while in High Point's pulpit had been warm and positive. Their missions committee had subsequently agreed to provide $100 monthly support for her teaching ministry in Turkey.

Her only regret was that her own father would probably never consent to come hear her share God's Word. There it was again . . . that need for parental blessing! She sighed. *Don't hold your breath, Katrina.*

Thursday, 12 June, 0800 local time
Los Angeles International Airport

KATRINA HAD FLOWN SEVERAL TIMES between San Bernardino and San Francisco and once, as a child, she had flown with her parents to Spokane to attend a family reunion. But that was it. Now she waved farewell to her former roommates who had driven her to the airport and stepped aboard her United flight to New York.

The flight attendant, dressed in navy blue slacks and vest top over a white blouse, glanced at her ticket. "Straight ahead and to your right. Enjoy your flight."

"Thank you," replied Katrina.

Her seat was located in the tourist section on the inside aisle. Settling in, she saw that half of the Boeing 767's seats were empty, including the two middle section seats on her left. That was okay with her. She had too much on her mind to want to engage in conversation with strangers.

This would be a good time for writing in her new journal, a parting gift from one of her classmates. Maybe she could even catch a nap. The final nights in her own bed had been restless and lack of sleep was beginning to catch up with her.

Five hours later, at John F. Kennedy, she began the long transfer from domestic to international terminals, finally arriving at the gate from which her flight to Rome would depart. All this with forty-five minutes to spare. Katrina sat down to catch her breath and watch the ebb and flow of fellow travelers. Before long, her Alitalia Boeing 747 flight was called, quickly filling to capacity. Soon after takeoff, drinks were served, followed by a meal of beef, mushrooms, carrots and beans, salad, and dessert. Katrina had only nibbled at her food on the earlier flight and she was very hungry.

Seat 48F was located near a side exit identified by the word "Portofino" on the door. The good news? It was in the no smoking section. The bad news? The smoking section was immediately adjacent to the open space in front of the exit and soon became occupied with a hoard of inveterate smokers who saw this as a wonderful place to converse while enjoying another cigarette. Since most of her fellow travelers were Italian, Katrina was unable to form a complaint. She thought about speaking to an attendant, but didn't want to create a scene. As it turned out, she didn't need to.

Her seatmate suddenly leapt to her feet from out of a sound sleep, pointed her finger accusingly at the offenders, and shouted at the top of her voice, "Non fumatori! Non fumatori!" Her dark eyes flashed as she stood her ground, feet spread wide, hands on hips, until the last of the tobacco transgressors, filtered tips in hand, had slunk guiltily back to their seats in the forward section.

She then turned her wrath on the flight attendants, glaring fiercely while admonishing them for what Katrina could only assume was their failure to keep the aisle clear. At last, the woman turned, winked at Katrina and smiled mischievously, giving a signal with her hands that in baseball would have indicated everybody was safe. The woman sat down and resumed her posture of sleep. They could continue on to Rome now.

The plane landed at Leonardo da Vinci Airport at about eight-thirty. Katrina had hoped for at least a glimpse of the great old city, but it was not to be. Rome was too expensive for a stopover. She looked at her watch. Her connecting flight to Istanbul was still three hours and ten minutes away from departure.

Katrina found her way through passport control, stopping for a moment in front of the Customs Administration Office to get her bearings. For a while she wandered through La Galleria, looking at store windows, silently pronouncing names both familiar and strange. *Tabacchi-Profumi-Liquori. Barbiere. Caffetteria & Bar. Poste Ufficio. Banco.* It was still hard for her to grasp that she was actually in Italy.

An hour of wandering through the high-priced Galleria shops brought Katrina the realization that Duty-free did not always signal great bargains. At last she made her way to Gate 23 and checked in early. After a stop by the ladies room, she ambled across the waiting area and sat down on a welded steel rod bench under a ZONA NON FUMATORI sign.

Strange. Why would they install something so uncomfortable as these benches for travelers? It's like perching on a fence.

A man sat down beside her and promptly lit a cigarette. She tapped his arm and pointed to the sign, at the same time repeating the words out loud, "Non fumatori." The man glared at her, then moved away. She was learning!

Watching people come and go, she became conscious of how different she must look. Tall and willowy of figure, Katrina's sky blue eyes, fair skin, and blond hair were definitely in the minority here. Her gaze kept drifting back to the woman who sat across from her, reading an Italian fashion magazine.

Possessing a flawless face, with dark eyes, high cheekbones, full lips and a tawny complexion, she wore a pinstripe charcoal suit jacket over a cerulean-colored blouse, matching miniskirt and dark heels.

Katrina tried to imagine how any traveler could be so put together this early in the morning. *Maybe she's a model looking at her own pictures.*

But it was her hair that captivated Katrina's attention more than any other feature. *How can hair be that black? Almost a blue-black. It's absolutely stunning!*

When she heard the first call for her flight, Katrina took a deep breath and gathered her things together. Reaching into her carry-on for her boarding pass, she started toward the gate.

A shiver of excitement ran through her body. Istanbul was now less than three hours away!

Twelve. Ibrahim

It was late afternoon in Istanbul's notoriously hot prelude to its summer season. Oak and ash trees extended leafy arms across the boulevards and parks, stoically awaiting their liberation from the oppressiveness of the day's heat. It was a vigil that appeared to be ill-fated. The air was sultry and heavy with no sign of a break in the humidity. People moved slowly across the campus, seeking whatever shade they could find on their way to cars, taxis, and buses.

Ibrahim glanced around one last time before locking the door to his office. Dropping the key into a small brown envelope with his name scrawled across the flap, he adjusted his grip on a cardboard box filled with books and papers. Strolling down the hallway toward the exit, he slipped the envelope through a slot in the door marked Administration. Just beyond, at the open door to another *fakülte* (faculty) office, he paused.

"Ahmet," he called out softly.

A middle-aged man smoking his pipe looked up from the papers on his desk. "Ibrahim, nasilsiniz?" *Ibrahim, how are you?*

"Tesekkür ederim, iyiyim, Ahmet, babanizin ölümüne çok

üzüldüm." *Fine, thank you, Ahmet, but I'm sorry about your father's death.*

"Thank you."

"Was it sudden? I had not heard that he was ill."

"Cancer of the throat. Too many years of enjoying his cigarettes," the professor replied, releasing a mouthful of pipe smoke to the already blue-gray air above his desk. Ibrahim chose not to comment on the oxymoronic nature of Ahmet's remark concerning the cause of his father's death and his own self-contradicting action.

Instead he asked, "How old was he?"

"Sixty-seven."

"Allah's will."

Ahmet shrugged. "Perhaps. Who can know?"

It was common knowledge that Professor Sötlü was at best a "pragmatic" Muslim, one whose face was rarely seen inside a mosque. Religion, in his view, was a benign part of life's baggage that he dutifully carried in order to preserve his professional status.

"You're leaving today?" Ahmet asked.

"Yes, I catch the night train to Ankara at eleven o'clock. A member of the team is picking me up there in the morning. I should be on site ready to go to work the day after tomorrow."

"How much time off has the University given?"

"Until the end of December."

"Are you excited? I hear that it's a new dig."

"Yes, very much so. Field work is a great deal more exhilarating than the classroom. And, yes, it is a new project. The team has been working for about three months. They've begun to suspect that it's bigger than was anticipated at first."

"Who's heading it up?"

"Doctor Bülent Üzünal. Do you know him?"

"No."

"He's an assistant director at the Anatolian Civilizations Museum in Ankara. He'll continue on site for two more weeks. Then I'll assume the duties he carries for the remainder of the season. We'll continue exploring and digging at least until the snows come. The rest of the time will be spent sorting out what we've found."

"A big responsibility for such a young man."

Ibrahim looked away in embarrassment. "Yes, I'm very fortunate. It's my first time to serve as overseer for such an important project."

Ahmet turned the pipe bowl upside down and tapped it gently in a nearby ashtray. "I envy you, but not much. Getting away from grading papers and unmotivated students sounds like heaven. But, sweating under the hot sun and digging on my hands and knees all day sounds like hell. Better you than me."

"This is why you teach art history, and why I must go out and dig something up for you to explain to your students. No?"

The two friends laughed as Ibrahim turned away from the door.

"Be careful," Ahmet called out, waving his hand. "Don't get lost in your underground city and forget to come home."

"And you as well. Don't drink too much raki or you may confuse Rami Ulmer with Marc Chagall in one of your irresistible lectures."

"Good advice, my virtuous friend. The sad thing is that my students would probably never know the difference!"

THE CLOCK ON THE RESTAURANT wall said nine-fifteen by the time Ibrahim had finished the *kuzu rostosu,* a leg of lamb braised with vegetables, and *söbiyet,* a kind of baklava filled with pistachios, washing his meal down with a glass of white wine. After paying the bill, he carried his suitcase across the boulevard to a boat dock where several small ferryboats rocked gently on the water.

"Hos geldiniz." *Welcome.*

The solitary crewman greeted him without looking up, at the same time reaching for his luggage and stowing it just inside the cabin's open door where Ibrahim glimpsed two other pieces against the wall. The evening still felt warm and sultry as he climbed the steep steps to the outdoor deck on top of the enclosed passenger area.

A half-dozen people casually talked with companions while sitting on folding chairs scattered randomly across the deck. One man leaned against the railing, staring at the lights that shimmered along the nearby bank, apparently deep in his own private thoughts. Beyond the watery darkness, more lights marked the opposite shoreline.

As minutes passed, three additional passengers came aboard. Then, with hardly a sound and no announcement, the boat backed away from the dock and headed in an easterly direction along the Golden Horn, the freshwater estuary separating Stamboul, Istanbul's Old City, from Beyoglu in the north. The crewman who had greeted him reappeared to take drink orders from his passengers. Ibrahim ordered a Coke and, when it appeared, was pleasantly surprised to find that it was cold. Soon they were passing under the Galata Bridge on their way toward the Sea of Marmara.

Once past the bridge, the sixteen-mile Bosphorus strait that connects the Black Sea with the Sea of Marmara came into view on the port side. Serving as Istanbul's watery main street, it was filled even at this hour with tankers, warships, cargo vessels, oceanliners, and ferryboats. In the distance, he saw a steady stream of lights crossing the Bosphorus Bridge and disappearing inland along the Çevre Yolu. By the time he had downed the last of his Coke, the captain was maneuvering the vessel into the dock at the Haydarpasa train station. In a matter of minutes, Ibrahim had traveled by sea from Europe to Asia.

An hour later, he settled into a clean, comfortable upper bunk on the night train. An Iranian businessman named Hasami was snoring away in the lower bunk before Ibrahim could get the light turned out. He felt the train begin to move just as he laid his head on the pillow.

The train rolled steadily through the night, away from Istanbul, past the cities of Bilecik, Bozhüyük, and Eskisehir. Once in the early morning, Ibrahim got up to visit the *tuvalet,* checked his watch, and fell back into the bunk. It was broad daylight when he opened his eyes again. The Iranian was shaking his shoulder.

"It's morning," Hasami admonished, his Turkish heavy with a Persian accent. "Time for breakfast."

Groggily, Ibrahim rose on one elbow and looked out the window. The landscape was green and hilly. "Where are we, do you know?"

"We passed Beylikova a while back. Should be in Ankara within the hour. They're serving breakfast now. Better hurry," the

Iranian called over his shoulder, as he stepped into the narrow passage and headed off in the direction of the dining car.

Ibrahim quickly donned his clothes, brushed his teeth, and doused his face in lukewarm water before following after him.

The dining car was busy, but the Iranian had saved him a place. An attendant in a dark blue jacket flopped a paper plate onto the table in front of him, containing a bagel sealed in plastic and a small marmalade cup. Ibrahim looked dolefully at his "breakfast" as the sour-faced attendant poured warm water into a paper cup. The water sloshed over the sides as he pushed it onto the table alongside the plate. He paused for a second, looking steadily into Ibrahim's eyes, as if daring him to make some disparaging remark. Instead, Ibrahim smiled.

"It's not exactly the Istanbul Sheraton," he said pleasantly, "but I guess it will have to do until we arrive."

Disappointed at his inability to pick a verbal fight, the attendant shuffled off to test some other passenger's disposition.

The Iranian rolled his eyes as he sipped at the tepid liquid. "Nice fellow."

Both men chuckled as they looked out the window. By this time the countryside had given way to an increasing number of shanties scattered haphazardly along the tracks. Soon, one-story tile-roofed houses were jumbled together with high-rise hotels and gray-cement office buildings, arranged like so many disorderly boxes in a warehouse of humanity.

Ibrahim glanced at his watch. It was nearly eight o'clock. Right on schedule.

Saturday, 14 June, 0820 local time Ankara, Turkey

THE TRAIN STATION WAS NEARLY EMPTY. Only a few people came and went. Ibrahim made his way along the tracks, keeping an eye on the bent old man tugging at the heavily laden baggage cart. Inside, he identified his solitary case and tipped the man whose ensuing smile revealed dark gaping holes between tobacco-stained teeth.

On the front steps leading to the parking lot, he called to a shabbily dressed man carrying a large tray of *simit* on top of his head. The purchase completed, he bit into the soft pretzel-like bread while glancing about to see who might be there to meet him. At that moment, a blue pickup truck with a canvas top came racing across the lot and skidded to a stop alongside Ibrahim.

"You are Dr. Sevali, yes?" the driver called.

"Yes."

The man jumped down from the truck and hurried around to where Ibrahim stood. "My name is Çali. Please accept my apologies for not being here when your train arrived, *doktor.* The traffic in Ankara during the rush hour is terrible. Here, let me take your bag."

Çali lifted the suitcase over the tailgate and then opened the passenger door. "You are rested? We have a long journey ahead. If all goes well, we should arrive by midafternoon. I know that Doctor Üzünal is looking forward to your arrival. He tells us that you are one of the best archaeologists in all of Turkey."

"One can afford to be overly generous with compliments when he's as gifted and talented as Dr. Üzünal," Ibrahim answered, attempting to fit his feet around a small petrol can on the floor.

"I'm sorry for the inconvenience," said Çali, as the truck bounced out of the lot and onto the street. "The back of our vehicle is filled with food and supplies for the camp. So we must carry a little extra petrol in the front with us. Just in case."

Ibrahim moved closer to the open window to avoid the fumes emanating from the can. It was going to be a long day.

OVER THREE HUNDRED KILOMETERS and some seven hours later, the pickup truck bumped its way off the main road south of Derinkuyu and headed west on the village road to Kilçilar. A short stretch beyond the tiny village, they turned off the road and onto a vehicle path. In the distance, Ibrahim could see the huddle of black, Bedouin-style tents that surrounded the archaeological site.

Minutes later, to his great relief, they jerked to a stop between two army trucks. Nearby, he saw two jeeps and a dark-colored Land Rover. Ibrahim brushed unsuccessfully at the sweaty grime caked on his shirt and waited for the trailing cloud of billowing dust to settle around them. It was even more primitive than he had imagined.

There wasn't much to see . . . some tired-looking vehicles. The black tents in which members of the team made their homes away from home. Work areas with wooden tables and benches beneath canvas stretched and staked out to mitigate the sun's rays. Two men in work shorts and a young woman dressed in jeans and a loose-fitting T-shirt were at one of the tables, assembling what appeared to be an array of broken pottery pieces.

A field kitchen with the usual pots, pans, and metal utensils, together with a makeshift plank table balanced on top of two empty barrels on which to serve the meals cafeteria-style. To one side of the tent camp was a large water tank resting on a wooden platform and, adjacent to that, what appeared to be outdoor showers and several chemical toilets.

As he walked around to the front of the pickup truck, he spied what he had come to see. There was the cave entrance, half hidden from his view by one of the black tents. He started toward it when out of a nearby tent came a man he recognized. Ibrahim smiled as he turned to meet him.

Dr. Üzünal looked like an archaeologist ought to look. His sun-bronzed face was accentuated by nearly snow-white hair and a large mustache. Ibrahim guessed that he had changed clothes this morning. The olive-colored shorts and freshly laundered shirt looked clean, perhaps even pressed. Unusual out here.

"Ibrahim! Welcome to our hole in the ground!"

"Merhaba, Dr. Üzünal." *It's a pleasure.*

"Nasilsiniz?" *How are you?*

"Tesekkür ederim, iyiyim. Siz nasilsiniz?" *Fine, thank you. And you?*

The two men greeted each other with hands on shoulders and cheeks touching, first the right, then the left. Up close, Ibrahim detected something unexpected in Dr. Üzünal's face. A pinched look, extra crow's-feet at the edge of his eyes. "What is it, doktor? You don't look well."

Dr. Üzünal stepped back and smiled weakly. "One cannot expect to fool the critical eyes of a fine archaeologist."

"It's nothing serious, I hope," Ibrahim responded sincerely, gazing questioningly at the man he admired more than any other.

Dr. Üzünal put his arm around Ibrahim's shoulder and they started toward the tent. "Come in out of the sun. Let's have something to drink and we'll talk."

He motioned Ibrahim into his tent. In many ways it was fitted in typical Bedouin fashion, just not as nicely. Instead of colorful rugs, cheap blankets and canvas covered the earth. A sleeping cot with sheet and blanket was off to one side. In the center stood a small stove, vented by a pipe rising out of the top and turned at a ninety-degree angle to enable its exit high up through the side of the tent. A table, two chairs, and a small bookshelf crammed with books and papers were opposite the cot on the side nearest the entrance.

"Home, sweet home, as they say," said Üzünal, glancing around the tent. He reached for a large can with a picture of red apples wrapped around its circumference and proceeded to pour its contents into two glasses. "You'll bring your things in here once we've drunk some *meyve suya.*"

"Begging your pardon, sir, but your hospitality is not necessary. I'm happy to bunk down with members of the staff until your departure." Ibrahim glanced around. "My presence will crowd you, especially if we try moving another cot in here."

"We'll bring another cot in for tonight and tomorrow night. After that, you can remove it. I will be gone."

They stood quietly for a moment.

"I don't understand," said Ibrahim, breaking the silence at last. "What are you saying? You didn't answer my question earlier regarding your health. Is something wrong?"

There was no answer.

"Durumum kötü mü?" *Is it serious?*

Üzünal stared off over Ibrahim's shoulder for a moment. Then he drew back his gaze to look squarely at his new colleague.

"Disim kanser, Ibrahim." *I have cancer.*

Ibrahim let out a long, slow breath. "I am sorry. What is the prognosis, my friend?" he asked finally.

"I'll have surgery early next week in Istanbul."

"Istanbul? Not Ankara?"

"The tumor is pushing against the left side of my brain. It will require two specialists, one coming down from the top of my head and the other through the nasal area. Worst case, I may lose some vision. However, they believe they've discovered it in time to carve out the entire tumor with minimal side effects. Then, depending on what they find, I'll undergo radiation treatments. The best they can tell me is that I'll be out of commission for three or four months."

"I'm sorry," said Ibrahim again, his tone filled with deep feeling for his friend and mentor.

"Meanwhile, it means that you have to get up to speed much more quickly than we anticipated. You worked with excellence on the Adilcevaz project last summer. I watched you carefully. I don't say this lightly, Ibrahim, but I'm convinced that you will one day be recognized as Turkey's most distinguished archaeologist. Perhaps in all the world!"

Ibrahim raised a hand and started to protest in embarrassment.

"No, don't interrupt me, please. I know that you do not need another father. You have a proud father, a man of the soil, in your home village of Lisla, a great man, even though we've never met. I say this because a lesser man would have driven you to the fields to work with your hands instead of seeing your potential and making certain that you received a fine education.

"To me, however, you've become a *protégé par excellànt,* one who can carry this work of recovering and interpreting the ancient things to the whole world. Your father is the kind of man who made our nation what it is today. But you, Ibrahim, and other rare and gifted souls like you, will make it what it must become tomorrow."

Ibrahim opened his mouth to speak, but again the good doctor waved him off.

"I and my peers have watched your career with great pride and interest. At the age of thirteen you were learning Arabic, Syrian, Chaldean, and Coptic. By the time your *üniversite* training was finished, you were also proficient in Greek and Hebrew. You speak English and French well enough to enable you to lecture abroad, which you have done at various times in the past three years. You studied under the best teachers in our country, as well as in Grenoble and Paris. And now, at the age of twenty-nine, you're about to become the director of what may well be the monumental discovery of our time with regard to Cappadocia's underground cities!"

"I . . . I don't understand . . ." Ibrahim stammered, further embarrassed at the recounting of his youthful accomplishments and, at the same time, inquisitive about the sudden burst of excitement in Üzünal's voice.

"In good time, my impatient friend." Üzünal smiled, keenly aware of the curiosity factor he had purposefully slipped into the inquiring mind of the young archaeologist. "Now it's time to get your things and bring in the extra cot. You need rest. Tomorrow I'll show you what we've found thus far. You have much to learn about overseeing this project."

"Have you . . . told the rest of the team that you'll be leaving?" Ibrahim asked hesitantly.

"Tonight at dinner. I wanted to wait until you were present. It will make for a more orderly transfer of leadership."

Ibrahim nodded, then reached over and touched the man's arm. "Is there anything I can do for you, Dr. Üzünal?"

"You can make me proud of my profession. I've a special feeling about *Kilçilar*. We've named this project after the last village you passed on your way here. It's ours now, to pursue until it reveals the truth about mankind's story in ways that only our kind of discoveries can!"

Thirteen. Ibrahim

Sunday, 15 June
Kilçilar, Turkey

Ibrahim thought the after-dinner meeting had gone about as well as one could expect. The other team members had also been shocked at the news of Dr. Üzünal's illness. They all had come to value his stern but fair leadership and his scholarly approach to the task at hand. They also respected the dignity with which he treated each one of them, right down to the carriers.

Ibrahim was introduced to the group as they crowded in around the tables under the eating area's canvas cover. They listened as Dr. Üzünal took pains to carefully outline Ibrahim's background and accomplishments and to express his own complete confidence in the young archaeologist's ability to assume the role that he would shortly be vacating.

Ibrahim then greeted the staff, expressing his deep sense of gratitude at having been invited by Dr. Üzünal to come work with him, and his own regret regarding his mentor's illness and early departure. He pledged to carry on the same policies and procedures, and encouraged them to join with him in honoring Dr. Üzünal by continuing to give their best to the project.

Afterward, he was introduced to each of the key men responsible for *Kilçilar.* Ibrahim met Tahsin Cem, an architect from Ankara whose task it was to map out the cave's tunnels and record the location and specific details of each discovery, large or small. Dr. Gürer El, a quiet, unsmiling man, balding and diminutive in stature, was an epigraphist from the Anatolian Civilizations Museum. The fact that he was there indicated to Ibrahim that something of interest must already have been uncovered. He was anxious to know what it was.

Dr. Üzünal continued to explain, for Ibrahim's benefit, that at *Kilçilar,* some fifty workmen had been recruited, mostly from the surrounding area. As projects go, this was not a large group, but certainly not a small one either. Ibrahim guessed rightly that it was probably the maximum number that could effectively work in the confining underground spaces. These men were further divided into small teams consisting of a pickman, a spademan, and three or four basketmen or carriers, as they were most often called.

The pickmen were chosen on the basis of experience and superior intelligence. Most of them had been employed on other projects over the years. They were not so old that they had grown blasé and uninterested, nor too young to be in authority over others on their teams. With a special trenching tool, the pickmen scrupulously cut away at centuries of dirt and were usually the first to discover things. It was up to them to expose an artifact without damaging it.

The second man on the team worked with a long-handled native spade. It was his job to scoop up the loosened earth and place it in containers to be disposed of by the carriers. If the pickman missed anything, the spademan should be the one to see it.

The carriers were mostly older men or young recruits without experience. Theirs was a simple task: remove the full containers to a designated area outside the cave, pour them out, and come back for more. It was tedious and thankless work. Still, the pace they kept was something on which the progress of the whole project depended.

For that reason, Dr. Üzünal encouraged Ibrahim to occasionally sit with the carriers during lunch or dinner and associate with them on a personal basis. Good will and understanding between the project director and the carriers was important.

Pursuit

There were two foremen, one from Italy and the other from Israel. In addition to their native languages, Rocco Valetti and Benjamin Hurstein both spoke Turkish and English fluently. They were of average build, muscular frames, and very intelligent. The Roc was well endowed with jet-black hair and skin the color of desert gold. Hurstein, affectionately referred to by his fellow workers as Ben Hur, was fair of complexion and retained only a few wisps of white hair under a wide-brimmed cowboy hat.

As Ibrahim observed the two of them together, he had the impression of a set of sturdy salt and pepper shakers. He discovered that Hurstein also spoke a little French and Spanish, and was conversant in Deutsch, a heritage from his parents who had survived the Dachau death camp during World War II.

Next to the archaeologist himself, Ibrahim knew that these two men were *Kilçilar's* most important people. He observed them as they conversed, understanding that he would be dependent on them for the conduct of the diggers and the ultimate success of the project. He relaxed somewhat as Dr. Üzünal complimented each man, noting that his mentor had worked with them before and seemed well pleased with them both.

The foreman, of necessity, had to be the most qualified man on the ground. He was a teacher who could train the rest in their job specialty. He was a jack-of-all-trades who could take over for those under him whenever needed. He knew exactly what his teams were doing and was able to evaluate the quality of each worker. He was capable of inspiring the workers to do their best out of pride, not from threats or coercion. He was an artful bargainer who settled disagreements and kept everyone in good spirits. He was all of these things if he was good. Dr. Üzünal assured Ibrahim that The Roc and Ben Hur were the very best.

It was ten o'clock when the pleasantries concluded. Dr. Üzünal's face showed lines of weariness and his shoulders slumped slightly by the time he and Ibrahim reached their tent. The low, constant hum of the generator would cease at ten-thirty. Any further need for light until dawn necessitated the use of flashlights or battery-powered table lamps. He showed Ibrahim where the flashlights and batteries for the lamp on his desk were stored.

Water for brushing teeth came from a container with a small spigot, located by Dr. Üzünal's desk. A visit to a nearby chemical toilet completed preparations for bed. Dr. Üzünal explained that fresh water was delivered daily by truck, except on Fridays, and stored in the large tank. At the end of the workday, for one hour the men were permitted five-minute individual showers in a common area. The two men finally said goodnight and within minutes both were snoring lightly.

The following morning, Ibrahim was reminded that running a field expedition involves much more than the literal excavation itself. Dr. Üzünal spent the time cramming Ibrahim with details that should have taken a week to assimilate. He showed Ibrahim how to make out the pay sheets, reviewed the correspondence and account files, walked through the list of vendors and the process for housing and feeding the camp. Names and numbers of key people at the Museum in Ankara, including his own personal phone number, were duly noted.

By lunchtime, Ibrahim was feeling overwhelmed with the administrative details. He had not been involved in this aspect of a project before, but decided he would much rather be where he was than have to face what was ahead for the good doctor.

After lunch, Dr. Üzünal stood up and slapped Ibrahim on the shoulder. "And now, my young colleague, let's leave all this paper-pushing and do what archaeologists are trained to do! You've tasted of our 'household chores' and have patiently tried to act interested in the part of this work that takes more of our time than ever it should. So, are you ready to have some real fun?"

Ibrahim's face lit up. "Yes!" he replied with enthusiasm.

"All right, then, follow me. I'm going to wear a light jacket. You brought one along, I trust?"

Ibrahim nodded.

"Good. Get it. You'll need it once we are inside the cave."

They gathered up jackets and flashlights. Ibrahim hurried to keep up with Dr. Üzünal's quick steps as they walked to an area about twenty meters from the cave's entrance. Here, a canvas stretched on poles covered another large work table. Tahsin Cem and Gürer El were working at either end. Tahsin was mapping out sketches that identified exactly where each item had been found. Dr. El, the only man on the team who insisted on being called *doktor* instead of by his first name, was concentrating on what appeared to be a small piece of stone.

"A clay tablet that was found on Level 2," Dr. Üzünal explained, his voice low so as not to disturb El's engrossment. "We have uncovered what appears to be a small library, though we're not yet certain just how extensive it is. In a few days we'll have a makeshift kiln set up, enabling us to bake and cleanse the tablets; then Dr. El should be able to tell us more."

"Any ideas yet?" asked Ibrahim.

"Ideas, yes, but they're so unusual that it's too early to draw any specific conclusions." Üzünal's tone became somewhat evasive and his eyes crinkled from squinting out of the direct sunlight into the shade that surrounded the table. "Come, let's go inside. I'll talk, you listen."

Ibrahim smiled. He enjoyed the older man's brusqueness.

They entered the cave together, but Ibrahim soon dropped a step behind to accommodate the narrow passageway and the carriers who were steadily moving past them toward the exit. A string of lights dimly illuminated the dark interior. There was a feeling of pleasant coolness as they continued farther and farther in. Reaching a sharp turn to the left, Üzünal stopped.

"It took us a couple of days to open the outside entrance, once we knew for certain where it was located. I think its closure was the result of natural causes, though the ancients were known to hide their entrances to the underground cities. Anyway, once we got past the initial rock and rubble, it was almost as you see it to this point. Perfectly preserved. Very little excavation work needed."

"How did they do it?" Ibrahim's voice was filled with wonder as he stared at his surroundings.

"Amazing, isn't it? I know you've been in several other 'cities,' but you haven't seen anything yet. Check the turn just ahead of us. We encountered a closed section here that took several days to clear. The result of a natural cave-in. Nothing exciting, just rock and dirt. But it gives you an idea of what you may encounter in the weeks ahead. Come."

They passed by the turn and stooped to go through a low tunnel about twenty meters in length and just wide enough for one person at a time. Some carriers waited patiently as they moved beyond and into what appeared to be a good-sized room.

"Look here," said Üzünal. "We know from what we've found at

Derinkuyu and Kaymakli that the entrances to these underground cities were generally closed by huge mill stones to keep out danger, most generally Arab raiders. Here's the first such stone that we found at *Kilçilar.* And see the darkness on the wall? The residue from fires that burned here. This was a kitchen. The people who lived here ate common meals together.

"Fires were permitted only in the kitchens in order to preserve oxygen. Because of the constancy of underground temperature, this posed no real comfort problem, even when the cold winters arrived above. In fact, even candles were used sparingly. Much of their time was spent in total darkness. Hard to imagine what it must have been like.

"You can see over there that smoke from the cooking fires left a residue of soot. And up there? That hole is an air vent. We haven't taken the time to try to see where it goes, but I can guarantee it's not straight up. Some of these vents go on forever in various directions, again making it hard for the enemy to discover them. Before we are through, Ibrahim, you will have seen dozens of similar air passages. And look how small in circumference this one is. How did they manage this?"

Ibrahim could not think of a response.

"There's more to be seen on this level when we come back. Be careful over here now. We're going down some steps."

"Do you have any idea as yet just how deep these tunnels go?"

Üzünal stopped and turned to Ibrahim. "I wondered when you would ask. Of course, you can tell we've been going down in elevation since entering the cave. But this is the first set of steps that we've encountered. They take us to Level 4. Our teams have already reached Level 6 and the end is not in sight! You know that Derinkuyu consists of seven levels that descend to eighty-five meters beneath the earth's surface? Well, we have reached sixty already!"

"You've made outstanding progress to have been here only three months," Ibrahim commented, as he watched carriers make their way up the stone steps from somewhere below. "I only hope that I can continue in the same manner."

"At first, we had enough workers. But no longer. You'll need a larger crew, Ibrahim. Even now, I can tell the work is starting to slow because of the distance to the exit from where we are working." As the last carrier moved past, Üzünal touched his arm. "Come, the way is clear now. We can go down."

Carefully they proceeded down the narrow earthen steps, occasionally balancing with one hand against the wall. At the bottom, the steps opened into another large room.

"What we've just passed, to get to this point, has already given up stone and bone tools as well as some limited human, plant, and animal remains. I didn't take the time to show you, but later you'll want to browse the artistic objects on the walls just above us. Two specific living areas I will show you on the way back. We have yet to confirm, but I believe they represent at least two, if not all three, stages of the Paleolithic Age."

Ibrahim's eyes widened at that revelation. "Am I correct then in saying that the Karain cave, south of here, is the only one in Anatolia where all of the Paleolithic or Stone Age phases are represented?"

"You are. So, if what we've found here is corroborated, that in itself constitutes a major find, not just for Turkey, but the entire Middle East. We live in the land of earth's earliest civilizations, as you know. We've already forwarded some of the smaller items to Ankara for study."

"How long do you think it will take?"

"Who knows? A major problem with all of this continues to be the accuracy of our dating methods. An era that began nearly two million years ago and continued until ten thousand years ago is difficult to measure. But, these items will be compared with the material we've uncovered in the Lower Euphrates region and on the renewed excavations going forward right now at Karain and Yarimburgaz."

"How far down did you find them?"

"So far everything in the Paleolithic Age that we have discovered here in *Kilçilar* has been in deposit layers that go no farther down than twelve meters. We're already well past that depth now. Remember, the farther down we go, the more recent should be our findings. The likelihood is that the initial cave has been here for hundreds of thousands of years. Then others came along and began burrowing further into the earth. These caves have taken centuries to dig."

"And exactly who did it and why is still a mystery, isn't it?" Ibrahim sighed.

"That's true in part, but we're learning more and more all the time," Üzünal said, pointing to a corner of the room as he moved in that direction. "For example, look over here. These are items that one of the pickmen uncovered recently. Tahsin was sick or he'd have mapped this and we'd have them out of here already. They'll be up on top tonight or tomorrow for sure."

Ibrahim knelt down and stared at the stone figure of a mother-goddess represented as a woman giving birth to a child. Next to her, a small handmade pottery piece, brown and black in color and about two-thirds intact, was displayed beside a flint dagger with a bone handle.

"See these depressions in the cave floor? Over there, we opened one up. This was the living quarters for a Neolithic family or maybe a group of families. These are graves and what you see here are gifts for the departed. At the Çatalhöyük excavation, we found that this Age group had buried their dead children under the floor of the rooms themselves. Adults were buried under benches. Here at *Kilçilar,* this looks to be very similar."

"So, these people would have lived in this room somewhere between 6800 to 5700 B.C.?"

"Exactly. The amazing thing is that the subsequent dwellers in these caves didn't destroy the evidence of their ancestors. I was especially surprised to find this goddess, knowing how the early Muslims and Christians felt about such things. At least in the case of the one grave we've opened so far, it appears these artifacts survived because they were buried with the body itself and not simply placed near or on top of the grave. However, that still doesn't account for some of the other findings."

They continued to stroll through the seemingly endless maze of tunnels, stair steps, and underground rooms, examining several with only the illumination of their power flashlights. Finally, Dr. Üzünal looked at his watch. "It's four-thirty. We'd better head back. I promised you a quick look at our Stone Age display. I have one other area I want to show you as well. I think by now it goes without saying to be very careful when you come back alone. It's easy to get lost down here. Until you are familiar, do be careful to watch where you're going."

"Where are we now?"

"This is Level 5."

"I'll get a map from Tahsin."

"Good. Tomorrow, after I'm gone, you should arrange for Tahsin to take you to Level 6. We're almost through a blocked area there. The Roc and Ben Hur have been at it with the crews for three days and I've been told they're almost done. Now, follow me. There's something important up ahead on Level 3."

They walked single file for about ten minutes in silence, listening to the sound of their boots on the cave's floor and its earthen steps while making their gradual ascent. At last, they came to the first of three dome-shaped rooms, each about the size of a large living room.

Dr. Üzünal smiled as he watched the expression on Ibrahim's face.

"Incredible!" Ibrahim whispered, taking a deep breath and releasing it slowly. "Absolutely incredible!"

Fourteen. Ibrahim

Sunday, 15 June, late afternoon
Kilçilar

"Is this what I think it is?" asked Ibrahim. On stone benches, shelves, and on the floor he saw oval-shaped cups, globular jars, large vases, and bowls of every shape and description. There were terra-cotta figurines of the mother-goddess in a variety of poses.

"If you think that these artifacts are primarily from the Chalcolithic Age, and that they were created somewhere between 5400 and 4750 B.C., you are correct. We've not removed anything from this or the other two rooms beyond. They are just as we found them."

Ibrahim tingled with excitement, surrounded by this treasure of ancient artifacts, all collected in a single room. He started to say something when his eye caught a bronze statuette of a stag, and yet another of a bull. On an earthen shelf about three feet from the floor stood a silver and gold idol of a woman. He reached out his hand toward it, then drew back and turned to Dr. Üzünal.

"But how could all these have been found here in the same room? This idol and those there have to be from the Bronze Age, the third and fourth millenniums B.C. They are from a much later period than some of these other rarities." As he spoke, his eyes fell on a small bronze figure of a woman nursing a child. Then he paused to touch an iron and gold dagger and a small gold pitcher.

"How, indeed? You've asked the right question, Ibrahim," observed Dr. Üzünal, his practiced eyes running over the treasure that spread out before them. "It comforts me to know that I have recommended a wise man as my successor here. 'How can this be' questions are the most important of all to one who would be a great archaeologist. I'm sure you will solve the puzzle in time. Meanwhile, come. There is more to see."

They entered the next room, similar in size, through a narrow opening about half the width of a door. Ibrahim instantly recognized two baked clay ring-vases, now popular with tourists who visit Turkish ceramic shops, but representational of the fourteenth century B.C. Hittite era. On a low earthen bench lay at least a dozen gold stamp seals from the eighteenth century B.C. Ceremonial vessels in the shape of bulls baked in clay, gods and goddesses, and a set of gold signet rings were on display.

Ibrahim walked to the far side of the room and knelt to examine a number of clay tablets, some broken apart but still able to be matched. He looked up at Dr. Üzünal.

"The Hittite language in cuneiform script?"

"Yes. When we found these, we sent for Dr. El. He's the expert." Üzünal's face grew grave as he mentioned the epigraphist's name. He lowered his voice though no one else was around. "Be careful, Ibrahim. El is the best at what he does, but the man is a fanatic fundamentalist. He may cause you trouble."

"What sort of trouble?"

"Well, he's already complained to me about having women in our crew. The girl you saw yesterday is a student volunteer from France. Two of her friends are due in next week. They are from the University in Paris and will be here through the summer. El doesn't like it. I think that may be only the first of several issues he calls you on."

Ibrahim nodded thoughtfully. "Thanks for the warning."

Dr. Üzünal shrugged and motioned him toward the last room.

"Wait," exclaimed Ibrahim, his eyes falling on two objects standing next to each other by the narrow passage. One was an ivory statuette of a seated lion, with its head turned over the left shoulder. The other was an ivory winged demon. "These are not Hittite Imperial art."

"You have a good eye, my young friend," answered Üzünal with a pleased tone in his voice. "What do you think?"

Ibrahim studied them carefully, without touching them.

"I'm going to say that this is Urartian in origin."

"Very good! Excellent. Right you are!" exclaimed Üzünal.

"But what are they doing here? The Urartians were centered in Eastern Anatolia and they disappeared after the Medes and Scythians invaded in the sixth century B.C. There's no record of their having come to this region."

"It's wonderful, eh?" Üzünal chuckled, rubbing his mustache. "You have many mysteries to solve. Come, we must hurry. It is getting late."

By now, Ibrahim felt numb from having witnessed the stockpile of antiquities contained in the first two rooms. He was not prepared for what he saw as they passed through another narrow entrance, this one low enough to force them to bend down as they entered. He looked around in amazement. In the matter of a few feet, they had stepped forward five thousand years! They stood in what was obviously the remains of an ancient Christian church!

On several occasions, Ibrahim had visited cave churches in the Cappadocian region. They were all that remained to remind mankind that people of deep Christian faith had, at one time, lived and worshiped here. Some of these carved stone sanctuaries had frescoes or at least simple markings of the cross or the Christian symbol of the fish. Most of the frescoes were faded and in some cases, sadly marred by the hideous markings of modern graffiti, making their meaning and identification difficult and sometimes impossible.

Such was not the case here. What he saw were perfect displays of ancient art, preserved by entombment.

"Eighth century?" he asked at last, his eyes consumed with the beauty of the room.

"Perhaps, though it could be as early as the sixth, maybe even the fifth century A.D. Its preservation is quite remarkable, wouldn't you say?"

"An understatement, Dr. Üzünal," Ibrahim said reverently. "I've never seen anything like this!"

Centered directly overhead, the dome-shaped ceiling revealed the face and upper body of Jesus Christ in multicolored mosaics, with lighter shades of brown and blue emerging from His face and spreading like a sunburst across the spherical covering.

Ibrahim was mesmerized by the face. It was not the usual medieval portrayal of a sad or passive Jesus. It seemed uniquely alive and human in its expressiveness. The eyes were warm and inviting, the facial contours suggesting a faint smile. His hands were open and extended, scarred with nail prints.

"The artist was incredibly talented," Ibrahim exclaimed. "He almost looks alive."

Ibrahim was reminded of his favorite portrayal of the Prophet Jesus. It was "The Christ Pantocrator," a mosaic above the entrance to the inner narthex of the Kariye Monastery in Istanbul. This depiction, however, went far beyond the Kariye mosaic in presenting the human figure while still retaining a sense of deity. The mosaic ended at the upper walls and was transposed by brilliant frescoes in reds, browns, and greens that filled three of the four stone walls. The frescoes displayed the ancient artist's conception of things he had read or heard from the Christian Bible.

On the far wall were scenes depicting the birth of the Christ Child, along with His dedication at the temple and His baptism. Across the back of the church, Jesus could be seen healing a sick woman and raising Lazarus from the dead. The near wall showed Him entering Jerusalem on a donkey, His death on the cross and His resurrection and ascension.

It was all right here. Preserved in near perfection by the dryness and constant temperature. Protected from man's desecration by tons of earth and rock. Concealed from prying eyes by centuries of darkness. An amazing discovery!

The wall without frescoes remained as natural as the day that nameless workers had hewn out the room. It was obviously the front of the church. What looked to be a stone altar was located at the center, inscribed with the Christian sign of the fish, a chalice and a loaf of bread carved in relief on what would have been the side facing people who gathered to worship. The scene representing the birth of the Christ Child was also the place for baptism, in a stone basin hollowed out of the wall. His eyes picked out several long, narrow depressions in the floor.

"More burial sites," he mused out loud.

"Yes," Üzünal agreed, his tone a foreshadowing of trepidation regarding the uncertain future that was his own now. "Possibly their community or spiritual leaders? We don't know. What do you think?"

"Right at this moment, I think that I know very little indeed."

Üzünal grunted in agreement. It was the correct answer.

The remainder of the floor appeared to have been hewn out of solid stone. It was crudely finished, uneven, yet the stones had been worn smooth by myriad bare and sandal-shod feet of the faithful. Beyond the tile ceiling and painted frescoes in this room, there was a noticeable absence of icons.

"You have much to care for, Ibrahim, and much yet to discover and interpret in the days ahead," his gloomy tone now replaced by wistfulness. "I wish I could remain to seek the answers with you."

"I wish and pray for the same, dear friend," Ibrahim said sincerely, placing an arm around his mentor. "May Allah grant you a quick and complete recovery."

Dr. Üzünal stared up at the mosaic Jesus. "He was one of the greatest prophets."

"Indeed," responded Ibrahim, as they stood shoulder to shoulder in the center of the room.

"When I was a child," Üzünal continued with a faraway look in his eyes, "my mother became very ill. My father told me later that they thought she was going to die. Some kind of bronchial disorder, though I'm not sure exactly what. Then, suddenly, the next day she was well and tending to her family."

"What caused such a recovery?"

"My father is getting up in years now, but he has been a devout and highly religious Muslim all his life. That I can say emphatically. However, one day he told me that whenever his parents were in serious physical need, they prayed to the Prophet Jesus. They believed that He was a great healer."

"That's not exactly prescribed Islamic practice," chuckled Ibrahim.

"Not exactly," agreed Üzünal, "but that's what he claimed to have done with my mother. I've since heard of others doing it as well. And now that I'm facing the . . . the possibility of this illness cutting my life short, I find myself giving thought to praying to Jesus for my healing."

Ibrahim turned until he could see Üzünal's face clearly in the artificial light. He was staring up at the mosaic. "You're serious, aren't you?"

"Never more so," was his simple answer.

"But I'm told that many Christians today do not believe in . . . what do you call it . . . divine healing? They insist that the stories of Jesus' healing power are myths created out of the ancients' own need to believe in the miraculous. Others say it was true only as long as He was alive."

"Like Muslims, many Christians do not believe in many things," answered Üzünal with a sigh. "But does a lack of belief, whether harbored in a Muslim or a Christian heart, make fact a fabrication?"

Ibrahim was silent. He stared at the face on the ceiling. He could almost swear that it was looking back at him. Into him. *Could it be . . . could such a thing be possible?*

Dr. Üzünal shook his head, as though suddenly reentering reality. "Enough of this. I've bothered you much too long with my personal ponderings. We must hurry or we'll miss dinner."

They crossed the stone floor to the exit, where Ibrahim waited momentarily for Dr. Üzünal to duck through the small doorway. As he stood by, Ibrahim's eyes fell on three iron pegs driven into the wall. About waist high, on either side of the opening, they seemed incongruent, conflicting with the balance of the room. *What are they? Why are they here?* He wanted to ask his tutor if he had noticed them before and knew the answer, but he hesitated. Now was not the time for more questions, given the mood he had just seen expressed by the man.

Perhaps we all become introspective as we approach the reality of death in a personal way, not simply as something "out there" to be faced some other day. Ibrahim did not know. He was twenty-nine, the picture of health, and preparing to unearth the greatest discovery of his career. It was not the time to be thinking about death.

Not his own anyway.

Not yet!

Fifteen. Katrina

Sunday evening, 15 June
Istanbul

Katrina sat on the edge of the bed, rubbing her tired feet, as she looked out the window of the tiny, third-floor hotel room. There wasn't anything to see really, other than the paint-chipped wall of the building next door. Well, that wasn't altogether true. If she stood at the window, she could look across the narrow alley, where a large and colorful Turkish rug remained draped exactly where it had been when she left the hotel that morning, after completing her usual devotional time of Bible reading and prayer.

The evening before, she had seen a heavyset woman, her pudgy face peeking out from under a faded scarf, wrestling the freshly cleaned rug over the gray cement escarpment and then smoothing it out to dry. Now, Katrina was pleased to see the rug was still there. Somehow it "belonged" in her mental picture of what life in this place was all about. There was something intimate and personal about a rug, even more so than the clothing she had seen hanging from an outdoor line that morning.

Here people walked, sat, talked, ate, lived out the important moments of their lives on rugs. They were also symbols of wealth. Katrina could see why, after pricing a few while strolling through

111

the Covered Bazaar earlier that afternoon. It was a shopping experience worth writing home about, though she had purchased only a few inexpensive items.

A merchant standing outside his shop door, beside a window that presented a gaudy display of gold rings and bracelets, had seemed happy to have someone to converse with in English. He informed her that this largest covered market in the city had been founded by Mehmet II in 1461, and expanded several times until 1701. Sixty-five covered streets, a mosque, seven fountains, even a well . . . and 3,300 shops!

It seemed to Katrina that the wealth of the world was on display in this incredible place. Others apparently agreed, for she was told that doors were closed promptly at seven every evening and throughout the night fifty guards patrolled the two *bedestans* where the valuables were kept and sold.

She had also walked through the nearby *Misir Çarsisi,* the Spice Market, Istanbul's second covered marketplace, with its eighty-six shops featuring a mind-boggling array of spices, many she had never heard of before. The two sites had consumed most of her afternoon, finishing off her second and last full day in the Republic of Turkey's largest city.

Katrina's hotel was located in Istanbul's oldest section, enabling her to walk to several of the historic sites. It couldn't have been better. Her camera was in constant action as she strolled around Sultahmet Square.

In California, something a hundred years old was either torn down or declared a historic monument. How incredible it seemed to stand at the hippodrome, begun by Septimius Severus in A.D. 203 and completed by Constantine I in 325.

That first day, she had happened onto an English-speaking tour group at the Sultanahmet Mosque and listened to their guide's narration. It is known popularly as the Blue Mosque, he had told them, because of the lavish blue-green revetments created to finish the interior. Today, its 260 windows gave off a warm, natural light reflecting a bluish color throughout the massive inner court. And again, she saw rugs. They were important, even in religion.

Early afternoon had been spent at the Museum of Turkish and Islamic Arts, especially in the Ethnographic Department in which a cross-section of Turkish folk life is presented, as well as in the Rug Department, containing specimens from the seventh to the nineteenth centuries.

Katrina had been aware of the powerful Christian heritage of this land, spearheaded at its outset by the Apostle Paul and his friends. She was currently rereading the Acts of the Apostles, especially the accounts of travels in these ancient lands. Still, she was surprised at her emotional unpreparedness in confronting so many relics of Christianity's near-forgotten past.

Her feeling was underscored by a visit to Hagia Sophia, the most renowned of the Byzantine cathedrals and the best-known Christian church in Istanbul, first constructed between 325–360. Since then, several fires and earthquakes had required rebuilding ventures. After the Turkish conquest of Istanbul in 1453, it had been converted to a mosque. In the end, Hagia Sophia was declared a national monument and a museum by order of Atatürk in 1934.

After wandering for some time throughout its cavernous halls, Katrina walked toward the exit at the southern narthex portal. Pausing, she looked up at a mosaic of the Virgin with the Christ Child in her arms. To her right, the Emperor Constantius Magnus offered a model of the city to the Virgin. At her left, Justinianus was presenting a model of the Hagia Sophia.

A sudden chill came over her, causing an involuntary shudder. The flame of Christian truth had been extinguished in this place, remembered now only as a relic of the past. To her added sorrow, she was rapidly learning that this was true in most of the churches throughout Turkey. The Christian message of Jesus' love and forgiveness, that had made so great a transformation in her own life, seemed hollow and empty here. *But how can that be?* She shivered again and hurried to get out of the building.

She managed to include a tour of the Topkapi Palace, with its infamous sultan's harem quarters. On the way back to her room, she lingered long enough to descend into *Yerebatan Sarnici,* a huge underground cistern first constructed during Constantine's reign in 306–337, to ensure the city a water supply during a siege. She was told that Istanbul's excellent symphony orchestra would be conducting summer concerts in this subterranean Basilica Cistern, as it had been known in the Byzantine era.

As the shadows lengthened, she reflected with amusement on

her most harrowing experience in Istanbul, navigating her way across the city by getting on and off buses and the *dolmus* "shared taxi" arrangement of minibuses and vans. She had learned with good reason why the word *dolma* meant "stuffed."

KATRINA CAST A FINAL GLANCE out the window at the rug. Its colors were merging now with the shadows. She entered the petite bathroom and began freshening up for dinner. The past two days in Istanbul had served as a parenthesis in her life journey, an interval in which to stow away the familiar and gather up new sights, sounds, and smells that were the future. At least, her future for the next twelve months.

She reached for the key, then stopped partway into the hall. Turning, she surveyed the tiny room, with its half-open travel bags, her precious boxes of books, and the still-damp underclothes that hung from the traveler's clothesline she had purchased before leaving Los Angeles. A feeling of satisfaction materialized at the thought of what she had accomplished these last few days.

Her initial fears were gone. She felt light-years ahead of her starting position in self-confidence. And why not? She had made it halfway around the world, survived a taxi ride from the airport with a driver who spoke no English, melded into an exotic and foreign culture, eaten cuisine that was both fascinating and bizarre, and loved every minute of it. She was not ready to leave!

But the parenthesis was almost over. Her flight to Antalya left in the morning at ten o'clock. She sighed as she closed the door and started down the stairs. Tomorrow would be a new day in more ways than one.

At dinner in the basement dining room of the hotel, she joined an older woman from a small village near Glasgow, and a young Swiss couple from Bern, whose stated goal was to travel around the world. After polite introductions and some small talk, the Swiss woman asked if the others had heard about the bombing.

Neither the elderly Scot nor Katrina knew anything.

"It happened this afternoon at the Covered Bazaar."

"Are you serious?" asked Katrina incredulously. "I was there this afternoon."

"When did you leave?"

"Let's see. I went from the Bazaar to the Spice Market. It must have been about three-thirty when I caught the bus."

The Swiss woman raised an eyebrow and grinned. "You are one lucky girl. It went off at exactly three-thirty! I know because we stopped at a little bar for a drink with a Turkish friend of ours and she saw it reported on television. Several people were killed. I don't know how many. And a lot of injuries. It was pretty big, I guess."

"Who could have done such a thing?" Katrina grasped her fork tightly, the food on her plate suddenly forgotten.

"The last we heard, no one has laid claim to it yet, but our friend is certain that it was the PKK. They've done it before."

"The PKK?"

"I'm not exactly sure what the initials stand for. It's some sort of radical Kurdistani group bent on turning the nation from a secular to a religious state. You know, like Iran?"

Katrina nodded silently, her thoughts still back at the Bazaar and the *bedestans,* crowded with men, women, and children. She thought of the merchant who had regaled her with tales of the Covered Bazaar's history. Had the bomb gone off near his store? What about the lady from whom she had asked directions? And her little girl? Were they among the victims?

"Hey, are you okay?"

Katrina started and then smiled at the young Swiss. "Yes, sorry. I'm all right. It was just such a surprise . . . you know? To be so close, I mean, and not even know it was happening."

Shaken by this unexpected reality, Katrina continued to pick at her meal and make small talk with the others, comparing notes as to what each person had seen that day. At last she excused herself and climbed the stairs to her room. Once inside, she carefully locked the door and began the job of repacking. It went quickly and before long she was ready for bed. Turning out the light, she padded barefoot to the window for a final look.

Total darkness enveloped the alley. She could no longer see her rug nor feel its comfort.

The old fears were back, plus some new ones. The self-confidence about which she had earlier congratulated herself had disappeared.

Katrina lifted the bedcovers and slipped between them. Her

thoughts were of home where, all of a sudden, she desperately wanted to be. A small tear trickled down her cheek and fell onto the pillow.

She fought to push the friends and family she had left behind out of her mind, knowing in her heart that they were too far removed and with no way to comprehend what she was feeling. Still . . .

How much time had passed? Was she asleep or awake? Something was emerging from her jumbled thoughts of home, friends, fears. Slowly at first, but with reassuring warmth, her mind filled with an incredible Presence!

She recognized Him instantly, though He looked both different and familiar while gazing down on her. She could see only His upper torso. He was clothed in brown, with hues of red and black throughout His robe.

As she stared up at Him from her pillow, His bronzed face became surrounded by a crystalline blue light that continued to increase in brilliance. His eyes drew her and with open hands He beckoned. *Those hands look so terribly scarred, and yet beautiful somehow.* She wanted those hands to touch her. He came closer. *His face is so expressive . . . His mouth turns upward with just the hint of a smile. He looks pleasant . . . so loving . . .*

She could hear Him speaking, though His lips did not move to form the words. And she understood! Others were busy with their own lives. If she looked to them, they would urge her to end her foolish journey and return home. But He wanted her to go on. *No. It's more than that. He needs me to go on. It's important to Him.*

Katrina's lips responded in whispered prayer. Then, without any warning or any sound, the vision exploded with a flash of blue light, bursting into the shimmering luster of a thousand stars.

She closed her eyes to its brilliance. When she opened them again, He was gone.

For a long time she lay in the dark, wondering . . . smiling through tears.

Tomorrow would indeed be a new day!

It was the last thing she remembered before dropping off into a deep and restful sleep.

Sixteen. The Shepherd

**Monday, 16 June, 0135 local time
Near Mt. Ararat in eastern Turkey**

Îlhan arose from his bed of blankets spread on an earthen floor that had first been strewn with rugs. The woman beside him stirred as he got to his feet. He gazed at her with tenderness. Her long, dark hair spread across the pillow like petals of a flower. *She is like a painting,* he thought. Mehlika, "a face like a full moon." The urge was strong to enter the bed again, to awaken his moon flower with caresses and feel the warmth of her lips against his own. Reluctantly he backed away, lifted the flap of the black tent, and stepped outside.

Îlhan's dark skin and curly black hair quickly melded with the night. He moved with the easy agility of an athlete or an outdoorsman. In his case, it was both. He had been a good student and a champion wrestler in school. This, together with his infectious laughter and the haunting music he played on his handmade flute, seemed contradictory to his passion for the life of a nomad. Yet this poetic life was all he wanted, all he cared about beyond his wife and their two children.

The faint smell of sheep rode the night's breezes as Îlhan listened to the restless movement of his flock. He looked up at the

117

whitish moon that rode its preordained orbit through the sky, shiny cold, carving a path through a thousand stars that glittered brightly overhead.

Directly behind him, Mt. Ararat rose nearly 17,000 feet from the Eastern plains, her perpetual snows and icy white glaciers visible in the moonlight. Her grandeur signaled an indifference to her surroundings. In the glow of the moon, she appeared poised to leap into the heavens.

İlhan knew that daylight would reveal another side of Ararat, making visible her streams and rivers and even waterfalls of coal-black lava, frozen in time, symbols of a corruption that he himself had rejected. He knew the world was going to hell and he wanted no part of it. That's why he was here.

Far to the south, the dark waters of Van Gölü awaited the dawn. The huge lake lay in the silent embrace of the volcanic mountains that towered above it. Due east of İlhan's tent, the grubby little town of Dogubeyazet huddled on the flat plains, heavy with the smell of sheep dung in its miserable streets, a dismal picture of Eastern Turkey's sad reality that decreed poverty as the main business of the people.

Farther still from İlhan's tent, but still a daily presence, were the former USSR member countries of Gürcistan, Ermenistan, Nahcivan, along with Iran, Iraq, and Syria, all ranging along the northern, eastern, and southern borders of his homeland.

A gust of cool air whipped briskly at his shirt, reminding him of the dreaded snows only a few months away. Once the winter storms set in they would leave towns and villages cut off for days at a time, with temperatures hovering at -45˚C [-49˚F]. He preferred the near intolerable heat of summer.

It was a harsh land, but that's the way he wanted it. He had come here to build a life for his family. It was a place to be alone, to meditate, to do freely as one pleased. Yet, even here, those freedoms were being threatened.

Tonight he watched while the menace replicated itself once again on the plains below his tent. First came the thin line of dust from Iran's border. Soon thereafter the sound of engines grinding their way over rough, roadless terrain. The three military-style trucks moved in single file, purposefully avoiding the main road. They proceeded without lights, but remained clearly visible to

Îlhan's elevated position before stopping just short of the southern highway to Van. The same as on three other occasions since he had moved his tent home to this remote location.

The occupants were standing around now, lighting cigarettes, talking and laughing among themselves. An exchange was about to take place. Îlhan had suspected on other occasions what was happening, but this time he wanted to be sure. Why, he was not certain. He had no intention of getting involved. Mark it up to human curiosity, to the fact that these people were doing their "business" in his front yard.

Moving with the unerring stealth of a hunter, his feet never dislodged a stone or betrayed his presence. He stopped approximately fifteen meters from the first truck and settled in behind a large rock. Soon he saw four farm trucks lumbering up the road from Van, pulling off at a signal from one of the waiting men.

In these darkest hours after the late summer's midnight, illuminated only by a half moon and bright stars, the seven trucks were well hidden in a low gully. Îlhan watched and listened.

From his position behind the rock he heard each voice clearly. The men from the first group of trucks were speaking Farsi, the language of Iran. While he was not fluent in Farsi, he understood enough at least to deal with smugglers who occasionally brought their sheep across the border to sell illegally. But when the conversation below suddenly changed to Turkish, Îlhan was surprised that the spokesperson for the Iranian group was not a man at all. It was a woman!

"You are Leila Azari?"* asked the Turk whose back was turned to Îlhan's hiding place.

"I am. And you are . . . ?"

"I am Yücel," was the response. "I'm pleased to meet you. We've heard about your exploits and have looked forward to our meeting since being told you were coming."

"You are prepared to deal?" the woman asked, ignoring Yücel's attempt at chivalry.

"I am."

"You know, of course, that these weapons are being sold to

---

*Leila Azari is a major character in *October's Child* by Ward Tanneberg, Victor Books, 1995.

you at much below our cost. We do this to help the cause in which you struggle. It is our cause as well."

"I understand. We're most grateful."

"Good. We will be watching to see how you put them to use. The money please?"

Yücel removed a small suitcase from the lead farm truck and handed it to the woman. She opened it and fingered the contents briefly before closing the lid again. "You've done well. It's all in U.S. dollars and German marks?"

"Yes. Difficult to come by these days, but yes. Just as you requested."

"Then have your men help mine and we'll transfer the load."

"Permit me to see one of the crates opened please."

"As you like." Her voice sounded impatient. She called to a man leaning against the fender of the nearest army truck. "Sayyed, pull down one of the crates and open it."

The man moved around to the back of the truck.

"No," Yücel spoke sharply. He pointed to the last truck. "I want to see one from there, please."

The Azari woman gave Yücel a cold glance and then motioned with her head to the man called Sayyed. He walked to the third truck, pulled out one of the crates, and lowered it to the ground. With a pry bar he broke it open. Yücel rummaged inside the box for a moment and then backed away. "Thank you. Everything seems to be in order."

The woman said nothing further as she lit a cigarette while the others moved swiftly to transfer their purchases.

Îlhan watched, his eyes darting back and forth as wooden cases were unloaded from the first truck and reloaded to one of the farm vehicles. He was almost certain what was in the boxes, but he wanted to be sure. At the pace they were working, the men would soon be done unloading the first truck. He would have to move quickly. Crawling out from behind the rock, he circled his way around to the last Iranian vehicle.

The crate that had been opened moments earlier was still lying on the ground behind the truck. Îlhan glanced inside and pursed his lips. Just as he had feared, it was filled with guns. AK47 automatic rifles! He looked up into the back of the truck and saw a large plastic box. Reaching up he flipped open the catches on the lid and eased it up. A Stinger missile! He had handled similar weapons during his training days in the Turkish Army. Carefully he put the lid back and snapped down the locks.

"What are you doing?"

İlhan froze!

Turning slowly, he came face to face with the woman he had observed earlier. She held an automatic pistol in her hand, pointed directly at him. Her eyes were menacing. İlhan's mind raced frantically for some way out.

"Yüsel told me to be certain the missiles were in this truck," he said at last, speaking to her in Turkish.

The woman eyed him with a coldness that confirmed to İlhan that he was a dead man. Then slowly she lowered her gun.

"You tell your Yüsel that everything we promised and that he has paid for is here!" She spit each word out angrily. "We do not play games with you!"

"Evet, evet. Özür dilerim!" *Yes, yes. I apologize!*

İlhan moved quickly, away from the rest of the workers. The woman turned in the opposite direction. Quietly as he had come, İlhan disappeared into the night.

He crossed the highway on a run and was halfway home when he heard the first loud shouts behind him. *The woman must have talked to the Turk and realized I didn't belong there!*

Adrenaline fueled his heart and limbs as he climbed the hill, still mindful of the need for quiet movement. It would be a disaster to disclose his location now. He arrived at the tent breathless, almost running Mehlika down at the place where she knelt by the door.

"What is happening, İlhan?" she asked anxiously. "I awoke when I heard voices. You were not here!"

"Quickly," İlhan whispered breathlessly. "Wake the children, but make certain they're quiet."

"What is it?"

"Just hurry. I'll tell you on the way. We're in danger!"

Mehlika ran to the children's tent while İlhan stumbled inside and dropped to his knees in front of a small wooden chest at the side of their bed. He reached underneath a cloth pile, stored for Mehlika's sewing projects that she sold to foreigners passing by on their way to climb the mountain. His fingers wrapped around the grip of a well-oiled handgun that he sometimes used to scare wild dogs or bears away from the sheep. Stuffing an extra round of ammunition into his pocket, he ran back outside.

Mehlika had returned, pushing two sleepy children in front of her. İlhan swept the oldest up with one arm. Mehlika noticed the gun in his other hand and her eyes widened with apprehension.

"Come," İlhan whispered. "Follow me. We're going up the mountain."

For twenty minutes they climbed as rapidly as they could before arriving at the place İlhan felt certain they would be safe. He often sat in this small cave, using it as a shelter from the heat, while watching his sheep graze along the mountainside.

Down on the plain, the distant rumble of truck motors could be heard and three . . . no, four sets of headlights could be seen leaving the area, two headed south toward Van, and two going west on the highway to Erzurum. He strained to see if the Iranian trucks were moving, hoping they had already started back to the border, but there was only the darkness. He couldn't be sure.

All at once, far below the perch on which his family shivered in the cold of the early morning, he spied a flicker of light. What was it? Then İlhan saw the flames. He cursed, letting out a groan of anguish, knowing in an instant what was happening.

"İlhan?" Mehlika stared up at her husband. She had never seen such anger and hatred on his face before! It frightened her. A hardness had come over her gentle husband. His eyes burned with a terrible passion as his strong arms drew her and the children close.

"It's the tent," he said, his voice hoarse with emotion. "They set fire to our tent!"

"But why?"

Before he could answer, gunfire rattled the night, its dreadful echo resounding in the darkness. Short staccato bursts. Over and over. Automatic weapons. Shooting at what? And as quickly as the question came to mind, so did the answer.

THE BLACKNESS OF THE NIGHT at last gave way to the dull gray of impending dawn. As always, Mt. Ararat became the wilderness bully, fending the sun's earliest rays away from her western slopes for several more hours.

This morning, the mountain could not smell the charred remains of a burned scar on its foothill where once a gentle man and his family had made their humble home. Nor could she taste the blood that flowed from dead and mortally wounded sheep. She could not understand what stirred in the solitary shepherd's bloodshot eyes as he surveyed the horror that was his home.

One had to be human to smell and taste and know inhumanity. To know that hell visited where peace once had reigned.

Even here in this stark and inhospitable wilderness, Îlhan had not been able to keep his family from the consequences of evil. His pursuit of a simple, peaceful life for himself and his family had been crushed. He was unable to express the grief he felt. He could only look upon slopes that fell upward to touch the sky and mourn the painful loss of his options.

His days of serene quiescence were finished. He could no longer stand by and watch evil break Allah's commandments at the very entrance to his tent.

He called out to his wife and children who awaited his signal on the ridgeline high above this abject profanation of their life's accomplishments. He saw Mehlika waving her hand. She had heard. In a few short minutes, she and their children would see. And their hearts would break along with his. Sadly, he looked at the confusing jumble that stretched across his foothill, choking back an angry sob.

Îlhan was motivated at last!

Seventeen. Kristian

Monday, 30 June, 2200 local time
San Francisco

As I walked to my apartment house, wispy fog puffs swirled over the city, bringing a gentle luminescence to the otherwise dark backdrop of the night. I unlocked the door and stepped inside, glancing at my watch while opening the mailbox. It was ten o'clock. I withdrew two utility bills, three nondescript pieces of bulk mail, and my first letter from Kat.

She'd been gone more than two weeks by this time and seeing her familiar handwriting beneath several exotic-looking stamps and postal markings evoked feelings of relief and curiosity. There had been no reassuring phone calls, and never a day passed that I didn't think about her, wondering if my kid sister was all right.

I actually developed a daily habit of scanning the newspaper before going off to work. Then I checked the newsroom computers for what might be happening in that part of the world. So far, there had been nothing other than a ten-line story about a bombing somewhere in Istanbul. That was it. I wondered if Kat even knew it had happened. Turkey is no big deal in the American news media.

I fumbled for the door key while climbing the stairs. My apartment is just off the first landing. Once inside, I flipped on the light, dropped the mail on the countertop that separates the kitchenette from the living area, opened the refrigerator, and pulled out a beer. The tab popped easily and, leaning back against a sink full of dirty dishes, I took a big swallow.

I know it's hard to believe in this day and age, but there's no dishwasher in this apartment. It's one of the reasons I got the place so cheap, although, in San Francisco, "cheap" is a relative term. When I started working at KFOR, I was barely beating the minimum wage. Of course, later that changed and it's about to change again, but it's all still too new to think about buying anything, though I guess with what they're going to pay me, I can certainly afford it. The thing is, I want to spend my time focusing on the show, not mowing grass. Anyway, this new lifestyle is going to take some getting used to. And so are some of the people in it.

But, with a salary that's going to hit six figures every month, maybe I can live on the beach. Or in Beverly Hills even. Up to now, my dream has been to live in the Marina district, with a view of Alcatraz, surrounded by million dollar Victorians built on soil fluid enough to make them serious nominees for the next great San Francisco earthquake disaster.

I didn't bother opening the utility bills. The bulk mail got a cursory shuffle-through before getting tossed into the nearby wastebasket. That left Kat's letter. While slipping my thumb under the envelope's flap, and carefully tearing away the seal, I closed my eyes and let out a heavy sigh. This had not been a good day. It started out okay, but went downhill from there. For that matter, so did last night.

I looked forward to this letter from Kat. It was a welcome respite from the week's tensions. Withdrawing the several sheets of pale blue stationery with its familiar handwriting, I noticed that it was postdated a week ago.

Dear Kris,

Hi, big brother. I've now been in Turkey for ten of the most exciting and exhausting days of my life! It's incredible! You've just got to see it to believe it. The flight over went smoothly, considering how little I know about traveling by air. I'm learning fast, believe me. Maybe this fall I can offer my students a course in "How to Survive Airplanes and Airports." What do you think?

I stayed in Istanbul for two days. It's the most wonderfully exotic place. I'll not bore you with the details, but I tried to see everything possible in that brief amount of time. Would you believe I had just left the Covered Bazaar when some fanatics set off a bomb inside? Scary, huh? I didn't know it had happened, though, until someone mentioned it at dinner. It motivated me to get my things packed and move on, that's for sure.

The Hedleys, who oversee our school, are wonderful. He was born in Ireland and she comes from Chicago. They're in their late fifties and have lived in Turkey for seventeen years. They worked with a Christian school in Izmir until two years ago. That's when they felt led to start a new school here in Antalya. It's a struggle, but I think it's going to go well. The reputation of the other school has helped them in gaining acceptance here. And having Euro-American roots seems to be a plus too, at least in the minds of many of the families we will be serving.

The Turks continue to defy my preconceptions. Most are very warm and friendly as soon as they know you truly care about them. Not many handlebar mustaches and I've not seen a single flashing sword!

I hope you can meet my roommate one day. She's twenty-eight, teaches French, Deutsch, and speaks English with a French accent that is cute beyond words. Her name is Michelle de Mené. I know . . . you want her picture first! Forget it, big brother! Eat your heart out while trying to imagine what she looks like. I'll say this, though. For a schoolteacher, she's not bad. And smart too. I'm already planning to study French with her.

It's warm here, feels almost tropical, although they say it will be more temperate come this fall. Did I tell you that Paul and Barnabas visited this place? It's all in the Bible. Check it out. Acts 14:25-26. Being here seems like a dream, a fantasy, and I keep thinking that one day I'll wake up and life will be back to normal.

You can't tell that I'm excited, can you? I really believe that

God has led me here, if only to have the experience of teaching the Bible for a year to young people who, for the most part, have never even held one in their hands.

I hope your new television show is coming along well. Please write and tell me all about it. We have no phone where we live, but you can reach me at the school by leaving a message. That's the good news. The bad news is that, if I'm not there, I may have to call you back collect, so be prepared. I've written Mom and Dad a letter. If you see them, say that you heard from me and that I'm fine. Don't mention the bombing incident, though, okay? I didn't tell them about that.

I remember you in prayer every day, big brother. God is interested in you and in what you're doing. I know He is. So am I. I miss you!!!

Love,
Kat

I glanced over the pages again before folding them back into the envelope. What a sister! Quiet, obedient, studious Kat. Who would have thought that she'd be the one to venture off to some exotic, faraway place to work for God? Dad ought to take pride in the fact that he has at least one kid serving the good Lord. Why can't he accept that?

As for me, well, Kat may think God is interested in what I'm doing, but I doubt it. My guess is that God doesn't watch television, and if He ever does, He probably wouldn't like our new show anyway.

After my second yawn, I went to the bathroom, brushed my teeth, pulled off my clothes, and fell into bed. Exhausted. But, as soon as my head hit the pillow, both eyes blew wide open and I stared up at the darkness . . . same as last night. Only this time I didn't throw anything. I just lay there . . . thinking about the night before this one . . . and the day after . . .

TOM KNIGHT IS A CHARACTER. And with that assessment, I'm being tactful. The guy is divorced, in his mid-forties, slightly overweight, not terribly personable, and occasionally mentions a woman named Leslie. Claude says that she's a starlet who's been living with Knight for the past few months, one of several who have paraded through his bedroom since his divorce. Watching the guy's squinty-eyed face is a lot like looking at a television screen without a "clicker" to turn it on and discover what's inside. What do women see in him anyway?

Having said that, it took only the first day to convince me that he knows this business inside and out. His demeanor is authoritative and to the point. In a way, working with him reminds me of the first days in school each year when the teachers and principal are trying to get the upper hand. Tough and demanding at first, but with the promise of easing up once things are under control. I haven't gotten to the "easing up" part yet.

His assistant, Carole Upton, is slender, doe-eyed, about five-five, chestnut-colored hair, and has a beauty mark on the left cheek of her very attractive face. I was especially taken by her voice. It's one of the best . . . very expressive. I would say it's good enough for radio, and blessed with a light accent from somewhere besides California. When I first met her, I thought Midwest. Turned out to be a good guess. She's no airhead, that's for sure. Very serious and professional. At least that's the initial impression I came away with.

From the outset, Carole has never hesitated to jump into discussions regarding show format, guests, topics, anything except the more mundane matters of contracts, guest fees, and sponsors. On these, her tendency is to defer. At first, I thought it was a lack of expertise, but of late I've decided that it's pure boredom. I get the feeling that there are some things on which she just doesn't care to waste her time.

Anyway, after a week and a half of working together, and knowing that Tom was leaving in a couple of days to go back to L.A., I invited them to join me for dinner at a nice restaurant. Both pled weariness of the "dinner out" routine and wondered if they could come to my apartment instead.

I figured part of their interest was curiosity over how I looked in my lair. That's okay. My place is no showcase, but it'll show them that they've got to accept me as I am. Besides, living by myself since I split from the home scene has whetted my interest in cooking to the point where there are some things I'm pretty good at, so I said okay, gave them directions, and left early to stop by the store.

By the time they arrived, I was putting the finishing touches on a filet mignon dinner that embodied my best efforts. A side of Caesar salad, a vegetable that my mother would have been proud of, and a French estate bottled cabernet sauvignon that she would not have approved. Coffee after dinner, served with a dish of melon-flavored sorbet. It was fun to cook with others around to help eat the finished product.

After dinner, we sat in the living room and talked at length about the network's current stable of sitcom stars, not one of whom I had personally met. The longer the conversation went, the more I felt like a small-town boy getting ready for his first trip to the city. Finally, Tom gave his watch a bored look and excused himself, saying that it was nine-thirty and he had an early morning meeting with Claude.

I noticed Carole hesitate ever so briefly before pushing herself up from the small couch on which she and Tom had been sitting. She began searching for the shoes she had kicked aside earlier. It was enough of a dawdle that I heard myself saying, "It's still early, Carole. If you'd like to stay a while longer, I'd be happy to see you back to the hotel." Both of them were staying at the St. Francis near Union Square.

Pausing for a moment, as if mulling over the offer, she resumed her place on the couch, smiled gratefully, and waved good-bye to Tom. For a split second I thought I saw a "look" flash between them and then it was gone. Probably my imagination. As he was leaving, Tom and I agreed to meet the next morning at ten in KFOR's conference room for another planning session.

When I turned back to face the very attractive Carole Upton, sitting on my not so attractive couch with an empty wine glass in her hand, I was suddenly flustered, feeling surprisingly inept and adolescent.

"More wine?" I asked, awkwardly searching for a way to jump-start the conversation, now that Tom was gone. The realization hit me that this was the first time the two of us had been alone together.

"A little, if there's some left."

She held up her glass. Our fingers touched as I steadied the glass and poured. Her hair brushed across her shoulders in a manner that looked both sensuous and chaste at the same time. Backlight from the table lamp danced through the chestnut strands, framing a face that appeared even more beautiful in my living room than it did at the station.

The dress she had chosen for the evening showed off the kind of Southern California tan that is the envy of every fog-bound San Franciscan. The lime silk fell gently over the contours of her body, underscoring her slender, well-proportioned frame.

"Will it hurt our working relationship if I say that you are a very lovely lady?" I asked, placing the bottle on the counter and starting back to my chair.

Her laugh was genuine, not coy and not brazen either, while the look she gave was that of one used to receiving compliments.

"Not at all, thank you very much," she responded, motioning with her hand. "Please, come sit over here with me."

I settled into the place that Tom had vacated, turning slightly to regain eye contact.

"You've not said anything about it before, but I'm guessing your accent is Midwestern. I'd say Iowa."

"Yes and no. Yes, I'm from the Midwest—Topeka, Kansas. Daddy manages a retail computer store there. And you? Nobody ever seems to be a native of California. So where?"

"Washington State, near Spokane. A little farming community. We moved a couple of more times after that and finally wound up in Baytown."

"That's in the East Bay, isn't it?"

"Right."

"Tom tells me you're a preacher's kid."

I searched her face, as I had done so many times before whenever someone threw that tag at me, looking for some inkling of condescension, but none was forthcoming.

"Yeah, I'm a PK all right," I admitted. "Church three times a week, plus Sunday School and a lifetime of parsonages. The whole bit."

"What denomination?"

"My dad was ordained by an ultraconservative Brethren breakaway group and since has always pastored small, but very independent, fundamentalist churches."

"I know about 'independent.' I'm a Baptist," she responded with a twinkle in her eye. "At least, I used to be. A certified, sun-ripened, born once in the hills and several more times in the church Southern Baptist. When I was growing up, I don't remember a Sunday morning that didn't end with an altar call, and umpteen verses of 'Just as I Am.'"

We both laughed at those remembrances of our religious youth, and I felt myself beginning to relax.

"Did any of it take?" I asked, finding it hard to believe that this beautiful, worldly-wise woman had ever been close to the same kind of "old time religion" that I grew up with.

"Oh, sure," she chuckled, taking another sip of wine. "I went to the altar every summer during youth camp. And I was baptized . . . you know, dunked in the river? We Baptists never do anything halfway."

"Trust me," I answered ruefully. "I understand."

I finished my glass and set it on the coffee table. How much of that stuff had I put away tonight? I couldn't remember, but I was starting to feel a bit lightheaded from having sipped well past my quota. At that moment, Carole changed her position, turning more toward me, uncrossing and crossing her legs again and resting her arm on the back of the couch. The consequence of this shift brought her closer to me by four or five inches.

Her hand accidentally moved against my shoulder and then pulled away as she continued talking. In the same instant, I felt her foot brush my leg. She seemed oblivious. A few moments later it was back again, resting just above my ankle. It was getting harder for me to concentrate on what she was saying, though she still seemed unaware of the physical contact. In the middle of a story about the Sunday she and two friends smuggled frogs into their church and dropped them into the baptistery just before the morning service, she leaned forward, tossing her head in laughter, and placed her glass on the table next to mine.

It was an awkward move from her position and threw her slightly off balance. Just enough as it turned out.

To catch herself, she put out her free hand. It fell onto mine. I reminded myself again that this was nothing more than an accidental touch and we were simply two working associates becoming better acquainted.

At least it seemed that way.

I glanced down at the long graceful fingers, each one crowned by a perfectly polished nail. As I did, the room became very quiet.

Nothing was said and she didn't move her hand. Instead, she smiled as I searched her eyes for a signal of some sort. Sensing no inclination otherwise, and enticed by the faint scent of her perfume, I leaned forward and we kissed. Lightly at first. Her lips tasted of the wine. Then we kissed again. When at last I drew back, I was wondering whether to apologize or give thanks.

She smiled sweetly as her arm fell from the back of the couch. She moved nearer until her head came to rest on my shoulder.

"That was very nice," she said softly.

It was all the encouragement I needed.

The clock on the dashboard of the taxi attested to the hour being twelve-thirty when we finally said our good-byes. I waited on the sidewalk in front of the St. Francis until she was past the doorman and well into the lobby. She turned and waved before disappearing around the corner.

"Back to where I came from," I said, sliding into the rear seat of the cab.

"Nice lookin' lady, amigo," the driver commented.

"You noticed."

"Who could help it?" he smiled into the rearview mirror. "She your girlfrien', no?"

"A lady I work with."

"Oh," he said, drawing out the vowel sound and nodding his head knowingly. "I bet you look forwar' to goin' to work every day, eh, amigo?"

I smiled and leaned back. I didn't want to talk, not to this guy or anyone else. I just wanted to savor the last few hours. When we arrived at my place, I paid the fare, tipped the driver, and took the steps up to my door two at a time. Once inside, I surveyed the remnants of an evening that had definitely taken an unexpected turn. The very serious and professional lady from L.A. had turned out to be warm, witty, and willing.

I cleared the remaining dishes into the sink, setting the empty wine glasses on the counter. Tomorrow would be soon enough to wash up. I looked at the couch for a long moment before crossing over to the bedroom.

We could have spent the night here, I thought. *There were no "yellow lights" from her at any "intersection" we crossed. She's beautiful and intelligent. And it's amazing how much we have in common.*

I tossed my shirt and pants across the top of the dresser.

So why am I sleeping alone tonight?

I threw back the covers and fell into bed. No clear answer was forthcoming.

I closed my eyes. But, it was not the witty, intelligent, sensuously beautiful Carole Upton who jumped onto my mental screen. I opened them again.

Pounding my fist into the extra pillow, I threw it at the wall!

It was my dad again!

. . . Now, twenty-four hours later, I was back in bed, clutching the same pillow I had thrown at the wall the night before. This time I hugged it to my chest and thought back over the previous night and the day following. *Why can't I shake the old man's hold on my life? About the time I think I've preempted several seasons worth of unwanted religious upbringing and finally programmed in a new lifestyle, there it is again.*

Admit it, Lauring. You wanted Carole to stay over last night! And she would have too, if you had asked. All it would have taken was a signal. Yet something held you back. It wasn't fear of rejection. No, it was something else.

I turned over onto my back, pushing the pillow under my head.

Guilt! It always comes down to this, doesn't it?

Dad sure knew how to give us kids the gift that goes on giving. Guilt. The church's ugly word. He really laid it on us, didn't he? The problem is, all the stuff Dad preached at us is from the Bible. God's "Holy Infallible Word." But, is it really? I mean, who actually knows anyway? I sure don't and at least I'm honest enough to admit it.

I'm okay with the idea that it's one of the world's great literature pieces. No question. Can it be that's all it is? Lots of intelligent people think so, from the professors to the psychics. They relegate the Bible to a collection of myths and stories embellished by generations of people who needed something to believe, in order to survive. Now it's a new age. We know enough today to make personal value and lifestyle choices based on what is right for us. It's an individual thing, isn't it? At least that's what they say.

Come on, Kris, get with it. You've pushed this idea yourself. It's what you think, isn't it? It's not just what others have told you. The idea of objective, ultimate truth is passé. New, progressive thought has to supersede a bunch of ancient ideas conceived centuries ago and half a world away, by people who are still at each other's throats.

So last night shouldn't have mattered to anyone but the two of us. Should it?

No. Of course not. It was my choice and I blew it!

All right, Lauring. The lady has class. Don't let the fact that you'll be working together slow you down. And forget guilt! You know it's what you both want. Go for it!

What was it, ten . . . fifteen minutes later? I tried lying perfectly still, emptying my thoughts. Relaxing. Drifting . . . off to sleep . . .

The dream again . . . it has to be . . . so strange . . . her face completely blank . . . long blond hair . . . is it . . . no, not Carole. Who, then? . . . she's real . . . someone . . . her hand . . . she's touching my face . . .

Eighteen. Kristian

Tuesday, 01 July, afternoon

The result of Tom Knight and Claude Jardin's early breakfast was to recommend cancellation of live productions of the "KL Show" for the rest of the summer. Instead, they proposed that tapes of previous shows be presented under the banner, "The Best of KL." This would give me time for a short vacation. And most of the show's crew were being reassigned once we shut down. This would let them get started on other projects before the busier fall season set in. It sounded reasonable, so I said okay. Claude agreed to get together with Regina and work out the details to coincide with my new contract.

Then, Tom, Carole, and I worked on plans for the new show until lunchtime. Writers needed to be selected. A band leader would have to be auditioned and hired. A studio location had to be secured and outfitted, since any suitable locations were currently used by late night programs.

That factor alone influenced the decision to kick off the new show in January. Tom thought this would give enough time to create a studio suitable to our needs. Even the name of the show was not finalized. My mind was zipping along like a Sunday morning freeway. There was so much to be done.

Pursuit

I was concerned about personal input into this and all the other stuff that was bound to surface in the days ahead. Tom assured me there was no reason to worry. I should take two weeks and go to Hawaii. They would be in touch whenever a problem arose. I would be regularly apprised of ongoing decisions and contacted for input while on vacation. As if to settle the issue beyond any possibility of argument, Tom promised that he would fly out to join me each weekend. We could work on the show and get in some golf at the same time.

Reluctantly, I agreed. I was tired, no doubt about that. Keeping up with a five-day-a-week show for two years had used up a lot of the creative juices, to say nothing at all about the sheer physical energy. A couple of weeks playing golf and sunning on a Maui beach sounded better and better.

So, next week would mark the end of the "KL Show," the most popular television talk format ever to hit the Bay Area. It was kind of like burying a friend who died prematurely. The thought of it being over brought with it a range of mixed and melancholy emotions.

After lunch, we were joined by Claude as we batted ideas back and forth around the conference table with regard to content and special guests. That's when the day started downhill. Before thirty minutes had passed, I felt myself growing increasingly unhappy about the way things were going.

It was the complete opposite of last week's planning sessions in which ideas and guests had included the names of leaders in political, educational, scientific, and business fields, current best-selling writers, and a sprinkling of movie stars who would be plugging their new films. Some of the names were not terribly new, having appeared often on the late-night circuit, but it was a start. I was certain the list would get better. However, this afternoon's discussion wasn't better at all.

"Hey!" My feet hit the floor and I leaned forward, both hands on the table. Until now, I had tried to remain fairly passive, stuffing most of what I didn't like, acquiescing to the pros. "Stuffing" is a fairly normal practice for me, a lesson well learned under my father's tutelage. Everyone looked my way.

"What's this we're talking?" I asked in a bit of a huff. "Last week we were headed down a major thoroughfare. Today we're off the map, talking about sleaze TV. What happened to the higher ground we were pushing for a few days ago?"

I saw Tom look across at Claude and then shift his gaze to Carole as he cleared his throat.

"I suppose you could call it sleaze," he said, calmly looking in my direction. "But whatever you call it, we need it. Otherwise, we'll be dead in a month."

"Why?" I demanded, as my initial tic of anger began gathering itself together for a real blowout. "This is not the late, late bad movie, Tom. We're slotted right after the early evening network news, for Pete's sake. The kids are just getting up from the table."

"And we're going up against 'Extra,' 'Hard Copy,' and 'ET,'" Tom responded. "Look, Kris, you may be young, but I know you're not naive. Up to this point in your career, you've had no competition. You stood head and shoulders above anything else on the local scene. But, come January you're in the 'big time,' buddy, and don't you forget it. You've got to start thinking Leno, Letterman, Raphael, Lake, and at least a dozen others out there. They've already established their track records *and* their places in the network sun. If you don't come up with some stuff that really 'zings,' you'll be off the air before you get started!"

"No pressure though, right?" I retorted sarcastically.

"You know what I mean," Tom answered, waving his hands as if to call a truce.

I was not ready to surrender yet. "Ricki Lake is already taking a hit on several stations," I countered. "I read where a dentist down in Texas has taken her on like he did Donahue because of their constant excessive and explicit sexual content. Family values and all that good stuff. I think the dentist even got Dr. Dobson and his Focus on the Family supporters to back him."

"Are you afraid of Dobson and his cohorts?"

I hesitated for a moment before answering. "'Afraid' is not the word, Tom. I guess I just don't think we need to stir up the religious right and get them all over our case during my first season on the network. I've had a little experience in the world of religious fundamentalism. For that matter, so has Carole."

I looked over at her, hoping for some support. She had been sitting back in her chair, quietly observing the heating of our disagreement. Now she leaned forward. *Good. She's going to speak out.*

"I know what you're referring to, Kris," she began, clasping her hands in front of her. "These people can be powerful adversaries. Censorship, though they don't want to call it that, is at the top of their agenda. But I also hear what Tom is saying, and I have to go along with him on this. I think both he and I understand this business better than you do. We've been in it a lot longer.

"I know you dream of discussing important issues and interviewing knowledgeable people on various subjects. It's a wonderful idea. I think we can do some of that if we don't come off too 'eggheadish.' Don't give up on it. But, we've got to catch the eye of the viewers with something that appeals and says, 'Watch us, we're on the cutting edge!'"

So much for support from her corner. I stared at Carole until she looked away, at the same time trying to calm my exasperation. I was being yanked around and that's one of the things I really don't like.

"So you think," I looked down at the notes I had been scribbling for the past few minutes, "that the 'Tenderloin Hookers of San Francisco' does that? And you want to follow it up with 'Husbands and Wives Who Advocate Open Marriages' and 'The Argument for the Legalization of Prostitution in America'? What's this going to be, Tom? 'Weird Sex in America Week'?"

"I take it that you don't think much of our current list of possible topics?" Tom said with a thin smile and a steely look in his eyes.

"What I'm trying to say is that sex is a worthwhile subject now and then, one we ought to cover. But can't we do it in a more legitimate way than this? Don't you think that our audience is bright enough to respond to something less tawdry than the Chippendales and streetwalkers from San Francisco?"

"No, I don't, if you really want to know." Tom's voice was edged with hostility now. "I really don't think much of the audiences watching us these days. Their intellect is sub-par. Their taste is gauche. Their appetite is voracious. And the only right they're really interested in is the right to switch channels!"

"Well, I don't agree with you," I began.

"So, what do *you* want this to be, Kris?" Tom interrupted with a sneer, sitting back in his chair, eyes snapping with disapproval. "Are you hoping to launch a national pulpit in order to espouse 'family values'? Are you secretly wanting to one-up your father?"

Before I knew it, I was on my feet, leaning across the table.

"Look, I don't care who you are or what you think, *Mr.* Knight. You leave my father out of this! If you want to trade insults, we'll meet privately and go after it. I'm willing to work with you and everyone else to build a great TV show. Just don't try to manipulate me. And don't drag my family into something that doesn't even concern them. I won't put up with that!"

I glared at Carole who was also standing now, with a worried look on her face. I felt Claude's hand on my arm. He must have thought I was going across the table and, now that I think about it, that might not have been a bad idea.

"Come on, everybody, let's sit down and cool our jets here. Both of you, try to be rational about this. It's been a long day." It was Claude's voice.

"No!" I responded sharply. "This discussion is done for today. I'll be back at ten in the morning. Right now I'm going to get some air and then get ready for this afternoon's taping."

"Would you like some company?" asked Carole, moving around to the end of the table.

"Thanks, but no thanks. I need some time alone."

As I went out the door, there was utter stillness in the room behind me. I could feel three pairs of eyes burning holes in the back of America's newest and most disconcerted television talk show host, one who had just experienced a taste of corporate babble. Say whatever he wants to hear, then do whatever they please!

What have I gotten myself into?

Nineteen. Ibrahim

Monday, 25 August
Kilçilar

The warm days and pleasantly cool nights of the high plateau summer at *Kilçilar* were passing swiftly. The morning that Dr. Üzünal and Ibrahim had said their good-byes, the entire crew had gathered to bid their beloved and respected leader farewell. There had been many promises to pray to Allah on his behalf and sincere wishes for his recovery.

Now, in the last week of August, the clearing of the labyrinth of tunnels and rooms continued to yield up the mound's underground secrets, as it had throughout the summer.

True to his word, when friends and colleagues visited his bedside after surgery, Dr. Üzünal twisted their arms with enthusiastic promises of a significant archaeological find in the Cappadocian high country. Already, news of the Paleolithic Age findings and the recovery of the Hittite tablets had reached the staff of the Anatolian Civilizations Museum in Ankara. This, combined with Dr. Üzünal's untiring "bedside manner," had resulted in enough additional funding to add fifty new carriers, and work was once again progressing steadily.

Two weeks before, they had reached an eleventh level, at a

depth of one hundred ten meters, deeper than any excavated underground city to date. Here a well was uncovered, fed by an underground stream that provided the critical element for sustaining human life in this subterranean refuge. Samples were sent to Ankara where it was confirmed that the water quality was mountain pure and drinkable. Ibrahim's enthusiasm was limitless as the size and scale of this subterranean city began taking on unprecedented proportions.

Dr. Tuncer Kuzik, an anthropologist whose expertise was in the Paleolithic period, had already confirmed that *Kilçilar* was yielding artifacts representing all the Lower, Middle, and Upper phases in this earliest of anthropological periods. This by itself was significant, something that had been found only once before in Anatolia, at a considerable distance southeast of *Kilçilar,* in the cave of Karain.

A weekend visit by two other archaeologists and the director of the Museum of Archaeology in Istanbul had culminated in a lively discussion with regard to the origins of Turkey's amazing underground villages, towns, and cities. The others seemed eager to hear Ibrahim's views, even though they were considerably older and more seasoned in the field. Gradually, he accepted it as a sign of their respect for his skills and their acceptance of him as an unusually gifted colleague.

When did he think these settlements were first established? And, in particular, this very one?

Who built *Kilçilar* and why?

How long did he think it had been occupied?

When had it been deserted for the final time?

One of the archaeologists, personally familiar with the underground cities of Acigöl, Agirnas, and Kaymakli, pressed a theory of similarity between these sites and that of a cross-section of scorpion and ant holes. Did Ibrahim think it possible that they might have been formed by gigantic ancestors of these species during previous geological eras?

Ibrahim tried not to smile at that theory, for he saw the man was not joking. Then he reminded his guests that there really was no final data available to answer their questions.

In doing so, he referred to a small section of the book of Ksenefon-Anabasis, written near the end of 4 B.C., in which it is mentioned that some Greeks stayed overnight in an underground city in the Derinkuyu region. It confirmed the existence and use of such cities in that era, but there was no documented record earlier than this.

Perhaps these Greeks had stayed in the tunnels that criss-crossed in a tangled web beneath modern Derinkuyu. Perhaps, he conjectured as the men nodded appreciatively, they had even stayed at *Kilçilar*. One thing was certain. These hollowed-out cities had been the ideal shelter, enabling tens of thousands of fleeing Christians to defend themselves against marauding Arabs from 642 and following.

Back at *Kilçilar,* workmen discovered two tunnels in the fifth level, extending in opposite directions. At first, nothing much was made of it. They were simply additional manifestations of the same endless maze that Ibrahim's team had unearthed in preceding weeks. Before long, however, Ibrahim and Tahsin Cem had convinced themselves that the east tunnel might very well extend all the way to Derinkuyu, while the western tunnel appeared to head steadily toward the region surrounding the town of Güzelyurt.

Ibrahim ultimately made the decision to abandon the east tunnel and concentrate their efforts to the west. Worker resources were already spread thin, due to the size of the city. There was no getting around the pressure that Ibrahim felt. If he was wrong, he might well be abandoning a major archaeological wonder. Besides, Derinkuyu was closer and it made more sense to go in that direction. But something induced him to do just the opposite. As a result, over two weeks earlier, a team of twenty had begun pushing their way through the West Tunnel Road.

It was quickly confirmed that the tunnel went away from the main confines of *Kilçilar.* Furthermore, the passage clearly had been designed with potential invaders in mind. It was narrow enough so that no more than two people could pass, even at its widest points. This made it difficult for the carriers as they moved back and forth. And, the ceiling was low, making it necessary for all but the shortest workers to bend over as they walked through. Numerous sharp turns had been designed into the tunnel, clearly for self-defense. Still, it led the workers with undeniable certainty on a westerly course.

Just when Ibrahim had been about to abandon the West Tunnel Road, due to the distance being traversed by the carriers, an escape passage was found approximately one kilometer away from *Kilçilar's* main entrance. This enabled the workers to establish a new and much closer deposit area for the fallen rock and rubble. In order to conserve time and energy, at some places in the tunnel where cave-ins had occurred, openings were created that were just large enough for one person at a time to make his way through. An additional electric generator was also installed and, because of the low ceiling, lightbulbs were stretched as high as possible along the side of the tunnel.

As the enterprise continued with the enlarged crew, Ibrahim's paperwork increased in direct proportion. Like so many other entrepreneurial souls bent on accomplishing great things, he detested this aspect of leadership. He longed to be in the middle of the task, digging and discovering for himself some new reminder of the people who had occupied this place. Recently, however, such opportunities had been rare. This was one reason why tonight Ibrahim had decided to pay a visit alone to *Kilçilar's* third level.

The other was the nagging reminder of the conversation with Dr. Üzünal during his first visit to the ancient church. He had been startled at his mentor's intimation that he might pray to Jesus for his healing. Üzünal had not even used the Prophet's customary Islamic name, Isa. He had referred to Him by His Christian name, Jesus.

Ibrahim had become increasingly fascinated by that incident, especially in light of the rapid recovery that Dr. Üzünal was now experiencing. The tumor, confirmed actively cancerous by extensive preoperative testing, had been lodged in a dangerous position against the brain.

Upon its removal, however, the physicians were both puzzled and amazed. Their conclusion was that the tests had been erroneous. The tumor was totally benign. It was removed in its entirety and the prognosis was updated to forecast a complete recovery.

Ibrahim had spoken with him several times on the telephone concerning his health, and the status of *Kilçilar,* asking his advice on certain key decisions that were imminent. One had to do with the West Tunnel Road. Dr. Üzünal advised him to retreat from investing such a high percentage of his workforce in that tunnel. September was approaching. By November, the season would be over and bad weather would prohibit further work until spring.

Ibrahim listened intently, normally ready to yield to the wisdom of his elder. Yet there was a restiveness, an uneasy feeling that came over him whenever he was about to acquiesce by closing the tunnel phase down. And so it remained ongoing.

It was not until three nights ago, however, that he had finally found a place in one of their conversations to casually ask the question that had lingered in his mind for weeks, "Did you pray to the Prophet Isa for your healing?"

After a short pause at the other end of the line, the answer came from a voice full of emotion, "Yes, I did, Ibrahim." There was another pause, this one longer than the first. Then Dr. Üzünal continued. "Ibrahim? I believe it was Jesus who turned my circumstance completely around! I know that my tumor was diagnosed several times as malignant. The doctors were absolutely certain. Yet, when they arrived on the scene in my brain, it was benign. What can you make of it? I am not enough of a theologian to know if what I did was correct. I will leave that to the imams. I only know that I am convinced my faith prayer to Jesus did it!"

It was a remarkable confession from any Muslim, but doubly so from the lips of one so esteemed. Ibrahim had been unable to shake it from his thoughts. Had a divine miracle really taken place in the body of his mentor? Tonight, that speculation was the real catalyst that drew him to the underground house of worship, long after the rest of the camp and its weary inhabitants had given up to the sounds of the night.

The generator had shut down, in order to save precious fuel. Ibrahim made his way through the entry tunnel's darkness with a flashlight in hand. He was familiar with the route by now, having passed this way on numerous occasions. It felt different at night, however, knowing that he was alone inside this earthen mound.

For what seemed to be a long while, there were only the disquieting sounds of his own footfalls and the raspy expelling of air from his lungs as he trudged through the passageway. Instead of added tension and uncertainty, however, the farther he went, the more relaxed he became.

When he came to the entrance, he paused for a moment, shining his flashlight through the narrow opening. Finally, bending low, he stepped inside.

Throwing light around the room, he could see that it was just as it had been on his initial visit. Beyond the sanctuary's opposite wall, the two adjoining rooms had yielded up most of their treasures after each piece and its location had been carefully identified and mapped. This place, however, had contained no idols. No traces of the usual human presence. Only the frescoes that graced three of the walls.

He walked around the room slowly, examining each fresco with a critical eye in the powerful beam of his flashlight, recognizing some of the Bible stories, but not all. He understood the scene depicting Mary and the Holy Child. He was also familiar with Christianity's version of the cross and resurrection portrayed on the opposite wall. He stood staring at the scene illustrating Isa as the healer. He could not recall the actual story in the picture and suddenly found himself longing for a Christian scholar to interpret some of these scenes.

Finally, Ibrahim looked up at the darkened ceiling. He had saved the best for last. He stood in the center of the room and slowly moved the beam up the wall until it illuminated the first tiles in the ceiling mosaic. *I'm like a small child,* he thought, running his tongue over lips that were dry with excitement.

My heart is pounding. It seems that I shouldn't be here. Not like this anyway. As an archaeologist, yes. But . . . what am I tonight? Why am I here? What am I searching for? I think the imam would forbid my being here in light of my feelings. Who knows? Is this the way a Christian might feel if he slipped into a mosque late at night where it was only himself and Allah? I wonder.

The face has a moving quality about it . . . so lofty, yet extraordinarily human. And the eyes.

Ibrahim felt as though he were being drawn upward into the eyes, absorbed by them, lost in them. The narrow beam of his flashlight refracted the colors in such a way as to seem ethereal. Ibrahim shook off a sudden chill. He looked away for a moment and then back again. *I almost have to remind myself that this is the work of an artist and not the real person!*

There was no doubt that this was the finest work of mosaic

religious art he had ever seen coming from the Christian Era. Perhaps from any age. He ran the beam of light over the extended hands, marked with the residue of crucifixion. But it was the face that drew him back. *Such kindness. And gentleness. Yet it's full of strength and . . . something else. Curiosity, perhaps? I can't help thinking of it as the face of a man I would genuinely like to know.*

Ibrahim trained the beam onto the face as he shifted to his left for a slightly different perspective. He was near the front of the church when he stumbled, his ankle giving way to a crack on the uneven floor. He pitched in an awkward sideways motion onto the stone altar while his hands flailed wildly in a vain attempt at regaining his balance. The flashlight flew from his grasp, clattering against the unadorned stone wall behind him, just before it disappeared altogether!

Twenty. Ibrahim

Ibrahim fought for his breath as he slumped painfully against the stone altar. Pushing himself up, he rolled into a sitting position on the floor, then sagged back against the altar's base. Each breath was painful. He felt along his rib cage . . . ouch . . . there! His head dropped in consternation as he groaned softly.

"Now I've done it. What a stupid thing to let happen!"

Enveloped in complete darkness, his only sense of direction came from his position against the altar. He knew that he was facing the back of the room. Cautiously he turned to the left, testing his mobility as he turned.

Where do you suppose that flashlight went?

He ran his hands back and forth across the rough floor without success. As he pushed himself into a crouching position, a sharp stab of pain brought another moan. Eyes clinched, he concentrated on shallow breathing. That helped a little.

The darkness was total. He touched his hand to his nose but could not see it. Disoriented, he shuffled his feet until he was standing, gingerly putting weight on his left ankle. It hurt, but he could tell it was not broken.

At least that's something. Now what?

Turning about slowly, he caught a faint glow coming from near the front wall. Strange. If it was the flashlight, as it had to be, it was not at the floor level, but in a waist-high location. Carefully he felt his way around the stone altar. A few more shuffle-steps and he was at the wall. His hands traced over the rough-hewn surface to a small opening, about three or four meters from where he remembered the baptismal font to be located.

Peering down into the opening, he saw the flashlight still glowing, its beam directed toward the bottom of a small crevice that no one had noticed before. Reaching in, he carefully withdrew the light with a sigh of relief. At least now he could find his way out. *What is that?* As he drew his arm out, his hand rubbed against something soft.

He turned the beam back onto the crevice and could see why he had not noticed it earlier. It was hidden from sight by the way the stone wall twisted back into itself at the crevice opening. It also appeared to have been crusted over and concealed still further by a layer of fine dirt. If it had not been for the flashlight, Ibrahim never would have noticed it. Curious, he pressed his face against the stone and squinted through the opening into a small natural pocket in the stone. It was no deeper than an arm's length and there was indeed something there. But what? Reaching in, he carefully pressed his fingers into the crumbly substance and pulled a few small fragments back into the light. *It must be an animal skin of some kind! But how did it get here?*

He shined the light in again. His fingers had disturbed the substance enough for Ibrahim to see another object. It looked like a small clay jar. *Might something have been placed here for safekeeping? Was this some sort of ancient storage locker?* The opening was large enough for Ibrahim's arm or the light, but not both. When he reached inside, it was impossible to see.

With great care, he pushed his hand into the crevice, gently brushing away the remains of what he thought might have been an animal skin pouch or purse. Then he touched it. He wrapped his fingers around a small container, the pain from his fall all but forgotten in the excitement of finding something that everyone else had missed!

Easy. Careful now. Don't drop it or crush it.

He eased his hand out of the crevice ever so gradually, clutching the fragile prize while at the same time trying not to hold on too tightly or bump it against the sides of the opening. *There! I have it!*

Ibrahim leaned against the wall. In spite of the cool temperature, a drop of perspiration found its way into his eye. He could feel the dampness under his arms as well. *Nothing like a little pain and excitement to get the body going.*

Turning the light onto the object in his hand, he saw that it was a small cylindrical container made from kiln-fired clay. Peeling back the cover, he looked inside.

"Yes!" he exclaimed, the sound of his voice reverberating excitedly through the chamber. "There's something in here!"

He paused for a moment as silence surrounded him once more, broken only by the sound of his breathing.

"I'm taking you with me, little lady," he said, holding it up to the light. Its surface was smooth and unmarred except for a small chip along the base. "You'll sleep tonight in my tent and tomorrow we'll see what you have to say to us."

Ibrahim tucked the vase into his jacket and started to leave. Then he remembered the soreness in his ankle and the annoying pain that speared through his side, gripping him like a vise whenever he turned a certain way. He grimaced as he bent to exit through the opening by which he had entered the underground church. Never mind. It was a small price to pay for this nocturnal adventure!

Thirty minutes later, Ibrahim had swallowed some pain pills and was stretched out on the cot in his tent, concentrating on making his body relax. He thought of what excuse he would make to the others for his injury.

He did not want to explain why he had gone to the underground church in the first place. Nor did he wish to discuss his reasons for removing an artifact from its original location before photographing it. He had done it on impulse. No other reason. There was something about that place . . . and, besides, he wanted to examine the contents of the jar for himself before revealing his discovery to anyone else. With his finger on the switch of the battery light by his bed, he paused for one last look.

He couldn't help but think of his prize as endowed with womanly qualities. She stood in solitude at the center of Ibrahim's work table, encircled by a faint ring of cave dust. Her smooth, graceful lines were still there, just as they had been when first taking shape on some nameless potter's wheel. Still, a part of her original beauty had faded, the price paid for silent centuries of faithfully fulfilling her *raison d'être*.

The longer Ibrahim gazed at her, the more she appeared distressingly naked and forlorn, like a prisoner of war facing the inevitable indignity of being forced by her enemy to give up the secrets she had so staunchly guarded.

He turned out the light and in the darkness, he wondered.

It is probably nothing more than bills of lading, discarded by some Greek businessmen mentioned in the book of Ksenefon-Anabasis.

He chuckled at the thought. Still, he had a feeling. Call it the professional's hunch. Intuition. Whatever.

He closed his eyes as drowsiness began setting in. The pills were taking effect.

Twenty-one. Ibrahim

Tuesday, 26 August, 0755 local time

The steady put-put-put seemed to be coming from a great distance until his mind cleared itself sufficiently of deep sleep. The longer he lay there, the louder and more distinct it became. *Where am I?* Then he recognized the steady drone of the camp generator, a sound grown so familiar during these last weeks that it usually went unnoticed.

Ibrahim's eyes opened to the light of a day that obviously was well under way. He reached for his watch. Nearly eight o'clock. He had overslept! Exhaustion after a restless night had kept him from hearing the noise of the crew members during breakfast and in their preparations for another workday. He started to get up, then fell back on the cot as a sharp reminder of his journey into *Kilçilar* during the previous night took his breath away.

"Dr. Sevali."

Ibrahim started at the sound of his name.

"Are you all right?"

He turned his head and saw *Kilçilar's* epigraphist, Gürer El, standing just inside the entrance to the tent.

"Yes, I'm fine, Dr. El, but I've overslept, haven't I?"

"It's very unusual for you. Normally you are one of the first

151

up. When we didn't see you at breakfast, Dr. Cem and I were concerned about your welfare. You are not ill, then?"

Ibrahim rolled onto his side, dropping his feet to the floor. Carefully he pushed himself up to a sitting position.

"I couldn't sleep last night, so I went for a walk. Twisted my ankle and I think I may have cracked a rib."

Gürer El came closer, his face knitted with concern. "I am sorry. Where did it happen?"

"Out beyond the camp, I couldn't say exactly," Ibrahim replied evasively.

"You should see a doctor."

"I think you're right. I'll have Çali drive me to the clinic in Güzelyurt. They can check me out and I can take care of a few errands while we're there. I should be back before dinner."

Ibrahim watched Dr. El as he spoke. El was not looking at him. Instead, he was staring at the small jar on Ibrahim's table. Ibrahim caught the furtive movement in El's eyes. *He's wondering where the jar came from and what's inside. Well, so am I, so we're even on that score.*

"In fact," said Ibrahim, "if you would find Çali and send him to me, I'd appreciate it. Is there anything else, Dr. El?"

El's face was somber as he shook his head. "I'm glad it's not more serious, Dr. Sevali. I will find him for you right away."

Wide awake now, Ibrahim was pulling on his pants when Çali poked his head through the tent door. "You called for me, boss? Dr. El said you hurt yourself."

"Yes. I want you to drive me into Güzelyurt to the medical clinic. It's nothing serious. I fell last night and I think a rib or two might be cracked. That's all."

"No problem. Can you sit up or do you need to lie down in the back?"

"I'll sit up front with you, Çali. It would be too great a loss not to enjoy your companionship while we're on the road."

Çali's face broke into a huge grin. "I agree, boss. I'll make you comfortable and keep you entertained, okay?"

"Okay, but just a minute."

Ibrahim picked up the jar from the table and placed it in the bottom file drawer, locking it securely when he had finished.

"All right, Mr. Ambulance Driver, let's go."

IT WAS ALMOST DINNERTIME when Çali and Ibrahim returned to the camp. After visiting the clinic, Ibrahim had made several phone calls and Çali shopped a list of supplies given him by the cook before they left. Stepping down from the vehicle, Ibrahim was greeted by The Roc and Ben Hur, coffee cups in hand as they came to meet him.

"Hey, doc, how're you doing?" Rocco called out. "I hear you took a fall last night."

"Yes, I stepped where I shouldn't have, I guess. I'm okay, though. Just a couple of cracked ribs and a sore ankle. Tomorrow I'll be fit and ready to go. I've survived the worst of my recovery by spending the day on the highways and byways with Çali at the wheel!"

The Roc and Ben Hur roared with laughter. They had ridden with Çali before.

"How did we do today?" asked Ibrahim.

"Nothing too much," Ben Hur answered, dropping his cowboy hat on the hood of the truck and running his hand through sweat-streaked hair. "The West Tunnel just keeps on going. I think you were right, Ibrahim. Every day that passes says to me that we'll eventually poke through the floor of the mayor's office in downtown Güzelyurt."

"And won't His Honor be surprised?" Rocco added, as he poured the remainder of his coffee on the ground and reached for a cigarette. "My crew is working on a cave-in on Level 7. We should break through in maybe another day or two."

"Good. You are both doing great. As for me, I think I'll go lie down for awhile. Çali, would you arrange to have some food brought to my tent when dinner is served? Tomorrow, I'll feel more like company. Tonight, I just want to eat something and turn in."

"No problem, boss," Çali answered. "I'll bring it personally. What you want to drink?"

"Whatever we've got that's cold, thanks. I'll see you all to-morrow."

The others nodded and turned in the direction of the mess tent. Once inside his own tent, Ibrahim removed his shirt and ran a hand over his side, feeling the tape the doctor had wrapped him in under the dubious pretext that it would help the healing process.

With great care he stretched out on the bed and tried to convince the muscles he had held tense for so many hours that it was all right to relax now.

He had just dozed off when he heard Çali's voice outside. "Dinner is served, boss." Çali ducked into the tent bearing a tray with chicken, beans, yogurt, and iced-tea.

Ibrahim glanced at the food. "What? No cloth napkins? No flowers? And where's your bow tie, Çali?"

"Hey, boss," Çali grinned, "if I had known I was going to be your waiter *and* your driver today, I would have come dressed for success. You got to give me more warning next time."

"I promise," Ibrahim rejoined with a grunt of satisfaction. "And thanks. You made me laugh too much for my own good today, but I appreciate it anyway. See you in the morning."

Çali backed out of the tent and, for the first time that day, Ibrahim was both awake and alone. He peeled the skin away from the chicken and bit into it with surprising relish. He had eaten nothing the entire day, while downing two good-sized bottles of water on their trip. All at once, he was very hungry! After polishing off the main course, he opened the bottle of pain medicine prescribed for him by the physician, popped two pills in his mouth and washed them down with the last bit of tea.

Setting the tray and its utensils on top of the filing cabinet, Ibrahim squatted, unlocked the bottom drawer, and took out the jar. Although it was still light outside, he turned on the battery light and moved it to the center of the table. Carefully, he removed the cover of the jar and peered inside.

Ward Tanneberg

• • •

REUTERS. August 10
Turkey's Prime Minister continues to search for ways to bring about a coalition with leaders from several of the nation's smaller splinter parties after having suffered a third rebuff by her most likely partner, the conservative Motherland Party [ANAP]. ANAP, together with every other mainstream party, looks with apprehension at the possibility of early elections. It is generally believed that the fundamentalist Refah [Welfare] Party, with its strong backing from Iranian sources, will do well if this takes place.

The President of Turkey is required by law to schedule elections by early in November. Meanwhile, the caretaker government grows weaker by the day as the nation's serious political vacuum continues. A new labor strike is threatening to close Turkey's major ports. A walkout has been tentatively scheduled for Sunday night. Talks continue with the government's negotiating team.

• • •

Twenty-two. Katrina

July/August
Antalya

When Katrina arrived at the airport in late June, Dorothy Hedley was there to meet her. Katrina decided instantly that she liked this woman.

"Call me Dorothy, dear," she said as they greeted one another. "There are too few of us to impress and too much that needs to be done not to go by our first names here. The students will call you Ms. Lauring, but to the rest of us, you'll be Katrina. Is that all right?"

"It's perfect, Mrs. Hed . . . Dorothy. And thank you for meeting me. It would have been quite all right to have sent someone else. I know how busy you must be."

"Thank you for sending your picture so that I didn't have to stand around with your name printed on one of those awful cards. By the way, you are lovely, my dear, and we're very excited to have you join us in our work here."

As they conversed on their way, Katrina sensed the warmth and enthusiasm of a woman who rewarded each new day with spirited participation. It bubbled from her lively and witty conversation. By the time they arrived at the apartment that would be her home for the next twelve months, Katrina had already begun letting go of her tensions, luxuriating in the pleasure of conversation with another American. One with similar values, beliefs, and life experiences. Similar and yet vastly different.

She noted that in September, the Hedleys would begin their eighteenth year in Turkey. Their devotion to and love for the people of their adopted land was undeniable.

Ian Hedley's reddish-brown hair with a touch of gray complimented the Irish ruddiness of his face, his ready smile and huge hands that made him look more like a longshoreman than a school principal. His muscular build reminded Katrina of a stock car, not as sleek and as showy as an Indy, but ready to race. He stood about even in height with Dorothy whose snow-white hair, a face that was filled with laugh wrinkles, and tailored dresses, reminded Katrina of Barbara Bush.

One day when she mentioned this, Dorothy laughed and said that others had suggested this before. "There may be many differences between us, my dear, but two stand out. One, she married the president while I married the principal. And, two, I don't have a dog named Millie!" Dorothy had been educated in the United States and Ian received his graduate degree in education at the University of Iowa. Both of them had also mastered the Turkish language.

Some of the faculty were nationals and two others, besides Katrina's roommate, were Europeans. One woman, a widow in her forties, was an American citizen who had taught for nineteen years in Des Moines' public schools. When her husband passed away following an extended bout with cancer, he left her with enough insurance money so that, invested wisely, she was able to live on its modest income.

She had first learned of the new school the Hedleys were starting through an article in her church newsletter. Except for short vacations in Canada and Mexico, Beverly Stonehill had never been out of the country before quitting her job, putting her house up for rent, and coming to Turkey. Nevertheless, she had proven that she had a heart for God, and was more than willing to adapt to the food, the culture, and most importantly, the people.

During Antalya Girls School's first year, she had taught a

combination second/third grade class in which fifteen bright-eyed Turkish girls had tested her teaching skills and her patience. She passed with flying colors, as did each of her students. Then she had decided to stay on for another year, much to the Hedleys' delight. During the summer months she tutored several students needing special help and, along with her own language studies, still managed to slip in a week's sailing trip along the Mediterranean Coast.

She and Katrina soon became good friends. Katrina told her one day how she admired her spirit and attitude. Beverly responded, "It hasn't always been this way. I felt really sorry for myself during George's illness. When he died I went into a deep depression. To go on was just too painful. Then one Sunday afternoon, I read about this school and the need for teachers. I suddenly found myself there in my living room, crying and wishing that I could do something like this.

"I thought about it and prayed well into the evening, after which I made this daring decision, something I'm definitely not noted for. I've always been the steady and reliable one. Maybe 'predictable' is a better word. Assessing my situation in life, I realized that our children were both grown and married. I want to be a grandmother someday, and a good one too. But I decided I wasn't going to sit around and wait for them to make me some grandchildren to play with. So, I contacted the Hedleys, and here I am.

"I've found something with these children, Katrina. The longer I live the more I realize that what's really important is what we can give away in order to help others become all they can be. After I'd been here a few weeks, I asked God to forgive me for feeling so sorry for myself. I invited Him to use what talent and skills I have to bring Him honor and to make a difference in the world."

Katrina felt both privileged and inspired to be associated with people like Beverly Stonehill. This was also true of Michelle de Mené. Having a roommate drawn out of a hat for you by someone can be a tricky thing. Katrina knew that this relationship could make or break her attitude toward everything else. She thanked the Lord each day for Michelle.

Her dark eyes were accentuated by short black hair and a golden complexion. Born twenty-eight years earlier in a small town on the Normandy coast of France, she had moved with her family to Nice when she was eight.

Not at all religious before moving to the south of France, her parents became Christians through watching the lives of their closest friends, who also happened to live in the same apartment complex. One evening at dinner, her father and mother announced that they were accepting Jesus Christ as their Savior and Lord and informed Michelle and her brother that they would be doing so as well.

It was not a decision driven by emotion or persuasive preaching. It wasn't even Sunday, Michelle noted laughingly. She described it as being more tribal in nature, rather like the chief of the village becoming a Christian and expecting all the villagers to do the same.

She recounted to Katrina that her father was uncertain as to how to carry through on it and so invited the neighbors over, explaining to them what had been decided. Katrina could picture the scene as Michelle described this intimate, yet rather matter-of-fact approach to gaining eternal life. The Christian neighbors were elated and led each member of her family through the sinner's prayer. Later, they asked her parents where they would like to go to church. Michelle's father answered, "Wherever you go. We have not been to a church in many years."

When the neighbor family eventually inquired as to what had prompted their decision, her father replied simply, "You did it. We've been watching you and have seen the positive effects of faith in you and your children. It made us hungry to be like you in this way!"

It was a delightful story and one, Katrina thought, that should be replicated by Christians everywhere. Unfortunately, such accounts were rarer than one would like to think.

During the balance of the summer, Katrina continued to absorb her new surroundings, walking the steamy palm-lined streets, laughing with delight on the day she discovered that McDonald's had also made it to Antalya and, in general, becoming increasingly familiar with her new environs. The surrounding agricultural region proved to be a constant source of fresh fruit and vegetables. And a gorgeous natural harbor, with its unpolluted sky, also made the city a favorite destination for thousands of tourists, Turkish and otherwise.

Pursuit

Dorothy, who taught Anatolian History—the history of Asian Turkey, brought Katrina up to date on the region's background. She reminded her that Asian Turkey has always been at the center of human history. It is the land of the Garden of Eden, between the Tigris and Euphrates rivers. Noah's ark is said to lie somewhere on Mt. Ararat, in eastern Anatolia.

Antalya had not been founded, however, until early in the second century B.C., by Attalus II of Pergamon. It passed into Roman hands and was visited by Emperor Hadrian in A.D. 130. Soon after, it became a Byzantine city and remained so until 1207 when it was conquered by the Seljuks. The Ottomans took over in 1391. From that time onward, it was content to simply preen itself each day in the sun while admiring its own natural beauty.

One Friday afternoon late in August, Katrina and Michelle went for a walk along Atatürk Caddesi where it curves down past Hadrian's Gate, a monument built in honor of the ancient emperor's visit. At the end of the street, overlooking the sea, they lingered in Karaali Park, admiring its stately palms, beds of flowers, and splashing fountains.

Leaving the park, they continued through the Old Town, stopping now and then to delight over an especially charming Ottoman house, before heading toward the ultramodern yacht marina. Along the way, they fell in with a group of American tourists who invited them to go on a yachting trip along the coast the next day.

Returning that evening to the apartment, they excitedly packed a small bag with swimsuits and lotions, all the while congratulating themselves on their good fortune. This would be a grand way to end the summer. And the best part, it was free!

During the night they were awakened by a noisy thunder and lightning rainstorm that swept in from the sea and soaked the city, causing water to run through the roof and into their sitting room. The next morning the landlord surveyed the puddles that covered most of the tile floor, shrugged and assured them that by opening the door and windows to the warm outside air, it would be dry by afternoon.

They were concerned as to whether the trip might be called off, but when it came time to set sail, the day was drenched in sunlight with not a cloud in the sky. There was undisguised ebullience among the passengers on board as they walked the deck of the wooden vessel and talked of other boat rides in other places on other days like this. It didn't take the sun-worshipers long to stake out their places on the forward deck, strip down to their swimsuits, and stretch out to catch some rays.

However, once they cleared the harbor, the turbulence of the open sea became an immediate issue. Waves eventually reached four and five meters, causing the boat to pitch and yaw relentlessly. It wasn't long before enthusiasm among the passengers began to wane. Soon they were lined up along both rails, heaving their personal choice of breakfast into the deep blue sea. Eventually, the skipper cut the trip short. The residue of the night's storm had proven too formidable.

They sailed into the harbor at Kemer and stood by while the tour guide went by taxi to Tekirova to fetch the bus that was waiting for them there.

Those who were able, including Michelle, ate a lunch of fish, spaghetti, and bread prepared by the crew on the yacht's stern. Those who were unable, including Katrina, wished that they had chosen another way to spend their holiday. But by the time their bus had negotiated the narrow coastal road and they saw the lights of Antalya coming closer, everyone was in good spirits again; they had shared an adventure together, something to talk about when they returned home. The group gathered dockside to say good-bye to Michelle and Katrina who thanked their hosts for inviting them. Maybe next time it would not be quite so rough!

In this manner, August sweltered into September. The summer had been full of pleasant memories and the near incident with terrorists in Istanbul was all but forgotten. It was too beautiful here to think of Bosnia, Beirut, or other troubled places. And, the opening day of school was only a week away.

Her chance to join with the Hedleys, Beverly Stonehill, Michelle, and the other *fakülte* in making a difference in a group of young strangers was finally here. Seven days from now, she would stand in front of her students and welcome them to her ninth and tenth grade Bible and English Literature classes, and a session in Conversational English. A heavy load for a first-year teacher, but Katrina felt up to it, and the thrill of new beginnings was growing inside her.

Twenty-three. Ibrahim

Tuesday, 26 August, 1945 local time
Kilçilar

The opening was barely large enough for his hand. His fingers coaxed and tugged ever so gently until the contents lay on the table beside the jar. Ibrahim ran his tongue over his lips as he set the container to one side and gazed at the thin scroll before peeling away the linen wrap. Then he worked at opening two parchment sheets on which there appeared to be a letter. A third, smaller sheet had been rolled inside the rest.

Ibrahim's heart pounded as he looked at the parchment. These were definitely not bills of lading, but what were they? The parchment was amazingly well preserved, kept dry in the jar and free from moisture in its subterranean stone locker. The characters were an ancient form of Greek, one which his linguistic studies enabled him to interpret.

Adjusting the light, Ibrahim bent closer and began reading. He had barely passed over the first line when he stopped and took a deep breath. *No. It cannot be, but . . .* he stared at the words before taking out a pad and pencil . . . *I know who this writer is! Yet, I don't believe it.* He began writing down the translation:

Simon Peter a servant and apostle of Jesus Christ

Is this possible? Can this really be a letter from Saint Peter?

Deciphering the parchment text was slow work. There was no punctuation and words occasionally ran together, causing Ibrahim to backtrack several times before he finally finished transcribing the contents of the letter. He held his translation under the light and read it again:

to my dear friend and fellow apostle John shepherd of the flock in Ephesus I bring you greetings from Jerusalem I will be leaving soon on my way to Rome and hope to be able to pass through Ephesus for a visit In fact it seems imperative to me that I see you once again perhaps for the final time As I have told you before I am possessed with troubling thoughts concerning some of the church's earliest teachings regarding our Lord Jesus but there is no one in whom I may confide these things I write to you now in strictest confidence and with deepest respect my dear friend We have not many years left and the truth about the Master must be established beyond all doubt I received your letter some weeks ago informing that Mary has gone from us to be rewarded in heaven for her faithful deeds It is one more reason to search out what she has left behind Perhaps you alone can help me determine what to do with the most perplexing question of all that now remains locked forever in his mother's womb You yourself have written and often spoken of Jesus as God's only begotten Son Yet I cannot overcome the problem that if he was indeed begotten then he must have had a beginning of existence This means that there must have been a time when the Son was not and if such is the case it sets the eternality of Jesus at issue and raises other questions as well regarding the true manner of his birth I cannot but believe that we must clarify and possibly modify our earliest teachings In this regard Is it not more truthful to state that the Logos is an intermediate being who stands between the Creator and creation I know we spoke to him after his death I am certain that it was truly he who came to us again and that he is resurrected from the dead But what else do we not know We are not learned Pharisees John We are only fishermen and now what once seemed simple is clouded over with ambiguity and illusion We must speak dear friend I fear that the future of the church and its teachings rests with us and that we are unworthy of the great responsibility The years have made my hand unsteady as you know I have asked brother Mark a faithful coworker to assist me with this letter and have sworn him to secrecy about these concerns So that you know these are my own true and personal thoughts you will recognize my signature by my own hand May God's peace and blessing be upon you and all those you serve chosen of God and dispersed throughout Phrygia Asia Bithynia Galatia Cappadocia and Cilicia I pray we will see each other soon to discuss these things

Ibrahim stared for a long time at the signature. Then he checked his watch. It was nearly midnight. With care he reread each line. He was confident that his translation was accurate, but he was dumbfounded at what he had just read. The Apostle Peter, considered by many to be the first Pope, most revered leader of the Christian faith, was confessing to doubts regarding the doctrine of Jesus Christ that has been traditionally accepted by the church for centuries? Astonishing!

What about the smaller paper? Ibrahim leaned closer and saw that it too was written in Greek and appeared to be a letter. He quickly ascertained that this one was not from Peter.

Auderius of Antioch to my dear friend Eusebius Bishop of Nicomedia I write this brief note to you to affirm that my servant Ziyaettin bears an important document that I and others have authenticated as having been dictated and signed by the Apostle Peter It was retrieved from the library of the Apostle John in Ephesus by Estian a student of theology who lived for a brief time in Ephesus We here fully accept it as expressing the mind of the great church leader in his later years and send it to you with all due urgency given the forthcoming Council at Nicea I have heard that you intend to defend Arius I remember with fondness our early days in Antioch when the three of us sat under our teacher and mentor the great Lucian Our prayers here are for victory over those who have since deposed Arius as a heretic This letter from the Apostle Peter should silence our enemies once

and for all and help set the church on its true and righteous
course May you be blessed of God in all you do and may our
dear friend and God's true servant Arius be reinstated to his
rightful place of influence

Ibrahim leaned back in his chair and rubbed his eyes. The dull pain in his ribcage gradually returned him to the present. The lamp was starting to dim. He reached into a box on the floor by the file cabinet for a replacement battery, all the while mulling over what he understood so far.

The Apostle Peter he knew about. Also John, the apostle who had been exiled to the island of Patmos where he had had a great vision that was later included in the Christian Bible. Ibrahim also knew that a Council had taken place in Nicea, early in the fourth century, although he had no idea what drew the church leaders there or what had resulted from their gathering. The other names mentioned in the text were not familiar to him.

How on earth did these letters find their way into this cave? The fourth century predated the mosaic Jesus and the painted frescoes by at least two to four hundred years! The jar must have been there all along, hidden in the natural stone wall. Did the Christians who created the underground church know of its hiding place? Surely not, or they would have destroyed it. And yet they didn't destroy the idols and art objects in the other rooms, did they? Some of which would surely have been reprehensible to them. Why not? Who were these people? How did they think?

Question after question filled Ibrahim's thoughts, but he had few logical answers. *What kind of archaeologist am I, anyway? I could very well have just made the discovery of the century. It's a dream come true! So why don't I run outside and wake up the camp?*

"Because there are still too many questions," he muttered under his breath.

Carefully he laid a transparent plastic cover over the parchment letters and put them, together with the jar, in the file cabinet. The penciled translation he folded and stuffed into his pocket. Undressing, he put his clothes over the back of the chair in which he had been sitting for the last several hours. Before stretching out on the cot, he again checked the time. His watch said two-thirty. Ibrahim yawned as he turned out the light.

Pursuit

THE SHADOWY FIGURE STOOD halfway between the latrine area and the tents. A match flared, its flame touching the end of a cigarette. For an instant a face was visible, pensive and brooding, eyes peering steadily ahead, contemplating the faint glow of light in the canvas tent a half dozen meters away. A breath of smoky air extinguished the flame, leaving only the cigarette's red glow to point out his presence.

A short time later, the light in the tent dimmed and then went out altogether.

The cigarette glowed brightly twice more before disappearing under the toe of an unlaced boot.

Twenty-four. Ibrahim

Wednesday morning, 27 August

By the time he had finished breakfast and checked with The Roc and Ben Hur about the day's activities, Ibrahim had made up his mind. Coffee cup in hand, he headed for his tent.

"How do you feel this morning, Dr. Sevali?"

"Much better, thank you, Dr. El."

"You rested well?"

"Very."

"Is there anything I can do for you today?" El asked with unusual politeness.

"No, just keep on deciphering those tablets."

El nodded imperceptibly.

"Have you found anything special in the tablets?" asked Ibrahim.

"I am working on what appears to be an interesting myth, perhaps a favorite story of these people at that time. I can't be certain as yet. I'll let you know."

"Thanks." Ibrahim turned and started to walk away.

"And you, doctor. Has there been anything new brought to your attention?"

Pausing, Ibrahim turned back to his epigraphist.

"No, nothing that would be of interest. Mostly payrolls and bills for food and equipment. I think you have a much more fascinating day ahead than I do."

"That's too bad. I'm sure you must get bored with all the administrative details that go with being the director of a project such as this."

"It is a handful, I'll say that. Anyway, thanks for your kind offer. I need to go, but I'll drop by later. I would be very pleased if you would show me your myth."

Ibrahim turned and this time continued walking away from the man he had come to dislike, all the while wondering what had prompted this conversation. Gürer El rarely spoke unless spoken to, and smiled even less. He treated everyone with indifference, and complained profusely when something offended his fundamentalist beliefs.

Ibrahim smiled grimly as he reached the entrance to his tent. *Well, Dr. Üzünal warned me, didn't he?*

His most oft-repeated complaint had to do with the three young female students from Paris. During the first week that all three were in the camp, El had complained bitterly that their presence contributed nothing meaningful to the overall goals of the project. This, in spite of the generally accepted practice of injecting young, new blood into the science of archaeology by means of student internships that afforded hands-on involvement in projects like this one.

When it became obvious that Ibrahim would not back down on this matter, El's complaints took on a less philosophical and more practical bent. One day he began arguing with Ibrahim in front of Tahsin and Ben Hur.

"Having these women here adds unnecessary expense to the budget," he said caustically, though Ibrahim knew that the man actually understood little or nothing about the financial aspects of *Kilçilar.*

"We're always looking for more money," he went on, "and these women burden our project by requiring separate quarters and a private latrine."

"That is not something they asked for," Ibrahim interjected. "We volunteered these items to them."

"And then there is the troublesomeness of their using the

same showers as the men," El continued, as if he had not heard Ibrahim's observation. "It's not just the inconvenience, it is a moral issue. Some of the younger men are being tempted by these women using the same showers as the men!"

Ibrahim struggled to keep from laughing at this, but couldn't resist a jab at El's overbearing pompousness. "And some of the older men? Are they being tempted as well?"

Dr. El glared at Ibrahim, his mouth opening and then closing, momentarily at a loss to respond. Then he sputtered a restatement of his belief that it was unreasonable to include women, especially "foreign" women, in the camp. Ibrahim reminded El that each time women were in the showers, a sign was posted to alert the men, and that they were fully dressed before entering or leaving. Under the circumstances of life in a camp like this, what more did he think could be done?

During the entire discussion, Tahsin and Ben Hur stood by silently, their only contribution being an occasional amused glance at each other while their leader patiently dealt with the "problem."

When the matter of dress was mentioned, El started off again. "These foreign women do not respect our culture. They wear clothing that reveals their bodies immodestly. I have seen them in men's pants and even in shorts. This should not be!"

"I understand what you are saying, Dr. El, and I respect your views. But you must remember that these women come from a country and a culture that sees nothing wrong with the way that they dress. In actuality, they have worn nothing more or less than what many of our young Turkish women also wear these days. However, it will please you to know that I've asked our guests not to wear their short shorts, out of respect to our male-dominated fraternity here at *Kılçılar.*"

"And that is precisely the point, doctor! A devilish Western slime is spreading across our land, drowning out the sanctity of our moral and religious values. Movies and television and magazines, all from the West! Our women are watching and beginning to think they can be and do whatever they please. Unless we return to the fundamentals of our Islamic faith, our nation will soon be a wasteland of Western heresy!"

"We are a secular state, Dr. El. Our nation's father, Atatürk, very wisely led our people to separate mosque and state. He saw that to do otherwise would be folly. This is not Iran, may Allah be praised. Our destiny is not controlled by a handful of mullahs. Turkey is a land in which women are being educated to read and write. They can carry on an interesting conversation. They can vote. They can even run for office. The fact is, they can *be* and *do* what they please. And I for one see nothing wrong in this."

Dr. El and the others were silent.

"And now, I think our conversation has reached an end. We've spanned the distance from latrines and showers all the way to the state of the nation. It is the beauty of our land that we are able to argue our differences and yet work together and live in peace, don't you agree?"

Ibrahim put his hand on the epigraphist's shoulder. "I respect your views, Dr. El, and especially your skills. I promise that I will do what I can to make your participation with us a pleasant experience. So, what do you say we get on with the work at hand?"

Once inside his tent, Ibrahim brought out the cellular phone that had only recently been added to the camp's inventory. Until midway through the summer, the nearest telephone had been located in Derinkuyu. Just one more inconvenience that was now history. He dialed the number and listened.

"Günaydin." *Good morning.*

"Üzünal Doktor görüsebilir miyim lütfen?" *May I speak with Dr. Üzünal, please?*

"Aradiginiz kimse burada yok." *The person you are calling is not here.*

"This is Ibrahim Sevali at the *Kilçilar* excavation. May I ask when you expect Dr. Üzünal to return?"

"Ah, Dr. Sevali. I didn't recognize your voice. This is Sabri. He mentioned that you might call. Unfortunately, there is no way to be in touch with him. He and my mother have gone north for two weeks to fish and rest. Anything to get him out of here. He is quite anxious to be back at work, but the doctor says he must wait. They are somewhere around Yenice in a cabin on the river. They have no telephone, but if they do go into the village and call here, would you like to leave a message?"

"Yes. Please tell him to get in touch with me. It's very important or I would not bother him."

"Of course. I understand."

"Everyone is well?"

"Yes. Father continues to amaze the doctors. He is a walking miracle. My mother is also well and we are very happy for them both."

"As are we here at *Kilçilar*. Okay, Sabri. Hos bulduk." *Thanks.*

"Allahaismarladik." *Good-bye.*

Ibrahim sat on the edge of the cot, holding the phone and thinking about what to do with this unexpected development. He had decided the night before to confide only in someone he could trust.

On the one hand, he was excited about what this discovery might mean to his career. If verified to be an authentic letter from Peter, it would result in unprecedented recognition among his colleagues. His name in journals recounting his great discovery . . . lectures . . . a book, perhaps . . . media interviews. It all sounded very heady to an archaeologist who had not yet reached his thirtieth birthday.

However, there was a dark side to this as well, one that caused Ibrahim to move cautiously. To begin with, he wasn't sure what had happened at the Council in Nicea more than sixteen centuries ago. But holding onto a document by the man generally acknowledged to be the most revered person in the Christian church, outside of Jesus Himself, his need to know was a responsibility that became weightier by the hour.

What will happen if one of the world's greatest religions is suddenly undermined by the doubts of one of its founding fathers? To what ends will the leaders go in my own Islamic faith to further upset the delicate balance existing between the world's religions if the contents of this letter are made public? Even the Jews will be affected, if for no other reason than a probable downturn in tourism from a public grown disenchanted with their faith.

Perhaps the church would be able to shrug off the doubts and fears of one man. In his heart, however, Ibrahim knew that this was not just any one man. This was *Peter!* He sat without moving, suddenly struck by the overwhelming magnitude of his situation. His hand moved back and forth across the telephone as the face of a person he had not thought about for some time took shape in his mind.

They had become acquainted through a mutual friend at a dinner in Istanbul. Each had taken an instant liking to the other. Both were teachers, though coming from vastly different backgrounds. Instead of it being a handicap, however, their differing worlds seemed invigorating and bracing. Though they had met on only two subsequent occasions, there had developed between them a strong mutual esteem. *Yes, he might be just the person.*

His friend had moved from Izmir to Antalya more than a year ago. That much he knew. Perhaps the easiest thing would be to call the former employer for the new number. No, instead, he first would try information. A few minutes later, Ibrahim was speaking to the operator.

"Antalya telefon etmek istiyorum." *I'd like to make a telephone call to Antalya* . . . "No, I'm sorry, I don't have the number . . . Yes, thank you. I wish to speak to a Mr. Ian Hedley, please."

Within a matter of minutes, he smiled at the sound of a familiar voice on the line, one that still carried the light Irish accent that Ibrahim found as pleasant today as the first time he had heard it.

"Ian, it's Ibrahim Sevali."

"Ibrahim! What a wonderful surprise, lad. And to what do I owe the joy o' speakin' to my favorite archaeologist? It's good to hear yer voice."

"And yours as well, my friend. I'll get right to the reason for my call. I'm working on a field project near Derinkuyu. We have just recently opened a new underground city here. The other night, I found something that . . . that I'm uncertain as to how to go about handling. I can't say anything further over the telephone. I need to see you in person. Is that possible?"

"I should think it would be if you can come this way. We're in the process o' puttin' the final touches on our school's openin' next week."

"Of course, I understand. It's not too great an imposition?"

"An imposition? O' course not, lad. Ne'er where ye're concerned. I'll be lookin' forwar' to a visit. When will I be expectin' ye to arrive, then?"

"The day after tomorrow?"

"Fine. Will ye be needin' to be picked up somewhere?"

"No, but I do need your address."

Ian Hedley gave him the address of the school and instructions as to its location.

"Thanks. I wouldn't bother you if this were not important, Ian. I need some of that Celtic wisdom of yours."

"Ah, 'tis the best in the world, lad. It ne'er comes any better anywhere. 'Tis a sad thing that too few folk realize it."

Ibrahim was chuckling as he pushed the cut-out button.

Friday, 29 August, 1600 local time Antalya

TWO DAYS LATER AT FOUR in the afternoon, Ibrahim handed over the fare and tip to the taxi driver and, with overnight bag in hand, he walked through a gate that opened onto a courtyard, its striking feature a garden carpet of floral colors spreading out from beneath four large palm trees. The buildings were single story and plain, although they appeared to have recently received a fresh coat of paint. The air was muggy and dark clouds hung threateningly overhead.

Ibrahim pushed the main entrance door open and walked into a small foyer. There did not seem to be anyone about. Hallways went in opposite directions off the reception area. Hesitating, he looked both ways, then chose the one to the right. He walked along slowly, looking into each room as he passed by. He was two-thirds of the way down the hall when he heard a noise.

Following the sound, he paused at an open doorway. A woman was standing on a stepladder in paint-stained shorts and blouse tied at the waist, balancing a container with one hand while pushing a roller along the top of the wall with the other. For a moment he watched in silence, admiring her long, tanned legs and lithe form as she stretched upward to reach the corner. Unaware of his presence, the woman remained focused on keeping the roller's fresh paint on the wall and away from the ceiling.

At the precise moment that she drew the roller back to the container for more paint, he knocked on the open door.

"Tünaydin." *Good afternoon.*

"Oh! You startled me. I didn't know anyone was there."

"I'm sorry," Ibrahim answered in English.

"That's all right. What can I do for you?"

The woman's hands and arms were speckled with paint and there was a smear on her cheek. She had an open and friendly smile, accentuated by a pair of striking blue eyes that studied him through wisps of straying blond hair.

"I'm here to see the principal, Mr. Hedley."

"You came in the main entrance?"

He nodded affirmatively.

"Back the way you came then. His office is the second door on the left in the other hall."

"Thank you," Ibrahim said, lingering a second longer to admire this lovely creature perched nonchalantly on the ladder, before retreating slowly from the doorway.

"Unfortunately, he's not in," she added. Ibrahim stopped abruptly. "He was called away on a family emergency. However, I believe Mrs. Hedley is there now and I'm sure she'll be able to help you."

"Thank you," he said again, frowning as he mulled over this bit of unexpected news.

"Would you like for me to go with you?"

"No, it's all right. I can find my way. You've been very helpful."

"No problem," the woman said, turning back to the task at hand.

Ibrahim retraced his steps, crossed the small lobby, and started down the opposite hall. True to the painter's word, the second door to the left was marked Principal. He knocked.

"Come in," said a feminine voice that he recognized.

Ibrahim opened the door and waited until Dorothy Hedley looked up from a desk awash with paper. Her white hair was pulled back and tied in a short ponytail and she wore an aqua dress.

"Ibrahim!"

Dorothy dropped her pen and rose from the chair, moving quickly around the desk until she was standing in front of him.

"Oh, it is so good to see you again," she said, enfolding his hand in both of hers. "Come in. Let me take your bag."

"No, it's all right, Mrs. Hedley. I'm very happy to see you.

You're looking well."

"And so are you. You've lost some weight, though."

"Camp food."

"But still as handsome as ever!" Dorothy exclaimed, kissing his cheek. "Ibrahim, I am so sorry that Ian is not here. It was only a few hours after you called that we received word. His father suffered a serious heart attack. He's up in years, of course, and the doctors don't give him much hope. They told Ian that if he wished to see his father alive again, he would have to hurry home."

"I'm very sorry."

"Unfortunately, we had no way of contacting you. Oh, I just feel terrible knowing that you've come all this way and Ian is not here. He told me that you had something urgent you wished to speak to him about. Please, let me get you some tea. Have a seat."

Ibrahim sat in one of the wooden chairs opposite the desk while Dorothy poured water from the teapot that warmed on a small hot plate near the window.

"This couldn't have come at a worse time for Ian," she declared, handing the small glass cup to Ibrahim. "School begins next week. I'm trying to get as much done as possible. Our teachers have been touching up their rooms and getting everything as ready as we can. But, I do miss him being here to take charge. Tell me, Ibrahim, is there anything that I can do to help in this situation? I'll be talking to Ian by telephone this evening. Is there a message? Would you like to speak with him when he calls?"

Ibrahim weighed the options as he took another sip of apple tea. Finally, he looked across at her, his brow deeply furrowed with the concern he could no longer keep hidden.

"I have found something, Mrs. Hedley . . . "

"Please, Ibrahim, it's Dorothy. I'll feel much better if you call me by my first name."

"Yes. All right, Dorothy. I remember how you and Ian feel about 'formalities.' As I started to say, at the underground city that we call *Kilçilar*, I have found a parchment, dating back to the fourth century."

"Oh, my, that sounds exciting. Have you been able to translate it? Of course, that's a silly question, given your linguistic abilities."

"Yes, as a matter of fact, I have translated it. That's really why I'm here. I needed to talk to someone with a Christian background who could tell me about this document's historical significance. I respect Ian highly and thought perhaps he could help. Now, I guess that will not be possible."

Dorothy sat silently for a moment, hands folded on the desk.

"You need to speak with someone knowledgeable in Christian history?"

Ibrahim nodded.

"There is someone . . . a teacher who came to us this summer from the States. She's a seminary graduate with an outstanding academic record, and she will be teaching some of our Bible courses this year. Her major was biblical studies with a minor in church history. Both Ian and I have been impressed with her. She's very bright and conversant in the history of the Christian church. Perhaps you could talk with her. In fact, she may have a better handle on what you need to know than Ian would."

Ibrahim said nothing as he finished his tea and set the glass on the desk. Then he looked up at Dorothy.

"I really wish Ian were here," he said earnestly, a worried look on his face. He paused for a moment before continuing. "Can this teacher be trusted to keep any conversations we might have in confidence?"

"Oh, I'm sure that will not be a problem."

"Then if you recommend her so highly, perhaps it will be possible for me to talk with her?"

"Just a minute," Dorothy said as she walked over to the door. "I think she's still in her classroom. At least she was a half hour ago."

Opening the door, she called out, "Katrina? Are you still here?"

"Yes, I am," came the muffled reply.

"Would you come to my office, please? I have someone I'd like you to meet."

"Just a moment. I'll be right there," the voice answered again.

Dorothy turned back to Ibrahim. "The longer I think about it, the more I believe this may very well be your best alternative to speaking with Ian. Find out as much as you can from her, and if you still need to speak to him, we'll call later."

"All right. I truly appreciate what . . . " The rest of Ibrahim's thought remained unspoken as a woman appeared in the doorway in paint-stained shorts and blouse knotted at the waist, wiping her hands with a towel.

"Katrina, thank you for coming," said Dorothy. "I have a dear friend of ours I want you to meet. He has some questions that need answering and, unfortunately, Ian is not here. Because the information he is seeking is in your field, I thought perhaps you might be able to help. Katrina Lauring, this is Dr. Ibrahim Sevali."

Katrina brushed at strands of hair that persisted in straying across her face. Her eyes sparkled with curiosity as she held out her hand.

"How do you do, Dr. Sevali? I apologize for my appearance, but I was not expecting to meet anyone this afternoon. It's nice to see you again."

"Again?" Dorothy looked puzzled. "Have you two . . . "

"Ms. Lauring has already answered one of my questions today, Dorothy," laughed Ibrahim, "and it proved correct. I stopped by the room in which she was working and she directed me to you. If she is equally as knowledgeable in Christian history, I have no doubt that she'll be able to assist me with what I need to know."

Dorothy and Katrina joined him in laughter.

"Is it possible for you both to join me for dinner this evening?" he asked.

"Oh, I *am* sorry, Ibrahim," answered Dorothy. "There's nothing I would enjoy more, but as you can see, I have a long way to go before we are sufficiently organized for opening day. And with Ian absent, there is no one else. Are you free to go, Katrina?"

"I feel that I should stay to help you, but yes, I would be happy to have dinner with Dr. Sevali," Katrina responded with a smile. "But first I need to get this paint and grime off and change into something appropriate. Can I meet you somewhere? Say at seven o'clock?"

"If I know where you live, I will be happy to meet you there."

Katrina glanced at Dorothy. She nodded reassuringly.

"Very well, then," Katrina smiled, glancing at her wristwatch. "I live just two blocks from here, up the hill on the left. It's a two-story building. Just before you reach the corner, you'll come to an alley covered with cobblestones. Walk up the alley about twenty meters. You'll see an iron gate on the right underneath a large tree. Ring the buzzer and I'll try not to keep you waiting."

"Thank you, Ms. Lauring," said Ibrahim, bowing slightly, "for the privilege of your time. I'll see you at seven."

"'Bye, Dorothy," Katrina paused as she entered the hall. "Don't work too late. Michelle and I will help you tomorrow if you need us."

"Thanks. I'll let you know. Go now, and do enjoy your evening."

Twenty-five. Katrina

1858 local time

It was just before seven when the buzzer sounded at the gate. The fact that this security measure was in place had been reassuring to both Katrina and Michelle when they first moved in. The downside lay in the fact that the accompanying speaker system, enabling them to talk to whoever was waiting at the gate, did not work.

Katrina took a last quick look. Her hair fell loosely around her shoulders, attractively framing the classic Nordic face that returned her gaze from the mirror. She wore a simple short-sleeved, white linen dress and heels. Katrina was mindful of her natural beauty, but not in a self-aggrandizing way. She saw herself and every woman as stewards of their bodies. Whatever level of physical attractiveness had been granted was a gift from God to be nurtured through care and conditioning, tempered by the knowledge that true loveliness is lit from within.

"'Bye, Michelle," she called, as she opened the door. "I won't be late."

"Au revoir, mon amie," her friend called back from the tiny kitchen they shared together. "Have a good time."

Halfway down the steps from their second floor apartment,

Katrina saw the Hedleys' friend waiting patiently at the gate. She waved.

"Hello again, Dr. Sevali."

"Good evening, Ms. Lauring."

Katrina keyed the gate open and passed through into the alleyway. They fell into step together as they walked toward the street.

"Our taxi is waiting. I forgot to ask at the school what kind of food you prefer. Is Italian satisfactory?"

"Very. You couldn't have made a better choice."

"Good. I'm not so familiar with restaurants in Antalya, but Françesco's on the Beach was recommended by the bellman at my hotel. Shall we give it a try?"

"It sounds delightful and I am hungry. Painting my classroom this afternoon gave me a real appetite."

"Then we shall see to it that you have a suitable meal. Here's our taxi." He held open the door. "Please?"

Thirty minutes later they were seated at a window table, looking at an overcast sea in the gathering darkness. Françesco's was a well-established restaurant, patronized by locals rather than tourists. The dining area consisted of a large room, plainly decorated, overlit and decidedly noisy.

The menu turned out to be more Turkish than Italian. After reviewing the various options with Katrina, Ibrahim ordered *marul salatasi* and *iskender kebabi,* a Romaine lettuce salad and lamb roasted on a vertical spit, before being cut into thin slices and served on a bed of rice.

"What would you like to drink?"

"Mineral water will be fine."

"Maden suyu sodasi lütfen," he said to the waiter, holding up two fingers.

At eight o'clock, Ibrahim and Katrina looked up from their conversation, startled as the noisy atmosphere around them suddenly quieted. They watched as the room that had been a "caterpillar" began its surprise metamorphosis into a "butterfly."

Lights were dimmed. A pianist on the opposite side of the room embarked on a hauntingly romantic melody. Waiters made their way among the tables with trays of candles protruding from wax-covered wine bottles. Starting with those at the outside and working toward the center, it was carried off with elegance. Shortly, a waiter stood by Katrina's side, placing a bottle at the window's edge of their table while another lit the candle with a long tapered torch.

"Afiyet olsun," he said, expressing the Turkish equivalent of bon appetite.

"Tesekkür ederim," both of Françesco's first-time patrons answered at the same time. *Thank you.*

"You speak Turkish?" Ibrahim asked in surprise.

"You've heard about the extent of it," she said laughingly. "I've been working on 'survival Turkish' since my arrival in June. On top of that, my roommate is trying to make me more fluent in French. I'm not sure if I will ever become truly conversant, but I'm determined to give it a try. Where did you learn to speak such excellent English?"

"In school and on my own. Languages are what I do best. Fortunately, they are central to what I enjoy doing the most."

As their eyes adjusted to the candlelight, the pianist continued playing at the far end of the room. In a matter of moments, the atmosphere had taken on a decidedly intimate and romantic air. Ibrahim shifted a bit nervously as their waiter returned with the salads.

"I hope that the atmosphere is not too uncomfortable, Ms. Lauring. I apologize. I have not been to this place before."

"No," she answered quickly, with a wave of her hand, "on the contrary. I love it. You made a good choice. And if this salad is any indication, the food is going to be as delicious as our surroundings. One thing, though. I'd find it even more pleasant if you'll call me Katrina."

"Katrina," he repeated softly, as if testing the word on his tongue to see if it belonged there. "And you must call me Ibrahim."

"Fair enough."

"You are Swedish in ancestry? From the name and your appearance . . . "

"Mostly Danish. My paternal grandparents emigrated from the old country as teenagers. They were married in Chicago and then moved west, farming in South Dakota before moving to eastern Washington State. At least, that's what I am told. They died before I ever had a chance to know them. Mother is half

Danish, half Norwegian, so the Scandinavian gene pool is full and overflowing. My parents met in college."

"What do they do?"

"Besides raising my brother and me, they have pastored churches all their married lives. They live in the Bay Area now . . . near San Francisco."

Ibrahim smiled and nodded. "It's very beautiful there, I'm told. I've been to America, but only to New York and Chicago. And I was so busy that sightseeing was not a high priority."

"You said on the way over here that you are a professor at the University of Istanbul. We were sidetracked in the conversation before you had a chance to tell me in what department."

"I'm a professor of archaeology."

"How exciting," Katrina exclaimed. "That's something I've always been interested in. I want to spend a summer on an archaeological dig someday. I've read so much about it, and listened to some fascinating lectures, but have never actually been to a site."

"Then you must come to *Kilçilar*. There I can show you some of Turkey's most exciting archaeological findings." Ibrahim's eyes flashed with excitement. "In fact, it is *Kilçilar* that brings me to Antalya."

Just then the waiter reappeared with the main courses.

"Tell me about your family, Ibrahim," Katrina inquired, "and about how you decided to become an archaeologist."

For the next half hour they chatted comfortably back and forth over the *iskender kebabi.* As the dishes were being removed, Ibrahim ordered *kazandibi* for desert, a pudding with a caramelized base, and *sütlü çay,* tea with milk.

"You are not having much in the way of 'Italian cuisine' this evening, in spite of the name of this place, but I trust you've enjoyed your meal anyway?"

"The food has been wonderful, Ibrahim, and the conversation has been delightful as well. It's a pleasure getting to know you."

"And you as well. This comes as a complete surprise, I must admit."

"How so?"

"Well, first of all, I intended to meet with Ian. Of course, that was not possible."

"I am sorry . . . "

"No, no," Ibrahim exclaimed reassuringly. He leaned forward, the candlelight creating light and shadow on his face. "Though I would have been happy to see my old friend once more, as it has turned out, I've had an even more delightful evening with a new acquaintance. One I hope I will be privileged to see again."

Katrina smiled but said nothing.

"Now I must ask you some of the questions that brought me to Antalya in the first place," he said seriously.

"And I must tell you before we begin that I'm feeling very nervous and inadequate, Ibrahim. I'm fresh out of seminary and not at all sure that I'll be able to help. I only wish one of my professors were here," she added, though not with any real conviction in her voice. She was secretly luxuriating in this unanticipated evening with a handsome and extremely intelligent stranger.

Katrina listened attentively as Ibrahim explained the background of Cappadocia's underground cities in general, and *Kilçilar,* in particular. The longer he spoke, the more she felt his mounting excitement. The man's intensity engaged her totally, as he described with his hands as well as with words what he wanted her to see.

She became fascinated with the story of *Kilçilar* and its treasures. Her imagination bogged down at the thought of thirty thousand persecuted Christian believers living together for months at a time in such a place and she wondered why she had not heard of this before. She was also amazed that such a young man, only four years her senior, could have been entrusted with so much responsibility.

Eventually, Ibrahim described finding the clay jar, leaving out his private reasons for having made the late night pilgrimage in the first place.

"Inside the jar was a manuscript. It is in the form of a letter written in Greek and addressed to Eusebius of Nicomedia. Do you know anything of this man?"

Katrina sat for a moment without moving. Her mind traced back through her early church history studies at Tower Seminary.

"Church history is a love of mine," she responded at last, "but I feel like a real novice. I do know of such a man, however. Actually, there were several men in the Christian church's history by that name, but only one from Nicomedia. He was a bishop who gained prominence at the Council of Nicea in 325. I'm familiar with this because I had to do a major research paper on this Council."

"This Council is also mentioned in the letter," Ibrahim interrupted. "I am familiar with the name and place, but not so much with what happened there."

"It was called by Emperor Constantine to deal with Arianism, a heresy that threatened to divide the church. As I remember, very few bishops from the West came to the Council. Most were from the Eastern church. The main issue was a man named Arius, who had already gotten 'the axe' a few years earlier."

"The axe?" queried Ibrahim. "What is 'the axe?'"

"One of our American colloquialisms," laughed Katrina apologetically. "It means to be thrown out. Fired. Or, in this case, deposed or excommunicated. Is that better?"

"It is good, this axe," Ibrahim mused, "though I think it has more French connotations than American." He moved his finger in a cutting motion across his throat.

"Anyway," she went on, "the bishops met to deal with this matter of Arianism. In essence, it was a denial of Jesus Christ as the eternal Son of God. Arius said that if Jesus was the 'only begotten Son of God,' then there had to have been a time when He was not. Thus His existence came from 'nothing,' and not from that which was, in its very essence, God Himself. Are you tracking with me so far?"

Ibrahim nodded thoughtfully.

"Okay. In a nutshell, Arianism was knocked out by a bishop named Athanasius, a wealthy Egyptian with a Greek education. He was a skilled theologian with a journalist's instincts when it came to the pen. Remember, Arius taught that Christ the Logos was not the eternal Son of God, but a subordinate being. Along comes Athanasius who says, 'You're wrong, Arius. The Scriptures teach the eternal Sonship of the Logos. They say that the world was directly created by God, and that the redemption of the world and of men is made possible by God in Christ Jesus.'"

By this time, Ibrahim had withdrawn a small notebook and pen from inside his jacket and was writing furiously. Eventually, he paused and looked up.

"Go on," he said anxiously.

"Well, that's about it. A creed called the Nicene Creed was formulated at this Council. It's thought that this Creed was probably taken, in large part, from the baptismal creeds of the churches in Antioch and Jerusalem. It mainly emphasizes the idea that the Son is of 'one substance' with the Father. Theologians like big words. The one they use for this is 'consubstantiality.' It simply means that the Son is of the same substance as the Father."

"Were these men the 'white hairs' of the early church?"

"That's a curious question, now that I think about it, given our own youth at this table. Athanasius was young, in his twenties, when he began expounding on these matters. I'm not sure about the others."

Ibrahim pushed his notebook aside and sat back in his chair, staring at the table. Katrina said nothing, sensing that the handsome young archaeologist sitting across from her was far away in his thoughts. She waited patiently until he stirred and reached inside his jacket once more. This time he pulled out a folded piece of paper which he laid on the table and smoothed out with his hand.

"Have you ever heard of one named Auderius of Antioch?"

Katrina shook her head.

"Ziyaettin?"

"No."

"Estian."

"No. Sorry."

"Lucian?"

Katrina thought for a moment.

"There was a Lucian of Antioch, who became head of the Antiochene School of Theology. He was considered highly controversial because of some of his theological views. As I recall, he was a literalist in the interpretation of Scripture. He opposed the allegorical methods of people like Origen. He believed in the preexistence of Christ, but insisted that it had not been from all eternity.

"And, you know, now that I think about it, Arius was one of his students. And so was Eusebius, for that matter! Eusebius is even referred to as the father of Arianism by some, because of his tremendous influence during that time. He signed the Creed at Nicea, all right, but afterward engineered one of the five exiles of Athanasius and led a widespread reaction against the Creed. Later on, he became the patriarch of Constantinople or Istanbul. Around 339, I think. Ultimately he was martyred in Nicomedia."

Ibrahim gazed soberly at Katrina in the light of a candle almost consumed to the lip of the bottle.

"That's all I know, Ibrahim. Does it help?"

"It does indeed," he said slowly, fingering the paper in front of him. "I have translated the manuscript that I found in the cave. It mentions Lucian as having been the teacher of Auderius, the man who writes a note attached to the main letter. Auderius also identifies Eusebius, the man to whom the letter is addressed, as a classmate. He further states that Arius was also a student with them at the same time."

"Then who are the others?" asked Katrina. "Have you any idea?"

"Ziyaettin was apparently a servant of Auderius who was carrying the main letter to Eusebius. Estian is identified by Auderius as a student in Ephesus who found the main letter in a library in Ephesus."

"You keep mentioning another letter," Katrina said inquiringly. "Are you saying that Auderius was sending a letter with his letter?"

Ibrahim nodded slowly.

"To whom was the main letter written?"

Ibrahim remained silent, staring into her face.

"I'm sorry," she said finally. "I take it that the main letter brought you here to see Ian. If it's not something that we should discuss, please don't feel embarrassed."

"I . . . I want to . . . discuss it," Ibrahim responded haltingly. "I did not have that intention when we came to dinner. But I respect your knowledge and am having a sense about you . . . that you would be able to keep a confidence if it was important."

"I'd like to think that I would keep a confidence, even if it was not important. I grew up in a pastor's home, remember? I knew a lot of things that I probably should not have, but I never caused my parents grief by speaking out of turn. When a confidence is shared, until permission is given, it remains locked up in my head or my heart, depending on where I have to store it."

Ibrahim smiled.

"Then I must trust you without further hesitation," he said simply. "Help me again, Katrina. Are there not letters included in the Bible from the Apostle Peter?"

"Yes, two of them, in the New Testament."

"Do you know to whom they were addressed?"

"Sure. The second letter is easy. It was written to the church at large, with no specific group designated. But his first letter was directed to Christians in Pontus, Galatia, Cappadocia . . . " She hesitated when the name suddenly clicked in her mind as being the region in which Ibrahim was working, and her voice faded as she concluded with ". . . Asia and Bithynia."

"Do you understand where all those places are located?" Ibrahim asked softly, as he leaned forward.

She nodded and whispered, "Turkey."

For several seconds neither of them moved as they looked across the table at each other. The stillness between them formed an invisible bridge over which their thoughts rushed to meet. Katrina was the first to break the silence and her voice was low, but overflowing with incredulity.

"Are you telling me that you've discovered a letter . . . *from the Apostle Peter?*"

"Yes, that's what I'm saying."

Katrina was at a loss for words. Finally she asked, "To whom is the letter written?"

"To the Apostle John."

Ibrahim's calm pronouncement rang like a thunderclap in Katrina's mind.

"Are you serious? To the . . . to John? Why, Ibrahim, this is absolutely breathtaking! I can hardly believe what you're telling me. A letter from the Apostle Peter to the Apostle John. Are you sure that it's authentic?"

"Of course, it must be studied by experts for verification. But there's no doubt as to what the letter says. I am the expert in that regard."

"Unbelievable! This is utterly fabulous, Ibrahim. Why, it will be the find of the century. How absolutely wonderful!" Katrina clapped her hands with excitement. Then slowly she sat back and studied the face of the man who had just revealed to her his steppingstone to greatness. He was slumped in his chair, looking somber and suddenly depressed.

"What's the matter, Ibrahim?"

"You will not be so happy, Katrina, when you read the letter."

Earlier elation was abruptly replaced with a disquieting uneasiness. As Ibrahim signaled the waiter, Katrina glanced away and was surprised to see that most of the evening's patrons had already left. She looked in disbelief at her watch. Eleven forty-five!

"We should go," Ibrahim remarked as he examined the bill and paid the waiter. "They'll be closing in a few minutes. But first, I want you to read what I have translated. Please?"

He handed over the penciled notepaper that had lain between them on the table throughout their conversation.

When she finished reading, she handed it back without a word. Gathering up her purse, she stood and stared out the window into the black darkness that had earlier been the Mediterranean Sea.

"Let's get out of here," she said finally.

"Are you all right?" asked Ibrahim, his voice filled with concern.

"No. But I'm just the first among millions."

As they started for the door, Katrina wiped at a sudden dampness on her cheek. It was the tear she had stubbornly refused to shed while sitting in front of Ibrahim. Yet, she knew the tear was just like the letter now tucked away in this Turkish archaeologist's pocket.

No matter what she did, it would not be denied release!

Twenty-six. Katrina

Saturday, 30 August, 0110 local time

It was after one o'clock by the time Katrina slipped the key into the iron gate that protected the stairway to her apartment. She felt spent, emotionally used up. A lovely evening had shattered like an heirloom vase, leaving her with a feeling of overwhelming loss.

By seven the next morning, she had managed to doze only fitfully on a bed that looked as though it had been occupied by a wrestler. With a groan muffled by her pillow, she pushed herself up and out, shuffling to the bathroom and staring into the mirror. Blue eyes rimmed in red stared back through strands of matted and disheveled hair.

You're a mess, Kat.

Just then Michelle's voice summoned her from the kitchen. "Breakfast in five minutes, mon amie."

"I'm not hungry."

"Un jus de fruit, un oeuf á la coque, des toasts, y du café noir. Que c'est bon?" *Some fruit juice, a boiled egg, toast, and black coffee. It's good, don't you think?* "Especially for someone who got in as late as you last night. Vous avez quatre minutes." *You have four minutes.*

"C'est trop grand," Katrina called out. "Seulement du café, s'il vous plait." *It is too much. Only some coffee, please.*

"Ah, mon amie, you've not totally forgotten the precious and beautiful words you have learned of the language God prefers to speak when He is tired of Hebrew. C'est bon. Maintenant, dépêchez-vous! Vous avez deux minutes." *It is good. Now, hurry up! You have two minutes!*

Katrina turned on the tiny shower and stepped in, pulling the curtain after her. She stood still, letting the tepid water spray across her face and run in tiny rivulets over her body.

"I'm putting it on the table."

Katrina grinned at the persistence of her roommate. It was what she needed this morning. Quickly she washed, rinsed, and turned the water off. Moments later she emerged, wrapped in a light robe, her hair hanging straight and limp at her shoulders.

"Hi, Michelle."

"Well, well. And how's my favorite drowned mouse this morning?"

"Tough night."

"Bad date?"

"I told you last night, it wasn't a date," Katrina protested, as she pulled a chair back from the table and sat down. "I was filling in for Ian actually. Ibrahim ... Dr. Sevali needed some information that happens to be in my field of expertise."

"Mmm."

"That's all it was. Really."

"Mmm."

"Come on, Michelle."

"The lady doth protest too much. She better start praying instead," Michelle urged with a knowing look. "The food is getting cold."

They bowed their heads as Katrina gave thanks.

Michelle spread marmalade on a piece of toast. "So what is this 'Ibrahim' of yours? Old? Young? Exciting? Dull? What?"

Katrina smiled as she peeled the shell away from the soft-boiled egg. "You know what I like about you most, Michelle? It's all that French subtlety. You beat around the bush and never come right out and say what's on your mind."

Michelle made a wry face. "You know what I like about you

most? It's all that American naiveté. You exude this remarkable freshness and innocence. Did you grow up wearing a little nun's habit and singing, 'The hills are alive with the sound of music'?"

They burst out laughing.

"Oh, you *are* good for my soul," Katrina answered. "How I wish you could meet my brother. He'd love your humor."

"Then I wish I could meet him," Michelle responded brightly. "If he is half as wonderful as you say, you must promise that someday I will meet him."

"I promise."

"Now, quit stalling," Michelle pleaded. "Tell me about last night."

"Okay. Ibrahim is twenty-nine and a professor of archaeology at the University of Istanbul."

"Sounds stuffy," Michelle commented, as she bit into a second piece of toast.

"Well, he's anything but stuffy," Katrina defended. "He's handsome and very intelligent and is the director of a field project in Cappadocia. It's in the central part of the country. I've got to get my map out and find the place. The project is called *Kilçilar*. That's the name of the nearest village. What he's working on was once an underground city."

Katrina went on filling in her roommate with all the information she could about Ibrahim and his work, as well as the restaurant at which they had spent the evening, all the while carefully avoiding any reference to the jar and its distressing letters.

"Do you think that you'll ever see him again?"

Katrina glanced up at the clock above the sink. "Yes, actually, he's calling for me at ten o'clock."

"Is he really?"

"There are some additional matters he wants to discuss."

"I'm sure!"

"Michelle! Be nice! He just wants to talk about his project."

"Mmm."

"Then he's taking me to lunch and I should be back early this afternoon."

"Mmm. That's another thing I admire about you Americans."

"What?"

"You're not nearly as naive as we French think and a lot more ingenious than we give you credit for."

Katrina wadded her napkin and threw it at Michelle.

AT EXACTLY ONE MINUTE BEFORE TEN the buzzer sounded and Katrina, dressed casually in pants and blouse, and hair woven in a French braid, met Ibrahim at the gate for the second time. He was wearing a sport shirt, blue jeans, and a beat-up pair of Nikes.

"Günaydin," he smiled as they shook hands. *Good morning.*

"Merhaba," Katrina replied. "Nasilsiniz?" *Hello. How are you?*

"Tesekkür ederim, iyiyim. Siz nasilsiniz?" *Fine, thank you. How are you?*

"Tesekkür ederim. Ben de iyiyim," she replied. *Thank you, I'm fine too.* "I've also used up my Turkish vocabulary, so don't get any ideas that we're going to spend the day talking like this."

"I'm very impressed," Ibrahim said, as they walked to the street. "In fact, you are an amazing person, Katrina. I do appreciate your taking more time to speak with me today. I know you are preparing for the beginning of school, so I'll try not to use up all your free moments."

"I'm enjoying it," Katrina responded. Then, thinking once more of the letters, she sadly added, "At least most of it."

Ibrahim glanced over at her, but she was staring off into the distance. He understood.

"Here is our taxi. Let me ask, have you visited the Antalya Museum yet?"

"No."

"This morning I thought we might go there for a short visit. I think you will find it very interesting."

"I went to a museum in Istanbul, not all that far from where you teach, now that I think about it. It's difficult, though, when everything is presented in a language you don't understand."

"That's one of the reasons I want you to see this place. I've been there before. It's quite . . . how do you Americans say . . . user-friendly? Your students will probably be making field trips to this place during the school year, and you'll find it easy to join in because the exhibits are arranged superbly and each is clearly labeled in English. Would you like to do this?"

"Sure."

"Afterward, I thought perhaps we could return to the Old Town and walk around a bit. There are many little cafes in that area. The temperature will be moderate today, so we can sit at one of the outdoor tables, if that pleases you."

"It pleases me," she answered, entering the taxi. "I've had a cup of Michelle's coffee already, but let's find a place that will make us the real thing. A genuine cup of coffee sounds really good to me."

"Then we'll search until we find some 'real coffee.' And when we do, you may have all you want."

Their taxi drove them along Orgeneral Kenan Evren Bulvari, the main coastal road, to the western end of the city where, for the next two hours, Katrina discovered that visiting a museum with someone as knowledgeable as Ibrahim can be a rare treat.

They began with the Stone Age and continued along the Bronze Age artifacts, each exhibit representing the spectrum of Turkey's history. As they walked, Ibrahim explained the respective Greek, Roman, Byzantine, Seljuk, and Ottoman eras on display. Each section contained innumerable smaller objects as well as more monumental sculpture and statuary from the various time periods. The exhibit that Katrina loved best was the ethnographic collection that presented all manner of urban and rural life in Anatolia. There was even a section devoted to nomads.

She found herself understanding Ibrahim better as he equated some of the rural displays with his own family history. Here was a brilliant young archaeology professor talking without apology about his humble roots. She found it easy to imagine him as the little boy he described, sitting on the verandah with his father, absorbing the stories and legends of the land as the world passed by their front door.

Later they walked through the narrow streets of the Old City, inquiring at two cafés before finding one that would accommodate them with 'real coffee.' Ibrahim opted for tea instead, insisting that he did not care that much for coffee. Especially Turkish coffee.

"Regular is okay first thing in the morning, but the 'Turkish' tastes like the bottom of the Euphrates River," he declared with a grimace and a mock shudder.

The flow of their conversation from the previous night had returned easily. They enjoyed each other's companionship and their intellectual compatibility. Even those spaces where no words were spoken, lurking like vacant lots between people ill at ease, were for them like quiet meadows.

Their conversation eventually returned to the letters, as Katrina knew that it would. The pleasantness of watching and listening while couples strolled by on this sunny Saturday afternoon gave way to the reality of what concerned them both.

"Have you thought further about them?" Ibrahim asked, leaning back in his chair.

"How could I not?" answered Katrina soberly. "I tossed and turned all night. What are you going to do now?"

"That's originally what I came to discuss with Ian. I respect his wisdom and truthfulness. He's a fine man and a strong Christian. I thought perhaps he could shed some light on the names and the content of the letters. You've done that for me. I also wanted to ask him what he thought would be the impact of Peter's letter on the public."

Katrina sat quietly, listening.

"What do you think, Katrina? What will happen when people hear of it?"

"If my reaction is any indication, I believe it will be devastating."

"How so?"

"Think about it, Ibrahim. If Peter was really in this frame of mind, no one ever knew it. Though he once denied his relationship with Jesus, there's no further indication of any breakdown in his faith or courage. He's a hero to the church. Maybe the doubts expressed in the letter can be chalked up to a growing senility, but I didn't get that feeling from reading your translation notes. I wish that I could see the actual letters."

"You also know Greek?" Ibrahim exclaimed with a surprised look.

"I can read New Testament Greek. But, really, I was just thinking out loud. I've never tried reading from an original document as you have done. And I certainly don't doubt your accuracy. I just think it would help to actually see the text. I'm probably grasping at straws here. Was he a closet 'doubting Thomas'? He's suggesting personal misgivings regarding doctrine that has been established dogma in the church for centuries. The thought that Peter might doubt that Jesus is the eternal Son of God, possibly relegating Him to some lower form of intermediary between God and man, strikes at the very heart of the orthodox Christian faith. It's just incredible!

"For centuries, Christians have lived and died for this. It's what we've examined and come to believe as truth. In Jesus, God and man uniquely commingled in a way that has never occurred before and never will again. He stands alone in mankind's history, Ibrahim, as man's Creator and the sole source of his redemption."

Ibrahim sat silently, watching and listening as Katrina spoke.

"Another incriminating issue that critics will leap upon is the implied cover-up. Peter writes to John about his concerns, but no one ever hears about them until now? The letter should probably have been burned, but it wasn't. Did John and Peter really discuss these matters face-to-face? There's no record of such a meeting, but if it did take place, what conclusions did they reach? Were they different than we've accorded to them all these years?

"Then, a couple of centuries later a student supposedly finds this letter while searching through John's memorabilia at Ephesus. He passes it on to this Auderius character who forwards it to a bishop for presentation as argumentative evidence at the Council of Nicea. But something or someone prevented it. What happened? Why was it never offered up? How did it wind up in a cave in Cappadocia, hundreds of miles from Nicea?

"Did someone fear what I fear and decide to hide it? There are so many unanswered questions here, Ibrahim. But one thing is for sure—if this letter had made it to the Council of Nicea, it might very well have changed the entire course of church history!"

"There's also a consideration you haven't mentioned," Ibrahim added.

Katrina looked steadily into Ibrahim's eyes.

"It's the response of the Muslim world."

"You're certainly the expert there, Ibrahim. I'm just starting to get acquainted with your world, so what do you think it would be?"

"Our religious leaders would be elated. Especially those who are members of the Shi'ite sect of Islam. You are familiar with them? You've seen them in the streets since you arrived?"

"I've seen some of the women in their chadors. I can't tell about the men from the way they dress."

"In Iran these people control the government. It's a religious state. Here in Turkey, we hold the mosque and state to be separate, similar to what you are familiar with in American religious life. As you've seen, I'm sure, our Turkish women have many freedoms. Most do not wear the chador, opting for a more European look. Still, the Shi'ites are very strong and continue to gain support in our land. For many of us, this is hard to understand. There's an urgency among a large minority who want to return to the way things were in the past. At least, to the way they imagine things to have been.

"I know from what you've said that your religious beliefs are fairly conservative. You may not like this, but when I read of the efforts of some of your so-called 'religious right' to infiltrate the government with their conservative mores and values, I can't help but equate them to what the fundamentalists are attempting to do here."

"Conservative Christians in America don't blow up shopping centers to make their point," Katrina commented dryly, thinking back on her exposure to the actions of radicals in Istanbul.

"Is that true? What about the bombing of abortion clinics and the murder of doctors who act in the role of abortionists?"

"That's different," protested Katrina. "Those people are oddballs. Religious kooks. No true Christian would affirm such heinous acts."

"Nevertheless, from our view at a distance, these people seem to be gaining greater visibility and power than at any time in recent history. The same can be said to be true among Muslims.

"Here, the fundamentalists' influence is growing. In America, you have basically a two-party system. During our last elections, there were more than twenty registered political parties. Between most of these groups, the differences are really inconsequential. But what happens? Each one bleeds votes from the other. That makes it possible for the fundamentalist Shi'ites to have a much greater influence. Recently, in Konya and in several other smaller cities, this political-religious group has been voted into power. If their influence continues to grow, I fear for the future of democracy in our country.

"We are ninety-nine percent Muslim here and most of our citizens respect and tolerate those of other faiths or cultural backgrounds. All we ask for is mutual respect. We are not obsessively anti-Christian or anti-Western or even anti-Jewish."

"Then how is it that the countries of the world that are predominantly Muslim have all declared themselves to be at war with Israel?"

Ibrahim shrugged. "Not *all* the countries, but admittedly this is a problem. Turkey recognizes the nation of Israel. I don't have the answer to your question, and it is a fair one. Only that reason must one day prevail over the heat of passion."

"Amen to that," breathed Katrina softly. "But how, with all our differences, can that ever happen unless people enter into a personal relationship of faith and forgiveness through Jesus Christ?"

Ibrahim remained silent for a moment, as though he were thinking of what Katrina had just said.

"We Muslims have a deep respect for the Jesus of the Bible," he answered at last. "To us, he's one of the twenty-four prophets, stretching from Adam to Mohammed. I'm no theologian, Katrina, but I know there are many parallels in your beliefs and mine.

"For example, we believe that John the Baptist was sent to proclaim the coming of the Word, which was Jesus. The Koran tells us of the angel's announcement to the Virgin Mary that she would give birth to a son. 'His name shall be Masih Isa Ibnu Mariam, honorable, honorable in this world and the world to come,' is the way it reads. In Islam, the name most often used for Jesus is 'Isa.' But we are speaking of the same person.

"We also know that He was born in Bethlehem, and of no human father. He was virtuous, meek and kind, a great miracle worker, especially in matters of healing, and was endowed with the Holy Spirit in a unique way. We believe that He even raised the dead to life again, that He was rejected by the Jews, and ultimately ascended to heaven. He's coming a second time to destroy His greatest enemy.

"There are two specific areas in which we're not in agreement, however. At least two of which I'm aware. Islam does not accept the Christian idea that Jesus died on the cross. Nor is there an acknowledgment of His divinity. So you can see that the Apostle's letter will bring the Muslim world to its feet cheering and saying,

'See? We've told you this for centuries. And this proves it. We've been right all along!'"

"It will cause the faith of many Christians to be destroyed or, at the very least, to be deeply unsettled," Katrina admitted. "To be perfectly honest, it even shakes my own faith to think of Peter giving voice to such doubts."

"What else will it do?" Ibrahim asked, as he pointed a finger in her direction for emphasis. "It could well bring economic chaos. If Christians leave the church, many of your religious institutions will close their doors. Lines will be drawn even more deeply between fundamentalists and the rest of the Christians, just as lines are being drawn here. Truth be known, the Muslim fundamentalists hate us more than they do you. And hatred is a cancer that spreads quickly and with deadly results.

"Even the Jews will be affected, if for no other reason than economics. Christian pilgrims will stay away in droves, and tourism, which is Israel's second most profitable industry, will suffer irreparable damage. Perhaps now you can see why I'm so deeply concerned about this discovery. I wish now that I'd never found that jar. The world would be better off not knowing the truth of this matter!"

"Do you really believe that, Ibrahim?" Katrina instinctively reached over the table and took his hand. "Is the world ever better off not knowing and facing up to truth? How can we be afraid of it? Jesus once said, 'I *am* the truth.'"

Ibrahim was silent, but did not move his hand away. After a few moments in which no words were spoken, it was Katrina who pulled hers back.

"I know one thing for sure," she continued. "If what I believe can be proven false, I for one want to know about it. I could not bear the thought of living my life under the branches of a tree rooted in deception and error."

"So what do you think I . . . what should *we* do about this?"

"I think the first thing we should do is pray and ask God for wisdom and divine direction, don't you?"

Ibrahim nodded, though he had to admit that this was a new thought. It did seem right in this case, however, and why he had to suddenly be reminded of the power of prayer by a Christian was a bit of a mystery. Then a curious question came to mind. *Do you suppose we are talking about praying to the same God?* He opened his mouth to ask and then stopped. This was not the time nor the place to get into a theological debate. At least not yet.

"I must return to *Kilçilar* tomorrow," Ibrahim said reluctantly. "And I know you've got to finish preparing for the opening day of school. It's a long journey, but would you be willing to visit the site?"

Katrina's eyes danced with excitement at the very thought.

"It would give you a chance to see the underground city and to observe an archaeological site firsthand, something you said earlier you'd like to do. I want you to read the letters for yourself. Perhaps you'll find something in them that I've missed. You most certainly will 'feel' the hearts of the writers. That I can assure you. And from experience, I can testify that viewing the real object is far superior to notes or pictures."

"I'd love to visit," Katrina answered quickly. "I just don't know how it would be possible at the moment. Ian is gone. School is beginning. I'm new and I wouldn't be comfortable asking for time off."

"Permit me to ask. We could do it next week or the one following. If you left early on Friday, you could be at the site by nightfall. You'd be able to go into the caves and also examine the letters on Saturday. Returning on Sunday, you'd miss only one day of classes." Ibrahim looked imploringly at Katrina. "It will be a long, hard trip, but it would mean a great deal to me if you could do this."

"Then let's talk with Dorothy together," Katrina answered supportively. "She'll be in her office this afternoon. Are you willing to share with her the reason for your request?"

Ibrahim nodded. "I have the utmost confidence in the Hedleys. That's what brought me here in the first place."

"All right, let's explain what you have in mind. If she says okay, I'll do it."

"Thank you. You don't know how grateful I am," said Ibrahim, sounding relieved at her willingness to consider helping further.

No, I probably don't. I also have no idea why I'm becoming involved in this at all. What's going on here, Lord? Why me?

• • •

ASSOCIATED PRESS. September 3.
U.S. and European governments are urging the curtailment of foreign business travel in Turkey until further notice. Sources cite safety of foreign citizens as the primary reason. Three French businessmen were gunned down in the streets of Ankara on Tuesday morning. Their assassins were subsequently tracked down and killed in a gun battle lasting three hours.

In the early evening of the same day, a bomb exploded near the main entrance of an Istanbul hotel generally frequented by American and European tourists. Seven were killed and three injured. Two of the victims have been identified as Japanese, three others as German. It is not known if Americans are among the dead or wounded. Names are being withheld until families are notified. Security personnel are being increased at all major hotels in the city.

• • •

Twenty-seven. Kristian

I think everybody in the world should be granted two weeks in Hawaii. A "pilgrimage to Paradise" for the body and soul. I'm still a traveling novice, having done most of mine under the aegis of Uncle Sam. It's not that I don't like going to new places. I've just never had enough green in the kitty before now. It certainly feels different to sleep in $200-a-day rooms and have plenty of pocket money left over for the souvenir stores.

I snorkled some, played golf and tennis, dozed in the sun some, and walked around a lot. The weather was warm, not too humid, and late afternoon breezes off the ocean introduced each delightful evening.

I sampled restaurants in Lahaina and in several of the hotels that line Kaanapali Beach. I even managed to knock off four novels, three that were well written with good plots and strong characters. The last one was a no-brainer by a woman who is on our list of possible guests for next year. If she's anything like the novel, I'll pass.

The very first morning I woke up thinking, *I can afford all this now.* I dialed food service from my bed and minutes later was sipping a steaming cup of Kona coffee and munching on croissants. There's no doubt that I can get used to this!

Tom called a couple of times, but never flew out. I don't think I really expected him to, even though he said that he would. These high-powered, show-biz types seem to say a lot of things they never intend to act on.

I don't know if this is true where Carole is concerned. Her roots are deep in the same soil as mine, but where is she going with her life? For that matter, where am I going with mine?

I was attracted to her, even though she did tick me off at our last planning meeting in San Francisco. There have been no phone calls from her and I didn't make any. Besides the physical rest, I needed time to think without the constant interruption of others. Especially an "other" as physically appealing as Carole.

Then, on my last night . . . it happened again!

The same ethereal, intangible light figure . . . fading in . . . then out . . . an apparition . . . materializing in my dream . . . with a vacant emptiness where her face should be . . . the hair . . . long and blond . . . like Kat's . . . but it's not Kat . . . yet, so familiar . . . who are you? . . . Do I know you? Are you from my past . . . or my future? Will I see you on a street corner someday . . . and then lose you again. . . . Strange . . . have I lost you before?

WHEN I RETURNED to Los Angeles, I was eager to plunge back into the endless rounds of budget meetings, planning sessions, and hiring interviews. It was already September, and there was so much to be done before the first of the year. Not the least of which was finding a place to live.

Every afternoon, that first week back, I drove past dozens of exclusive residences and condominiums before finally settling on a place about five miles from network headquarters. It was a new, upscale three-story apartment and condominium complex with tennis courts, a fitness center, three large pools, and separate Jacuzzis scattered through beautifully appointed grounds.

The Brenton was a gated community, still new enough that several units were available. I managed to secure a two-bedroom model on the top floor. The lease was longer than I wanted, but it did take the pressure off deciding where to buy. And, though I tried not to think about it in these terms, it also gave me an out if the show crashed and I turned up in America's increasingly crowded talk-show-host litter box.

"ALL RIGHT. LET'S LIST THE ASSETS."

Tom Knight was sitting at the end of the conference room table behind papers and books that were spread as far as he could reach. "I want to hear from everybody but Kris on this."

Connie Sandlewood, an attractive young secretary assigned to work with Tom, sat to his right. The thought crossed my mind that she would probably be next in Tom's harem lineup. If she wasn't already.

To her right was Jim Stanton, the head of Entertainment. Carole sat between Stanton and Carey Marsten, our new lead writer, who would be working with me and heading up a team of six whose job it would be to ensure that each show's five-to-seven-minute opening monologue was filled with pointed and peppery journalistic humor. On the opposite side of the table, Sid Maples from Productions had just been joined by Karla Rivers, head of Affiliate Relations and Sales.

"Somebody take the lead," Tom ordered gruffly.

"Some pretty good guests are already shaping up," Stanton began, checking over the list of confirmed and maybes that Connie had presented to the group.

"Guests are ancillary."

"What do you mean, Tom?" asked Stanton in surprise.

"Remember what Carson used to say?" Tom paused and let his eyes shift across his audience. No one could remember. I doubted that anyone had a clue about what Carson used to say, including myself. It was just Tom's clever way of asserting himself as the undisputed expert at the table.

"'These shows are not about the guests. They are about the guy behind the desk.' That's what Carson said. And he's right. So what sort of assets do we have to work with behind *our* desk?"

"Well, I think we've said it before," Stanton began again. "Kris has this boyish look on camera. He comes off like every mother's son or grandson. I think he'll appeal to the younger crowd, but he's going to be a real winner with the older ones too. He looks wholesome . . . kind of like a milk ad."

Everyone laughed, except Knight who never laughs at anything. Stanton winked at me.

"Thanks," I responded dryly, just loud enough for Stanton to hear.

"We know he picked up some broadcast experience on campus radio while he was in college." It was Marsten who spoke up. "That has stood him in good stead. And speaking of that, he has a degree in communications."

"And what will that buy us?" grunted Tom, tossing his pen onto the table.

"You said to list the assets. Here we are listing them," Stanton shot back testily.

"Humph. What else?" Tom appeared to turn his attention away from the others as he stared at a piece of modern art hanging on the wall behind Sid. I thought this was probably also a ploy to make the others ill at ease.

"His army experience gives him authenticity with the Armed Forces people."

Back and forth across the table people pitched their view of the "assets." I wasn't used to being talked about like a new car on the showroom floor. One thing for sure in this business, every day throws you a new learning curve.

"Small town and big city identity."

"His experience at KFOR in San Fran."

I hate it when people down here shorten that word. Calling it Frisco is even worse. A true native or an authentic adopted son knows the word is Francisco. It's the respect one gives to the beautiful City by the Bay.

I had to remind myself that I was in L.A. now, Dodger and Angel country. Home of the Lakers and the Mighty Ducks. Maybe I could shift loyalties to the Lakers, but . . . the Mighty Ducks? Get real! Only in Disneyland. Oh, well. Maybe I was just a San Francisco snob at heart.

"He's quick on his feet. Lightning fast with ad libs. Has an aw-shucks kind of cynicism."

Cynicism about what? I wondered, as the listing continued.

"I think we've found a star who will feel comfortable to the mass viewing audience . . . *and* their mass prejudices." Everyone turned to look at Carole.

"What do you mean exactly?" Tom asked, his attention now focused on the assistant producer-director.

"I mean that during the last two weeks I've watched five "KL Shows" a day. I've taken them apart and put them back together again. Some were bad. Most were good to above average. And a few were masterpieces. Carson was right. It *is* all about the guy behind the desk.

"Kris comes off as honest and intelligent, but not boorish. He never loses the audience or the guest during interviews. People see him as being able to relate to them, whether they are the working man or the professional. Not everyone can do that. His humor is clean, but he runs it out as far as he can without becoming overtly offensive. He pokes fun at anyone and everything. And then he gets serious when it's called for."

Carole leaned forward, resting her hands on the table.

"I watched him work actors, politicians, professionals, educators, even bicycle messengers, which I understand he was once himself for a short time. He's got the ability to handle that kind of breadth and still hold it together. And that asset makes him acceptable to the viewer when he tackles their bents and prejudices. He gets away with a lot when it comes to the controversial issues. And I don't mean in a tacky or tawdry sort of way. He makes you think."

As she sat back in her chair, eyes moved from Carole over to me, as though some of them were seeing me for the first time. I could tell they were thinking about what had just been said. For some, I was sure, it shed new light. Actually, I was as surprised as anyone that Carole had taken that much time to study and analyze her new project. Maybe she was going to make a good producer-director. It was getting a little embarrassing, though, so I lifted both hands in the surrender mode and shrugged.

"Anyone else?" Tom pulled us back on track.

No one spoke.

"Okay. So what are the downsides?"

"No studio site yet," Carole observed. "That decision has to be made yesterday, Sid. We can't keep being put off!"

I saw Sid Maples scribble something on a notepad and hoped it had to do with Carole's comment. I was getting more and more uneasy about the Top Brass' indecision, or maybe it was just their basic lack of concern about the production location.

"I think we're closer on that, Carole," he smiled as he looked up. "Maybe by next week. Week after at the latest. Politics and keeping everybody happy, you know."

"We want to be kept happy too, Sid," Carole smiled sweetly in return.

There were other issues. My age. My lack of major network or comedy room experience. No real exposure outside the Bay Area. Ideas were batted around as to how to minimize these drawbacks. Guest shots on the late night shows and interviews on the network's news magazine programs were suggested. Sitcom cameo appearances. Pitch the TV magazines. Press conferences. Newspaper ads, including a full page in *USA Today*. Place it on Friday to appear the entire weekend before the premiere show.

I shuffled and squirmed in my chair. I'd been reading *USA Today* in my hotel every morning in Hawaii. *And now they want to put me in it? Is this really happening? What will it be like with my face plastered all over America and everybody wanting a piece of the action?* Excitement and panic started to gnaw a hole in my stomach. *What if this turns out to be a huge flop?*

"Okay, Kris." Tom's voice was drawing me back to Realityville. "I'd like to finalize our meeting today by hearing from you. What do you have to add to what has been said? Have you had much opportunity to think about your goals for this show?"

I waited for a moment until everyone turned in my direction. The thought crossed my mind that the outburst in San Francisco had not been mentioned since I got back. Maybe the point had been made and we'd all moved on. I hoped so.

"First of all, modest soul that I am, I agree with everything good that has been said about me." There were some good-natured chuckles as I continued. "And I know the downside issues are all capable of being dealt with, especially the matter of my age. Not to worry. After I've been at this for six months, I'll have aged ten years. Two years from now, I'll look like Grandpa on a "Walton's Mountain" rerun!"

Everyone laughed. With the exception of Tom Knight, of course.

"Do you think people will find you in the 6:30–7:30 time slot, Kris?" asked Karla Rivers. "That's what our affiliates and the sponsors want to know."

"Are you suggesting that my target audience does not understand the complexities of channel surfing?"

More laughter.

"Is it going to be too big of a stretch in your humor quotient to bridge the age difference between you and our older target audience?" Karla persisted.

"I don't know, Karla. You all seem to be keeping up okay and I've been talking to my parents for twenty-eight years, so you be the judge."

Another round of guffaws. They were starting to warm up.

I looked across the table just in time to catch traces of a slight grin cracking Tom Knight's otherwise blank-screen veneer. Then he began gathering up the papers scattered in front of him, a sure sign that we were almost done.

"Seriously, there is one thing. I hope that besides making people laugh we can occasionally stir up public opinion and even overheat their minds on some issues. Things like censorship. Right to life. Euthanasia. Ethics issues in business, politics, science, wherever. Truth and integrity out there where everyone has to live it.

"That may sound a bit heavy, but if it's paced properly I believe these are the things people want to talk about today and they are ready to do it intelligently, thoughtfully, and even humorously. I'll tell you what I think. I think that if we weren't the pioneers here, one of the other networks would be fighting, clawing, scratching, and kicking to do it first. My dream is to have people talking about last night's show the next morning while they're standing around the water cooler."

Tom was stuffing the papers into his briefcase now.

"Okay, I see it's time to break up. Thanks for letting me listen a lot and talk a little this afternoon. I've learned some things just tuning in to the rest of you. Oh, by the way, there is one item that nobody has thought to mention."

Everyone was standing now, stretching and gathering their things, anxious to be on their way. They paused and looked at me again

"The show still needs a name."

Glances around the table.

"Make a note, Connie," said a bemused Tom Knight. "Kris thinks the show might need a name. I, for one, agree."

Twenty-eight. Katrina

Friday, 12 September, 0715 local time
Antalya

Her bus left the terminal on Kazim Ozalp Caddesi early in the morning. She gazed out of the window from her seat near the front, her eyes still smarting from leftover sleep. As the sun climbed to the top of Antalya's tree-lined streets, it exposed pearls of dampness collected on palm leaves and roofs and roadways from last night's rain.

A quick look as she boarded had disclosed that hers was the only Euro-American face among the passengers. A sudden wave of loneliness swept over her as she stared at the passing scenery. Alone in a land that was not her own. No one to share the adventure. And with it came the return of a question that had surfaced numerous times before. *What in the world am I doing here?*

The week following Ibrahim's visit had been a busy one for Katrina. On Sunday morning the staff began the day with a small Christian worship service. The entire faculty was present with the exception of five Turkish teachers in the elementary grades, all of whom were Muslims.

Other than three international students, one from Canada and the other two from Germany, the AGS student body was Muslim.

This meant that Christian teachers faced a much greater challenge than did the Muslim *fakülte,* and several had already begun to look to their Islamic counterparts for insights into cultural differences and customs. Katrina had found the national teachers to be very professional, fully qualified in their teaching skills, and delightful to work with.

Initially she had wondered what the reaction of supporters back home might be if they knew there were Muslim faculty members in a school that was being touted as a Christian outreach ministry. Dorothy explained that there were simply not enough international teachers to go around and so, of necessity, they had negotiated the services of some local instructors.

This morning, the staff had sung without musical accompaniment, shared together in a time of informal conversational prayer, and listened as Dorothy Hedley brought to them a devotional message from Acts 13.

She reminded them that the Apostle Paul and his companions had arrived here at Antalya-Perga from the island of Cyprus on their first missionary journey. It was also here, for reasons left unmentioned in Luke's telling of the story, that John Mark deserted them and returned to Jerusalem.

Later, as they prepared to launch their second missionary foray into the same general area, John Mark expressed a desire to rejoin their ministry team. Paul's companion, Barnabas, showed greater sympathy for his nephew's offense, but Paul refused a second chance for their young companion and ultimately this matter split these early missionary workers. Barnabas and John Mark sailed for Cyprus, while Paul chose his friend Silas, and traveled north through ancient Syria and Cilicia. It was not until much later that Paul and John Mark were reconciled.

The staff listened intently as Dorothy talked further about the importance of responsibility and accountability in relationships, reminding them of how difficult they are to build and how easy to tear down. After a while, she engaged the others in a lively discussion centered around the application of this biblical principle to their own immediate circumstance.

Dorothy then asked them to join hands in a circle and led in a prayer for their health, safety, and personal fulfillment as they worked with students and families throughout the year. Their worship time concluded by praying the Lord's Prayer together in unison. As their voices blended with the "Our Father . . . " it seemed to Katrina one of the most holy moments she had ever experienced.

A friendly camaraderie had followed over a simple meal, with the afternoon given to discussing educational plans and problems, last-minute classroom needs, and the unique challenges of expressing Christian faith and love in a predominantly Muslim world. Dorothy cautioned them that while the majority of Muslims in Turkey at least nominally accepted their presence, there were religious and political extremists in every city, including Antalya, who despised the fact that they were permitted by the government to be here.

By early evening, assignments for the following first day had been given, and *iyi aksamlars* or goodnights said, along with offers of "Help if you need it," as the AGS staff left for their homes.

Michelle and Katrina spent the rest of the evening in their apartment going over basic Turkish phrases they had been learning since their arrival. Though all classes were to be taught in English, an effort would be made by each international faculty member to respect Turkish culture, traditions, and language.

Two hundred twelve students were registered in the elementary through high school classes. This was considered an outstanding response to a school in its second year of operation, and it affirmed the reputation of the Hedleys and their work in Izmir.

Katrina did a quick review of her introductory Bible class lecture and discussion notes. Her eight o'clock class of ninth graders would be followed by grade ten. Most of the first day would be taken up getting acquainted with her girls and giving a brief overview of what the Bible classes would cover.

Third period was designated as Katrina's teacher prep time, for which she was grateful, though some of the veteran instructors indicated it was mostly a time to work with students who had questions or were finding some aspect of their studies difficult.

During fourth and fifth periods she would introduce the tenth and twelfth grades to a course referred to simply as English. This was the subject she felt the least comfortable with and anticipated that it might prove to be her most challenging task.

Nervously, she flipped through the pages of her *Annotated Teacher's Edition of Adventures in English Literature,* renewing acquaintance with such names as Shakespeare, Chaucer, Wordsworth, Tennyson, and the Brownings. When she accepted this assignment, Ian had helped her understand its importance for these Third-World students, some of whom would undoubtedly become tomorrow's leaders in a society profoundly influenced by Western concepts.

Edited by William C. Bassell of Staten Island, New York, the teacher's manual was already proving to be a lifesaver, even before her first session. Each page presented the text read by students prior to coming to class and surrounded this material with anecdotes, additional insights, and discussion questions that she would be able to use during the actual classroom presentation.

Conversational English made up the last period of the day and had been left up to her own discretion as to methodology. She had chosen a Berlitz-style approach during which students would not be permitted to speak anything other than English in the classroom. Since most of them already had at least a rudimentary understanding, she did not anticipate it being a difficult assignment and looked forward to it with relish.

Day one came and went without any major catastrophes. She and Michelle spent the dinner hour excitedly recounting the day's events. And so it had been for the remainder of the week.

On Wednesday, Katrina announced to Michelle that she was leaving on Friday to visit Ibrahim at the *Kilçilar* excavation site. Dorothy had agreed to take her Bible and English classes. Conversational English would be canceled while she was absent. After her initial surprise, followed by several "Mmm's," Michelle's face took on a serious look.

"This isn't just a visit between two people who like each other, is it?" she asked.

Katrina shook her head.

There was a long pause.

"It is something he's found that you can't talk about?"

"I'm sorry, Michelle. You are my dearest friend here, but I've promised Ibrahim to remain silent. As soon as I can, you'll be among the first that I confide in. I can tell you this much—I really need your prayers. I'm not at all sure where this is going, but it is very important." Katrina paused and then added, "And that's probably the understatement of the century!"

Michelle had continued to stare at her curiously and with a good deal of puzzled concern, but said nothing. Nor did she bring up the subject again. . . .

For several hours now, Katrina's bus had lumbered along a two-lane highway into the mountains where the landscape changed from a subtropical urban coastland into a bucolic setting of rustic pine, reigning over a kingdom of scrub brush and dusty undergrowth.

It was going to be a long journey. Even the shorter route on which she would return was a full day's drive. But, on her way to *Kilçilar*, she had determined to take the route north to Isparta. There she would transfer and head east to Konya and Aksaray where Ibrahim was to meet her. It was an itinerary full of significance—she was on the very route taken by the Apostle Paul on his first missionary journey!

Katrina settled back and reread Acts 13 and 14. Closing her New Testament, she let her imagination trek with Paul as they drove north through the region of ancient Pamphylia. After changing buses, she continued on past Egidir Gölü, one of the area's largest and greenest lakes, to the locale of Pisidian Antioch where one day Paul had stirred the entire city with his preaching.

Late in the afternoon, they passed through Konya. She observed many drab and gray high-rises in this industrial center, known during the Roman era as Iconium. It was here that Paul was stoned by outraged citizens. Ibrahim had warned Katrina not to wander off alone here, since this was still a center for political and religious radicalism.

She knew that Lystra was only a short distance from where her bus threaded through the maze of heavily trafficked city streets. Lystra was the birthplace of Timothy, one of Paul's young converts who joined the great apostle's ministry team during his second missionary journey.

By nightfall the lights of Aksaray could be seen in the distance. Though tired from the journey, Katrina had found it an incredible day of silent communion with the Lord and also with some of the great saints of the New Testament. After viewing the rugged mountain terrain and the high desert plateau over which Gospel pioneers had journeyed on foot, her veneration of these stalwart saints knew no bounds. She could now visualize their tenacity, faith, and utter dedication in living color.

At eight-thirty she stepped into the aisle, clutching the small bag she'd packed for the trip. Descending from the bus, she was at once aware of how cramped and weary she felt. She stood uncertainly, hesitating before making her way into the small terminal building. Then she saw him.

Ibrahim was jogging toward her from the street entrance.

"Iyi aksamlar, Katrina! You made it. And what a journey you must have had." He greeted her cheek to cheek. "I suspect that you are tired, no?"

"Yes," she replied wearily. "I'm exhausted. But it was worth every mile. Thank you so much for arranging my itinerary. It was a once-in-a-lifetime experience I shall never forget! But, as we say in America, I've 'been there, done that.' It should hold me for a while. At least until I go back on Sunday."

"I wish there were an easier way, but your return bus trip is really the best way to go without hiring a private plane."

"Not to worry. I'll make it fine. This way I get to see the countryside."

"This is all you brought?" Ibrahim gestured toward the bag.

She nodded.

"Please. Let me take it for you. Come with me. Your chariot awaits."

Katrina groaned. "How much farther is this place?"

"About an hour's drive," Ibrahim answered. "No more."

"Good, because I don't think I have more than an hour left in me. At least, not in a sitting position."

Ibrahim chuckled as he helped her into the Land Rover. "There's a small bag with a sandwich and something to drink there in the seat beside you. I thought that you might not have eaten."

"You thought correctly. I am hungry. And you?"

"As you say in America, 'Been there, done that.'"

He stowed her bag in back and climbed in behind the wheel. As they pulled away from the curb and into the flow of traffic, Katrina leaned her head back against the seat and closed her eyes, reflecting with some small surprise on how good it felt to be with Ibrahim once again.

It was nearly nine-thirty by the time the Rover bounced to the end of the rutted road and came to a stop at *Kilçilar*. It was this last bit of rough road that awakened Katrina.

"Oh," she exclaimed with a feeling of embarrassment, "I'm sorry. I didn't mean to fall asleep."

"You needed the rest. For you it has been a very long day on top of what I imagine has been a very full week."

"You imagine correctly. The first week of school and my first 'official' attempts at teaching."

"How did it go for you?"

"Well, I think. The children are delightful."

"Good. Our country needs people such as you to love our children and guide them into the next century."

They were standing in the darkness now by the vehicle. Katrina shivered.

"It's cold up here. I guess I've gotten used to Antalya's warm mugginess. How high are we?"

"I think something less than eighteen hundred meters, I'm not exactly sure," Ibrahim answered. "What is that . . . about six thousand feet?"

"No wonder it's crisp and cool!" Katrina exclaimed, pulling her sweater more tightly about her shoulders. "This feels like Tahoe in my home state—a ski resort."

"Let me take you to your sleeping quarters. You'll be staying in a tent with one of the young students from France. They speak English, though, so you'll have no problem communicating."

"Okay. Lead me on to my Stone Age penthouse and I'll catch up to you at breakfast. And Ibrahim . . . " she paused, thinking better of what she was about to say, and concluded with, "Thanks for coming to get me."

She felt his hand rest lightly on her arm as they walked toward her tent. With each step her desire to respond in some way increased.

To move closer. To place her hand in his.

Something to signal what she was feeling. What *was* she feeling?

I hardly know this man and my heart beats like a schoolgirl's over an innocent touch. He means nothing by it. He's just being polite. Katrina smiled. *Okay, I like polite.*

"This is it." His voice pierced her reverie. "Here, take this pencil flashlight. One of the beds is occupied. The other is yours."

"Thanks. You get some rest too. I'll be fine." Katrina waited. His hand lingered on her arm. Suddenly he let go, as though he had just realized they were standing still and no longer walking. Stepping back, his hands now dangled loosely and his face became visible in the moonlight. Before she could say anything, he turned and walked away.

Minutes later, lying on a cot that had most likely been made ready by her sleeping tentmate, Katrina sought to shut off her thoughts and go to sleep.

This is crazy. Focus, Kat, focus. You're here to examine some ancient letters. That's it. Nothing more is ever going to come of this. It cannot.

Katrina tried squirming her way to a more comfortable position under the sheet and blanket that covered the canvas cot.

Maybe it's the unusual circumstance that has drawn us together. Like mothers with newborns or men in the heat of battle.

She lay quietly.

And maybe it's this thin plateau air whistling through my empty head!

At last her eyelids grew heavy and she nuzzled her pillow one last time as a final thought danced off the stage of her consciousness and the curtain fell.

It's not just the letters, though, is it?

CONCEALED IN THE SHADOWS, he remained absolutely still.

Listening.

Watching.

Planning.

He was near enough to hear the woman preparing for bed, but the flap was closed and no light was visible inside. Unable to see her, he turned his attention to Ibrahim, hands in pockets, walking slowly across the way until he disappeared into his tent. A moment later a small battery lamp threaded a yellow ribbon of light out onto the ground in front of the tent's open flap.

At last, satisfied that everyone was settled down for the night, he turned and made his way toward the cave entrance.

Twenty-nine. Katrina

Saturday, 13 September,
0730 local time
Kilçilar

The next morning, Katrina was surprised and embarrassed to discover that she had slept through the breakfast hour. Renée Patry, the young student in whose tent she had awakened, roused her with the delivery of a small pot containing two very black cups of coffee and a tray with fresh bread slices, butter, and jam. After briefly introducing herself, she apologized that she was running late and jogged off to her work.

Katrina perched on the edge of the cot and poured the steaming liquid into her cup, letting its heat warm her body, melting away the residue fatigue. Setting the cup aside, she searched through her bag for clean underclothes before stepping into a pair of jeans and donning the cotton shirt she had packed in Antalya.

Squeezing paste onto her toothbrush, she began brushing vigorously, rinsing with water from the covered pitcher on the small wooden tray table between the two cots. That's when she noticed a small French New Testament on the stand behind the

217

pitcher. Her countenance lit up with surprise and pleasure.

Then, looking around and seeing no other option, she spit the toothpaste and water under the edge of the tent. From the looks of the small patch of dirt, she decided that it had been done before. Thinking how nice a hot shower would feel, she settled for dousing water on her face and, after drying, engaged in a hurried makeup process in front of a travel mirror.

All at once, the sound of loud voices jarred her, causing her to look up. People were shouting to each other outside her tent. The urgency in their voices made her drop her things and duck through the tent door into the bright morning sunshine.

Ibrahim was running from the direction of the cave with another man hard on his heels. He barked out an order, gesturing toward the vehicle parking area. The man veered off in that direction.

"What's wrong?" Katrina called out anxiously. At the sound of her voice, Ibrahim slowed slightly, then stopped altogether.

"It's Renée, the girl in whose tent you are staying."

"What happened?"

"A large boulder fell from the side of the passageway, just as she was walking by."

"Is she hurt badly?"

Ibrahim's look was one of grave concern.

"It hit her from the side. She looks . . . it is not very good." Just then the Land Rover in which Katrina had arrived the night before skidded past, bouncing crazily over the rough ground on its way to the cave entrance.

Katrina felt queasy. She started to ask if there was anything that she could do, but Ibrahim interrupted.

"Excuse me," he said, as he turned toward his tent. "I have to alert the clinic that we're coming."

She watched two men emerge, carrying a stretcher between them. Several others followed after them. Katrina moved closer. Standing near the waiting Land Rover she glimpsed Renée's still form under a blanket. Only her face could be seen, but it was enough.

The girl had sustained a crushing blow to the right side of her head. Her ear lay partially severed and the bones around her eye looked pulverized. Her face was grossly contorted, streaked with dirt and hair matted in the moist blood and torn skin.

Sickened, Katrina averted her gaze and began to pray, all the while thinking to herself, *She just brought me coffee. How could this have happened?*

As the Land Rover left for the clinic, Katrina walked over to Ibraham's tent, where he was finishing his call. His eyes acknowledged her presence as he signed off and dropped the unit inside the tent door.

"I'm sorry." Katrina's voice sounded small and tentative.

Ibrahim shook his head.

"I don't understand," he said. "We've been careful to shore up wherever it was necessary. She was walking a tunnel we use every day. In fact, the other workers had already passed through this morning. There has never been a problem. Then, out of nowhere, a stone tumbles and . . . " His voice trailed off.

Workers were continuing to emerge from the cave, standing in small clusters, smoking and talking and occasionally glancing over in their direction. Ibrahim was obviously shaken and he stared off in the distance without saying anything further.

Katrina sat down on a large rock and waited. After what seemed an interminable period of time, Ibrahim sighed heavily and turned his gaze back toward her. His smile was forced and filled with sadness.

"Çali will see that they get her to the clinic as quickly as possible. He's a good driver. She is one of Ben Hur's workers. He went with the others to attend to her."

"There were two other women in the vehicle."

"Fellow students from the University of Paris. Here for the summer. Well, there's nothing more we can do now. Stay here while I talk to the men. I'll return as quickly as possible and then we'll look at the letters."

It was nearly an hour before Katrina saw Ibrahim walking back, head down and hands in pockets. There was a puzzled look on his face as he paused at the tent door.

"I think everyone is back at work now. I'm going to the clinic to check on the girl. But let's get you started on the reason for your being here." He motioned her inside the tent.

"If you want to wait, it's all right," Katrina said. "I know this is a difficult time."

"Katrina, something is very wrong here."

"What do you mean?"

"I mean I went back with Rocco . . . one of the foremen . . . to where the stone fell on Renée."

"And. . . ?"

"When we examined the stone, we saw markings."

"What do you mean?"

"Markings," Ibrahim repeated, "like a pick or a wedge perhaps? I couldn't tell. They're small, almost indistinguishable. But they are there."

"You're sure? Could they have come from some of your earlier excavation work?" asked Katrina.

"Perhaps . . . that's what Rocco suggested. But it's not in a weakened location. Everything around it is firm and solidly in place. It seems unlikely to me that under those circumstances, and of its own accord, a stone just suddenly decides to give way. Besides, while we were examining the area I found this." Ibrahim reached into his pocket.

"What is it?"

"It's a piece of wire," Ibrahim answered, handing it to her. "It was in the dirt near the rock."

"Are you suggesting that someone actually meant for this to happen?" Katrina asked, pulling the short length of wire taut. "This is odd looking. What could it be for?"

"It's detonator wire."

Katrina stared at him. "An explosion? Why would anyone do such a thing?"

Ibrahim's eyes were flintlike, his jaw set. He went to the file, opened the bottom drawer, and withdrew its contents.

A small terra cotta jar. And the letters.

Placing them on the table he looked up at Katrina.

"Perhaps these could be the reason," he answered.

Thirty. Ibrahim

"But no one knows that you have these letters," Katrina exclaimed, bending over the table to see for herself the apostolic missal and its companion piece. She was surprised at the clean and clear manner in which almost every word retained its readability this many centuries after the original inscription.

Ibrahim said nothing as he watched Katrina's eyes move to the ancient text. In spite of the way the morning had gone so far, he smiled at the vibrancy in her demeanor.

"Do they?" Katrina was suddenly mindful that Ibrahim did not proffer a response. She looked at him questioningly, waiting for him to say something.

"I'm not certain," he said at last, sighing heavily.

"What do you mean?"

"Before I visited with you in Antalya, I placed this jar and the manuscripts here in this file," he began, motioning toward the half-open drawer. "I locked it and kept the key with me. But now I'm almost positive that someone has seen the letters."

"What makes you think that?"

"Everything was still there when I returned," he continued, "but something was different. For most of that first day, I couldn't say what it was. It was just a feeling, an uneasiness that wouldn't go away. Then it hit me. By the day's end, I knew what it was."

He sat on the edge of the bed with his hands on his knees.

"It was hardly noticeable. Whoever came into my tent was extremely careful not to leave a trace. But he missed it too."

"What?" asked Katrina, now fully absorbed by thoughts of deceitfulness and treachery. "What was missed?"

"It didn't come to me until I started to place the documents in the drawer again. It was the text. When I first withdrew the letters the text was reversed. Let me show you." Ibrahim took the parchment letters and held them over the open drawer. "If I lay a document that I'm working on in the file without putting it in a folder, I place the text so that it faces the open end, not the back. Then, when I reopen the drawer, whatever is there can be instantly read without standing on my head to see it."

"You *always* do this?" asked Katrina.

Ibrahim smiled. "I know. It sounds boringly methodical. Like something a bookish archaeologist might do. Habit is a powerful thing and I am a creature of habit. Certain habits help clear the clutter and keep me organized. But I remembered. When I opened the drawer after returning from Antalya, the text was facing away from me, not toward me."

"Are you sure?"

"Absolutely."

"Then someone must have a key. You're certain that you locked it before leaving?"

"Yes. Someone else must have a key to my file. Or, they're skilled in the art of lock-picking."

"If that's true, how can you leave the documents in the same place? What if they come back again?" Then Katrina had another thought. "Is what you have done . . . concealing the letters until now . . . is it illegal or anything?"

"It's a director's prerogative to control a project's findings and the timing of their announcement. Obviously, there are ethical guidelines that one must follow, but the director always has the final say. No, nothing I've done is illegal. Unorthodox, perhaps, by the exclusion of my fellow colleagues up to this point, but definitely not illegal. If I were to willfully destroy these artifacts, or sell them for profit, then I'd most certainly and rightly be culpable."

"But if this did happen as you believe, then these things are not safe here."

"And where would you suggest that I place them?" Ibrahim turned to face the open entry. "It wouldn't be proper to remove them from the site without first acknowledging their presence. There are few safe places at my disposal in these primitive conditions. And I've not been certain of my suspicions . . . that is, until today. Now, I'm convinced that someone is out to sabotage our efforts. And I think I know who it is."

"Who?" asked Katrina, her eyes never leaving Ibrahim's face.

"As yet, I shouldn't say. It's inappropriate to accuse someone simply because I have a feeling. And before I share my suspicions, I must first confront that person, in order to give him opportunity to clear his name." He was watching Katrina carefully now as he spoke. "Is this not the way of Christians, as well as Muslims?"

His question caught her off guard.

"I'll grant you that it's the way the Bible teaches us to conduct ourselves in such matters," she answered at last, gathering her thoughts. "I think it's in Luke's Gospel that some repentant soldiers came to Jesus one day to be baptized. They posed an interesting ethical question. 'What should we do?' they asked, wanting to know what He expected of them as His disciples. 'Don't extort money and don't accuse people falsely,' was the answer He gave, touching on two things for which these men were notorious.

"Later on, the Apostle Paul admonished Timothy to 'not entertain an accusation against an elder unless it is brought by two or three witnesses.' I see your point and I agree with you whole-heartedly. Growing up in a pastor's home, I've observed how doing otherwise brings embarrassment and, at times, irreparable damage to people's reputations when they're unjustly accused of wrongdoing."

Ibrahim looked away and then back again before responding.

"I think that my view of Christians has been skewed. What I've observed in the lives of more than a few who profess Christianity does not speak well of them or their religious beliefs. Yet, in the Hedleys I've seen the conduct of their everyday lives to be something that I myself wish to emulate. Honesty. Integrity. How do you Americans say, they are 'walking their talking'?"

"Close, Ibrahim."

"Good," he replied, smiling again. "And now I find these characteristics in you. The words of Jesus and the great Apostle Paul that you have just spoken are the reason I must have proof before I can justifiably accuse. You know, I think we are very close as Muslim and Christian in the things for which we stand."

"I have to agree with you," answered Katrina, "and I'm amazed to hear myself say that. I never imagined having any common ground with a Muslim."

"It's true for me as well, when I've considered those I knew who called themselves Christians. The Hedleys were the first to cause me to consider things differently. When you see a life really lived according to the teachings of Jesus and the Bible, it's the best witness of all, wouldn't you say?"

They were quiet for a moment, each looking at the other, considering what they had just shared.

"What can I do to help?" Katrina asked at last.

"I'm going to the clinic to check on Renée. I shouldn't be gone more than two or three hours."

"What do you think are her chances?"

Ibrahim frowned. Then he sighed and shook his head. "While I'm gone, you'll have opportunity to go over the letters. See if I'm correct in my translation. Examine them freely. When I return, we'll go into the underground city."

"Are you certain that you want to leave me here alone with these letters?"

Ibrahim looked at her quizzically, then smiled as he moved to the tent's open exit. "I am certain."

"What if I decide to destroy them?"

Ibrahim's countenance was sober as he returned her gaze.

"A part of me wishes that you would," he answered.

IT WAS AFTER THREE O'CLOCK when Ibrahim returned to the site. He wasn't driving the vehicle he had gone away in, but rode as a passenger in the Land Rover with Çali and the two women who had gone to the clinic with Renée. Behind them came Ibrahim's truck with Ben Hur at the wheel.

Ibrahim saw Katrina sitting on a canvas chair in front of her tent and walked over to her.

"How is she?" Katrina asked, getting to her feet.

Ibrahim shook his head.

A veil of sadness dropped over Katrina's face. Tears surfaced quickly. Her shoulders slumped in anticipation of what was coming.

"She's gone. In fact, she died before they were able to reach the clinic. I reported her death to the local *polis* and I just spoke with her parents by telephone."

The young girl had shared her tent with Katrina just a few hours ago. The student with whom she had spoken only a half dozen words had brought coffee and bread to Katrina's bedside and then waved good-bye as she ran to catch up with the others. A bright, thoughtful girl. Their lives had barely touched, and suddenly she was gone. It didn't seem possible. Katrina whispered as she wiped her eyes and looked away, "Au revoir, Renée. A bientot." *Good-bye, Renée. See you later.*

Just then Rocco ambled over with a bottle of Coke in his hand. He drew a long swallow as he stopped in front of Ibrahim.

"We've got problems, boss," he said matter-of-factly, wiping at his face with one of his shirt sleeves. "Some of my workers say they're quitting."

Ibrahim looked at him sharply.

"Why?" he asked.

"They say it's the curse."

"The curse?"

"Yeah. You know, the stories the villagers have talked about from time to time since our coming here. They've been handing this stuff down to each other in village folklore for generations. You should have seen how tough it was at first for Dr. Üzünal to get some of the locals to work with us. 'People who go to the hill disappear,' they said. 'Not even their bones are seen again. It is the curse!'" His voice took on a mocking tone as a sarcastic grin crept over his face. "There have always been a few who've kept the stories alive among the other workers. Now, it looks like the girl's death has pushed them over the edge."

"How many?"

"Don't know for sure, but I think you better talk to the men after dinner tonight."

Ibrahim nodded. Then he looked at Katrina.

"If you're going to see the underground city, perhaps we should go now. We have about two and a half hours. If we hurry, you'll at least have an idea of what it's like inside. We can get up early and explore further tomorrow if you like, before you have to leave."

"Would you rather stay here?" Katrina asked, concern registered in her voice. "This hasn't been a good day for you, I know. And I understand. I can always return to *Kilçilar* another time."

"It's all right. You've come a long way and I want you to see it. We'll go now, at least for a while. Rocco, I'll address the men tonight after the meal. Find out who wants to quit, if you can. Maybe I can head them off by appealing to them personally. I'll catch up with you at mealtime."

"Okay, Ibrahim. Remember to be careful."

Ibrahim turned back to Katrina. "Do you have a sweater or jacket you can bring with you?"

She nodded and ducked back into the tent. A moment later she reappeared with a bulky knit cotton sweater tied around her waist. Together they walked toward the entrance. Katrina's mind suddenly flashed back to the beginning of the day. Renée Patry had hurried away from her along this same path. Involuntarily, she shivered.

"Are you all right?" asked Ibrahim.

"I'm fine," she said, wondering all the while just how fine she really was.

Moments later, side by side, they entered the underground city of *Kilçilar*.

Thirty-one. Katrina

1530 local time

As the dimly lit tunnel enveloped them, Katrina became conscious of the strange coolness of being inside the earth. It was her first experience in a cave. She unwrapped the sweater from around her waist and slipped it on over her head. Her next noticeable sensation was the total absence of air movement. There was no breeze, only the serene sentience of an "other world" as they followed a path worn smooth by a parade of humanity seeking refuge.

They walked briskly, and with each step she tried to absorb the immensity of it all. How had this place, and the others like it that Ibrahim had told her about, ever come to pass? What terrible desperation had driven people to burrow into the earth like this?

Just inside the entrance, there had been room for three or four people to stand side by side together. As they went on, the tunnel narrowed quickly, causing Katrina to fall in behind Ibrahim. Occasionally they met a carrier or member of a digging team coming from the opposite direction. However, most of the work was going on deeper in the city and along what Ibrahim called the West Tunnel Road.

Initially, Katrina sensed Ibrahim's preoccupation with the day's happenings in the abrupt, almost mechanical way he

227

explained the purpose of different rooms or tunnels. Gradually, however, she saw him begin to relax. It wasn't so much in what he said as in his body language and tone of voice. The tension around his jaw line softened.

The further they went, the more centered he became on their walkabout. Looking and listening, Katrina was reminded of their visit to the Antalya Museum. Ibrahim was obviously at home in this place with his present discoveries and with mysteries that might be waiting around the next bend. And she was happy to be here with him.

Occasionally the passageway narrowed so that only one could squeeze through. They had walked a considerable distance and visited several chambers when Ibrahim paused in front of a narrow opening.

"Prepare yourself," he smiled back at her. "You are about to enter a very special place." With no further explanation he ducked low and moved on through. Katrina followed.

Once beyond the confining walkway, she stood upright and stared, awestruck. There were no words to adequately describe what she saw.

"With the exception of Rocco, you are the first Christian to come to this place of worship for many centuries," Ibrahim said with characteristic simplicity. "Welcome to the underground church of *Kilçilar*."

"I can't believe it!" she exclaimed, clasping her hands together as she looked around the room. She turned slowly as, one by one, the frescos presented themselves to her. Then, as she looked up, what she saw made her knees give way. She swayed and Ibrahim reached out to keep her from falling.

"Are you all right?" he asked, one hand on her arm, the other at her waist.

Her attention was riveted on the ceiling mosaic.

"O Ibrahim!" Katrina felt his arm around her and leaned back against his body. But her eyes never left the mosaic. "This is incredible! It's like . . . that is . . . Ibrahim, I've seen Him before."

Ibrahim looked up at the mosaic and then back at her quizzically. "No. It's not possible."

She smiled at the domed ceiling that held the mosaic face and upper torso of Jesus Christ.

"Even the colors! They're exactly the same!"

He looked up with fresh interest at the brown, red, and black mosaics that composed the face. Once again he felt warmth and friendship coming from the eyes. The artisan had managed a depth in them that Ibrahim could not escape each time he visited this place.

He glanced down at Katrina from behind her, his arms loosely around her waist. She leaned her head back against his shoulder and smiled as a tear trailed down her cheek. "What do you mean, Katrina. Where do you think you have seen this before?"

She felt their closeness, but did not move. Ibrahim's arms were strong. It felt good to stand like this, resting against his body. And she could not escape the gaze of the face above them. Nor the hands . . .

"In Istanbul," she said softly. "In my room."

Mystified, Ibrahim waited for her to continue.

"I had a dream, Ibrahim. A dream . . . a vision . . . I don't know. It's nothing I've ever experienced before. I went to my room after dinner on my last night there, feeling very sorry for myself, all alone and in a strange place. The temptation to just turn around and go home was overwhelming. Then I began to pray and, all at once, I saw . . . Him!"

She pointed toward the ancient ceiling.

"It wasn't just a picture of Jesus that I might have remembered from a magazine or the front of a Bible." She tilted her face toward Ibrahim and rested her hands on his at her waist. "I swear to you, it was this exact replica! These same identical colors. The same eyes. And I remember that the corners of His mouth—they were turned up in this same unusual way. He was smiling. His hands were extended toward me. His lips didn't move, but I heard Him speak."

Katrina turned to face Ibrahim. "I know it sounds crazy, but He was urging me not to turn back. I had this overwhelming sense of being needed. At the time, I thought it was regarding my work at the Girls School. And, maybe it is. Only . . . why am I here now? In this place? Under the same face of Jesus that I saw in my dream . . . or whatever it was?"

The light from the bare bulbs reflected off the frescos, giving the room and her countenance a soft reddish hue.

"This is all so weird. You must surely think I'm demented or something."

"I think," said Ibrahim tenderly as he took her hands, "that you are a most extraordinary woman."

He moved closer to her.

"And I feel very clumsy and awkward right now, because there's a great deal of beauty on your face and emotion coming from your heart—and I'd like very much to kiss you. But I don't wish to offend or do anything that would cause our friendship to become less comfortable."

Katrina did not answer. Nor did she resist as he put his arms around her. Her eyes closed. His lips touched hers lightly at first, and then with tender gentleness he drew her to him. She felt the pounding of her heart against his chest. Her hands encircled his neck as she responded in dazed but delighted wonder. Above them, the eyes of the mosaic Christ seemed to emanate affection and love toward the man and woman who stood below in the ancient underground church.

"I'm very fond of you," Ibrahim said softly, as she tucked her head into the curve of his shoulder. "I didn't expect anything like this when first we met. Thoughts such as these were far from my heart. I've never had feelings for someone like this before. I . . . I don't know what more to say. You've known me for such a short time. I trust that I've not offended you, Katrina."

"Please. Call me Kat."

"Kat?"

"Yes. It's short for Katrina. There's only one other person who calls me by that name. My brother, Kris. It's been his term of endearment for me since we were kids. I miss the closeness that he and I have kept through the years. We've always been able to talk about anything. Whenever I've needed someone to share with about really important personal things, he's been my closest confidant.

"I know that's kind of strange for brothers and sisters, at least in my country, but it's been that way our entire lives. We've had our disagreements and fights, of course, but I really can't explain it. It's just always been there. That's what his nickname for me means to me.

"When I've needed a man's perspective, there's never been

any other I felt I could talk to so freely . . . until now. Maybe it's because I'm so far from my family. I know it's partly because I believe I could talk to you in the same way I've done with Kris. I'm probably not making any sense at all, but, what I'm saying is, I'd like for you to be the one other person to call me Kat."

"Kat," Ibrahim repeated softly. "I'm honored to join your brother in using this most intimate of names for a very special woman."

Lifting her head slightly, she looked up into the face and form of the mosaic Jesus, and smiled. "I've never kissed a man in church before. But I've always believed that Jesus was right there with me whenever I was on a date with someone. I knew the way I handled myself would either offend or enhance His and my relationship."

"And have we offended Him this afternoon?"

"No," she replied happily, looking up at the smiling Jesus. "Most definitely not."

They wandered around the room together, holding hands as they examined each fresco. Ibrahim then showed her the place where he had found the jar and the letters, explaining how it had happened.

"It's amazing," she declared, standing back and letting her eyes roam across the ancient chapel. "I wonder how it came to be in this place? If it was written by Peter, and more than two centuries later failed to arrive at its intended destination at Nicea, who put it here? You say this place could not have become a church for an additional three to five centuries. So it had to be hidden here before there was a church."

"You are very perceptive, Katri . . . Kat," said Ibrahim. "It's the same conclusion that I reached."

"Do you think that the Christians who worshiped here knew of the letter's existence?"

"That's a good question. Did they discover it elsewhere and bring it to this place? Was it here all along without their knowledge? I'm afraid we may never know the answer."

"Would the fact that the front of the church has been left *au naturel* while frescoes cover the other walls be an indication?"

Ibrahim stared at the gray stone wall. Then he turned to Katrina. "I think that is a very good question as well. I was under the impression that they might have left it free of artistry for religious reasons. But, what if that were not the case?"

"Have you seen any other churches from this period with a blank wall?" asked Katrina.

"No, none," was the reply, followed by a long silence as the two of them faced the ancient stone altar and wondered at what must have happened in this place. Worship services. Funerals. Baptisms. Weddings.

"Can we see some more?" asked Katrina. "I left my watch back at the tent, but if there's time . . . "

"Of course. I need to be back for dinner in order to speak with the men, but if we hurry, we still have enough time to go further down. I'll show you the well and the underground stream that feeds it. There's a new shaft that we opened up last week. It doesn't go far, but it will give you an idea of how we work."

Crouching down, they made their way out of the chapel and back to the main tunnel. Ibrahim was animated now as he described their findings on the various levels. Katrina was constantly amazed at what she saw and heard. They laughed as Ibrahim pointed out communication holes that he said enabled the wives to gossip with one another on different levels of the city while the men did the work!

Behind them, in the direction they just had come, a shadow fell across the path under the artificial light, and a dislodged pebble rolled slowly down the passageway, nearly reaching them before being smothered in the dust. But neither of them noticed.

Eventually they reached Level 11 and stood at the edge of a stone-rimmed well. Ibrahim shined his flashlight into the depths in order to catch the reflection.

"How far down to the water?"

"Only about two meters," replied Ibrahim. "It's fresh and as drinkable today as it was when first it was dug."

Katrina shook her head in admiration at the ingenuity and tenacity of the people who had at one time lived in this place.

"How did they know they would find water here?" she asked.

"That's something you will have to ask your Christian friends one day. We're certain that they are the ones who dug it. Come. Let me show you what we opened last week."

Ibrahim took her hand, leading her over to one side and into a narrow tunnel. Crouching down, they walked about a half-dozen meters before coming to a pile of rock and rubble. Here the string of lights ended. Ibrahim shone his flashlight at a small breach.

"This opening will be expanded if we find what we hope for."

"What's that?"

"Follow me. It's a tight fit, but you'll see once we've passed through."

They squeezed past the pile of rubble and through the narrow opening. About a dozen steps later they came to a space high enough to stand upright. This cavity was about two more meters in length and ended abruptly at a solid rock wall.

"Over here," said Ibrahim, shining his light to the left. Katrina saw a small hole, about a hand-width in diameter.

"Take the flashlight and look inside."

Katrina held the light next to her head as she peered into the hole through a wall about one meter thick. By moving the light back and forth as much as the hole permitted, she saw that it opened onto a large chamber. "Oh!" A startled cry of surprise escaped her lips. She steadied the light on a near-perfect human skeleton stretched at the base of the far wall.

"What is it?" she cried out excitedly.

"Who is it?" responded Ibrahim with a chuckle. "Maybe the keeper of the well?"

"I can't believe all this," Katrina exclaimed, turning back to face Ibrahim. "It's so unreal. You've uncovered an archaeological wonder in this place!"

"Right you are. We already know that this is Turkey's largest and most productive underground city. It sheds more light every day as we try to understand our history and that of the ancients who preceded us." He looked at his watch. "Oh, oh, we must hurry. I forgot the time. We can still make the dinner hour, at least before the workers are finished eating, but we need to leave now."

He smiled as he took the flashlight from her hand and turned back to the narrow opening.

Just then, Katrina heard a loud popping sound.

A split second later a thick cloud of dust and dirt, laced with bits of splintered stone, exploded into the tiny chamber amidst the frightening rumble of falling rock. An invisible compression of air threw Ibrahim backward against Katrina with a force that

Pursuit

knocked them both to the earthen floor!
 She tried desperately to catch her breath in the swirling dust.
 Her ears rang with excruciating pain.
 Then darkness swallowed them!

Thirty-two. Katrina

1737 local time

She couldn't breathe!

Katrina rolled onto her side, struggling to her hands and knees, coughing and gasping for air. In the darkness, she stumbled over Ibrahim's body. Was he dead or alive?

Yanking the sweater over her head, she felt for his face. With a hurried motion she wiped his mouth and nose clear, and then draped the sweater over him as a protective filter. The suffocating dust continued stinging and burning her eyes, tiny particles filling her mouth and nose. With the first signs of light-headedness came the realization that she had held her breath as long as she could.

The inky blackness was absolute and total!

O God, what am I going to do?

Though she could not see it, she felt the dust still thick around her and strained to hold her breath longer.

The hole!

In desperation she ran her hands over the dirt and stone wall until she felt the hole that she had looked through moments earlier. Covering it with her face, she sucked in air.

Her lungs tried to respond.

Coughing and hacking, she spit out dirt and phlegm and grime.

Dizziness enveloped her. *Don't faint, Katrina. Don't . . .*

A breath came at last, and with it enough clean air to keep her from collapsing.

Another breath. Then still another.

She stayed at the small hole for what she thought must be at least a minute. The ringing in her ears continued, but the pain gradually subsided.

Ibrahim!

She moved away from the hole, testing the air first with quick, short breaths. It was still filled with floating dust particles, but breathable now; she dropped to her knees to feel for Ibrahim in the darkness. Her hand ran over his chest. His heart was beating! His breath was shallow, but it was there.

Oh, thank God, you're alive!

Her hands told her that the sweater was covered with a thick layer of dust and dirt. It had done its job but was of little use now. She removed it and tossed it to one side, concentrating on getting the dirt particles away from his eyes, nose, and mouth. As she moved her hand across his forehead, her fingers felt a sudden stickiness. Though she could not see, there was no doubt as to what it was. Katrina explored a long gash with her fingertips. They came away wet with blood.

Tears ran through the dirt on her face now, while at the same time she tried not to panic.

Where is the flashlight?

Katrina scrambled around the tiny chamber on her hands and knees in the dirt. Her head banged against a wall. Still no flashlight. Then she heard a low moan.

"Ibrahim!"

She crawled back toward him.

"Kat?" His voice was hesitant and weak.

"I'm here, Ibrahim. Oh, thank God, you're alive!"

Kneeling over him, she put her hands on his shoulders and laid her head against his chest.

"Kat?" His voice was little more than a mumble. "What . . . what happened?"

"I don't know. I think there was a landslide or an explosion." Her voice was shaky. "I heard a 'popping' and then the entrance caved in."

"You are . . . all right?"

"Yes, but I can't find the flashlight."

"My . . . pocket . . . "

She felt him trying to move his hand.

"Your pocket?"

"Matches. They are . . . in my pocket."

Katrina ran her hand down his arm to his pants pockets. The left one was empty. But her fingers closed around a small box in the other pocket.

"I have them!"

Her hands trembled as she tried to slide it open and take a match out without dropping the rest. Feeling for the coarseness on the side of the box, she turned it over and struck the match against it. A tiny flame appeared like a flare bursting against a night sky. Darkness had joined the bits of rock and dust to suffocate and demoralize. The flame restored sight, and sight gave hope . . . at least for a brief instant.

Ibrahim tried to sit up, but fell back again, gritting his teeth against the pain. Katrina looked around frantically.

"I still can't find the flashlight!" she exclaimed frantically. "Ouch!"

She dropped the match as the flame burned the tips of her fingers.

Darkness!

Shakily she reached for another.

Strike it. This time get your bearings.

The flame revealed a small chamber, perhaps two by three meters in size. The way out was completely closed. They were sealed off from the outside world. She held the match close to Ibrahim and looked at the gash near his hairline. It was a good two inches long, swelling, and still seeping blood. Katrina wondered at its severity. It was not good, that's for certain. In fact, it looked awful.

Darkness again!

"Are you still with me, Ibrahim?" Katrina heard the trembling anxiety in her voice.

"I'm . . . yes. I'm with you, Kat," came the weakened voice from out of the darkness. "Here. Sit down and take my hand for a minute."

"Are you all right?" she asked, as she knelt beside him. She grasped at his hand as it brushed against her arm. "I mean, can you tell if there are other injuries besides that gash in your forehead?"

"I can't, but I'm going to try to sit up."

"No! Wait for a little bit. Can you move your arms and legs?"

"The parts are all there. But my collarbone—I think it might be broken. And I may have reinjured my rib cage."

Katrina ran her hand over his chest again and down either side. She opened his jacket and felt something under his shirt. "What's this?" she asked, pushing her hand beneath the shirt and touching an elastic wrap.

"When I fell . . . in the chapel the other day . . . I cracked a couple of ribs."

"O Ibrahim, I'm so sorry. Why didn't you tell me?"

"It's nothing. They are almost . . . at least they were . . . almost healed." His words came in short gasps. "I think . . . this didn't help . . . but I'm okay. We're okay. We're alive!"

"Yes," Katrina said fervently. "I can't tell you how good it is to know that you aren't . . . that you are . . . "

Katrina's voice broke as tears spilled over again, unseen in the blackness. "I'm sorry."

"It's all right. I feel badly to have brought you here. To have placed you in such danger. After what happened this morning, I shouldn't have been so careless."

"It's not your fault, Ibrahim. Someone is definitely out to stop what is going on here. You must have been right when you suspected that your file had been broken into."

Silence.

"Ibrahim?"

"Yes . . . I was . . . I was thinking."

"Will the others come looking for us soon?"

"When we have not . . . returned for dinner, yes. Rocco . . . and Ben Hur will come . . . they'll find us."

"But, there are so many tunnels and places where we might have gone. How will they know where to search?"

"There are . . . many of them, Kat. They'll spread out."

"What about our air supply?"

"I think we'll . . . be fine. Don't worry. It is close here . . . but air comes through the little hole . . . the one you saw earlier."

"It's what saved me."

"Yes?"

"I put my face against it and breathed through my mouth until the dust settled. It was so thick," she added, her mind flashing back to that brief moment of paralyzing fright. "I put my sweater over your face to protect you."

"I wondered what . . . you must have done . . . thank you."

"I'm going to light another match and check your head wound."

A moment later, the flame illuminated their underground prison. Clotting seemed to have begun, but blood still oozed from the wound. Infection had to be a concern. If only they had water. But that resource lay beyond a pile of rubble and stone.

"How much rock do you think has fallen in?" asked Katrina, glancing over at where they had entered.

Ibrahim's eyes followed hers. "Tons, I would imagine. Too much for us to move, but the men will do it in a few hours." He attempted to sound reassuring.

"How will they know we are here? Will they be able to hear us?"

Ibrahim did not answer.

Darkness again!

"Kat . . . I'm going to get up . . . please?"

"Wait! Can I help?"

"No."

She heard him groan, and with her hand felt him turning on his shoulder. Rolling to one side, he pushed until he managed to get to his hands and knees.

"Now you can help . . . I'm going to stand . . . but I want to . . . take your hand. It's hard to breathe . . . but I seem to . . . be fine otherwise. Okay. Here we go."

Katrina scrambled to her feet, never losing touch with Ibrahim. He grasped her hands with his right hand, pulling himself up until he stood just inches from her. As close as he was, she was unable to see even a shadow in the thick blackness.

"Where do you think your collarbone is broken?"

"I can feel it on the left side." He took her hand and guided it over a large bump just below the neck, wincing as she touched it. "At least it hasn't punctured the flesh."

Katrina shuddered at that thought.

"I need something to keep my arm immobile. Perhaps standing isn't such a good thing right now. I think I'll sit down."

Katrina felt him sway like a dancer in the dark. She held onto him as best she could as he sagged back to a sitting position.

"Are you going to pass out?"

Silence.

"Ibrahim?"

No response.

Katrina's hands shook again as she lit another match. Ibrahim's head slumped awkwardly to one side and his eyes were closed. He had fainted. Quickly she felt along his collarbone and found the swelling again, confirming an injury. Kneeling, and with one hand, she drew his left arm across his chest and folded the other onto his lap so that she would not accidentally step on his hand.

Darkness!

She pushed the matchbox into the pocket of her jeans. Then she reached for Ibrahim and fumbled with the pocket in which she had found them. There it was. She thought she had felt it earlier.

She removed a small knife and ran her fingers over it in the darkness. There appeared to be several blades folded. She thought that it was probably a Swiss Army knife, one like Kris used to carry as a teenager.

The first blade she tried was too difficult to open, but the next one came easily. Carefully she laid the knife flat on the calf of her leg, just behind the knee, and sat back. It remained in place where she could find it again. Then she began unbuttoning her shirt.

Working on her knees in the dark was not easy, but at least her feeling of total panic had been replaced by a more objective concern. With the release of the final button, she took it off and reached for the knife. Counting three buttons up, she laid the knife blade against the material and began cutting and tearing, hoping that when she was finished there would still be enough left for her to wear.

At last the shirt lay on her lap in two pieces. She put the upper portion on once again, buttoning it as before. The remainder, with its length of shirttail, was folded into a makeshift sling, which she ran up under his arm and tied off at the back of his neck. Unable to see what she was doing, everything had to be done by touch and by the imagery created in her mind.

Finally finished, she stood up and ran her fingers along the bottom edge of her shirt. Though the cut and tear method had left an irregular line, there seemed to be enough remaining to insure at least a modicum of modesty. And there was still the sweater. She had thought of using it for the sling, but decided its loose knit would tear and unravel too easily once she had cut into it. Besides, she could still wear it to keep warm.

Closing the knife, she slipped it into her pocket and reached for the box of matches. Sliding the tray open, she emptied them into her hand and began counting. *Nine, ten, eleven. Eleven. That's it.* Her hand closed around the precious sticks as she thought about the price she would be willing to pay for a full box right now. Better still, a flashlight. *It must be buried in the rubble.* Leaning back against the wall, she closed her eyes and shuddered to think how close they had both come to dying.

"Kat?"

The voice startled her.

"Are you all right?"

Her eyes were open now, though it made no difference at all.

"I must have dozed. I think . . ." She did not finish the sentence, but reached over and touched his shoulder. "How're you doing?"

"I'll be okay. I apologize. I must have passed out."

"Apology accepted." Katrina tried to inject a touch of lightheartedness into her voice. "I manufactured a makeshift sling for you. Does it help? You sound as though you're breathing a little easier."

"Yes, it helps. It does relieve some of the pressure. You're a good doctor, Kat, but how. . . ?"

"Let's just say that the University of Istanbul owes me a new shirt."

For a moment there was no response. "Perhaps you'd better warn me the next time you light a match," Ibrahim said at last, with a chuckle followed by a grunt of pain. "Oh, that hurts. Don't make me laugh."

"Serves you right, professor," she answered reprovingly. "Anyway, we only have eleven matches left. Besides, I saved the best part of the shirt for myself, so relax."

"Another one of life's disappointments."

"Ibrahim!" she laughed. "You must be feeling better. Or else that gash in your head went deeper than I thought!"

Katrina ran her fingers along his arm until she found his hand and held on to it tightly. "How long do you think before they find us?"

"Soon," Ibrahim answered unconvincingly. "It will be soon."

Thirty-three. Missing

"I wonder where he is?"

Ben Hur put his food tray down on the table next to Rocco. Tahsin Cem and Dr. El were sitting across from them. He glanced over the group of men gathered around the long tables and noticed the two French girls eating quietly at a table by themselves. He wondered what must be going through their minds.

"He'll be along," Rocco responded, taking a sip of hot tea. "He knows he has to talk with the men tonight. Maybe he's putting his thoughts together."

Gossip and rumors were being passed about in hushed tones. Some men ate quietly while others, in groups of three or four, huddled in animated conversation. Among the men there was a definite atmosphere of pessimism and dark gloom. Renée's death had certainly cast a grim pall over *Kilçilar*. Most of the men had liked her. She'd been a quick learner, very bright, and a hard worker.

"I stopped by his tent on the way over," said Tahsin. "He wasn't there."

"He is probably off somewhere with that American whore he met in Antalya," muttered Dr. El.

243

"Whoa!" exclaimed Ben Hur as he sat down. "That's uncalled for. Have you talked with Ms. Lauring at all?"

Dr. El did not answer.

"Well, I have," Ben Hur continued, "and she's a nice lady. She's a contract teacher in a private school. Studied church history and wanted to see a real archaeological site firsthand."

"Then why did she spend most of her day in our young director's tent?" queried El with eyebrows raised accusingly. "They were together in front of his tent when Çali and the others drove the French girl to the clinic. After Dr. Sevali followed them, she went into his tent and remained there for several hours."

"Maybe she wanted to lie down," Rocco interjected with a smile.

"Perhaps that's how she does her best work. On her back." El smirked wickedly as he pushed a fork through the pile of rice on his plate. "Did anyone check the showers? Perhaps they could be found over there."

"That's enough!" Ben Hur's sharp command drew stares from several of the men closest to them who stopped talking in order to watch. Rocco and Tahsin said nothing further for the remainder of the meal, but tension was clearly visible between the other two.

As soon as he finished, Dr. El carried his tray back to the field kitchen where he handed it to a helper before stalking off.

Ben Hur's gaze ran over the group once again. Still no sign of him. Nor of the teacher either, for that matter. It looked more and more like they must be somewhere together. One of his diggers approached.

"You said there would be a meeting?"

"Yes," replied Ben Hur. "Dr. Sevali wanted to speak with everyone after dinner. He's not here, though."

"I saw him late this afternoon. Maybe two or three hours ago."

"Where?"

"In the tunnel. He and the American lady were together. I think it was on Level 5. He spoke to me. They were headed down."

Ben Hur glanced at Rocco and Tahsin, then back at the digger.

"What did he say?"

"Just 'hello,' and that he would see me at dinner."

Ben Hur turned to Rocco. "Let's call the crew back together later. Meanwhile, why don't the three of us go in and make sure nothing has happened to them."

"You're a little jumpy, aren't you?" asked Rocco. "They probably just lost track of the time."

"You're too much of an Italian romantic, Rocco. Me? I'm a cynical old Jew. Especially after this morning. I've lived with my enemies long enough to know that few things happen by chance."

"Are you saying what I think you're saying?" asked Rocco, suddenly looking very sober.

"God knows," he answered with a shrug. "But it's up to us to find out. Come on. I'll tell the men the meeting will be later. Then we'll go find them. Okay?"

Rocco nodded as Tahsin got to his feet, wiping his mouth on his shirt sleeve.

Ten minutes later, having made certain that the power generator would remain on past its normal cutoff time, the three of them entered the cave.

"Do you think they might have gone into the East or West tunnels?" asked Tahsin, as they reached the junction.

"No. They were headed down. My guess is that Ibrahim wanted the teacher to see the well," Ben Hur answered.

"I agree, but let's give a yell anyway," said Rocco.

They shouted Ibrahim's name several times. There was no response. As they passed through each level they called out.

Twenty-five minutes later and out of breath, they stared across the well at one another. Their search had turned up no sign of Ibrahim or the teacher.

"I don't like this," Ben Hur grimaced. "I don't like this at all."

"Maybe we'd better check out the tunnels," said Rocco. "And there are lots of little side rooms on every level. If no one saw them leave, they must still be in here someplace."

Ben Hur nodded.

"Let's go up and get the crews. We'll fan out and check every nook."

"I'll get my maps," said Tahsin. "Assign a leader on each level who can read. We'll give them a copy to be sure they don't miss anything."

As they started back the way they had come, Tahsin gave a

last look around. It seemed darker than usual here at the well. Looking up he noted that two of the lights were broken out. That was not unusual. A worker probably hit them with something, but they should have been replaced. He shook his head and ran to catch the others.

Though each man was in good shape, the route was a continuous upward grade of twists and turns with an occasional row of stone or earthen steps here and there. By the time the winded trio reached the work camp again, it was well after seven o'clock and darkness was settling in.

Some of the workers were still lounging around the tables in the mess area. A few shouts drew the others from their tents.

"Dr. Sevali and the American teacher are missing!" Ben Hur explained carefully. "They were last seen somewhere around Level 5. We believe something may have happened to them and we need you to help us search."

One of the men stepped out from the group and came forward, a dark look on his face. Ben Hur recognized him as one of the carriers hired from the local village.

"Vehbi? What is it?"

"This morning the girl was killed," he said slowly. "Now Dr. Sevali and the American have disappeared. What if there is something in there that we don't know about? Perhaps our presence has awakened the ancient spirits once again. We who have grown up here know that others have vanished in this place. Our ancestors have told us, and since the work has begun here, our parents and grandparents remind us of this often. Perhaps they are right. Who is to say that this place is safe for any one of us?"

A low murmur rippled through the group and some shuffled nervously. Ben Hur looked around. This was exactly the problem he did not want to face without Ibrahim. Yet, here he was and the one thing they did not need at this moment was a revolt.

"I agree with you, Vehbi," he said, making an effort to use his most noncombative tone. "This has not been a good day for any of us. In fact, Dr. Sevali intended to speak to you this evening about Renée Patry's death. It was extremely unfortunate and we are all saddened by it. But for now we must put these concerns aside and concentrate on finding Dr. Sevali and the American. If they're hurt in there somewhere, then we need to find them as quickly as possible."

The two men exchanged hard looks before Vehbi nodded, and stood to one side. Ben Hur breathed a silent sigh of relief.

He and Rocco made leader selections. Search areas were assigned. Rocco would supervise the search on Levels 1–3; Tahsin on 4–5; Ben Hur on 6–8. Because Dr. El had not been with them earlier and was fresher, he was assigned 9–11, the levels farthest down.

Just then, Tahsin ran up with maps for each of the eleven levels, including the East-West Tunnels, and began handing them to the leaders. In a matter of minutes the men had gone back to their tents for flashlights and jackets or sweaters and reassembled at the cave entrance.

The four leaders conferred for a final time before splitting up.

"Dr. El," said Tahsin, "let me take 9–11 and you take 4–5. I grabbed some lightbulbs to replace the broken ones I noticed while we were down earlier."

"Give them to me. I'll take care of it."

"That's all right. I don't mind. I want to look around there again anyway. I had a feeling that something was different . . . but I can't put my finger on it. I'd like to check it out again, if you don't mind."

El shrugged.

"Okay, then," said Ben Hur, glancing at his watch. It was nearly eight. He motioned to the others. "We're set. Let's go, everybody."

Thirty-four. Katrina

"Are you awake?"

Ibrahim stirred.

"You need to stay awake. I'm worried about that cut on your head. How does it feel?"

"Like an overripe melon about to burst."

"Is it still bleeding?"

"I can't tell for sure. No gusher anyway. Maybe a slow leak."

Katrina relaxed a little. At least his breathing sounded better. And he made sense when he talked. She hoped that there was nothing serious internally. "How long do you suppose it's been?"

"I've lost track. In this blackness one loses a sense of time as well as balance. When we light another match, I'll check my watch."

"It seems like hours, Ibrahim. What if they can't find us?"

"They'll find us. Don't worry."

"Let's pray and ask God to help us."

Her words were greeted by silence.

"Okay, Ibrahim?"

She shook him gently.

"Ibrahim, please try to stay awake."

There was no response. He had slipped back into unconsciousness.

Tears again mixed with dirt and dust, stinging her eyes. She knelt down, placed her hand on Ibrahim's outstretched leg, and began to pray.

"I feel like the psalmist, God. 'Out of the depths I cry to You, O Lord; O Lord, hear my voice. Let Your ears be attentive to my cry for mercy.' I've never been in a situation like this. Here we are, Lord, buried in the depths of the earth. Someone has tried to kill us and unless You come to our rescue, they may succeed. Ibrahim needs Your healing touch. Please, Jesus, please take care of any internal injuries and stop the bleeding from the blow he's received on his head."

"Yes, Jesus . . . "

Katrina started at the sound of Ibrahim's voice.

"I believe You healed Dr. Bülent Üzünal. And I believe You . . . You can help us as well."

She reached for his free hand and covered it with both of hers, surprised at his prayer and yet warmed by it as well.

"Jesus," she continued, "we are also asking that You guide our rescuers to us soon. Help them to find us. And thank You for hearing these prayers that we pray in Your name. Amen."

"Amen," whispered Ibrahim. Then he continued, "O God! If I worship You in fear of Hell, burn me in it; and if I worship You in hope of Paradise, exclude me from it; but if I worship You for Your own being, do not withhold from me Your everlasting beauty. Amen."

"Amen," added Katrina. "That was beautiful, Ibrahim."

"It is a prayer written by a woman from Basra. Her name is Rabi'a al-'Adawiyya. She died in 801. She was one of the earliest Sufis in Islam."

"I have heard of Sufism, but I don't know anything about it. Can you tell me?" Katrina was not so interested in the subject matter as in keeping Ibrahim awake.

"Poetry is generally appreciated much more in the Islamic world than by Westerners, I think. And some of our greatest poets were from the sect of Sufism. Rumi, for example, was born a Persian in Afghanistan, lived in Syria for a short time, then settled in Konya where he died. He's buried in the Sultan's garden. You came through Konya on your way here, remember?"

"Yes," she replied. "Go on."

"The word 'Sufi' comes from the Arabic *Suf* which means wool. Sufis wear wool as a sign of rejecting materialistic things. They believe that through silence, solitude, hunger, and wakefulness they can attain the knowledge of God. They are most famous for their Whirling Dervishes."

"Those are the people who wear white robes and whirl about for hours?" asked Katrina, growing more interested in what Ibrahim was saying.

"Yes. They pivot on one foot as they circle—right hand upward toward heaven and the left hand down toward the earth. It's symbolic of the spinning planets that revolve around the Center, which is God."

"Do they use music when they whirl?"

"Not necessarily. The Koran doesn't make any pronouncements on music, but some have condemned it as sinful. Still, the followers of Rumi's *Tariqa*, the 'Sufi path,' used music and dance as a means of achieving divine oneness. They also utilize the Rosary in their times of meditation. It contains ninety-nine beads to be used in reciting the ninety-nine names of God in the Koran."

"You seem to know a lot about them. Are you a Sufi?" asked Katrina curiously.

"No. But, we studied their philosophy in school. And Rumi's poem, the *Methnawi*, is one of our great pieces of literature. He spent forty years composing it."

"Interesting."

"Kat, I know what you're doing. You are more interested in keeping me awake than in Sufism. But don't worry. I'll be fine."

Tenderly, she touched his forehead and moved her hand around the gash.

"I think the bleeding has stopped."

Ibrahim took her hand and kissed it. "Thank you for being so brave. I'm sorry I've gotten you into this."

"I'm not," she answered simply, and leaned forward until her cheek touched his. "But I need to do something."

She got to her feet.

"Going somewhere?" Ibrahim called out, half in jest.

"Maybe," she replied, hands stretched out, feeling her way as she shuffled slowly across the tiny chamber. "I have to do something, so I'm going to work on this little hole. It seems to be mostly earth and small stones around it. Maybe I can carve out a space big enough to crawl through."

"Be serious, Kat."

"I am," she said with determination. "I've got your knife. The wall can't be more than a couple of feet thick. Yes, here it is! I'll stick my hand through . . . okay, it's the length of my arm. Maybe I'm crazy, but I can't just sit here and do nothing."

"All right," Ibrahim said. "I'll help."

"You'll do nothing of the kind. You stay where you are!"

"So, you can't sit here and do nothing, but I have to sit here and do nothing. Is that what you're saying?"

"You hear really well."

"Western women!"

"What about Western women?" she asked, as she began chipping away at the dirt and rock.

"When a Western woman is trapped in a cave, she becomes very bossy."

"You've been a man too long," Katrina retorted. "Just sit back and keep talking or sing or recite some poetry. But stay awake. You know the old saying, 'A woman's work is never done'? Well, I have no dishes to wash and I'll scrub the floor later. Right now, I just want to see what can be done with this hole."

TAHSIN CEM AND HIS MEN continued working their way from Level 9 to Level 10. Their shouts echoed around the tunnels, the large lounge areas, and tiny rooms. Every place that someone could possibly be was investigated. So far the search had been fruitless. He hoped that the others were having better luck.

"YOU KNOW, IBRAHIM, WE MAY JUST have something here." The dirt and rock scratched away from the hole slowly, but her patience was paying off. "I can almost stick my head in now."

Ibrahim did not respond. In fact, he had been quiet for the last few minutes. "Ibrahim? Are you with me?"

She heard a grunt as he shifted to a new position.

"Yes. I am with you."

His voice sounded tired. Far away. Katrina thought that perhaps he had lost more blood than she had initially surmised. A few minutes later, she stopped to listen and was relieved to hear his heavy breathing. *For a little while I'll let him sleep. It must be getting late.*

She returned to her task. For the last several minutes she had been working the knife blade around a rock that felt about two or three times the size of her hand. She had already broken one blade, the large one, and had finally managed to release the one that served as a bottle opener. Its configuration and thickness worked well in this sort of soil. Eventually, she felt a slight movement in the rock. With renewed energy she dug and pushed and scraped until at last her raw fingertips pulled it free.

IT WAS NINE-THIRTY BY THE TIME Tahsin reached Level 11. He was discouraged. The word from above was not good. There had been no sign of the missing persons. Rocco's team had finished and joined El, who was wrapping up on Level 5.

He reached up and carefully twisted the remains of the broken lightbulbs out of their sockets. It was difficult with the second one. There was no bulb left, only the base. Carefully he worked until it moved far enough to get his fingers around. The rest came easily. With new bulbs, the lighting returned to normal.

Two men were on their stomachs, flashing lights into the dark pool of well water. Others moved into the few remaining areas where a person might be, but there was little optimism. As Tahsin cast a weary glance around the room, he was gripped by an uneasy feeling. *Something doesn't seem right here. What is it?* Standing back from the well, he studied the wall to his left. Then he lifted his map to the light. *Didn't we open up that section a few days ago?* He stared at the rubble and rock, then back at the map.

Yes. Here it is. We opened up a narrow passage into a tiny chamber. It's the one the workers were saying had a viewing hole that revealed some human remains. Other graves had been discovered and opened already, so one more skeleton hadn't caused any great excitement. Except for one thing. The digger declared that the bones were not buried. They were simply there on the floor. *Strange. But now there's no opening here. And there should be. You don't suppose . . .*

"Kemal," he said to one of the men, "go find Rocco. I think some of his men were working this area. Tell him that we may have found something, but that I need his help. Hurry!"

The man gave him a quizzical look and then ran off.

Fifteen minutes passed before Kemal and Rocco came puffing down the tunnel to Level 11.

"What have you got?" asked Rocco, his burly chest heaving from the exertion of the descent. Some of the men thought coming down through the levels was more difficult than going up.

"Didn't we recently open up a passage over there?"

Rocco stared in the direction that Tahsin was pointing. There was only rock and rubble where he knew there had been a passageway.

"Yes, we did. What's happened here? We opened this up a week ago. It only went as far as a small anteroom, so we stopped. There's a room beyond it, but it was sealed off, so we thought we'd come back and tackle it later." Rocco reached out and picked up a stone that appeared to have been split apart. "Why didn't we notice this when we were here before?"

"The lighting was bad in this area. Some bulbs were missing. It was dark enough that none of us noticed," Tahsin answered, pointing to the bulbs he had just replaced. "I heard there was a skeleton that could be seen in another room."

"Yes. I saw it myself and reported it to Ibrahim and Dr. El. They both checked it out as well. But our workers have been stretched thin, so Ibrahim and I decided to wait a few weeks. Maybe open it in November, just before we have to shut down for the winter."

"Do you suppose this could have caved in on them?" asked Tahsin as they walked over to examine it closely.

"I wouldn't have thought so." Rocco's face masked his true feelings. "There were no support beams or anything. But it didn't need them. The passage was narrow, mostly rock, some dirt."

"From the map, it looks to be about six meters in length. If this has backfilled totally, that's a lot of dirt and rock."

"Let's check with the others. They should be finished by now. If Ibrahim hasn't turned up, we'd better start digging."

"How long will it take?"

"Maybe twenty hours. Maybe longer. If they were in the

passage, we'll find them, but it won't be pretty."

"Could they be in that little anteroom you mentioned?"

"If it hasn't caved in as well."

"I thought you said that you didn't think this was a cave-in."

"Figure of speech," Rocco responded. "I *don't* think this was a cave-in."

"Then what?"

"I'd almost bet my month's wages that somebody touched this off on purpose. Like this morning."

Tahsin looked hard at Rocco, grasping the implications of what had just been said. Then he turned away. "I'll go get the others."

KATRINA WAS FINALLY ABLE TO SQUEEZE her head and shoulders into the hole. Doing so made her feel claustrophobic, however, so she drew back. Her digging project had caused a layer of cool sweat to form tiny dirt trails over most of her body. She could taste the perspiration and dust mixed together.

Ibrahim was sleeping. In spite of the jacket, his body temperature had felt cool to Katrina and so she had placed her sweater over him. Now she stretched her aching muscles in the darkness and started to feel her way to his side.

"Ibrahim," she spoke softly and shook his leg gently. "Wake up."

She felt him stir.

"Come on, mister, I need you to wake up! Are you with me?"

"Yes. I'm with you," he answered sleepily. "What's *Kilçilar's* newest female digger up to now?"

"I'm about to pay our next-door neighbor a visit."

She felt his sudden stirring and heard him try to stifle a groan.

"You have a hole big enough to go through? Are you sure?"

"Unless I gain some weight standing here talking to you. And, by the way, if we ever decide to do this again, I want better tools."

She could almost feel him grinning in the dark.

"Beginners can't be trusted with too many tools."

"Well, I'm keeping this knife as a souvenir. It's so bent out of shape that you'd stab yourself if you put it back in your pocket."

Ibrahim reached out his hand and touched her arm, sliding it upward until he felt her neck and face. It was damp. "You're sweating, but it's cool in here. I have your sweater. Aren't you cold?"

"Real women don't sweat. They 'glow.' However, I've been 'glowing' myself into a real sweat for the past however long it's been. I'll wait until I get through the hole and see what's there. If it looks promising, I'll take my sweater and you with me. Okay?"

"Okay, but be careful."

"I know there's a floor at the same level on the other side because I saw it earlier. And I know there is someone over there to greet me," she added, shivering at the thought of the human skeleton. "But, he's on the far side of the room so I'll be careful not to wake him up."

"I think it's time I got up and walked over with you."

"Good idea. Can you make it?"

Ibrahim's muscles had tightened and were sore from the shock of the explosion and his inactivity during the last few hours. "I feel like an old man," he said, "but if you help me up and let me get steady on my feet, I'll be all right."

"Can you tell if you've stopped bleeding?"

"For the most part, I think, yes. If it gets worse, I'll just have you do some 'soldier ant' surgery."

"What are you talking about?"

"It's an old Central African procedure. You take the wound and hold its edges together. Next, you put soldier ants on the wound. They instinctively bite down, lock their jaws, and seal the cut. Then all you have to do is cut off their thoraxes and tails, leave the jaws in place, and wait for several days until the flesh is healed."

"Ugh! How gross! Are you pulling my rookie leg, Ibrahim?"

"I don't have the strength to pull anyone's leg. It's no joke. Just native medicine at its best."

"Well, then, you'd better hope and pray that I don't have to operate. Come on now, let's get up."

Carefully Katrina put her arm around his back. Bending her legs she took as much of his weight as she could and helped him to his feet. He leaned on her heavily for a minute or two.

"How is it?" she asked.

"My head is swimming upstream," he replied, his voice sounding strained, "but the rest of me is headed out to sea."

Katrina began to giggle nervously. Then something inside spun out of control. The more she tried to stop, the more impossible it became. Soon they were both chuckling, with Ibrahim groaning over each spasm of laughter.

"I think . . . if we don't stop this . . . I'll have to sit down again," Ibrahim choked.

"I'm sorry," Katrina said apologetically, as she concentrated on regaining control while guiding them both through the pitch-blackness to the opposite wall where her freshly carved hole awaited. "I guess the psalmist was right."

"The psalmist? How so?"

"Because he said, 'When the Lord brought back the captives to Zion, we were like men who dreamed. Our mouths were filled with laughter, our tongues with songs of joy.'"

"Well, we're not back to Zion just yet," Ibrahim reminded her.

"But at least we're about to go next door. And here we are. Do you think you can help me? It's a tight fit. Can you push if I say 'push'?"

"I can do that."

"Okay," she said, her voice taking on a hollow quality as she ducked into the hole. "I'm starting through. Give me a push."

Ibrahim placed his hands on her hips and pushed. Pain shot through his head and chest. He thought he was going to faint again, but said nothing. Gritting his teeth, he continued to push. He could feel her slipping forward through the opening. Then he heard a muffled, "No more!" He held onto her feet and then felt them suddenly disappear.

"Are you all right?"

"Yes, I'm fine. Fortunately, I landed on my head. It's the hardest part of my body. Anyway, something here cushioned me when I dropped to the floor."

Ibrahim leaned against the wall, fighting back a wrenching spasm of pain and dizziness.

"I'm going to light one of our matches. Are you there?"

"Yes, I'm here."

The match flared. Out of the corner of his eye, Ibrahim saw its faint light in the room beyond.

Suddenly, every nerve in his body froze!

Her scream was chilling!

He pushed away from the wall and gripped the sides of the hole, staring blindly into it. The light was not there!

Thirty-five. Katrina

"Katrina!"

For a split second there was nothing. Ibrahim caught his breath.

Then another cry came out of the dark. "O God, O God, O dear God, help me!"

"Katrina! What's happening? What is going on?"

"Get me out of here!"

She sounded like a terrified little child. Ibrahim stared into the dark void, all the while listening to her muffled sobs.

He started to push his way into the hole, but fell back in pain. "I . . . I . . . can't. Light another match, Katrina. What is the matter?"

"I . . . dropped them. Ibrahim, I'm coming back. I've got to come back!" The panic in her voice told him that something had completely unhinged her. The next few seconds were crucial to them both.

"No. Wait. Don't move!" His voice was stern. "You've got to find the matches! They're all the light we've got. If you come back without them, we'll never find them again. Stay right where you are and look, Katrina. Feel around for them."

"That's what I don't want to do!"

"Have you moved since you dropped them?"

"No. I . . . I'm afraid to."

Ibrahim wondered at that.

"You must, Katrina. Get hold of yourself and do it!"

He heard a choking cough, but couldn't tell if she was still frozen in place or had begun looking.

"Oh, thank You, Jesus, thank You," he heard her say softly.

"Did you find them?"

"Yes. I . . . I'm sorry. I just . . ."

Her voice sounded small and weak.

"Light another match and let me help you back."

He could hear her fumbling with the box and he leaned as far into the hole as he could in anticipation of the light. His position increased the pain from his injured ribs, but he had to see. Suddenly the match flared.

"Oh, my . . . " Ibrahim swore under his breath.

Katrina stood about three feet from the hole, her hand shaking as she held the match away from her body. Her face and hair were matted with dirt. The remains of her shirt hung loosely several inches above her jeans. She was caked with dust and grime.

Her initial fright had turned to a paralyzing horror, her voice more the whimper of a small child after a fall, almost as if she were too timid to cry out. She looked at him helplessly, the dreadfulness of her circumstance written on her face, oblivious to the fact that the match was now burning close to her fingers. He gazed into the room in disbelief.

Row after frightful row of human skeletons! They were everywhere, filling the entire room.

One sat apart against the opposite wall, the lone skeleton they had seen from the anteroom. Now, however, he could tell that a smaller skeleton had fallen into the large one. The "cushion" that had broken her tumble into the room was the remains of several skeletons that lay just beneath the hole. Katrina's feet were frozen in the unexpected morbidness of a human burial ground!

Then, just as the flame reached her fingers, his eyes widened at what he glimpsed along the far wall.

"Katrina. The match."

"Ouch!"

She flicked it away and the now familiar darkness descended once again.

"Katrina. Listen to my voice. Remember where you saw the hole last. Move toward it."

"I can't," she choked the words out, still trying to regain control of her emotions. "I want to, but I can't."

"You're in shock, Kat. I don't blame you. How could anyone have anticipated what you have fallen into? But you can come toward me now. You must. Listen to my voice. Push your right foot forward. Now your left one. If you touch anything, it's all right. By not lifting your feet you won't stumble and you won't disturb anything too much. It's only a couple of steps. My hand is through the hole. Move yours this way until you find it . . . there . . . I've got you!"

"O dear God, help me. I'm so scared. Why am I so scared? They're all dead. I shouldn't be so scared. My heart. It's beating a hundred times too fast! I think I'm hyperventilating!"

He couldn't tell her to put her head down. She would be too afraid. "Here. Lay your face on my hand. Lean into the hole and rest for a minute."

"I want out of here. I want to come back through."

"Wait, Katrina. Just a minute. Let's get it together first before we do anything else." Ibrahim's mind was racing, his head throbbing. He could feel the tautness in her face as she laid her head on his hand. Gently he moved his fingers, massaging her cheek and under her chin. For what he thought must have been a minute or more, she did not move. She made absolutely no sound except for her breathing. At last he felt her lift her head.

"Okay. I'm coming back now."

"Wait. Listen. Let me come to you instead."

"No, Ibrahim, I just want to get out of this place. I'm sorry. I can't do this anymore!"

"That's just it. If I come to you, then maybe we can."

"Are you crazy? What are you talking about?"

"Kat, listen. I saw something while the match was burning."

"Yes, so did I. A room full of dead people!"

"But how did they get there?"

"I don't know and I don't care. Just get out of the way!"

"They must have come down the stairs!"

Katrina hesitated. "The stairs?"

"Yes. I saw stairs. On the far wall."

"You . . . are you sure?"

"Positive. It must be the way these people came here or were brought here. Maybe it will lead us out."

"And if it doesn't?"

"If not, we can always come back here and wait for someone to find us."

He heard her take a deep breath.

"I'm not having a good time right now."

"I know. I'm sorry. But you're an unbelievable trooper. And look at it this way. Besides making an incredible archaeological discovery that none of us knew existed here, you may have given us a way out."

"I don't care about any archaeological discovery, Ibrahim. I don't care if this is King Tut's brother's tomb!" Katrina paused, taking a deep breath. "Okay. So do you think you can make it through the hole?"

"No problem," he said, trying to sound more confident than he felt. "Here. Take the sweater."

At least his light-headedness had gone away. Ibrahim clamped his jaws together, took his arm from the sling, and removed his jacket, pushing it through the hole ahead of him. Finally, steeling himself against the pain, he leaned into the opening as far as he could. The hurt was intense as he pushed and clawed his way through, trying to favor his injuries. Unfortunately, it turned out to be an even tighter fit for him than it had been for Katrina.

"Give me a hand, Kat."

She touched the top of his head.

"My right hand is through. Take it and pull. But slowly."

"What about your collarbone?"

"Try not to jerk, but pull. I can't maneuver."

She began pulling, gently at first, then harder. He moved several painful inches toward her and then became stuck again.

"Okay, Kat," he growled, gritting his teeth against the pain, "reach under my arms and get a good hold. And pull!"

The pressure became intense. His total engrossment centered on a tiny mental dot. Just when he thought he was going to pass out, he felt his body move. An inch. Then another. All at once his shoulders and chest came free and he slid forward to the other side!

"Easy, Ibrahim, I've got you."

Her arms were locked under his now, pulling him the rest of the way. With a final effort he fairly glided out and tumbled against Katrina, causing them both to fall.

Ibrahim released a single groan between his clinched teeth. They lay silently in the darkness, pressed into each other's arms, as their breathing returned to normal.

Katrina's body shook as tension and anxiety rushed to escape every twitching muscle and open pore. Her heart pounded out a timpani beat against his chest as she gathered the will to move again, knowing that to do so meant reaching out and touching . . . what? Someone's leg or arm or face?

"You are a brave woman, Katrina," Ibrahim whispered, when at last he had caught his breath. "The bravest I have ever known."

He felt a shudder run through her.

"I'm really just a chicken heart," she responded, her face pressed closely to his chest. "It's been a while since I dropped in for a visit with a room full of dead people!"

Ibrahim chuckled. "That's one of the things I like most about you."

"What?"

"Your humor. Your ability to laugh when things get very hard."

"I don't know about that. It seems like I'm crying more than laughing lately. And I hate it when that happens. But thanks anyway."

"Are you okay now?"

"Are you kidding? How can anyone be okay lying among a bunch of skeletons?"

"I'm getting up now," said Ibrahim. "Here, let me help you. It will be all right."

He released his hold and gently helped her to a sitting position.

"You are cold?" he asked.

"I'm shivering. I'm not sure whether it's because I'm cold or just that I'm scared to death. Oh, no. Bad choice of words."

"Put this on."

He waited until she had pulled the sweater over her head. "All right then. Dig out another match. How many do we have left?"

"I think nine."

UNDERGROUND STAIRS

"Are you ready for a look around?"

He heard her let out a deep breath. "No, but here goes anyway."

The match blazed, its tiny light wavering unsteadily as the room took on a reddish glow. Ibrahim's gaze was drawn once again to the human remains that filled the large room. And then to the wall at the far side.

"Come on."

"What? Where?"

"Over there is a staircase. On that wall. See it?"

Gingerly they began stepping over and around skeletal structures that appeared to comprise every age group. There, propped against the wall were two adult skeletons with two children in between. Here in front of them, a row of about a dozen infants. Every part of the large room had been turned into a sepulcher, a tomb to house the remains of some indescribable human tragedy.

Darkness.

"Match number eight," said Katrina, as she struck it on the side of the little box of sticks that had, in the last several hours, become more precious to them both than they could ever have imagined. Holding it up in front of them, they continued their halting steps across the ancient mausoleum.

"Look," Ibrahim exclaimed. "Over there. What's that?"

They made their way to a hole in the floor and looked down.

"It must be a well," said Katrina.

"Apparently. And look," he said, pointing to the wall that ran at an angle to the staircase. A rectangular stone was situated two or three meters away from the wall. Directly behind it, cracked and faded with age, a poorly rendered face alongside a cross had been painted on the wall. The workmanship was crudely done, surely not by the hand of a skilled artist.

"An altar?" said Katrina.

"So it would seem. That, together with the well, suggests that these people were alive when they entered this room."

Darkness.

Then light again.

"Match number seven, Ibrahim. We're using up our supply too quickly. I don't want to get stuck in here in the dark."

"I couldn't agree with you more. Here's the stairs. After you?"

"Okay."

"Stay close to the wall and be very careful."

Ibrahim tried to see the top of the stairs as they began their ascent, but it disappeared into the darkness. There was no balustrade or safety rail, just open space on one side.

"Wait!" he exclaimed and turned to see where they had come.

"What is it?"

He held up his hand for silence, but his lips were moving. Just as the match went out, he turned back.

"Eighteen."

"What are you talking about?"

"We've come seventeen steps to reach this landing."

"So?" Katrina stood poised with match in hand, ready to strike number six.

"I almost didn't remember to count. Just in case we have to come back down in the dark."

Katrina sighed as she struck the match. "Never in a hundred years would I have thought to count these steps."

Nine more steps and they came to a large stone wheel.

"A door?" asked Katrina.

"Yes. Thankfully it's open. See? From the size of this thing we'd have a tough time opening it if the wheel was rolled into place."

They continued upward, each trying to grasp what had happened here at some point in the history of *Kilçilar*. Whatever it could have been, each stone step that led them upward into the darkness seemed scarred with sorrow.

Thereafter, a small landing came at every eighteenth or twentieth step. And, at every other landing, a similar stone wheel had been rolled to one side to permit passage. The open room had long since disappeared somewhere in the darkness below. They continued their climb on the steep narrow staircase, that was now a tunnel with steps leading upward through the earth. Ibrahim continued to count the steps. Katrina was counting matches.

"Ibrahim," she said, as darkness once again enveloped them. "We have only three left."

"We must be nearing the surface," he answered, grasping for words of encouragement.

"Should we try to walk for a while in the dark?" she asked.

"It will be safer to walk in darkness where we have already

been than where we have not," Ibrahim replied. "If it comes to that, we'll rest for a while and, if necessary, retrace our steps."

"How do you feel?" she asked, her hand touching his shoulder. "You didn't look good when we started. You must be exhausted by now."

The truth was that Ibrahim did feel depleted and weak from fatigue and injuries, but he didn't want to cause Katrina further anxiety. So he said, "I'm fine. A brief rest and we continue on."

They sat in darkness on the landing, feet dangling onto the step below.

"Do you know what the Koran says?" he asked at last.

"What?"

"God is the light of the heavens and the earth. His light may be compared to a niche that enshrines a lamp, the lamp within a crystal starlike brilliance. It is lit from a blessed olive tree neither eastern or western. Its very oil would almost shine forth though no fire touched it. Light upon light, God guides to His light whom He will."

"That's beautiful, Ibrahim," Katrina responded. "It reminds me of something the Bible says."

"What is that?"

"Jesus spoke to the people and said, 'I am the light of the world. Whoever follows Me will never walk in darkness, but will have the light of life.'"

"Then it would seem that Allah has spoken. Do you believe Allah knows where we are right now?"

Katrina paused for a second.

"Yes, I do. Although I have to admit that those parchment letters of yours have made me return to my beliefs for a spiritual reality check. The idea of Peter saying the things that are in that letter shakes me a lot. But, if I ever needed to trust and believe, that time has certainly come. I need the strength that can only come from a God who is really there.

"David, the king of Israel, once wrote, 'Where can I go from Your Spirit? Where can I flee from Your presence? If I go up to the heavens, You are there' . . . and, listen to this, Ibrahim . . . 'if I make my bed in the depths, You are there!' I think He knows exactly where we are."

"I won't argue with you on that," he grunted. "I just hope He knows the way out of here."

"Want to hear something else? I was quoting David in Psalm 139. In that same psalm, he went on to talk about God, saying, 'Even the darkness will not be dark to You; the night will shine like the day; for darkness is as light to You.'"

Ibrahim was silent, pondering what he had just heard.

"What are you thinking?" Katrina asked.

"I think I am impressed that you are a woman of great faith. I think I'm glad that you honor my heritage and belief in the Koran by not arguing or putting me down, but by answering to its truth and beauty. I think I am amazed at your knowledge of the Christian Bible and your willingness to include me in the things that it teaches. Thank you."

"You're welcome."

"Now tell me one thing."

"Okay, if I can."

"Is the darkness becoming as light to you yet?"

Katrina's laugh sounded hearty as, for a moment, her mind had been turned away from their predicament and onto spiritual truth.

"Not yet. But perhaps that won't be necessary."

"How can that be?"

"Maybe He already knows just how many matches we need."

Now it was Ibrahim's turn to laugh.

"Katrina Lauring, you are a lamp for my soul."

"I hope so," she replied, offering him an unseen smile. "Well, one way or another, God is going to get us out of here, Ibrahim. With that in mind, let's strike another match and be on our way."

"Good idea. If I sit here much longer, I'll be too stiff and sore to move."

Match number three flared for an instant and then burned steadily toward Katrina's fingers as the two modern-day troglodytes resumed their upward climb through the earthen enclosure.

Match number two shook briefly in Katrina's hand. Ibrahim watched as she involuntarily swallowed the dryness they were both feeling in their throats. Her eyes revealed unspoken anxiousness as they studied one another in the flickering light. The end of their match supply was at hand.

They continued climbing.

"And then there was darkness," Katrina declared as the match burned out. "I guess this must be man's reversal of the creative act.

God said, 'Let there be light, and there was light.' Well, Ibrahim, we've got one last match. I hope you remember how many stairs we've climbed because it looks like we'll have to make a return trip in the dark. I can tell you I'm not looking forward to . . . "

"Kat," interrupted Ibrahim. "Look!"

"Where? If you're pointing, I can't see you."

"Up there. Up the staircase a little further."

Katrina stared upward into the blackness in the direction they were walking. At first she didn't see it. Then, when she did, she was afraid to believe it.

"Is that . . . what I think it is?"

She felt Ibrahim's grip on her arm.

Together, they stared at an ever so tiny but brightly lit cleavage in the earth!

With the unlit match still clutched in her hand, Katrina felt her way along the staircase as Ibrahim followed close behind. Step by step until they reached the crack. The light that passed through the sliverlike opening cast a razor-thin beam across the narrow passageway. Katrina put her hand in its path.

"Beautiful," she said admiringly of the light against her palm.

"Amen!" agreed Ibrahim. He reached up with his free hand and felt around the crack. "The light has to be coming from one of the tunnels or the rooms. Now we have to make some noise and hope we are heard."

They began shouting. First Ibrahim. Then Katrina. Back and forth with brief listening pauses in between. After about ten minutes, Ibrahim whispered, "Shh. Quiet."

A voice was calling to them!

"Is that you, Ibrahim? Where are you?"

"We're in here. Follow the sound of my voice until you find a small crack. Here. I'll run something through it so you can tell that you've found us. He unbuckled his belt and gave it to Katrina. She reached up and began pushing it into the crack.

"It's too wide," she said, handing it back. "Mine is smaller."

She slipped hers from around her waist and began working it through to the other side.

"We've got it!" a voice called out. "We've got the belt!"

"All right!" shouted Ibrahim. "Yes. You've found us. Just dig below the crack and get us out of here."

Soon they heard more excited voices outside.

"What are you doing in there, Ibrahim?"

"Hey there, Rocco, what every good archaeologist does. We've been exploring new territory."

"Is Ms. Lauring with you?" It was Ben Hur's voice now.

"Hello, Ben Hur. Yes, she's here and she's fine. She's in better shape than I am, actually."

"That's what we all said the last time we saw you two together," boomed Rocco's voice, over the laughter and general agreement of the others beginning to gather on the opposite side of the earthen wall. "Now stand back while we punch our way through."

Ibrahim and Katrina retreated several steps along the tunnel staircase and sat down to wait.

"You were right," said Ibrahim, as he put his arm around Katrina.

"About what?" she smiled, letting her head rest on his shoulder while staring gratefully at the tiny beam of light a few feet away.

"God knew exactly how many matches we needed."

"But we have one left."

"Give it here."

"What do you want it for?"

"Give it here."

Katrina laid the match in his hand.

"This is why we have one match left."

He struck it against the stone step and watched it flare to fulfill its brief purpose. Holding it between them, he could see clearly the way that dirt and grime, sweat and tears, had produced patterns of fatigue and exhaustion in her face. But her eyes were warm, searching his own. She moistened her dry lips with the tip of her tongue and then formed the most beautiful smile he had ever seen. Reaching her arms around his neck she kissed him.

"I needed to see you like this . . . one last time . . . before we return to the outside world."

"I know," she said and kissed him again.

They settled back and listened to the glorious scraping, pounding, scratching symphony of picks and shovels digging their way toward them through the dirt and stone.

Ward Tanneberg

• • •

REUTERS. September 14
In southeast Turkey, the PKK and the army are locked in
still another bloody battle, the third major skirmish in
two weeks. Five foreign travelers were kidnapped in this
region three days ago. Their bullet-riddled bodies were
found today along the highway north of Hakkari. The
PKK has claimed responsibility for the killings and has
promised "death to all foreigners" in the future. Business
travel to this region is recommended for only the most
urgent and essential matters and then only by air.

In the western region of the country, political unrest is
on the rise. Demonstrations are seen almost daily in the
streets of Istanbul and Ankara. Crime is also on the
increase in major cities. In the back alleys of Istanbul's
Beyoglu tenderloin, there has been a significant rise of
late-night muggings of foreigners. Recreational travel in
Turkey is no longer sanctioned by the U.S. State
Department.

• • •

Thirty-six. The Shepherd

Her lithesome crescent form did not dance among the stars tonight. Instead, she sailed her orbit on a black sea, like a small boat on a great ocean, one whose presence is hardly noticed in the infinite watery waste. The mountain seemed enormous by comparison, silent in her majestic pose, a sentinel at this wilderness crossroads.

Hidden in her phantomlike specter, half a dozen meters from a scorched patch of mountain foothill, İlhan stared into the blackness below and listened to the low murmur of voices. In the distance he heard truck motors grinding northward along the road from Van. Soon after, lights came into view, four sets of them, cutting a yellow trail through the night. A handheld light near the highway flashed three times. The four trucks pulled off the road and into the gully where headlamps were turned off, replaced by flashlights and lanterns.

It was the same as he had witnessed on other occasions. The same talking and laughing. The same sharing of cigarettes. The

270

same low banter before the exchange of murderous weapons took place between Iran's fanatical right wing and Turkey's radical copycats. Weapons designed to hurl death and destruction at the sleeping citizens of Turkey's fledgling Republic.

Only one thing marked this night from the others. İlhan's smile was thin and cold as his eyes narrowed in anticipation of that difference.

The first shout came from out of the darkness bordering the outlaws' nefarious business at exactly one forty-seven, followed by expletives and outcries of surprise, then more shouts. Gunfire. Howls of pain. The rattle of automatic rifles echoing across the desert plain, their deadly staccato ricocheting off the mountain cliffs.

In two minutes the firefight was over!

Those left standing raised hands that signified surrender. Others lay silent on the ground in the grotesquely twisted patterns so common to violent death. The ambush had been carried off with precision by a crack Turkish Army troop detachment, hidden among the rocks and brush since well before midnight.

At a signal from the officer-in-charge, İlhan ran across the highway, his sharp eyes sweeping the mini-battleground. It took only moments to realize that she was not there. The Iranian woman, whose name he remembered was Azari, had not made the trip.

He walked over to where the Turk, Yücel, lay wounded among his comrades. İlhan stared at him wordlessly, then spit in his face. Nodding to the OIC that this was the leader of the Turkish outlaw contingent, he turned away and disappeared into the darkness, quickly forgotten by the few soldiers who had noticed him at all during the excitement.

Standing once again on his patch of scorched earth, İlhan stared across the plain in the direction of Iran. One less supply line trafficking death to his fellow countrymen. There were others, he knew, but he felt satisfaction in having helped to shut this one down.

"You were lucky tonight, Azari," he said softly, "but I do not forget you. Never. Someday . . . somewhere, if others do not, I will. You are a dead woman!"

Thirty-seven. Ibrahim

It was almost two o'clock on Sunday morning when the workers finally broke through. More than ten hours had come and gone since they entered the underground city.

Both Ibrahim and Katrina were driven to the emergency medical clinic in Güzelyurt where they were given beds for the remainder of the night. Tahsin, Rocco, and Ben Hur insisted that Ibrahim be transferred to Ankara for rest and a more complete physical evaluation. Dr. El remained silent in the background. The others suggested that Katrina should do the same, but she would have none of it.

"I'm on loan from my school. They expected me to return today and be in the classroom on Monday morning."

The gash on Ibrahim's head had been cleaned and sewn together. X rays revealed nothing beyond the original cracked ribs, though a good-sized bruise had formed on his chest, most likely from a stone flung by the explosion. His collarbone was fractured—another flying rock, no doubt. The doctor determined

272

that nothing further could be done for it other than immobilizing the arm on that side of his body and waiting for it to heal.

"You are sure there was an explosion?" Ben Hur asked again, his brow furrowed with concern as he stood by Katrina's bed. Rocco was also in the room with him. Tahsin and Dr. El were on their way back to the camp. As a result of the heavy pain medication, Ibrahim was already dozing in the next room.

"I'm positive," Katrina replied, settling back on the bed. She had just come from taking a shower and washing her hair. The long damp strands spread across the pillow in layers of yellow and golden brown.

"I heard a loud pop . . . it hurt my ears . . . and then there was this sound. You could hear the rock crumbling. My heart was in my throat and the next second we were blown off our feet! The dust was unreal and there were pieces of rock flying around. I thought we were . . . I didn't know if we'd make it."

"Ibrahim says that neither of you would have survived were it not for your courage and quick thinking. We're grateful, Ms. Lauring, that you were there. I know that sounds odd, but you understand what I mean."

"Mmm," she murmured, closing her eyes as the combination of her medication, the hot shower, and the gradual release of tension and weariness broke over her like a gentle ocean wave. The two men saw that she was fading and made a move to leave.

"We'll let you rest now," Rocco pledged in his softest voice, that still seemed too large for the size of the room. "Goodnight, Ms. Lauring."

"Rocco," she called out sleepily, as they started through the doorway, "Ben Hur, thanks for everything. You guys are wonderful. Really. And would you send someone with my things tomorrow? I'm desperate for clean clothes. There's a small bag on my bed in Renée's tent. Also, on the bed are the clothes I intended to wear tomorrow. If it's not too much trouble? And listen, guys, forget 'Ms. Lauring,' would you? The name is Katrina. But my really good friends call me Katy."

"Of course . . . Katy. I'll have Çali bring your things in the morning."

"I appreciate it. Thanks and goodnight."

Pursuit

THE ROOM WAS ALREADY BATHED in sunlight by the time Katrina awoke. The wall clock said ten twenty-five. She looked past the small food table toward a doorless closet that boasted a clothes rod, but no hangers. There were her clothes, draped over the back of a wooden chair, and her bag had been placed on the seat.

A half hour later, she stepped into the hallway wearing a red blouse and blue denim skirt. The door to the adjoining room was open, permitting her to hear low-pitched voices, one of which she recognized as Ibrahim's. She peeked into the room. Both Rocco and Ben Hur were standing next to Ibrahim who sat with his feet dangling over the side of the bed.

"May I?" asked Katrina, knocking softly on the door to announce her presence.

"Günaydin." *Good morning.* "Come in, please," motioned Ibrahim. He had on denim trousers and a cotton plaid shirt, open at the front and revealing fresh, new bandages that had been wrapped around his chest. He had obviously had a shower as well, and his arm rested in a newer and more stable sling. She noticed a newspaper in his lap.

Ben Hur and Rocco looked at her and nodded. None of the trio appeared very happy.

"How are you feeling, Ibrahim?"

"Much better. They gave me something for pain and I slept until almost nine o'clock."

"Great. That's probably what you needed the most. Oh, and thank you, gentlemen, for bringing my things. I didn't expect you to deliver them personally."

"It's nothing," Rocco smiled briefly. "We're always pleased to help a damsel in distress."

"And how are you feeling, Kat?" asked Ibrahim.

"Like I'd stepped in front of a moving truck. There are no places that are not sore."

"But you slept well?" Rocco inquired politely.

"I didn't know a thing until after ten," she smiled, at the same time continuing to detect a decided absence of cheerfulness in the room. "Perhaps I should step out? I have the feeling that I'm interrupting."

"No, please stay. Rocco, will you bring that chair around so

274

Katrina can join us?" Ibrahim's face was sober as he looked at her. "This concerns you as well."

Observing that the others were standing, she offered the chair from her room.

"Thank you, but we can't stay long. We're needed back at camp."

Katrina sat down. Rocco perched on the bed next to Ibrahim while Ben Hur, both hands stuffed in his pockets, stood stoically to her left.

"So what's happening?" she asked. "Why is everyone so glum?"

"This morning these men received a call from Dr. Süleyman Akin. He's the director of the Anatolian Civilizations Museum in Ankara. Since *Kilçilar* is sponsored by the Museum, he is for all practical purposes our boss. He was very angry."

"An understatement," muttered Ben Hur. "He was furious!"

Katrina looked from one man to the other.

"He asked for me, of course, but I wasn't there. He demanded to know what was happening at *Kilçilar*. More specifically, he wanted to know about certain letters that had been recovered from the site, one in particular written by the Apostle Peter. Of course, neither Ben Hur nor Rocco knew anything about such a letter." He glanced at the men, then back to Katrina. "I was just explaining to them how I made the discovery and the concerns I have had over how to deal with it. They know now that I asked you to come and examine the document."

Looking at the others, he continued.

"To finish what I was saying before Katrina joined us, initially I tried to contact Dr. Üzünal, but he was not available. Then, I went to Antalya to see Ian Hedley. He's an educator in whom I have implicit trust and I thought that his advice and perspective from the Christian viewpoint would be helpful. His absence brought Katrina into the picture.

"I'm sure there are scholars who will ultimately be more qualified to study the letters. But, for now, she is the only one I know and trust who can read ancient Greek, while applying her training and background in Christian church history to the matter of its contents. She, and now you two, are the only persons to whom I have spoken about this. But, when I returned from

275

Antalya, I felt certain someone had entered my files and examined the letters.

"And now," his voice was lined with bitter frustration, "this morning the whole world is aware of what has been found. All of my caution with regard to divulging its presence and contents has been for nothing."

He passed the newspaper to Katrina. She recognized the masthead of the *Turkish Daily News.* She had become familiar with it since arriving in Antalya. While giving priority to Turkish news, it also provided information on the world with stories from the AP and Reuters.

Among expatriates, however, the *TDN* enjoyed the reputation of being one of the world's funniest newspapers, due to its wildly contradictive stories and bloodthirsty sports page headlines. Teams did not simply lose; they were "smashed," "destroyed," "mauled," or described in defeat by other equally colorful terms.

In today's edition, on the front page, lower right-hand section, was a two-column photograph of an ancient papyrus sheet and the headline:

LETTER FROM FIRST POPE CASTS DOUBTS ON DEITY OF JESUS CHRIST

At the recently excavated underground city known as *Kilçilar,* an exciting new discovery has been reported. Among what some experts are declaring to be the finest artifacts ever assembled in one location, is included a letter reputed to have been written by the Apostle Peter, the Christian Church's first Pope.

The letter, written to the Apostle John, expresses grave personal doubts over the prevailing view of the Christian Church relative to its doctrine declaring Jesus Christ to be "coexistent and coequal with God." This teaching has long been a major roadblock to achieving greater unity among Muslims and Christians.

Kilçilar, named after a nearby village, is located within the "Cappadocian Triangle" between Derinkuyu and Güzelyurt. Due to its remoteness and a lack of general public information, little is currently known about the project itself, other than that it is sponsored by the Anatolian Civilizations Museum in Ankara. However, with the discovery of the letters, that will most certainly change.

Museum experts and Muslim religious scholars have yet to examine the letters in order to verify content and authenticity. Dr. Süleyman Akin, the museum director, had no comment.

TDN has learned that the project was turned over to Dr. Ibrahim Sevali, of the University of Istanbul, after Dr. Bülent Üzünal, the project's original director, was hospitalized with a brain tumor earlier this summer. The brilliant twenty-nine-year-old archaeologist, already known throughout the world for his giftedness in ancient languages, was unavailable for comment.

Katrina looked dismayed as she laid the paper on the bed.

"That's not all," said Rocco.

"What else could there be?" Katrina asked as she stared at the news photo, wondering what Dorothy Hedley and the teaching faculty at the Antalya Girls School would think when they read this news report. Those who knew of her connection with Ibrahim would surely recognize the name *Kilçilar*.

"Dr. Akin says that the reporter who contacted him initially for a comment on this story called again last night. He claimed to have information that indicated Ibrahim was acting improperly by failing to report the existence of these letters and other invaluable manuscripts and artifacts."

"That's absurd," Katrina exploded.

"As director, it's my right and responsibility to determine at what point a discovery should be made public," Ibrahim declared emphatically.

Ben Hur nodded his head in agreement.

Rocco shrugged his shoulders, offering an openhanded gesture of helplessness. "That may be true, but who will the public believe? You or the *Turkish Daily News*?"

Ibrahim looked down at the floor.

"Akin also said the reporter wanted confirmation that there had been three accidental deaths at the site yesterday."

Katrina's mouth dropped. "What are you saying?"

"That's the same thing Akin said. It was news to him. So the reporter told him that, according to his source, three people were killed in accidents yesterday. Two women and the good doctor here."

"You said that Dr. Akin was contacted by this reporter last night? Do you know what time?"

"Did he say?" asked Rocco, turning to Ben Hur.

"It must have been before ten. Akin said he tried to contact us after the reporter's first call. That was around six-thirty or seven. It had to be sometime before ten when the reporter called back with the news of your demise, because that's when Dr. Akin began trying to reach us again. We didn't answer because everybody in the camp was busy looking for you two."

"Did this reporter have names?"

"He did. Renée Patry, a student worker from the University of Paris, and Katrina Lauring, American schoolteacher and 'close friend,'" Rocco emphasized the words, "of Dr. Ibrahim Sevali. Rumor has it that you two disappeared together and are believed to have died in a cave-in. By now it's probably on the wires and in tomorrow's *TDN* as well. I can see the headlines now. 'ARCHAEOLOGIST DIGS OWN GRAVE. TEACHER STONED TO DEATH.'"

Rocco's attempt at humor fell on deaf ears.

"So the reporter had the names of the deceased before ten o'clock. Before either of you knew for sure what had happened!"

No one responded. In their concern over the news article, they had overlooked the time at which Dr. Akin had been contacted.

"Deep Throat."

"What?" asked Ibrahim.

"Oh, it just reminds me of when one of our country's past presidents, Richard Nixon, was forced to resign the presidency," said Katrina. "There was an informant who cooperated with the *Washington Post* and helped to bring about Nixon's downfall. His name was never revealed and he became known as 'Deep Throat.'"

"And you think we have a Deep Throat here at *Kilçilar*?"

"A different kind, to be sure, but what else? There must be someone on the inside who doesn't like you very much. They've rifled your files and exploited your secrets. Not satisfied with that, they intend to demean your reputation as a professional by insinuating wrongdoing. They may even intend to ruin your rep-

278

utation by inferring that you are a philanderer. Not that it will matter too much to you personally, if you are dead."

"A phil . . . what is this thing?"

"It's someone who is messing around. A flirt. A man who's long overdue for his 3,000-mile moral checkup."

Ibrahim stared quizzically at Katrina. Rocco and the stoic Ben Hur burst into laughter.

"Ms . . . I mean, Katy," said Ben Hur with a big grin on his face, "I don't know how Ibrahim here ever made contact with the likes of you, but I have to say that I'm glad he did. You'd make one whale of a *sabra* back in Israel."

"Do I presume that to be a compliment, Mr. Hur?" Katrina asked coquettishly. "As Ibrahim would say, 'What is this thing?'"

"It's a word we Israelis have coined from a particular kind of cactus. When we try to describe someone like you, we say she is a *sabra*. Tough and prickly on the outside, but soft and mushy on the inside. These are qualities that we admire."

"Well, thank you very much," she said, as she stood to her feet and kissed him lightly on the cheek, causing him to blush.

"Hey," fussed Rocco, "what about me?"

"You have too much inbred Italian willingness, Mr. Valetti. My mother told me about men like you and warned me to avoid them at all costs." She paused, noting his feigned look of disappointment, then leaned over and kissed his cheek too. "But for you I make this one-time exception."

Rocco beamed with delight.

Katrina's face became serious again. "I hope you both know how grateful I am that Ibrahim has you watching out for him."

The two foremen glanced away, embarrassed by her sincerity.

"Don't you worry your pretty little head," said Rocco. "Ben here and I won't let anything happen to him. Nor you either, as long as you're with us."

"Unfortunately, that won't be much longer. I've got to leave as soon as I can."

"Kat, do you think the Hedleys would consider letting you stay a few more days?"

Katrina looked at Ibrahim in surprise.

"Oh, I can't imagine it. They're shorthanded as it is and with my being gone, well, it makes it that much harder. Why do you ask?"

Pursuit

The others waited with Katrina for his answer.

"I've been thinking of several reasons. One, now that the letters are public information, I expect all . . . well, you know, everything is going to break loose. I could use some help right now. Second, if my reputation as a philan—whatever is on the line, your presence may help reassure those who need to know. In your absence, rumor will certainly gain a momentum all its own. And third, the likelihood of being invaded by the media appears to be closer than I had thought twenty-four hours ago. You've told me about your brother, Kris. Do you suppose he would be willing to come and help us?"

Katrina's mouth dropped again while Ibrahim went on to explain to the others who Kris was and what he did professionally.

"I'm not sure you understand, Ibrahim. My brother is a talk show host, not a network newscaster. He's a cross between a journalist and an entertainer. And he's in Los Angeles now preparing to launch a new show."

"But you speak highly of him and say that you trust him?"

"Of course, but then he's my brother. We're very close, as I've already told you. He's been the one man in my life with whom I've been able to share my innermost feelings until . . . I mean . . . why Kris, and not someone from CNN, for example?"

"Because you trust him. And I trust you."

The others nodded in agreement.

Katrina's mind raced to sort out the reasons needed to explain to these men why such a thing was impossible.

"I think it is good if you can do as Ibrahim suggests," said Ben Hur, looking very serious once again. "We are sitting on an extremely volatile situation here. The media is about to descend upon us. The Museum director is ready to fire all of us. And a murderer is running loose among us! We can use your brother's help, Katy. And yours too."

Katrina's eyes moved imploringly from Ben Hur to Rocco to Ibrahim.

"At least give it some thought. Now we have to excuse ourselves. Rocco and I want to get back to the camp and make certain the letters are safe. We're going to secure Ibrahim's tent and put a guard there around the clock."

"Good," said Ibrahim. "Kat, please let me talk to the Hedleys for you. And then call your brother to see if he will come."

Katrina's thoughts were swirling. Finally she looked at Ibrahim. "I'll speak with Dorothy. If she says no, then I must return."

"I understand."

"After that, I'll call Kris."

Thirty-eight. Katrina

1230 local time
Güzelyurt, Turkey

Katrina hung up the telephone and leaned back in the chair. She was in the clinic reception area where she had eventually been given permission to use the phone after showing her telephone credit card and offering repeated assurances that the call would be billed to her personally and not to the clinic.

When they were finally connected, Dorothy listened carefully to Katrina's account of what was happening. As it turned out, she had not read the *Turkish Daily News* as yet, but assured Katrina that she would as soon as they hung up. Katrina should remain at *Kilçilar* as long as she was needed. The outcome there precluded any other priority, as far as Dorothy was concerned.

"Besides, Ian returned last night," she told Katrina. "Between the two of us, we can handle your load and still manage to keep things under control for a while longer. Take as much time as you need. A week. Two. More if it becomes necessary. Oh, I just can't imagine anything like this! Nothing can be more important to God's kingdom right now than to seek the truth about what Ibrahim has uncovered there. If Peter did write that letter, well, it will turn the church world upside down, won't it? Has Ibrahim considered the possibility of forgery?"

"Yes, he's mentioned it. We also talked about the importance of getting an opinion from top researchers in the Christian, Muslim, and Jewish faiths. In fact, this was his plan before yesterday. He fears an upheaval in the religious world if there's too much time for speculation before an accurate, unbiased determination can be published. Now, with this news article . . ."

"I believe God has you there for a reason, Katrina," Dorothy assured her. "This whole thing is so very unusual . . . Ian being called away and everything at the very time that Ibrahim needed to talk with him. And then the Lord had you here to take his place and now He's using you for His own purposes there. It's all too uncanny for it to be otherwise."

Dorothy's reasoning was a new thought to Katrina.

"I can't imagine why, Dorothy. At times it all seems like a dream. Although last night up here was more of a nightmare. Why me? God needs some experts up here. I'm just barely out of seminary, for goodness sake."

"As has often been said, 'His ways are not our ways,'" Dorothy answered. "It's been said so many times because it's true, my dear. His plans are way beyond our own thinking. Look how He mightily used a young convert named Timothy who's from that very region where you are now.

"Remember, Katrina, God is not surprised by any of this. He knew it would happen before it came to pass. Just keep searching for the truth. And do be careful. Ian and I and the entire staff will be praying for you here every day. If there is anything we can do to help, please call."

"There is something. Would you ask Michelle to send me a couple of changes of clothes? A skirt, some blouses and jeans. And my jacket. It's in the bottom drawer of my dresser. I ruined the clothes I was wearing yesterday and I didn't pack for a long stay." Katrina gave her the *Kilçilar* project mailing address.

"I'll have her do it right away."

After saying good-bye, Katrina hung up the phone and leaned back in her chair. *What's going on, Jesus? I don't understand this at all. I feel so inadequate and inexperienced. I hope You realize what a novice You have here. You could've done a lot better. All I can think to say is, whatever You're wanting, please don't let me blow it!*

She reached for her address book in the side pocket of her bag, fixed with a rubber band to her New Testament. She opened it to the new phone numbers that Kris had included in his one letter of the summer. Katrina never complained about his lack of writing. She knew that he was busy getting settled and putting his new show together. Besides, he had called her once after the letter and they talked for forty-five minutes. She shuddered to think what that must have cost.

She checked the clock on the wall and decided it must be late Saturday night in Los Angeles. He should be home. Following the instructions for international calls printed on the back of her credit card, she dialed a glut of numbers . . . missed one and started over. On the third try she heard the phone ringing. Once. Twice. Three times. *Oh, no, he's not going to . . .*

"Hello?" The voice at the other end sounded sleepy.

"Hi, Kris."

"Kat? Is that you, Kat? Hey, it's good to hear your voice. You sound like you're next door."

"You too."

"What's up? I mean besides me, now."

"What time is it there?"

"About a quarter to three."

"Oh, oh. Sorry, Kris. I was thinking it was around midnight."

"I'll send you a timetable. Anyway, I'm glad you called. A nice long talk with my kid sister will make my day—or night, as the case may be."

"We'll 'make your day' on your nickel, big brother. As much as I'd like to accommodate, my budget won't allow it."

"So then, what's on your mind?" he asked jokingly. "I know you're too tight to just call me for no reason."

She paused.

"Kris, I . . . we need you."

"Well, here I am."

"No, I mean I *need* you. To come here."

Now it was Kris' turn to pause.

"Are you okay, sis?" His voice sounded tense and more alert. The casual banter tone was gone. "Are you in some kind of trouble?"

"Not legal trouble . . . at least, none that I know of. Although last night someone did try to kill me and the man I was with."

"What's that? Did I hear you correctly? Someone tried to *kill* you? A bomb at the school? What happened?"

"No, I'm not at the school, Kris. Right now I'm in central Turkey in a region called Cappadocia. It's the area the Apostle Paul visited on his first missionary journey. You remember from Sunday School?"

"So what are you doing there?"

For the next eight minutes she briefed Kris regarding meeting Ibrahim; the letters that had been en route to Nicea; the underground city where they were found; Renée Patry's death; Ibrahim's and her narrow escape, and the unexpected news article in the *TDN* this morning.

"It's sure to eventually hit the papers and television in the States, Kris. The *TDN* takes stories from the AP and Reuters, so I imagine they feed them theirs as well.

"Anyway, we think once the news media figures out the importance of the letters, they'll drop in by parachute if they have to. The remoteness of the area will be the only thing that slows them down. But not for long.

"The thing is, Ibrahim trusts me. I've told him about you, and he thinks you could advise him in dealing with the reporters. In fact, he said to tell your people that he will not work with anyone else from the network. He promises that if you come right away, he'll give you the complete story. It might make a great lead for your new show. Phones are already starting to ring in Ankara, after people here read the story and saw the photo of the letters this morning."

"Did you say those letters were headed for Nicea, but never got there?"

"Yes. Why do you ask?"

"No reason," Kris answered vaguely. "Anyway, our first show doesn't go until after the New Year holiday."

"Maybe your bosses would give you an earlier prime-time special or something."

She could almost hear the gears grinding as Kris mulled that possibility over in his mind.

"Where are you right now, Kat? This very minute."

Katrina hesitated, not wanting to upset her brother.

"I'm at a medical clinic, but I'm okay. Really. I just spent the night and was treated for a few cuts and bruises. I'll tell you all about it when you come. Can you come, Kris?"

There was a long silence. Then Kris spoke up.

"Give me a number where you can be reached for the next several hours. I have to make some calls. I know you wouldn't ask if this wasn't important, so I'll be there as quickly as I can. And you may be right. This could be great stuff. Hey, we might just set our opening night audience right on its ear. Like it's God's way of saying, 'I told you so.'"

"Maybe. Anyway, thanks, Kris. You won't regret it. I promise." Katrina repeated the numbers of the clinic and of Ibrahim's cellular phone. "Oh, and one more favor. Please?"

"No prob. What do you want now? A little side trip for a blowgun in Borneo? Or a yak in Outer Mongolia for the film crew to ride?"

"Sort of. But maybe not that easy," she answered. After pausing, she continued. "Would you mind calling Mom and Dad? I'd hate for them to read in *USA Today* that I had been killed while romancing Turkey's leading young archaeologist. I'm cynical enough about the business you're in to believe it could happen."

"Maybe the 'killed' part wouldn't be so bad," Kris responded dryly. "I think they half expected that anyway when you left the country. But the part about 'romancing' a Turkish archaeologist might drive our old man to an early grave."

"Kris," she appealed in a chiding tone, "be nice!"

"Okay, okay," he grumbled. "I'll call them."

"And not at three on Sunday morning, either."

"You take all the fun out of life."

"And you are still bad!"

"You noticed. All right. I'll call them before they leave for church. Meanwhile, I'll see what I can do about meeting up with you. I assume I'll have to fly through Istanbul. Travel agents will be on the golf course today, so let me see what I can do on my own. Check with your friend. Find out the name of the nearest airport. Commercial and otherwise. And some directions for driving too. I have that small map of Turkey you sent in your last letter. That should do me for now."

"Do you have a passport?"

"Can you believe that I just got it a couple of days ago? And an International Driver's Permit to boot. The network hotshots thought they might be needed sometime. Guess they were right, huh?"

"I think the Lord knew you were supposed to be here, so He's made certain that you are ready."

There was silence at the other end.

"Okay," he said slowly. "Then if God is my travel agent, it should be no problem getting a last-minute, first-class ticket. Right? Later, sis."

Katrina put down the telephone and walked back to Ibrahim's room. He lay fully dressed on top of the sheets, hands folded over his chest. From the doorway she watched the gentle movement of his chest. A smile stole across her face as her thoughts wandered back over their last several hours together. Their first kiss beneath that incredible mosaic Jesus in the underground church. Minutes later, hands touching in the dark as they struggled to survive. His arm around her. His face in the match light.

Their second kiss had been equally as sweet as they sat waiting to be rescued. Waiting on stone steps that had heard no footfall but their own for hundreds of years. Could this all really be happening to Katrina Sarah Lauring of Baytown, California? Ms. Lauring, the unsung, unknown, and inexperienced new Bible teacher at the Antalya Girls School?

She shivered involuntarily at remembrances of the room full of skeletons . . . and of Renée . . .

Her mind drifted back to their kisses again. She'd been kissed before. Not many times, but a few. Of course, there would always be Tommy. Wet and slippery, hardly wonderful, but thoroughly eager Tommy. She smiled to herself at the memory of Fluffy White Cloud Day.

Since Tommy, some suitors had been pleasantly shy. And others had come on . . . well, too strong. Like mighty conquerors. But this had been different. *Very* different. The thought of Ibrahim's lips touching hers gave her a warm feeling. Had it been the atmosphere of the ancient church? Or the undeniable relief she had felt when rescue was certain at last? Who could know?

At twenty-five, Katrina was still a virgin. Her choice. It was the way she wanted to live. No one-night stands. No uncommitted sexual relationships. No fatal illnesses resulting from promiscuity.

Life was too precious a gift for such convoluted twistings.

She was not a prude. The idea of passionately loving a man with her total being was a beautiful thought, a prospect she took pleasure in. But her relationship to Jesus continued to be first and foremost. She had given her life to the Lord years before and was even willing to remain unmarried, if that turned out to be God's plan for her.

These days, the way she saw it, the decision as to whether or not one casually engaged in sex was a matter every individual had to confront sooner or later. Through the years, several of her friends had taken their chances with sexually transmitted diseases and premarital pregnancies and were paying too high a price. If she did find true love, she intended to come to him on their wedding night healthy and clean. Even some of her seminary friends laughed at her "Cinderella" approach to life, but not many. Most shared her views.

In fact, among more and more friends her age, hers was a growing trend. Some, like herself, had made the decision to remain virgins, setting limits during teen years on how they would conduct themselves in dating relationships. She was not surprised that most of these were already committed Christians at the time, guided by God-inspired values. Others made the decision to say no much later, after realizing they were being used and abused by boys or men who insisted on sex as the price for a relationship.

Her thoughts and feelings ran together, like marbles on a board, as she studied Ibrahim's features. Handsome in a natural, unaffected sort of way. Respected by peers who had placed this twenty-nine-year-old in charge of what was turning out to be Turkey's most extensive archaeological find among its unique collection of underground cities. Sensitive and attentive to her feelings. A gentleman in every way. This was certainly not what she had expected.

Is he the one, Lord? Could I love this man?

The question came as a surprise. She thought back over their initial meeting, paint clothes and all. The dinner at Françesco's. The next day's fascinating walk through the museum. The outdoor cafe in Old Town where conversations flowed so easily . . .

"So how long do you intend to stand there?"

Katrina bumped against the door jam, jolted from her daydream. Ibrahim's eyes were open. He was smiling as he looked at her.

"I . . . I thought you were sleeping." She stumbled over her words, embarrassed to be caught staring, hoping that he had not imagined her thoughts.

He smiled.

"I was able to reach Dorothy."

"And?" Ibrahim pushed himself to a sitting position.

"And she understood completely. She told me to remain here as long as I was needed. A week. Even two. Michelle is sending me some extra clothes."

"That's wonderful!"

"You do understand that I must return as soon as I'm of no further use here. I've barely gotten acquainted with my students."

"Of course."

"I also spoke with my brother."

At this, Ibrahim threw his feet over the side of the bed, supporting himself on its edge with his hands. His eyes glowed with anticipation.

"Kris is coming. I gave him the clinic's phone number and also your cellular number. He'll call to let me know when and how he's getting here."

"That's terrific, Kat! I've been lying here thinking about all this since Ben Hur and Rocco left. The word is out. Soon it will be in more and more papers and on radio and television. Someone has taken the initiative from us and now we have to get it back. Why would anyone break into my private files for those letters, kill Renée Patry, and then try to kill us? We've found many wonderful things at *Kilçilar*, but now everything is beginning to revolve around the letters."

"Do you want an answer? Or have you already decided and are merely waiting for me to ask you to tell what you know?"

"Tell me what *you* think about the break-in."

Katrina thought for a moment.

"Well, it was done by someone who is very good at opening locks. There were no visible indentations or markings. Or, he must have a key. It has to be someone in the crew who saw you leave the cave late at night and wondered what you were doing. Has anybody asked suspicious questions?"

"I'm thinking about this."

"I can narrow the field of suspects. Who besides yourself can read the Greek text? Most of your crew wouldn't know if they were photographing the letters upside down. In fact, my guess is that there is only one."

Ibrahim nodded in agreement.

"And why kill poor Renée and then try to do us in? Jealousy? An old enemy? Someone who wants to stir up trouble by dipping village tales in human blood in order to cause fear and strife among the workers? Perhaps someone who thinks that with you out of the way they might be tapped to oversee *Kilçilar?* Maybe a religious zealot who sees this as an opportunity to embarrass the Christians by disclosing to the world the secret doubts and qualms of their most revered leader. How am I doing?"

"Very well," he smiled appreciatively. "Those are all genuine possibilities, in part or as a whole. But there's still something missing. A vital piece that I can't put my finger on."

"Are you going to Ankara for a thorough examination?" asked Katrina, ready to change the subject back to Ibrahim's welfare.

"No. I can't afford to be absent from *Kilçilar* for that length of time right now. I've agreed to remain here overnight again. Then I'm going back to the project. The doctor has studied the X rays further and says that everything internally appears ready to heal."

"Wonderful," said Katrina. "Actually, I'm impressed that such a small clinic as this has been able to care for you this well."

"Our country's medical facilities are not up to the standards you are used to in the States, but they are improving all the time. Since coming here, we've found the two doctors who service this clinic are very reliable. They tell me that my ribs are cracked but have not punctured anything. The collarbone will mend with time. When I'm released, they'll provide me with a pain medication. That, together with rest and being careful, is the prescription for a full recovery. By the way, how do you like my sutures?" he asked, touching the physician's handiwork lightly with his fingers.

"Couldn't have done it better myself. All except for the hole."

"The hole?" A concerned look flashed across his face as he instinctively reached up to feel his wound again.

"The one that lets all that stubborn obstinacy in."

Ibrahim's hand dropped to his side, a mock scowl offset by his sheepish grin. "I prefer to think of it as professional tenacity."

Katrina shook her head.

Thirty-nine. Kristian

Burbank, California

Looking back on it, I can see how things were building to a climax, but the two weeks before my phone rang in the middle of the night, it just felt like a good case of nerves mixed in with heavy doses of depression.

The more I thought about it, the more the length of the new show was keeping me awake at night. It was twice what I'd done before, and that had been pressure-packed. The time slot petrified me too. Here I was, losing sleep over the competition and I hadn't turned out my first show yet.

Can I really expect to succeed, taking on entrenched TV tabloid shows like "Hard Copy," "Extra," and "Entertainment Tonight"? Is there really a hope of finding an audience willing to deal me into their television deck of cards? To do what I'm about to do is crazy. I'm finally beginning to realize just how high the stakes are in this venture, at least for me. Is there such a thing as "mediacide"? If there is, I must be near to committing it. Everything is at risk here. If the show flops, my career will be shot down in flames before I'm thirty. Even Pat Sajak had "Wheel" to fall back on.

Why didn't I stay in San Francisco? What possesses someone

to stick his face up on the screen and take a chance on being rejected by an entire nation? I suppose the same thing that keeps you awake at night, hoping for its approval and acceptance.

Anyway, what I tell Tom Knight and the others at the planning table is one thing. What I'm feeling when I'm alone is quite another matter.

Alone. Now there's something else I have to deal with.

Being by myself has never been a problem before. But recently I've had that awful sense of being adrift in a small boat without an oar or a compass. The last few weeks have been filled with so many "what-ifs" and "possibilities." I can feel myself yearning for some concrete decisions. Stop the waffling. Enough already. Let's start nailing things down!

The good news?

A couple of important items have been settled. The "KL Show" title was voted down over my objections. I thought the name had some viewer identity from which we could benefit. The rest of the planning team believe that a whole new image is needed to lock in our audience and give them an attachment to the host. It was finally determined that the show would be called "Kris." I don't like it, but I've decided not to sweat it for now. "Kris"? Come on. There's got to be a better title than that!

The other item has to do with the set itself. Studio 14 has finally been chosen as the permanent location and a complete gutting and remodeling got under way last week. Old furniture and staging is being removed. Early yesterday I spent a couple of hours with the designers and the project manager making suggestions as to some changes I feel will improve the new set.

We shouted at each other over the noise of hammers and power tools while working out each of the items in question. The studio will include a main floor that slopes downward to the front edge of the stage itself. A balcony, tiered in semicircular fashion, will provide close-in seating and easy accessibility to the live audience. Throughout, comfortable theater seats are to be installed over newly carpeted floors.

Fifteen video monitors, each fitted with electronic applause signs, will be dispersed throughout the studio. Microphones hung from the ceiling will bring the audience's participatory response to the viewer at home. The bandstand is located to my left as I face the audience. Three cameras will shoot from the balcony and three more from the main floor, together with an additional camera on a boom. Two additional shoulder cameras will bring the total to nine, a far cry from the three I was used to at KFOR.

The stage floor will be surfaced with hardwood and the set's furnishings will include a desk and chair, a small sofa, and two matching chairs. Audio monitors will be placed strategically. The entire studio will seat 360 people, and do it with the intimacy of a comedy club.

I guess it was the need for making decisions, as much as a hunger for companionship, that motivated my invitation for Carole to join me at dinner. I gave her the option of eating out at a fine restaurant of her choice, or dinner at my new place. Why was I not surprised that she chose the latter? Since I was cooking, she opted to drive herself over.

Promptly at seven, while rinsing off a pot and placing it in the dishwasher—I even have one of those now—I heard the doorbell. She was standing in the entryway with a bottle of Napa Valley white wine in her hand.

"I think I smell seafood," she said, "and I thought you'd be missing the Bay Area by now, so I must have guessed right on both counts."

"You did, indeed. Come on in." I took the bottle from her and closed the door. "It's still pretty warm out tonight, isn't it?"

"It's wonderful."

Carole had on an ivory-colored short sleeve top and a long, lightweight, floral-print skirt. She carried a matching sweater on her arm for later. Her dark hair hung loosely around her face and the beauty mark danced gracefully on her cheek each time she smiled. Away from the studio, she was still every bit as desirable as any woman I had ever known.

At the studio? Well, that was something else again. Carole can be . . . difficult, to use a polite word. In fact, sometimes she can be a real pain in the wherever. Her ideas are often excellent though, and always definite.

She fights for what she thinks. Not a bad trait really, except that even when she is outvoted, you know she'll be back the next day with an ever-so-slight variation on the same idea with which she then proceeds to manipulate, rearrange, stroke, and occasionally curse her opponents into giving up and falling in line. She's a very formidable force among those who are forming the team to create and sustain this new show.

Having by this time discovered Carole's penchant for oriental food, I had decided on something the cookbook called a "Thai seafood firepot," a kind of Southeast Asian bouillabaisse, replete with clams, shrimp, and crab, simmered in lime juice and garnished with cilantro and onions. The meal began with fried wanton and wound up with fresh strawberries. It turned out quite well, if I do say so myself.

We were sipping the last of the wine when Carole leaned back in her chair and sighed contentedly. "This is a decided improvement over San Francisco," she said, letting her eyes move slowly from one part of the room to the other. With a slight movement of her wrist she swirled the glass in a circular motion.

"Yeah, I brought my chair from Smyth's 'going out of business sale,' and a couple of other small items with me. The rest I left with the landlord. Some of it was his anyway. All new stuff in here."

"Well, you can certainly afford it. Two hundred fifty thousand a month plus a nice fat ratings bonus is not too shabby, Kris," she said matter-of-factly, as she pushed back from the table and walked over to my new sofa. "At least not for starters."

The woman has class, I thought, watching as she moved gracefully across the room. I was surprised though that she knew so much about my deal with the network. I didn't think contracts interested her all that much. The $3 million a year, three-year contract was public information and in all the newspapers and magazines. But the ratings bonus is a small-print add-on, one that I figured was known only to a few.

The bonus is calculated on how well I do with the sixteen to twenty-five age-group on the one hand, and the over-fifty-five group on the other. No other major player has attempted to target such a widely diverse audience, but here I am, about to take it on.

The age demographics are the numbers used by advertisers when buying television time. If I average a 3 rating through the season with both groups, I get an extra $500,000. At 3.5, it's $1 million. A 4 rating gets a full $1.5 million, according to the bonus clause. If the rating is in the hoped-for range for one age-group but not the other, it gets cut accordingly.

In addition, the network put up $60 million for a three-year budget to cover all salaries, costs of production, and the newly renovated Studio 14. There's another $5 million set aside for approved prime time specials.

When I first heard these numbers, they blew me away. I thought only guys who could bounce a big ball or throw a hard fast one earned this kind of money. Then they told me Leno and Letterman make a whole lot more. I couldn't believe it. I felt like I was robbing a bank. Still, like anything else, I'm already starting to get used to it. But is anyone really worth all this?

"You are," she said, crossing her legs and leaning back into the sofa.

"I am what?" I said as I crossed the room and sat down next to her.

"You are worth it."

"What is this? First you seem to know all the details of my contract. Are you reading my mind now?"

She smiled with mock timidity. "Maybe."

I hoped that was not true. It would be embarrassing if she knew some of the thoughts I had dreamed about her.

"It's still hard for me to comprehend all that money. I used to make $25,000 a year and managed to live on it. Now I make more than twice that in a single week!"

"And this is only the beginning, Kris," said Carole, her eyes shining as she leaned forward. "Once you become a household name, the sky's the limit. You'll be making ten times more than you're getting now."

"Okay. Easy, easy. I don't want the bank to get a hernia carrying all my millions to the safe. By the way, how is it that you know so much about my contract anyway?"

"I work with Tom," she answered softly. "We have no secrets."

Our eyes met and lingered for a moment. I wondered if there was a double meaning concealed in her last remark. Though their relationship always seemed professional on the surface, I'd seen the way Tom's hand occasionally dawdled longer than was necessary on Carole's arm, and once I recalled observing them down by the Video Editing Department with their heads together and his arm around her waist.

Pursuit

Just good friends? Coworkers in Hollywood where everything is a little looser? Or is there something more? I looked away finally, conscious that she was still watching me. I got up and went into the kitchen, turned on the coffee maker, and got cups down from the cupboard.

"Do you mind if we talk about the show for a minute?" I asked.

"I can think of more interesting things to do, but if you want, go ahead."

Her tone sounded suggestive, but I let it pass.

"Do you remember in San Francisco, when you voted we dip into the sleaze bag once in a while in order to spice up our programs?"

"I remember."

"Then you also remember how I blew my cool that afternoon and walked out of the meeting. I figured you and Tom would be all over me about that the next day. But since then, no one has mentioned it one way or the other. I could use some closure. If, as you say, you and Tom have no secrets, what is his thinking about this? For that matter, what are your thoughts?"

While I was talking I looked across the room and reminded myself again just how beautiful this woman is. As I watched her brush back a loose strand of that silky chestnut hair, the thought of how nice it would be to have someone to come home to flashed through my mind. Especially someone like Carole. No more lonely nights.

"We have talked about it."

"And?"

"As I recall, a few weeks ago you indicated a desire to host nontraditional Hollywood stars, sports figures, news anchors, persons doing research in controversial fields, religious leaders, obscure stage actors. And you didn't want to do anything that glorified the misuse of drugs or that could be interpreted as vulgarity by today's middle class, or words to that effect."

"Right. I want to do journalistic comedy each evening that jabs at whatever is happening in the world's current events. I'll poke fun at people, but I'm tired of all this 'rip and tear' comedy stuff. I can be funny without cutting people to pieces. I know, because I've been doing it now for three years. So we mix together some sharp music from a small 'with-it' jazz band, add in interesting guests that include entertainers and people from fields that tap the younger crowd and seniors alike. And we come up with a format that reflects America's plurality, with attention centered on both problems and solutions."

"I applaud your noble desires," Carole responded. "I couldn't agree with you more."

"Great," I sighed with a deep sense of relief.

"But," Carole added, shifting her body to a different position, "while I agree with you that this should be our target goal, we still have to shoot some 'attention-getting' arrows into the crowd."

"What do you mean?" I suddenly felt as though we were back in the conference room where muscle-tightening occurred in my back and shoulders on a regular basis these days. I poured the freshly perked coffee. "You drink it black, right?"

"Right."

Actually, I prefer warm milk in my coffee, especially in the evening. There's a soothing quality about it. But "soothing" was still a question mark for the moment. I decided to leave it *au naturel.*

"I mean," she began as she took the cup from me, "the American public says one thing about its morals and values but lives out quite another. It's true there have been some loud protests over sex and violence on television. The politicos in Washington are getting as much mileage as they can from it, but it's mostly talk with very little clout to back it up.

"Look at the televangelists who have come and gone, Kris, fallen prey to the wiles of 'seductive women.'" Carole's voice carried a tone of obvious disdain. "And think about the pedophilia problems that have recently been exposed among Catholic priests. It's one of the reasons I decided to leave the church in the first place. It's not safe there! These so-called 'spiritual leaders' and 'family value thumpers' are the biggest sinners of us all."

"Not all of them are like that, Carole," I heard myself say, not quite believing I'd permitted myself to be cast as a defender of the preachers of the world. "Moral hypocrisy and criminal acts ought to be made public and dealt with. I couldn't agree more. But it's the minority that make the news, not the majority of church leaders, by any means."

"They're the naysayers who are trying to pin the increase in teen pregnancies and violent crime on us," Carole argued. "It's not right. Movies and television simply depict what society is, not the other way around. We're a mirror, not an influence."

"Come on, Carole, you can't really believe that," I retorted. "If television isn't the biggest influence-maker in the world, then why are the advertisers spending billions on us every year? They spend their money on us because they know the power of the medium. Of course, we're an influence. In many ways our influence is greater than the home, church, and government all thrown together."

"Well, we can't hope to be all things to all men now, can we?" she replied defensively. "Whose morals are we going to depict? Yours? Mine? Theirs?"

"There's no easy answer to that. But, I don't think thumbing our noses and saying 'Turn it off if you don't like it' is an answer. Television is too all-pervasive. Don't you think that we in the industry have to start working in good conscience? Making decisions about what we will or won't do based on more traditional human values?

"Since when, for example, do rape, robbery, and murder reflect the true values of our society? And when was the last time you saw television or the movies portray a happily married husband and wife as being passionately in love with each other? The only ones we ever see in bed together are not married, at least not to each other. Premarital and extramarital sex, subtly implied or graphically presented, is virtually all we're offering up today."

"So what are you saying?"

"I'm just saying . . . I'm saying that we don't have to keep glamorizing the dark side or the kinky side of sex in order to get an audience. I believe we can do something truthful, honestly reflective, and powerfully entertaining, without having to resort to the Chippendales or some whacko women for our guests. I don't want us to become dependent on sleaze topics that pander to minds never flying higher than an inch above the gutter."

"You're beginning to sound like your father."

I felt the veins in my neck tighten.

"My views are my own. You don't know my father, so leave him out of our discussion."

"But I do know your father."

I stared at her.

"What do you mean?"

"I mean that I've visited your father's church in Baytown. I've listened to him preach. I even shook his hand after the service."

I stood openmouthed, my surprise total and complete.

"What possessed you to do that?" I asked finally.

"The same thing that made me watch five 'KL Shows' a day for a couple of weeks while you rested in Hawaii. I want to know about you, Kris. I want to know *all* about you. You are going to be a great star!" Her voice had warmed again, filled with conviction.

Carole put down her cup and stood to her feet. Her eyes never left mine as she glided evenly across the room and encircled me with her arms. Her face pressed against my chest. I felt the warmth of her body passing through to my own. I held her, inhaling the freshness of her hair. Then her face tilted upward. Her lips were parted. The invitation was clearly given. I didn't have to guess this time.

But I didn't move to accept it either.

For a moment there was nothing. Then came a nearly imperceptible, but definite tightening of facial features as she pulled back and looked at me.

"What's wrong, Kris?"

"I don't know. You tell me."

"Tell you what?"

"Tell me why you're so desirable and yet . . . "

"There is no 'and yet,' Kris. You want me, don't you? I've seen it in the way you look at me. I want you too. I want what I know you want . . . now. Tonight. What can be wrong with two grown people wanting to be with each other?"

I took a step back, perplexed over my sudden hesitation.

"I'm not at all sure how to answer that question, Carole. For the last several years, I've listened a lot to the idea that if two people are mature enough to handle their feelings and truly care about each other, then whatever they want to do together is okay.

"In fact, I'll be very honest with you. When I invited you to dinner tonight, I guess I was hoping in the back of my mind that something like this might happen. I remember our evening together in San Francisco. I wanted you then and, you're right, that feeling hasn't changed. The problem is, I'm beginning to realize that my 'wants' are centered more in lust than love."

"So?" she responded unblushingly. "At least that's a start. Maybe in time there will be more. Let's just enjoy what we have for now and whatever else happens will happen."

"You don't understand," I answered. "That's not enough for me anymore."

Carole looked at me, puzzled.

"I don't get it. I'm not asking for a church wedding and a lifelong commitment, Kris. I just want to spend the night with you. That's all."

"That's it?"

"That's it."

"This is insane. I think there's a small stereotype reversal going on here. Men are supposedly the heavy breathers panting after one-night stands where no commitment is required."

"I just thought . . . well, I mean . . . " Carole fumbled for words, appearing uncertain now, for the first time this evening.

"You thought we'd spend the night together and go our separate ways tomorrow?"

There was no response. She just stood there, hands at her sides, in the middle of the room.

"To be totally honest, part of me would like that very much," I continued. "But we have to work together tomorrow. And the next day and the day after that."

"Are you . . . " she hesitated, "you know . . . "

"Am I gay? No. Trust me on that. But I've got to be honest with you. And with myself too. The truth of the matter is that I am confused right now. About you. About me. About us.

"We were raised differently, Carole. Our folks and the church gave us a different value system than we're talking here tonight. Since high school, I've dreamed of what is now coming to pass for me. All the stuff that success is supposed to bring. Fame, money, a home of my own. Somebody to love. Well, it's here. I've got it. And, now that it's here, what it all means is still a big question. Especially the 'somebody to love' part. I just wouldn't be able to handle a 'business as usual' relationship every day if we went ahead with tonight. I'm not like Tom."

"I can see that." Each word was charged with resignation and mixed with a growing anger.

"I've done some crazy stuff in my youth," I went on, trying to put the best face on what was quickly becoming an ugly moment, "and I've been lucky. I guess I'm finally starting to grow up or something. Why else would I turn down such a beautiful lady?"

Carole stepped back.

"I've got to go," she said, eyes glistening as she glanced first at her watch, then at me.

"Are we okay?" I asked, as she picked up her sweater and walked to the door.

She nodded. "I have to admit that I'm not used to throwing myself at someone and being turned down. You've just wasted the best offer you'll ever get, Kris Lauring."

"Hey, let's back up a bit here. We can still be good friends without being bad lovers. Can't we?"

"You are a different character, Kris," she answered coldly. "How did show biz ever come up with someone like you?"

I ignored that one and extended my hand. "I'll walk you to your car."

"Thanks, but don't bother. I can find it myself."

Without another word, she closed the door and was gone.

Forty. Kristian

I have to admit I didn't do a lot of sleeping that night. She was gone, but I couldn't get her out of my mind. Every time I closed my eyes, there she was, brushing back a playful strand of hair, playing more the role of model than assistant producer-director in her figure-flattering ivory top and flowers-on-black skirt. *Role-playing? Is that what it was?*

Early on Saturday morning I went to the studio and sat in my office jotting notes on the margins of several letters and memos so that Jill Aston, the young woman who was acting as my assistant for the time being, could construct the appropriate responses and I could drop by on Monday afternoon to sign them.

After finishing, I wandered out through the building trying to jump-start my emotions, stopping by Security to say hi to Sam, the always friendly African-American head of the department. I paused to look at some of the costumes and other memorabilia draped over mannequins and exhibited in the windows at Wardrobe. Usually, I'm too preoccupied to stop and check out the craftsmanship that others are contributing to my industry.

Taking the time to look more closely, I could see that real talent was apparent in the work on display. *Who are these people who spend their time behind these windows cutting, piecing, sewing works of costume art together? Without them the actors and actresses would be hopelessly incapable of doing their jobs. If Dad were running this show, he'd know these people all by name, wouldn't he? I could run into them in the cafeteria and not even recognize their faces. I need to stop by sometime during the week and visit for a few minutes.*

I continued walking. *What's going on with my head this morning? Here I am thinking about Dad again. Well, I can't blame last night on him. I did that one all by myself. Maybe that's why I'm feeling so morose.*

Even though it was Saturday, I noticed Tony sliding a key into the Graphic Arts Photography Department door. We talked briefly about nothing in particular and then he disappeared inside. I waved to Sandy Carlson as she walked across to a studio to do the weekend news for the network's local affiliate station.

Finally, bored and restless, I left.

The weather was warm enough and sunny, so I spent the remainder of the day back at my apartment complex reading by the pool. And thinking. It was the first time in days that I hadn't worked on some aspect of the show or pieced together the embryonic beginnings of a future monologue. I tried writing a letter to Kat. I owed her one, probably two, but I wasn't in the mood.

Carole kept moving sinuously back and forth through my thoughts. The attraction was very strong but, the more I thought about it, the more I had to admit it was almost wholly physical. She's bright and intelligent, but an enigma in so many other ways.

I made a mental note to ask Regina Levine about her at our meeting next week. Regina had some papers for me to sign on Monday. If anyone would know about Carole Upton, or any other Hollywood personality for that matter, she would. From the amount of time I had spent with her thus far, I was confident that she would've made a bang-up gossip columnist.

I dove into the clear, refreshing water, swimming back and forth until I was exhausted. Finally, pulling myself from the pool, I stretched out on a towel. *What's the matter with me? Why am I so restless?*

Later, as darkness settled over my spacious new home, I surfed back and forth through the television channels without finding anything worth watching. Sometimes I wonder if this world in which I've cast my lot really is a wasteland.

Pursuit

THE FOLLOWING SUNDAY MORNING, after coffee and the newspaper, I stared out the window for a long while. Finally, I put on a shirt and shorts and went for a walk.

About four blocks from my apartment, I started past a large church that I had noticed before. It is an attractive building, at the top of a gentle slope, surrounded by palm trees and flowering shrubs. The grounds are beautiful and today the parking lot was full. I glanced at my watch just as a huge church bell, mounted on a wooden frame off to one side, began ringing, signaling worshipers that it was time.

Almost before realizing it, I angled off the sidewalk and came to a halt, watching as the last of the parishioners hurried from their cars and climbed the steps. It's hard to explain, but all at once I had this intense yearning to join them. The fact that I wasn't dressed appropriately crossed my mind, but then I saw a young couple in walking shorts headed up the steps and my casual apparel felt more acceptable. Maybe I could slip in the back without being noticed.

A balding man in a blue sport jacket, tie, and gray slacks greeted me with a handshake, a smile, and the church bulletin. I watched his eyes for any sign of disapproval about the way I was dressed. If he was turned off by my being there, he didn't show it. I couldn't help but smile and wonder what old Deacon Harden might have done under similar circumstances, bless his stony little heart.

The choir and four people dressed in white clerical robes stood in the central doorway leading to the sanctuary. Two of those in clerical garb were women, which struck me as being a bit odd. I walked to the left and entered through a smaller side door.

There was an occasional empty seat, but the place was surprisingly full. The sign outside had identified it as St. Margaret's Church. I thought at first that it must be Roman Catholic, except I couldn't figure the women in clerical robes. Maybe the Pope had finally bitten the dust and altered his position on an all-male clergy. No, I would have heard about something that momentous.

I'd never heard of Saint Margaret and wondered who she might be. As it turned out, the bulletin didn't tell me, but at least I discovered that St. Margaret's was an Episcopal church and, according to the bulletin, it was "part of the original church founded by Jesus Christ with His Apostles." I guess you can't beat that for a recommendation, can you?

There were lots of 'gray hairs' in the congregation. That's what Kat and I used to call the seniors in Dad's church. But, interestingly, several young couples were scattered throughout as well. I figured that there must be a Sunday School for the children and youth because very few were with their parents.

In the pew directly in front of me, though, sat a young couple with an infant asleep in a baby carrier. She was beautiful, all dressed in white. The mother happened to turn around and caught my admiring look. "She's being baptized today," she said in a low voice. I nodded and smiled, trying to imagine Carole and me in their place.

I also thought it was good that Dad was not here to see this. Infant baptism was certainly not a part of his tradition, that's for sure. As far as he's concerned, if you're not wet all over, you're not baptized. It was an amusing picture that came to mind. The way he does it, this kid would be one drowned puppy!

I looked around. The building itself was not pretentious, but it was beautiful. The architect and the people had captured the charm and appeal of their surroundings by the use of clear glass windows on either side of the sanctuary, as well as from the top of the high-beamed roof line to about halfway down the wall behind the pulpit. There was a sense of openness to the natural beauty of palm trees and flowering shrubs that more than made up for the lack of stained glass.

Attractive bouquets of flowers were situated on either side of the platform, while across the wall behind a Plexiglas pulpit and below the clear glass windows, ranks of pipes signaled the presence of an organ. Having grown up in churches that always seemed to have a tired look about them, I found this place refreshing.

When is the last time I've been in a church? Aside from a few friends' weddings, not since I left home for college. I guess I've done a really good job of rejecting this part of my past, haven't I? So why the sudden urge this morning?

Just then the organ came to life and the people stood and began singing. How did they know what to sing? I glanced through the bulletin and discovered a list entitled, "Music for 10 A.M. service," and decided that we must be at the Processional

Hymn 569. I reached for a hymnbook and followed along.

Kat and I used to call it the "hum" book because so many people, particularly the men, didn't bother singing. That did not seem to be the case this morning. Almost everybody was singing along as the choir moved through the doorway and down the center aisle, led by a young lad carrying a cross and two small girls, each bearing a candle. The three dressed in white stood waiting to follow. I wondered what had happened to the fourth one.

"How ya doin' this morning?"

I started at the close proximity of the deep voice and glanced over my shoulder to see who it was. I know the color must have drained from my face. Here was the missing cleric. White robe, green stole, a cross hanging from around his neck. The whole bit. So was he waiting for some response? I swallowed in disbelief. Out of all the people present, why had he chosen to say something to me?

"I'm okay," I mumbled incoherently.

"Wonderful," he smiled, and gave my shoulder a firm squeeze before falling in behind the rest of the procession. As he moved past me, I could feel my eyes burning. I blinked back an emotion that, for some unaccountable reason, was threatening to spill over.

I watched him stop again, a few rows down on the opposite side of the aisle, to greet a young couple with a baby. The experience of his casual greeting and the sight of this man pausing long enough to speak to the young parents brought to me a rush of warmth and acceptance that I hadn't felt for . . . for a long time. I started to relax and even tried singing a little on the last verse of "God the Omnipotent," a song I'd never heard before in my life.

The service turned out to be totally different from anything I'd ever experienced. The rector, as the Reverend D. Collins Hanford was identified in the bulletin, greeted the people with the same enthusiastic warmth he had offered me. I got the feeling that this wasn't just another duty. This guy was really glad we were there!

As the hour progressed, different leaders led the congregation in the Eucharistic service. Now and then it was difficult to distinguish between clergy and laity. They followed an order printed in a Worship Booklet, excerpted from *The Book of Common Prayer.*

At various times, the ministers, clergy, choir, and people

united in the same actions and voiced the same words. I kept busy trying to follow along in the bulletin, the worship booklet, and the hymnbook. It occurred to me that to be a good Episcopalian, you really needed three hands.

The rector's message was short, only about ten minutes. He spoke of people who were standing about in life's hallways, waiting for an invitation to enter The Room. I knew that he was talking about me. I was in one of those hallways. The important thing, he said, was to accept people wherever we find them in life and then lead them gently forward.

I found myself comparing his message to one my father might have given. It lacked the biblical content Dad would have included and was decidedly shorter. Yet the simple truth of his message carried with it a profundity that was hard to escape.

The bulletin declared that this church was, among other things, an evangelical church, "proclaiming Christ Crucified and Risen and affirming the need for a personal commitment to Him." I understood this. It was the same message I had grown up with under my father's preaching.

On the opposite page, however, I noticed an announcement for beginner and intermediate level Line Dancing classes, an E.C.W. Fashion Show, and an AIDS Candlelight Vigil on the lawn in front of a nearby hospital. I smiled at this bewildering dichotomy. The "proclaiming" might be the same, but these announcements would never make it into Dad's church bulletin. Much too liberal for his tastes. *Maybe that's why I'm enjoying this so much.*

Suddenly everyone was standing again as the leader invited the people to recite the Nicene Creed. That such a Creed even existed had escaped my religious upbringing, and I was unsure even where to find it until the person next to me pointed it out in the Worship Booklet. I joined in the recitation.

We believe in one God,
   the Father, the Almighty,
   maker of heaven and earth,
   of all that is, seen and unseen.
We believe in one Lord, Jesus Christ,
   the only Son of God,

eternally begotten of the Father,
God from God, Light from Light,
true God from true God,
begotten, not made,
of one Being with the Father.
Through him all things were made.
For us and for our salvation
he came down from heaven:
by the power of the Holy Spirit
he became incarnate from the Virgin Mary,
and was made man.
For our sake he was crucified under Pontius Pilate;
he suffered death and was buried.
On the third day he rose again
in accordance with the Scriptures;
he ascended into heaven
and is seated at the right hand of the Father.
He will come again in glory to judge the living and the dead,
and his kingdom will have no end.
We believe in the Holy Spirit, the Lord, the giver of life,
who proceeds from the Father and the Son.
With the Father and the Son he is worshipped and glorified.
He has spoken through the Prophets.
We believe in one holy catholic and apostolic Church.
We acknowledge one baptism for the forgiveness of sins.
We look for the resurrection of the dead,
and the life of the world to come. Amen.

The beauty and power of those words was stunning. It was the essence of the Gospel message with which I was familiar, but concisely put in understandable terms.

Where did this come from?

I started to read through it again only to be interrupted by an assistant rector who now led us in the prayers of the people, in which everyone participated responsively. In my childhood church-attending years, the people used to pray out loud and all at once, but without unity of thought. I never understood what they were saying. Even the leader occasionally had a hard time being heard. This was somewhat the same, and yet strikingly different.

After the offering and Eucharistic prayers, the rector invited all baptized Christians, including children, to come forward and receive Holy Communion. I watched as the front rows of people started forward. Row by row they flowed into the outside aisles, kneeling at the altar, receiving communion, and then returning down the center aisle to their respective pews. I heard the choir singing "Breathe on me, Breath of God, 'til I am wholly Thine . . . " a song that I actually remembered from my youth. Then, a woman stepped forward to play "Sweet Hour of Prayer" on handbells. That one we sang a lot in my dad's church!

All of a sudden, I was aware of tears welling up in my eyes. I stuffed the worship booklet in my waistband, dropped the hymnal in the pew, and sprinted out the door and down the church steps with the sounds of choir and congregation singing the final hymn ringing in my ears.

Later that afternoon, I sat by the pool and pondered the morning at St. Margaret's. It had been an altogether different religious experience. An attractive place. An unfamiliar worship style. A comforting, yet disturbing encounter . . . with what? A denomination? A white-robed rector? A childish emotion? What? One thing was for certain. I had been given a Creed to contemplate that, if true, would not tolerate my sitting on the fence any longer. Not if I was determined to really be honest with myself. It required a personal vote. For or against.

I could almost hear Dad giving one of his impassioned altar calls.

Forty-one. Kristian

I lunged from pillow to telephone, hardly aware of what I was doing, and heard myself mumble an incoherent "hello" in the dark.

"Hi, Kris."

"Kat! Is that you, Kat?" I looked at the clock—quarter to three! "Hey, it's good to hear your voice." I knew there must be something wrong. Why else would she call at this ungodly hour? I rubbed the sleep from my eyes and in a matter of seconds I had the bed lamp turned on and was alert, listening to both her words and the strained tone of her voice. It was unspoken, but definitely there. At last came the opportunity to casually ask, "So, then what's on your mind?"

"Kris, I . . . we need you."

"Well, here I am," I responded, trying to keep a lightness in my tone.

"No, I mean I *need* you. To come here."

What followed for the next few minutes was so far removed from my list of personal possibilities that I had to pinch myself to be sure that I was not dreaming. Kat's story was incredible. My little sister? I could hardly make myself believe it. If it had been anyone else at this hour, with this kind of story, I would've hung up. But by the time we were finished, I was convinced I had to go.

I put the receiver back, rolled out of bed, and padded barefoot over to my desk. Off to one side lay the Worship Booklet from St. Margaret's. It was open to page 3. For at least the tenth or twelfth time since last Sunday, I reread the Nicean Creed.

What an incredible coincidence! I read it for the first time last Sunday and haven't been able to put it away since. Now, this Sunday, Kat wakes me up and tells me that old Pete may have been having second thoughts on all this stuff.

A wave of unexpected sadness broke over me.

It was like the time my best friend, who was seven, told me that he and his family were spending the holiday at his grandparents' house in the mountains. I went home and asked if we could spend the holidays with our grandparents, not certain what "grandparents" were actually, because I had never been around any of my own. The idea just sounded appealing. Mom became very pensive and somber as she informed me that I had no grandparents.

It left me with an empty feeling, the kind you'd have if an uncle you never knew suddenly died and left every relative a part of his estate. Everyone, that is, except you. You never anticipated anything in the first place; but, now that you knew of his existence, the disappointment over his demise and his lack of acknowledging that you were there in his thoughts, along with everybody else, hurt all the more.

When I asked why I had no grandparents, Mom said that they were all dead. Somehow that didn't seem fair, but I saw that it pained her to talk about it and so I never brought it up again.

"I think the Lord knew you were supposed to be here, so He has made certain that you are ready."

That's what Kat said when I told her that I'd just acquired a passport. I tried to push that one off lightly, but the events of the past few days were too notable to be tossed aside as "coincidental."

I reached for the phone again and dialed the airline's reservation number. "There's a flight leaving at eight o'clock," I was told. "There are two first-class seats available to New York. Alitalia will be your connection from there to Istanbul, via Rome. There are still two first-class seats available on that flight as well." I choked when she told me the price and then reserved both seats all the way. My watch told me that it was nearly three-thirty.

Next, I got Jim Stanton out of bed. Jim is the President of Entertainment and also happens to be my boss. I ran the details and possibilities past him for the next ten minutes. I didn't say so, but I was going whether or not he said yes. Fortunately for my expense account, and probably because he was half asleep, he agreed we should move on it.

"Normally this would be a News Department item," he said, "but if your archaeologist friend is giving us an exclusive and he'll deal only with you, then get out there as quickly as you can. I'll work it out with Eberbeck when he gets in from New York this afternoon. Take one of our camera guys with you. I'll see if we can break loose some more help from London. This just might be what we're looking for to launch the 'Kris' show."

I woke up Jack Millerton and fed him the details. He's forty-seven, twice-divorced, with one kid married and the other in college. That made him my first choice. No one to say good-bye to. He promised to be at the airport by seven with all his gear.

Tom Knight's home number was next. I needed to move quickly, but he should be informed about what was happening in order to plan for my absence during the week ahead. One ring. I glanced at my watch. Four ten. Two rings. *Hurry up and answer, Tom. I've got things to do.* Three rings.

"Hello?"

I froze for an instant.

I had expected Tom to answer. Instead, it was a woman's voice.

Was it Leslie, the starlet I'd heard about? Or had Connie Sandlewood finally succumbed to Tom Knight's unflagging charms?

"Hello? Who is this?"

Her voice was edged with both sleep and exasperation.

I opened my mouth but the words disappeared.

It wasn't Leslie whom I had awakened. It wasn't Connie Sandlewood, either.

But I knew who it was.

I swallowed back an overpowering urge to throw up and dropped the receiver back on the hook.

Let the two of them figure it out on their own on Monday!

Forty-two. Ibrahim

Monday, 15 September,
0630 local time
Kilçilar

The day of Kris' arrival began early for Ibrahim. Before breakfast, he met with Ben Hur and Rocco. Since the escape from *Kilçilar*'s amazing tomb of the dead, several things had happened.

After first confirming that the letters and the jar were still safe inside, the two foremen had set up a round-the-clock guard on Ibrahim's tent. As they discussed between them who could have carried out such a transgression, it didn't take them long to agree on their number one suspect.

Dr. Gürer El!

After talking it over the next day with Ibrahim, the three were in accord. As to motive, Ibrahim drew from Dr. Üzünal's initial warning. Somehow he had become suspicious and, when opportunity presented itself, had slipped into the tent and found the letters. Other than Ben Hur, there was no one else in the camp who had a scrap of capability at reading the ancient Greek. It had to be El. There was no one else. They were certain that the deed had been birthed in the man's fundamentalist Islamic fervor.

Ibrahim kept turning the matter over in his mind, wondering how Dr. El would receive his accusation. He did not relish the moment of confrontation with this man who was clearly his elder in years and in professional experience.

He had tried to reach Dr. Üzünal again to seek his counsel. This time it was the maid who assured him that the master of the house would be returning to his home the following Saturday. That was much too late; something had to be done before then. Ibrahim told the foremen that one of them would need to join him in meeting with Dr. El. They could decide which one. Rocco flipped the coin. Ben Hur lost.

The morning had awakened in the glow of brilliant sunshine. The air snapped with early autumn crispness as the crew left their breakfast dishes and straggled off toward *Kilçilar's* entrance for another day's work. Ben Hur and Rocco stood in front of the cave giving orders, patting first this and then that one on the shoulder, offering words of encouragement and instruction as the workers shuffled into the day's routine.

Rocco said something to Ben Hur, then slapped his shoulder before disappearing into the workplace. Ben Hur stood motionless for a moment, then turned and started back toward Ibrahim.

"You ready to tackle Islam's answer to the Hasidim?" asked Ben Hur as he came up alongside.

Ibrahim chuckled at that. He was acquainted with this most pious and ultraorthodox of Jewish sects and their commitment to a more mystical approach to Judaism. Originating in the seventeenth century in Eastern Europe, under the leadership of the Rabbi Baal Shem Tov, they were also the most visible Jews with their black hats, long black coats worn over tieless white shirts, and beards and side curls in their hair.

"Where did the Hasidim ever come up with their religious uniform, Ben Hur?" Ibrahim asked with sudden curiosity. "Do you know?"

"Sure. The style comes from late medieval Poland. Looks like it too, doesn't it? They wear those getups summer or winter. It reminds them that they are less than God and rids them of vanity. At least that's the idea. If you ask me, I think some of them have become more vain as a result, but that's neither here nor there."

"That's it? That's all there is to it?"

"Well, their clothing also depicts mourning over the temple which they insist will be rebuilt to accommodate the return of the Messiah."

"And when Messiah comes they can shed those awful clothes?"

"I'm not really clear on whether that's their hope. It certainly would be mine."

"How do you feel about all that?"

"The Hasidim? It's a free country. I don't care much for them, but I'm sure the feeling is mutual. I see them as modern-day Pharisees. A lot of them are too busy studying to work, and they refuse to serve in the military, citing religious convictions.

"For me it's different. Israel is my religion *and* my Messiah. I've fought Messiah's enemies all of my life and will probably be called on to do so again. And although I don't agree with those black-coated other-worldlings, I'll give my life to see to it that they, along with every other Jew, have the chance to live in peace and worship the way they want to."

"Anee mevin," Ibrahim replied in Hebrew. *I understand.*

Ben Hur nodded. He liked this Turk. Aside from knowing his craft better than most archaeologists with whom he had ever worked, Ibrahim was a good man. He gave those around him consideration and respect. First, for their professionalism and a job well done, and second, for their own uniqueness as human beings. Ben Hur saw it in the way he treated even the lowliest of the working staff. And he had felt it again just now as he stood beside him this morning.

"All right," said Ibrahim, "let's get this over with."

The two men strolled slowly toward Dr. El until they reached his table. Smoke curled up from the long ash of a cigarette propped on the edge of a small dirty dish. The canvas over the table flapped as chilly gusts of wind whipped around its stakes. All was quiet except for the wind and the small tool and brush that El was using to clear away the residue of the centuries from a Hittite tablet. He looked up from his work, but did not smile or greet them.

"Sit down," he said in a monotone, motioning for them to occupy the bench opposite him. He put the brush to one side and looked steadily into the unsmiling faces of his visitors.

"To what do I owe the honor?" he asked finally, folding his hands on the tabletop and returning their seriousness with his own unsmiling gaze.

"It's difficult to know where to begin," Ibrahim said. "I've asked Ben Hur to join us because I think it important to have a third party privy to our conversation."

"Humph," El grunted, as he glanced at Ben Hur. Ibrahim had the feeling that the man was not impressed with this Jew's credentials to be a witness to any discussion.

"Recently someone entered my tent without authorization," Ibrahim began. "This person not only entered without authorization, but very skillfully opened my locked file and removed its contents as well."

"And what might that have been?" Dr. El asked, his eyes never leaving the young overseer.

"The contents included an ancient vase and two letters dating back to the fourth century."

"Were they items from the underground city?"

"Yes."

"What were they doing in your file cabinet?"

"I placed them there out of concern over how best to handle their discovery."

"I see. You were not planning to keep them for your own purposes? I can imagine something as valuable as two fourth-century parchments might fetch a fair price from the right collector."

Ibrahim's eyes narrowed and his nostrils flared. Smuggling artifacts out of an archaeological site to be sold on the black market was not uncommon and was something each project director had to constantly guard against. The implication of wrongdoing on his part was unusual, however, and he was silent for a moment, struggling to regain his composure. The accuser had just become the accused. *He's a sly fox. I'd better be careful.*

"It's well within the prerogative of a project director to retain control over any artifacts removed by him or any member of his staff," said Ibrahim.

"Is it his right to keep the discovery to himself and fail to disclose his findings to anyone?"

"No," Ibrahim responded resolutely, "but he is given broad latitude in determining to whom he will make disclosure and when. That is his right and his alone. Would you not agree?"

Ben Hur had shifted so that he could see both men's faces, Dr. El's directly, along with Ibrahim's profile. He noted that El blinked at Ibrahim's last statement, but made no effort to answer the question. His hands were still folded in front of him.

"Dr. El, I regret that I must ask you this question," Ibrahim went on, "but I'm left with no choice. To understand the unusual value of these items, the person who entered my files would need the ability to expertly handle and read the ancient parchments. The content, as well as photos of the letters, appeared over the weekend in the *Turkish Daily News.* To the best of my knowledge, besides myself, there is only one here who has a working knowledge of ancient Greek.

"If I am wrong, this is your opportunity to correct me. Dr. El, did you enter my tent, examine the letters, and provide the *TDN* with the information needed for their news article? What do you say?"

"I say that you were wrong, Dr. Sevali. It was wrong of you to secrete those letters in your file. I do not believe for one minute that you intended to turn them over to the Museum. You saw their inherent value and I believe you determined to sell them, keeping the money for your own personal use."

"You can't be serious," Ben Hur exploded, his face turning a deep red. "Ibrahim has an impeccable reputation. As the leader here, there's nothing untoward in his action that I can see. Especially when it was something he turned up himself and that he felt was potentially inflammatory. I applaud the wisdom of his actions!"

"I would expect as much," Dr. El sneered contemptuously, his eyes burning with animosity. He leaned forward and gripped the side of the workbench. "In whom did you confide, Mr. Project Director? Your friend here? Or, did you suggest to our Mr. Valetti that the Vatican might be interested in what you found? No? Then perhaps you met with your American . . . female friend so that a deal could be consummated with a museum in New York or Chicago?"

"Enough!" responded Ibrahim, his voice hoarse as the muscles in his jaws worked overtime while he fought to keep from reaching across the table in anger. "You've stated your feelings quite clearly, Dr. El, but you have not answered my question. Did you enter my tent, break into my locked file, remove the letters in order to study and photograph them? Did you then contact the *TDN* and provide the information for their exposé?"

"And if I say that I did?" Dr. El asked, his lips curling into a tight, defiant smile.

"Then I ask if you are also responsible for the death of Renée Patry and for the explosion that was intended to send Ms. Lauring and me to our deaths?"

"You are a young liberal fool, Dr. Sevali," El snarled. "No better than your *yahudi* friend here. I hold no respect for you whatsoever. Allah will judge you for such false accusations, and I refuse to speak of these matters any further!"

"Then I have no other choice but to relieve you of your responsibilities, Dr. El. I'm asking you to vacate the premises. I'll report my action to the Museum officials in Ankara as well as to the police. What happens after that is up to them."

"You have no idea what we have here, do you?" Dr. El's voice rose as he spit out the words. "These letters will most certainly reinforce Islamic beliefs with regard to the Prophet Isa. All along we've said that Isa is not divine. Now you have in your possession a letter that invokes the same thought. One that is written by their key leader. Isa is not God come down in the flesh! He's a man, Sevali, like you and me. True Muslims have always believed this and now the great Saint Peter confirms it!"

"But the documents have not yet been examined by experts, Dr. El," Ibrahim rejoined. "To break into my locked file was criminal. And to release this story prematurely was a gross error in judgment on your part. It will only result in chaos throughout the religious world."

Dr. El stood up, his thin smile almost triumphant, while his countenance irradiated loathing and abhorrence. "On that I'm obliged to agree, Mr. Project Director. I hope you have a good time fighting off the wolves and rubbing this new coat of tarnish from your 'unblemished character'!"

El backed away from the table as the others rose from where they had been sitting. Ben Hur watched El shake his finger at Ibrahim and shout, "Your pandering to the non-Islamic religious world and refusal to reinforce the centuries-old beliefs that we hold as truth is unforgivable. In Allah's sight, you are dangerously close to becoming a heretic. If I have anything to do with it, that is indeed the brand you will wear for the rest of your life. How will you live with that? Heretic!"

"Dr. El, I've had enough of your acrimonious behavior. I regretfully must ask you to leave *Kilçilar*. I want your tent cleared by noontime. Ben Hur will remain with you until you've packed your things. He will drive you as far as Kayseri. I'll prepare a report, citing our discussion and my decision to relieve you of all duties. It will be forwarded to Dr. Süleyman Akin at the Ankara Museum. You will receive a copy. I'll also be reporting the incidents that have recently occurred here to the local police. I'm sure you will be hearing from them as well.

"Islam's modern disgrace is tied to the fanatic fundamentalism that permits you, and others like you, to engage in wrongdoing and then justify it in Allah's name. I do not intend to be a party to such distorted thinking. At the appropriate time and place, I'm sure that Dr. Akin will provide you with ample opportunity to present your side in this matter. Until then, iyi günler." *Good day.*

The two men glared at one another for a long moment. Dr. El's fists were clenched. The muscles of his jaw expanded and contracted furiously and he took a half step toward Ibrahim as though to physically assault him. Then, he turned abruptly and stalked off toward his tent. Ben Hur hesitated beside Ibrahim and put his hand on the young man's shoulder.

"He should never have been permitted to come here in the first place," muttered Ben Hur. "Don't worry. You did a good job. You handled yourself well. It is a hard thing."

Ibrahim sighed wordlessly and with hands in pockets, began walking toward his tent. He had now discovered yet another side of the responsibility that goes with being a leader. He didn't like it. Except that it did resolve things somewhat. *At least for now, we can concentrate on cutting our loses and finishing the job.*

By eleven o'clock, all that remained of Dr. El's departure was a cloud of dust behind the Land Rover loaded with his personal effects.

At twelve noon a cloud of dust trailed behind another van, this one headed into the camp. It was a film crew and reporter from CNN, making the first of what Ibrahim thought was sure to be numerous unannounced quests for information, stories, photos, and video sessions. He was not looking forward to this at all and concluded that Katrina's brother was getting in none too soon. If he was as good as Katrina insisted, then he would know best how to deal with the forthcoming packs of newshounds.

Forty-three. Kristian

1430 local time
Istanbul

By two-thirty Monday afternoon, Jack and I were greeted by an Irishman named K.C. Murphy, who had arrived from London three hours earlier. Together we walked through Istanbul's Atatürk Airport. Because of our first-class accommodations, we had been able to rest comfortably during the flight and felt about as good as world travelers possibly can, given that we'd been at this since early Sunday morning.

We confirmed our Turkish Airline flight to a city named Kayseri. Erkilet airport, we were told, was the nearest and only commercial airport around this *Kilçilar* place. I was able to reach Kat by phone to let her know our arrival time. After some initial confusion, during which we discovered that all domestic flights originated at another terminal by the name of Yesilköy, we boarded a THY Airlines bus and managed to show up fifteen minutes before takeoff.

The sun was setting over Central Anatolia's massive plain as the aircraft lined up for its final approach to our destination. For the last hour we'd been flying over Turkey's heartland, an enormous khaki-colored plateau, dotted with rectangular green

320

blankets and tiny clumps of doll houses cuddled together against wrinkled hills. As we approached Kayseri, the flight attendant pointed out to us the city's most impressive attribute, barely visible in the gathering darkness. It was the nearby snowcapped volcano, Erciyes Dagi, towering over an otherwise prosaic landscape at a height of nearly four thousand meters.

Forty-four. Ibrahim

1430 local time
Kilçilar

At two-thirty that afternoon, Rocco appeared at the tent entrance. Ibrahim looked up from the bed where he was resting before joining Katrina for the journey to Kayseri's airport. Her brother was due to arrive in a matter of hours.

"Sorry to interrupt, Ibrahim," apologized Rocco as he ducked his head to enter, "but I knew you would want to see what we've found."

He held out a clay jar, about eighteen inches long and five inches across. Ibrahim rolled to a sitting position on the edge of the bed.

"Where did you find it?" he asked, taking it in hand.

"Down in 'bone alley,'" Rocco answered irreverently. "We went ahead and strung lights down the staircase and into that room you found like you told us to. Man, that is really weird down there! I couldn't wait to get out!"

"I understand the feeling."

"I'm not sure how much you remember about the place . . . "

"Some things I'll never forget," Ibrahim interrupted, his mind creeping back down the ancient steps into *Kilçilar's* house of death.

"Anyway, I had one of the guys count the bodies as best he could," continued Rocco. "It may not be totally accurate, because some of the skeletal structures have fallen into one another. But, as nearly as we can make out, the count is five hundred and forty-seven!"

For a moment Ibrahim could think of nothing to say. He mind filled again with silent, bleached carcasses staring sightlessly at him through holes where eyes once were. He never dreamed the count would go so high.

"That's almost like opening a mass grave in Bosnia," Ibrahim said finally, trying to find some comparison. "Only there the bodies were just thrown together in huge piles. This is different, isn't it?"

"Different? I've never in my wildest nightmares seen anything that compares with this. It looks as though they simply sat down next to each other and died. There are no signs of chains or prison implements of any kind. Many of them are sitting there with hands folded over their abdomen. Man, I'm telling you, it is spooky! And there's one person who sat apart from the rest alongside the remains of a small child, maybe eight or ten years old, I would guess. That's where we found this jar."

Ibrahim's mind flashed back to the scene as he remembered it by matchlight. *A skeleton by itself. The single skeleton we saw through the hole. We thought that it was the only one.*

"Have you checked it out?"

"There's a scroll rolled up inside. We didn't look any further."

"Then, let's see what you've found."

Ibrahim moved to his worktable where he carefully laid the clay vessel on its side. The scroll within was wrapped in linen. Gently, he withdrew the contents of the jar until it lay on the table cover that he had spread underneath.

For the next few minutes, he worked skillfully at cutting and peeling away the protective wrap. It was very much like the covering he had found around the other two letters. He was careful to preserve the linen so that, together with its contents, it could later be subjected to laboratory radiocarbon studies to determine its historical time frame. While Ibrahim was still engrossed in the task, Rocco wandered over to the mess tent and in a few minutes was back with cups of hot tea.

Ibrahim's cup was still half full when, after nearly two hours of tedious work, Katrina stopped by the tent. Ibrahim looked up in surprise, then glanced at his watch, suddenly realizing it was time to leave for the airport. He explained what Rocco's men had found, showing her the scroll that was unrolled almost all the way. Katrina shuddered at the memory of that terrible place with its unexpected horror.

"I can't leave this, now that I've begun," Ibrahim said apologetically. "I'm sorry. It's much too delicate. I've got to finish unrolling the parchment."

"I understand," Katrina answered, her hand briefly touching his. "So will Kris. Don't worry. Çali is driving anyway. He knows how to get there. If the plane is on time, we'll be back before it's very late."

"Perhaps I'll have something to tell you when you return," Ibrahim said, as he walked with her to the tent entrance. Her nearness and the smell of her freshly washed hair suddenly distracted him, setting off an intoxicating impulse to take her in his arms. Such wild, emotional surges were unusual for Ibrahim. It surprised him and left him feeling unexpectedly shaken. Being near this woman was affording a whole set of new discoveries that had nothing to do with archaeology!

Rocco sat on the edge of the bed, watching. Ibrahim was certain the Italian had discerned his feelings and was bemused by the thought that Rocco would be the first to applaud such an impetuous act. Instead, Ibrahim simply took her arm and led her outside. Even that very proper touch sent a stirring arousal of tender affection coursing through him.

It was hard to believe. Until now he had been too engrossed in his professional life for more than a casual attitude toward women. Although close to his mother and sisters, he had had no serious loves. His studies and his work were his wife and children.

Now, with a swiftness that he could not have imagined, that was all changing. This American beauty had broken through to his heart before he realized it was happening, rendering him defenseless against her charms. It was unfamiliar and wonderful, upsetting and exciting, and most of all, nerve-racking. All at the same time.

"Be careful," he admonished her, with a look of seriousness.

"Stay with Çali. Don't wander off alone at night in Kayseri."

"We probably won't even be in the city," Katrina laughed as she took his hand in hers. "Çali tells me the airport is well outside of town. I'm so excited about seeing Kris that I can hardly wait."

Çali was waving to them from beside the van. "Let's go or we'll not be there in time."

"See you later," Katrina said as she ran toward the van.

Ibrahim stood watching until the vehicle was enveloped in a cloud of dust. Then he turned back to the tent. Rocco had stretched out on the bed, eyes closed. Ibrahim went to the table and stared down at the scroll. The edges had deteriorated with time and there were some loose fragments that had completely separated from the main portion. Overall, however, it appeared to be in excellent condition, the result of the constant temperature and dryness in the cave room.

The clearly written scroll consisted of two parchment strips stitched together and measuring about fourteen by forty-two inches. The ancient letters on the parchment were suspended from faintly ruled lines. Certain words along the edges were missing due to deterioration. It appeared at first glance that some lines might be missing at the top, but the bottom portion had been rolled inside and was better protected.

With magnifying glass in hand, Ibrahim began the wearying task of examining the text itself. Rocco awakened from his brief respite, excused himself at the dinner hour, and disappeared outside. Ibrahim did not even notice. He was lost in the emerging contents of the scroll.

• • •

RUETERS. September 15.
Monday evening, 09/15, at six forty-five, the Atatürk Airport fell victim to the latest round of terrorism being inflicted on this troubled nation's populace. Terrorists were able to drive a van loaded with plastic explosives to within one hundred yards of the main terminal and trigger detonators by remote control. Fortunately, the main charge failed to go off. Police rushed in and sealed off the area while bomb experts dismantled the deadly device. In a telephone call to the main office of the Turkish Airlines, the Kurdistan Workers Party [PKK] claimed credit for the disruption.

At eight o'clock the same night, a smaller but far more deadly explosion occurred in the Topkapi Bus Terminal, located on the European side of Istanbul. First uncon-firmed reports point to an apparent suicide bombing as a pickup truck, loaded with explosives, was driven between two city buses and detonated by the driver. Thirteen people are known to be dead and twenty-three hospit-alized with wounds, five of these critically.

• • •

Forty-five. Kristian

We found Kat waiting impatiently in the terminal with a pleasant-looking driver named Çali. She threw herself into my arms with the abandon of a long-lost sister which, in a way, she was. We had our personal things in hand, packed in carry-on bags that had been cleared through Customs in Istanbul.

The camera gear had been checked with baggage, however, and the driver insisted on remaining with Jack and K.C., until the equipment had been recovered and checked to be certain there were no problems.

Meanwhile, Kat and I stood off to one side and tried to catch up. It had been more than three months since we had last seen one another. Kat said that Dr. Sevali had been detained with matters at the work site and had sent his regrets at not being able to welcome us personally.

When we finally reached the main road and headed toward *Kilçilar*, Kat's description of the underground city and the story of their entrapment made the kilometers pass quickly. Later, she pointed out the little village the project was named after, and just as quickly we were past it, bumping over the last leg of our journey to the work camp itself.

"I can hardly believe this," I admitted at last.

"What?" asked Katrina, her head resting sleepily on my shoulder.

"That you are here, in the first place and, second, that I'm here with you. Just this past Sunday morning, I was resting comfortably in my own wonderful bed in my brand-new apartment. Since then, Jack and I haven't even seen a bed, much less stretched out on one. Exactly what time is it here?"

Çali spoke up. "It's ten twenty-seven, boss."

"Where did you get this guy?" I asked.

"I'm not sure, but he comes in mighty handy," Katrina answered with a smile and a pat on Çali's shoulder. Çali grinned into the rearview mirror. Moments later, the van rolled to a stop.

"Welcome to *Kilçilar,* boss," Çali announced, as he jumped down from the driver's seat. "You'll be staying in the 'Sheraton' tonight. I'll go make sure your room is ready, okay?"

Everyone laughed and then stood around, checking out the darkened tent village. This Çali was quite a character. His jovial personality put us all at ease and helped to smooth out the travel creases.

Forty-six. Ibrahim

2235 local time
Kilçilar

When he heard the sound of voices outside, he was surprised to see total darkness beyond the tent entrance. He looked at his watch. Ten thirty-five.

Wiping his forehead with his shirt sleeve, Ibrahim leaned back in his chair and sighed. During the last several hours he had disappeared into another world, one that found its existence in books and, at times, in his most repelling imaginings. It was with a feeling bordering on disbelief that he withdrew from that world and emerged from the tent, inhaling the crisp fresh air. His attention turned to laughter coming from the figures standing near the camp's parked vehicles. It seemed almost a sacrilege, out of sync with the funereal thoughts that lined his mind with grotesque shadows.

Then Katrina's face materialized out of the darkness. At the sound of her voice calling to him, something deep inside broke apart and floated to the surface of his soul. What if he and Katrina had been standing in this same place . . . at another time . . . for the final time . . . like the others?

A sudden flood of emotion overwhelmed him. Ibrahim wiped at the dampness in his eyes.

Forty-seven. Kristian

"Here he comes now," exclaimed Katrina.

I saw the figure of a man, momentarily silhouetted as he emerged from one of the few tents that was still lit at this hour.

Katrina ran to meet him as Çali hurried off to make sure the accommodations were ready for *Kilçilar's* newest guests. I watched as she held the man's hand for a moment before releasing it as they came toward us. It was easy to see that these two had become good friends. Just how close I was interested in finding out.

Kat introduced Jack, K.C., and me and we shook hands with Dr. Ibrahim Sevali, field director for *Kilçilar*. Though I knew his age already, I was taken again that such a young man was in charge of this important project. He seemed unpretentious and modest, yet obviously he was very competent.

Kat had mentioned earlier that he was well on his way to becoming one of the most respected archaeologists in Turkey, even though he was only twenty-nine. She said he was a genius, according to those who had worked with him on other projects. I wasn't sure how Turkish geniuses were supposed to act, but he seemed pretty normal to me.

I watched the two of them together in the darkness, their faces visible in the moonlight. The way she looked at him when he spoke told me that this might be serious. *How about that? She goes half a world away and gets buried alive with a young Turk. I wonder what happened in there anyway.*

After a few minutes of polite chatter, Dr. Sevali, who insisted on being called Ibrahim, showed us to our tent. We said goodnight and Katrina and Ibrahim walked away together. The last I saw of them, they were headed in the direction of her tent, holding hands.

There were three cots in our tent, none of which looked too comfortable, but Jack and K.C. were in them and under the covers, snoring in record time.

I figured they were both more used to sleeping wherever they lay down than I was, but I closed my eyes to give it a try. My cot sagged from having been slept on before by some overweight Turkish dude. In terms of comfort, it was barely a step up from the floor. The thought, *I'll never get to sleep on this,* was the last thing I remembered.

Had an hour passed? Or was it two?

I awakened suddenly, in a cold sweat, with the blanket thrown back and my heart beating furiously.

She had come again! The woman.

Her long blond hair falling down around her shoulders.

She reaches out to me in my dream and I strain to see her.

She feels close this time . . . closer than ever. The outline of her face fades in and out. Then in again. Her lips . . . I don't remember seeing them before . . . they are moving . . . full and young and red . . . she's saying something . . . what is it? . . . her eyes . . . only shadows where her eyes should be . . .

A shiver ran up and down my spine. I lay back on the cot, but I stayed awake until the sun crept into our tent the next morning!

THE SOLITARY FIGURE REMAINED unseen less than thirty meters from Ibrahim and Katrina, watching quietly from his position behind the mess tent. As they turned away, he raised a cigarette cupped in the fold of his hand, and drew from it deeply, listening to the quiet exchanges of conversation between the two.

He waited until Ibrahim said goodnight to Katrina in front of her tent and slowly shuffled off toward his own. Two more quick drags and the cigarette burned brightly each time before it was finally ground out under the toe of a boot.

Anyone standing nearby would have been startled by the pensive, brooding eyes peering steadily from beneath a dirty baseball cap. Probing eyes, darting from one person to another.

The eyes of a hunter.

One used to stalking human game!

Forty-eight. The Inscription

Tuesday, 16 September, 0930 local time

Ibrahim motioned for Katrina and Kris to sit on the bed. Rocco and Ben Hur took the chairs in front of his desk. He paused briefly, his eyes moving slowly from one member of his tiny audience to the next. Then he looked down and without further words of explanation or introduction, began to read:

> *. . . staggered in . . . a severe head wound . . . surprised four days before while visiting his mother and . . . wept as he spoke of their . . . the nights moving secretly . . . bandaged . . . wound the best . . . Nic . . . hovered between life and . . .*

"The parchment from this point is almost entirely intact," he assured them.

> *. . . reported that as far as the eye could see, there was only devastation. Homes lay in ruins. We knew it must be true. Smoke from towns and villages in the distance had risen for days until the entire plateau had turned an ashen gray and the fetid smell of death lingered everywhere.*

Pursuit

Nicetas confirmed that the rivers were awash with the bodies and blood of little children together with mothers and fathers who died in each other's arms. He witnessed scraps of human flesh still clinging to swords from which the blood had not yet dried.

Horses ran roughshod over those who lay mortally wounded in the streets. A tragic horror is once again revisited on our people. What have we done to deserve this, Lord? Our ancestors' story is already written in unrequited pain! How can You permit it to happen again?

Nicetas declares that it is the same everywhere. At the center of the village where his mother and father died, pieces of wood were heaped in huge piles by the forced labor of villagers who yet remained alive. The wood was then torched and as the fires grew hot, those who had stacked it were bound. Young men of fighting age were put to the sword immediately as were small children.

Their women faced even greater horror as, in the firelight and amid terrified screams for mercy, the vanquishing horde tore the remaining children from their arms and threw them alive into the flames.

They then engaged in further brutal savagery by beating and raping and killing. Some mercifully died quickly. Others were still alive as the hands and arms of laughing, grunting soldiers lifted their defiled bodies from the ground and threw them into the blazing pyre!

It is hard to imagine God is permitting such a thing to take place. We know only that our forefathers were persecuted for their faith in the Lord Jesus and, for whatever reason, their fate has become ours as well.

A new trail of smoke rises from a tiny farm village on the not-so-distant eastern horizon, serving as added warning to those of us living in the area surrounding Derinkuyu and nearby Güzelyurt that Cappadocia has once again fallen prey to merciless tribes invading from the east. We know that everything happening there will soon be visited upon us. We must act quickly, according to our predetermined plan, or be lost.

Fathers abandon their fields and gardens and run to gather

up the children. Mothers collect remnants of food and drink and then join the others in a mad rush for the nearest entrance to the underground city. The city is our only hope!

As one of the village leaders, I go ahead to help organize our flight as best we can. Pulcheria comes soon after, bringing with her our only child, our beloved Theodora.

Soon, long lines of frightened, anxious people crowd in front of these small openings into the earth's bowels. They proceed in an orderly fashion along the designated escape routes. The openings and tunnels that lay beyond are not unfamiliar to us. Our people have spent major portions of their lives digging, carrying, camouflaging, and supplying these underground chambers against just such a day as this.

It is well after dark when the last citizen slips inside. We hear horses' hooves thundering toward us in the darkness. There is no time left. The enemy is upon us. Those who might still be outside our secret shelter are lost!

Several of us hurry to fit the stone into the entrance, a process that is repeated along all the tunnel openings. This has been rehearsed many times and we know that, from without, these stones fit well into the rocky terrain. It will be impossible to distinguish them in the darkness and difficult even in the light of day. My heart pounds with fear, but I do not show it to the others.

We establish guard contingents near the entrances and then join the rest who crowd farther into the underground chambers. Candles are used initially until everyone is settled into their assigned groups and levels. Then the candles are extinguished, unless an elder or group leader permits. In order to preserve the quality of air, much of our life underground must be carried on in the darkness.

Communal kitchens are organized in prearranged locations. Our women take inventory of food stocks. We carry water from the wells for use on each of the levels. Young ones help the old to their living areas. It goes well with a minimum of confusion.

Here, deep beneath the surface of the earth, the only sounds are those made by our neighbors, friends, and families, shuffling back and forth along the unlit passageways. It is a strange world, altogether other than the one we are used to.

Pursuit

We settle in to wait out the enemy. And as time affords, I sit with Pulcheria and our daughter and write on this parchment the word of our flight.

By the end of the second day, group leaders establish the count of people quartered on the various levels. The number is twenty-seven thousand, three hundred and ten. Sadly, we understand this to mean more than twenty-five hundred of our brothers and sisters are not inside. Will some break under torture and reveal where we are hiding?

People on each level are designated a two-hour period in which to go to the church for worship. Those of us waiting to enter can hear our neighbors weeping and softly crying out to God for mercy. It is this way twenty-four hours a day! When everyone has had opportunity, we begin again. We know this to be our most important activity, even more than eating, for we know the Lord Jesus is our only hope.

Days and nights are marked by observers peering through tiny openings in the earth's surface, no bigger than a mole hole. From these locations they are able to inform us as to what is happening outside. To our dismay, today we are told that some villagers known to us were seen being tortured, raped, and slaughtered like sheep.

To make matters worse, the invaders have established their camp directly over our heads. They know we cannot have gone far. Search parties scour the nearby hills and valleys and caves.

On the fifth day, enemy scouts locate one of our secret entrances. They drag the stone away and try to enter, but the narrow configuration of our tunnels, with their many twists and turns, anticipated just such a defensive breach and our young men are able to fight the invaders back.

But now we are discovered! The worst is yet to come!

The enemy can be seen and heard at the observation points, scurrying like ants in their relentless effort to find us. On day seven a second entrance is compromised, but we are again able to drive them back. Realizing that they have found our refuge, but are incapable of driving us out, the invaders are settling down to wait.

On day twenty-seven, observers report that as many as half the troops visible to them are being sent on their way to rout

out other innocents in villages and towns beyond our own. But the remaining force continues to play the waiting game.

A careful check of food supplies indicates that we can remain underground for at least six, perhaps eight more weeks before our situation becomes desperate. This should carry us well into winter's early snows when untenable weather may force our foes to leave the area.

On day thirty-nine, further disaster befalls us! Early in the morning hours, level five reports sickness. It is a man beset with a high fever. Before many hours have passed, he is having great difficulty breathing and there is also a noticeable swelling in the groin. His condition becomes increasingly severe.

On day forty-one, the man on level five has died. But now, three more experience the same symptoms. Our medicines are short in supply and inadequate for the task. We are unable to stem the spread of the sickness.

On the same day the first man died, levels six and seven also reported cases of illness. By day forty-seven it is clear that we are facing some terrible and devastating plague. Every level has at least one, and several up to eight or nine who are severely ill. The sickness attacks both sexes and every age. There does not seem to be any cure. We are powerless to fight back!

At last, we have begun moving those who are ill away from the others. We take them down the long staircase to the lowest chamber. Water is available there and, at first, what food we can share is sent down. However, most are too ill to eat and at last the decision is made to provide those confined to that place with only bread and water.

On day fifty-two, Pulcheria has fallen to the illness. My heart is torn apart at the thought of it! My beautiful Pulcheria! Her hand burns with fever when I hold it. She will not permit our lips to touch as we say our farewell. The carriers lift her and I follow them to the dreaded staircase. Then she is gone!

Even that day's report of the season's first winter storm can do nothing to allay my sorrows.

Death is now a daily ritual. The longer we wait in this place, the worse it becomes. We carry the dying partway *down the steps until we are met by those from below still strong enough to take them from our hands.*

Prayers go up constantly from every part of our underground city. Grief and sorrow is everywhere. Yet, nothing works. It is all to no avail. Our place of refuge is rapidly becoming a tomb, not a city.

One week after Pulcheria and I whispered our love to each other, my beloved Theodora is stricken with the death fever. This is too much! How does God possibly think that I can bear this?

When carriers come to take her to the stairway, I refuse their help. I lift my dearest Theodora in my arms and, over their behest, walk to the steps that descend into the darkness from which no one returns.

My friends try to stop me, insisting that I am well and still needed as a leader. But I cannot stay. Pulcheria is somewhere below, no doubt sleeping the Great Sleep. My heart is broken at having sent her away to die without me. There was nothing I could do. Theodora and others still living needed me. But I cannot send little Theodora to live her last hours without staying close by.

I take a candle, my writing implements, and a water jar with us and start down the steps. The dying who meet us halfway beg that I should give her to them and go back. I cannot. I cannot let my Theodora go down into this hell without her father. At last they understand, as we weep together and I thank them. Then I follow them down each stone step, with my precious Theodora in my arms, on what will surely be our final journey.

At the bottom of the steps I pause to take in the horror. People have been arranged in rows. Many have already died sitting up, leaning against the walls until there are no more walls. New death rows have begun at the feet of our dead comrades.

I found Pulcheria, only to wish that I had been spared the hellish vision that was my dearest love. I know that her remains do not contain her spirit! The Apostle Paul has said that to be "absent from the body is to be present with the Lord." And yet I find it impossible not to stare across the room at her. This terrible ache inside my chest will not go away. I never seem to run out of tears! Why, God? Why?

Theodora died painfully and pitifully on what I believe was day fifty-nine or sixty. I cannot be certain anymore. There is nothing left for me now.

Since my arrival in this place, the putrid smell of death only grows stronger. The hopelessly sick are still carried down the staircase. I help care for them as best I can. And I write down my thoughts. For whom, I cannot know. Perhaps only for myself to keep sane amid the cries of the dying.

What time is it? What day? How long will the enemy remain? In this region of shadows and darkness where there is no light of day, I have begun measuring time by those descending the staircase. This too will soon cease.

In these past hours I have known my time is short. The swelling has begun, just as in the others. I recognize the beginnings of the fever, but say nothing to alert anyone.

I have come to believe that God has given me these writing implements so that I might leave some record behind for those who survive. I will spend the time left to me with our child, as I inscribe my people's collective experience and my own as well.

For years we have kept alive the knowledge of the ancients. When others demanded that we destroy the pottery, images, carvings, and idols made by those who lived here before us, we stood against them. Even so, with the letters.

We taught our children that there is no spirit power in idols of wood or stone or metal. We fight against principalities and powers of darkness and these things are nothing more than history reminding us how far we have come. From superstition to the Savior! And yet our present darkness shows how far mankind has yet to go!

It grows more difficult to think clearly and to hold the pen in my hand. The candle flickers. It is almost used up, as am I. So many things I do not understand. So many questions. But now I prepare myself for my spirit's final journey from this place to where I will find waiting my Pulcheria and our lovely Theodora. I am sure of it. This is my sustaining joy. Together we go to meet our Savior!

When the barbarians have gone and those who sorrow return in mourning to this charnel house, I pray these words will comfort your hearts. Take with you from this place the faith that sustains each one you find here, as we approach the end of things that we know.

We believe in one God, the Father, the Almighty, maker of heaven and earth, of all that is, seen and unseen. We believe in one Lord, Jesus Christ, the only Son of God, eternally begotten of the Father, God from God, Light from Light, true God from true God, begotten, not made, of one Being with the Father. Through him all things were made. For us and for our salvation he came down from heaven . . .

"The writing is difficult to decipher from here," Ibrahim said, looking up from the parchment at Katrina, Kristian, Rocco, and Ben Hur. "I think the last phrase reads 'by the power of the Holy Spirit.' That's all. The remaining marks are unintelligible."

"By the power of the Holy Spirit he became incarnate from the Virgin Mary, and was made man. For our sake he was crucified under Pontius Pilate; he suffered death and was buried. On the third day he rose again in accordance with the Scriptures; he ascended into heaven and is seated at the right hand of the Father. He will come again in glory to judge the living and the dead, and his kingdom will have no end.

"We believe in the Holy Spirit, the Lord, the giver of life, who proceeds from the Father and the Son. With the Father and the Son he is worshiped and glorified. He has spoken through the Prophets. We believe in one holy catholic and apostolic Church. We acknowledge one baptism for the forgiveness of sin. We look for the resurrection of the dead, and the life of the world to come. Amen."

Each person watched spellbound as Katrina, eyes reverently closed, recited what seemed to be a continuation of the unknown scribe's thoughts. Ibrahim and the others were silent when she finished, full of wonder at what they had heard and what they were experiencing.

"I memorized it at seminary," she concluded, her voice soft and steady.

"The Nicene Creed."

It was Katrina's turn to stare at her brother.

"You were repeating the Nicene Creed," Kris said again with quiet deliberateness. "The final testimony that the man was leaving for those who would come later to find them. He was writing down the words of the Nicene Creed when he died. Only, apparently no one came. No one found it . . . or them . . . until you discovered this place."

"Kris, how did you know?" Katrina asked wonderingly, still looking at her brother seated beside her.

"You mean the Creed?" He chuckled as he gave her shoulder a gentle squeeze. "I went to church."

"What?" She was smiling now, wanting to know more, baffled by Kris' cryptic answer to her question.

"I'll tell you later, Kat. I guess I'm like everyone else here. I've been searching. You know, for ultimate truth, life's real purpose, and all that. I've just been looking in different places than the rest of you. Anyway, trust me, this is really too uncanny. I need some time to figure out what's going on myself. By the way, did anyone catch the reference to 'the letters'?"

Everyone nodded.

"What do you make of it?" asked Katrina.

"I'm not sure," answered Ibrahim. "I need to think about it for a while."

Kris turned to Ibrahim. "So when do we get inside? A few hours' sleep on those cots last night did wonders."

"When can you be ready?"

"We're ready. Jack and K.C. have been checking the equipment since early this morning. They're out taking above-ground footage now. You say the word and we're right behind you."

"What do we do about our CNN guests? And I've received word from Ankara that other American and European network news teams are on the way. Some will arrive today. Others tomorrow. The Vatican is sending a film crew from Rome. A news team is even flying in from Brazil. It's going to be a madhouse before very long."

"Are you asking for my suggestion?" asked Kris.

"Please."

"Appoint Mr. Hurstein here as your media coordinator."

"Hold on," Ben Hur sputtered with surprise as he stood to his feet. "I don't know anything about the media!"

"You don't need to. I'll help on that score. What you do know is this place and the discoveries that have been made here. You also know how to organize people, and Kat tells me that you speak Turkish, Hebrew, and English fluently. Anything else?"

"A little French and Spanish," Ben Hur admitted, looking down at the tent floor. "And some Deutsch."

"Good. You're perfect. You may have to sign in Portuguese to the Brazilians and I don't know what you'll do with the Japanese, but everything else will be fine."

"Japanese?" Ben Hur's brow lifted with a start. "Are they coming too?"

"The Japanese are always coming. They never stay home. It's too crowded there," Kris grinned. "Be cordial but firm to every media representative. Explain that your boss can't permit a wholesale onslaught on the underground city. Make the reasons obvious. They'll scream and beg and threaten and plead, but they'll also understand. It's just that they have a job to do and want to scoop every other news network or magazine while doing it. Assure them that you're going to help them, that you'll treat them all equally and fairly. Tell them that they will receive every possible consideration. Just be careful not to promise more than you can produce.

"Today, because I'm here already and you've promised me some extra consideration in return for serving as your media consultant, I'd like to go in first. But today is all I'm asking for. With whatever media teams are here tomorrow, we'll form up a representative pool of cameramen and one reporter. Let them choose from among themselves. You might even think about changing crews every day. Assure them that they'll all receive the 'guided tour' as soon as possible.

"In any event, give access only to those who will cooperate by assuring that the day's footage and their full reports will be made immediately available to the rest. Anybody caught breaking that rule is out. Daily press conferences with Ibrahim or whoever he designates should be set up and coordinated under your direction.

"Meanwhile, one big problem out here is going to be logistics for entertaining your 'guests.' How long before we can get some more tents and food? These city slickers will have a tough time foraging for themselves in a place like this."

"I've been assured that the military will be here no later than tomorrow with tents, a couple of extra field kitchens, and additional food supplies," said Ibrahim.

"Good. Maybe we can accommodate any early birds for one night. Got any more extra beds?"

"A few, I think."

"Okay, then. If they don't all show up at once, it should work. We'll play that by ear. Does it sound okay so far?"

Ibrahim nodded, then glanced at Ben Hur.

"Zeh beseder," Ben Hur muttered.

"What?" asked Kris.

"I said, 'That's okay,'" answered Ben Hur with a slow smile. "I'd rather supervise the work crews, but I can handle these guys. Actually I did something like this once in Israel while I was serving in the army."

"So you've more hidden talents, my friend?" said Ibrahim as he stood to his feet, smiling. "Well, in a couple of days we'll give you a grade on just how wonderful you have been as the world's host. Actually, I know you'll be excellent. Use Çali as your gofer. Meanwhile, Rocco, you're in charge of all the work crews for now."

Ibrahim looked around the tent and sighed heavily. He started toward the exit, then stopped, turning slowly back to the others.

"Just a minute. There's something else. What about the staircase?"

"What do you mean?" asked Rocco.

"When you broke through to us, you didn't break down a door. You came through a wall. Correct?"

Rocco nodded.

"Events have been happening so fast that I'd forgotten about that until right now. While Kat and I were sitting there, waiting, I remember wondering why these stone steps come to that point and then no farther. Why build them if they don't lead to somewhere?"

Rocco and the others were standing at the tent door now, listening as Ibrahim directed their minds back to the landing where the rescue had taken shape.

"You think there's something beyond that landing?" Rocco asked finally.

"Of course. It all makes sense. We don't know what happened to the people who remained alive above the death chamber. But we can assume that some, if not all, finally escaped. The disease was still a dilemma for them, however. They knew that, whatever else, it was terribly contagious. Fear of contamination and more death would have prompted them not to return for their loved ones. They simply turned the room into a common tomb by sealing it forever!"

"That would account for the parchment still being there after all this time," Katrina exclaimed.

"Then there could be another tunnel yet undiscovered?" asked Kris, curious now as he listened to the reasoning of the others and felt their growing excitement.

"I'm sure of it!" Ibrahim said vehemently, pounding a fist into his hand for emphasis. "Rocco, get some workers over to that landing right away. Let's see if I'm right."

"Ibrahim, I know I've already said one day's headstart in the city is all I would ask by way of special treatment," Kris spoke with an apologetic smile. "But, would you consider keeping under wraps what you've just speculated? If nothing turns up, it was still a good idea. But assuming you are right, it would be great fun to take my crew into a tunnel that has just been discovered. If I could put something like this on television, catching the flavor and excitement I feel coming from you all right now, we could whet the appetites of a lot of young would-be archaeologists!"

Ibrahim remained silent, looking sternly at Kris.

"Already you ask for more considerations. If you think because you are Kat's brother and you are needed by me as a consultant for the next few days that you can expect to, how you Americans say, 'weasel out of me' more than we originally agreed upon . . ." his face suddenly broke into a broad grin, "you are absolutely right!"

"Thanks," Kris responded happily. "You won't regret it."

"Okay, let's go to work," Ibrahim concluded, as he walked out into the crisp morning air, the rest trailing along behind him. "We have a lot to do these next few days. By the way, Kat, your things arrived early this morning from Antalya. I almost forgot. They should be in your tent."

"A fresh change at last. It doesn't get any better than this!"

She ran off to her tent as the others scattered to their respective tasks. It was almost eleven o'clock when Ibrahim led Kris and his crew into the underground city of *Kilçilar*.

Ward Tanneberg

By their return at nightfall, Ben Hur was busy with two additional television crews, four writers and photographers from leading American and European weekly magazines, and reporters from two Turkish dailies.

Runners were carrying a steady flow of telephone messages from the nearby village. Dr. Üzünal was reportedly on his way at last, for which Ibrahim was grateful. He was feeling the effects of tension and the abuse his body had taken during the past several days.

And just before the first call to dinner, Rocco, covered with dirt and grime, appeared at Ibrahim's tent door to report that at five-twenty they had broken through what initially had been mistaken for the end of the staircase. It was as Ibrahim had surmised.

A tunnel lay beyond it!

Forty-nine. Kristian

2300 local time

As tired as I was, sleep still did not come easily. I simply couldn't turn off what I had seen.

This whole place is incredible! It's a dream that makes the catacombs look like a kindergarten. How did they ever turn something like this into reality? Ibrahim says there are probably scores of them yet unexplored around the country. Most of them in this region. If I had not seen it for myself . . .

And the church. Unbelievable! I can't get it out of my mind. When we went in to shoot this afternoon, I kept thinking of those people crying out to God for mercy. That Jesus mosaic is marvelous. Wait until Tom and Carole see the pictures. This one has to be an audience grabber!

I'm going to push Jim and Sid for a network special in December. We've got the perfect "after Christmas" show here. Viewership is light then. Old movies, reruns, and football. But with the kind of hype this baby is generating, we'll break the ratings bank! I'll call Tom tomorrow and start the ball rolling. He's probably still torqued about my leaving the country. Serves the conniver right. Carole too, for that matter. Anyway, we'll just wait and see where this one goes.

346

I tried sleeping on my left side, then on my right. I was tired, but the adrenaline was pumping, no doubt about it. I couldn't help letting my mind spin over tomorrow's tunnel. Ibrahim says that he and Kat will take us down to the sepulcher or whatever it is. He'll show us how they got in there in the first place. We'll track their journey up the stone steps in a reenactment scene, recording their feelings and fears along the way. Then we'll go into the new section. What a trip!

The news vultures have been gathering all day. I've tried to stay low profile, but word is out that I'm here in a "head start" program. They'll forget about it when the pictures and reports start coming out.

I hope we can . . . catch the . . . of the place . . .

It was ever so big. A huge black hole . . . space with no beginning and no ending . . . she floated in it . . . long blond hair against her shoulders. Her features . . . gradually taking shape . . . hands reaching . . . she wants me . . . and . . . I see her . . . I see her eyes . . . they are . . . blue, I think. Yes. I'm sure of it. Her eyes are blue . . . and what? Are you angry? Sad? What? Wait . . . don't go . . . please, don't . . . don't shut the door . . .

I awoke suddenly, sitting up and perspiring, but not because of heat. It was the dream again! Only this time I had seen her eyes! And her fingers were long, weren't they? A pianist? Maybe. Or the violin?

Who is she? We should know one another . . . shouldn't we?

I rubbed my hands together in a cold sweat!

Fifty. Katrina

Immediately after breakfast Katrina joined Ibrahim, Kris, Jack Millerton, and K.C. Murphy for the film reenactment of their earlier discovery and subsequent escape from the crypt.

"Ms. Lauring," said K.C. Murphy, as he stood in front of Katrina and Ibrahim, "we'll be wantin' some still photos of ye and Dr. Sevali o'er there by the entrance."

"Please, Mr. Murphy, the name is Katy."

"And I am Ibrahim."

"An' they're both good names, too . . . especially Katy," the Irishman smiled broadly, never turning his eyes away from Katrina. "It rolls off the tongue like a fine mist on Connemara's meadows. If only yer hair was a wee bit more the color of a sunset, ye could o' been born along the Atlantic's edge in Clifden or on Galway Bay. An' I'd be most pleased if ye called me K.C."

"My pleasure, K.C.," laughed Katrina. "Outside of my boss, you're the first *real* Irishman I've ever met, and you've not disappointed me in the least. You sound as though you're full of it!"

"Full o' what, darlin' Katy?" he asked, his deep brogue curling upward with artful innocence.

"Whatever it is that makes Irishmen so dashingly wonderful," she answered amusedly. "Now, let's go get the pictures over with."

Thirty more minutes passed before the outside photo shoot was over. Jack and K.C. seemed to like each other and worked well together. But the shadows surrounding the entrance and the sun's position had inspired the two photographer/cameramen to take extra care in making certain that what they had was acceptable.

Ben Hur was busy organizing the news media. By ten or so, he was taking the designated film crew into *Kilçilar.* At noon, Tahsin would direct a Q and A time with those who remained on top. To familiarize reporters with the city, he had prepared an overview map to be handed out during the noontime conference.

Because the Level 11 cave-in had not been reopened, they started by gathering at the rescue landing on Level 6 and retracing their steps downward. This trip down was much different. Temporary lights had been strung, enabling their descent with much greater ease.

Bare bulbs hung in the large death chamber as well, and Katrina was surprised at how much her earlier fears were diminished by their dim but steady glow. The sad display of human skeletons, however, was a ghostly reminder of the story deciphered by Ibrahim from the ancient parchment.

She found herself drawn toward the skeletal remains she had first sighted through the small hole from where she and Ibrahim had been trapped. They had names now. At least Theodora, the child skeleton, did. Though her father's name remained unknown, he would forever be a hero in Katrina's heart. He was The Writer who, even in death, had sought to leave a legacy of faith and hope for others.

A sudden flush of empathy and pity broke through her natural revulsion at the sight of so much human pain and misery. These skeletons were once real people!

Turning from the man and child, her gaze moved slowly across the grisly scene directly opposite. Row after row, a garden planted with the dead. She willed sinew and flesh on their bleached forms, though each remained motionless on the dirt floor. *Which one is Pulcheria? This one perhaps? Or is she that one over there? The Writer said that he positioned himself opposite her. But there are too many. I'm so sorry. We will never know.*

Katrina was absorbed in thought when, suddenly, something near her moved!

She shivered involuntarily and her heart leaped into her throat.

A pressure on her shoulder.

Wheeling about, Katrina stared at a shadowy form mere inches from her own! She cried out.

"Kat! Kat!"

Blindly she struck at the shadow with her fist.

"Kat, it's me. Kris. Are you all right?"

Katrina blinked and Kris' face came into focus, one hand firmly on her shoulder, the other gripping her forearm defensively. She choked back a sob, then another, as she slumped into his arms.

"I'm sorry, I'm sorry. I . . . you . . . frightened me. I was . . . for a moment I was with them, Kris. Oh, I'm so sorry. This place gets to me! All these people in their pain and their sadness. I really could feel it. I can't put The Writer's story out of my mind. And I wanted to find Pulcheria. I was trying to decide which one she might be when you startled me."

"Pulcheria? You mean The Writer's wife?"

"Yes."

They were both silent for a moment as Ibrahim and the two cameramen listened and watched.

"It seemed . . . kind of important, you know?" she said pleadingly, her voice thin and empty like a wire stretched too tightly. "But I can't tell which one she is."

"Yeah, sis," Kris responded huskily, "I know. It just doesn't seem right, does it? Where was God when all this happened?"

"He was right here with them."

Both of them turned to the source of the response.

"Isn't that what The Writer declared in his inscription?" Ibrahim continued. "The last thing he wrote about in this place was his confidence in the very presence of God. A dying man speaks only the truth. He expends his energy on that which truly matters, the things in which he believes and is convinced beyond all shadow of doubt. In the end, our friend here gave his last will and testimony in the words of the Nicene Creed. He was telling us that to him, anyway, the words of this Creed were the words of truth. That's what he believed. Nothing else mattered."

"To him it was truth," repeated Kris. "Does that mean infallible truth? Are we talking about absolute, undeniable, verifiable truth here? Or are you saying that *if* it was truth, it was only this man's truth? A hopeful wish? The dream of a dying man?"

The three turned toward each other now, intent on verbalizing thoughts that bounced off walls of dirt and stone like sermons proclaimed in a grand cathedral. Ibrahim shrugged and held up his hands.

"Where does scientifically verifiable truth stop and a faith that will not be denied begin?" said Ibrahim with a smile. "Remember, in order to discover things that are not yet, even the scientist must enter the realm of faith. But his faith is attached securely to what he already knows. For him, it's no fantasy leap into the dark. True faith is reasonable. True faith is logical. True faith brings a dying man's God into a hellish sepulcher like this so that they may walk out, together, into life eternal."

Katrina started to say something, but no words would come.

"You sound like a Christian, Ibrahim," Kris said finally.

"And you, my dear friend, sound very much like a Muslim," responded Ibrahim with a chuckle.

Katrina's tearstained cheeks glowed under the glare of the naked lights, as she moved next to Ibrahim and put an arm around his waist. With her other hand she drew Kris to her until the three stood together. They began walking toward the stairs, careful not to step on any of the bleached bones that marked their narrow aisleway.

"Are we that different really?" she asked. "Muslim and Christian, I mean?"

The others were silent for a moment as they slowly picked their way across the room.

"In many ways, not different at all," responded Ibrahim at last, "and in other ways, very. Perhaps it is in certain matters of understanding and thought that we differ most of all."

They reached the bottom of the staircase and paused, Katrina releasing her hold on the two men beside her.

"Do you mean our belief systems are different?" she asked.

"Can there be objective, infallible truth in a pluralistic society?" queried Kris, looking at the other two. "Or can there only be tolerance?"

"Tolerance is good," answered Ibrahim. "It's the first benchmark on the pathway to understanding. It provides us with a place to sit and think and listen to each other. Unfortunately, many are unwilling to walk together long enough to reach this first benchmark. Why this is so is one of the great mysteries and it's one of the main reasons that humanity is in such deficit.

"For example, during these last few months at *Kilçilar* I find myself longing to know more about the Christian view of Jesus. I know what my religion says. But I have the feeling there is more, if only it were possible for this Muslim to sit and think and converse intelligently with a Christian whom he could respect. But would such a conversation mean that he's forsaking his own religious heritage? Would his family disown him for such an inquiry? Might he lose face in his academic community? Perhaps his professional reputation might be in jeopardy.

"I would like for Christians, on the other hand," he continued, "to understand that a Muslim is one who has surrendered his or her whole being to the Creator of all things. In a very real sense, Islam means that Muslims have a responsibility to create a just society, one in which the poor and defenseless will be treated acceptably. Are we alike? In many things, yes. And in other things we are not. But it seems that we may all be alike in at least one thing."

Ibrahim paused and smiled at the others. "We are in pursuit of truth. Absolute and undeniable truth. I think that part of the secret in finding such truth is in realizing that there is much we do not yet understand. For example, the matter of faith."

"Now faith is being sure of what we hope for and certain of what we do not see," Katrina chimed in. "The New Testament writer to the Hebrews, 11:1. It's a great chapter on faith. One that everybody should study."

"Then I will," responded Ibrahim. "But will it speak truth to my Muslim mind and heart?"

"It will if you approach it with the same openness you apply to your archaeological profession. You search, find, examine, deduce, and then come to a conclusion. Faith is the same thing. We just have to look in the right place to find it."

"And where might that be?"

"The Apostle Paul says, 'Faith comes from hearing the message, and the message is heard through the word of Christ.'"

"Does that mean that Jesus' words are the only ones that can teach me about faith?"

"I'm afraid we've already reached one of those 'differences' we were talking about. Tolerance is needed in order to go on. As a Christian, I believe the evidence of Scripture and of history affirms conclusively that Jesus is the Son of God. He *is* God. Therefore, I can trust His words to be true truth. He was God incarnate in the flesh. Perfect God and perfect man. Unique in history. And because He is God, I can trust His message to bring faith. True faith, Ibrahim."

"Shoot!" exclaimed Kris suddenly.

"What?" asked Katrina, turning her attention toward her brother.

"Why didn't we get all this on tape? This is the perfect conversation to 'kick-start' some good parent-child discussion once they've watched our show. And I blew it! I got so engrossed in where we are and what we were saying that I forgot to do what I came here to do in the first place."

"Not to worry, laddie."

Kris turned to look at K.C. Murphy. His camera was on his shoulder. So was Millerton's.

"While the three of ye were philosophizin', Jack and me were shootin' up all kinds of film. Yer workin' with pros, laddie, not a pack o' amateurs like them pipsqueeks from the other networks!"

They broke into laughter. Then as quickly as it had come it was gone, replaced by the reverent feeling of awe that one has while visiting in a funeral home.

"Laughing in this place somehow seems like sacrilege," Kris said as they turned for a last look.

"Maybe it's okay," Katrina said, her eyes looking across the room and fastening onto the still form of The Writer and his child. "Perhaps if these people knew we were here, they would gather around to share with us what they know. I'm certain they could help us understand more of true truth. We've mingled our own tears with their pain and suffering. I don't think they'll mind if we mix a little of our joy with them too. I know one thing for sure."

"What is that?" asked Ibrahim curiously, as they started to climb the stone staircase.

"Heaven is more real to me now that I have stood in the pit of hell!"

Fifty-one. Kristian

1230 local time

At the top of the stairs I glanced back at Kat and Ibrahim. She had her arm through his as they turned to look down the long flights of steps.

"I imagine that I'll not see this passage again," Katrina said softly.

Ibrahim let his gaze rest on her face with . . . what was it? Understanding? Admiration? Love? I had the feeling that it was some of all of these.

"I really must get back to Antalya and my children," she declared, warmly returning Ibrahim's smile. "You understand?"

"Of course. You've missed several important days with your students in order to be here. I wish you could stay . . ." Ibrahim hesitated as though he had almost spoken embarrassingly and caught himself just in time. "I will miss you."

"I think everything I can help with is finished," said Katrina. "I want to go with you this afternoon, though. I want to know the thrill you feel when examining something new and untouched. But that's just for me, not for anything that I can give by way of assistance. And I can't impose on the Hedleys any longer. They've been so kind to release me for this time. Will you arrange for the bus? If not tomorrow, then the day after for certain? Tonight I'll

354

call to tell them when to expect me."

"Of course. It will be done."

"Kris, do you think you could come down to Antalya and see where I'm working? At least, where I'm supposed to be working?"

"I don't know, sis," I answered, as my mind ran over all the things I needed to do. "I've probably got two or three more days here and then I should head back. You know, 'The show must go on.'"

The words were not totally out of my mouth when I caught her crestfallen look. She was disappointed.

"But, I'll check with my boss," I continued quickly, "when we're close to finishing up here. If he gives me even one extra day, count on me showing up. If not, then I'll come back during the Christmas holidays."

"Would you, Kris?" Kat's face lit up with excitement. "Oh, if you could be here for Christmas, that would be wonderful! And you can meet my roommate."

"Another roomie?" I grinned, glancing at Ibrahim. "Kat has tried to fix me up with the 'Roommate of the Year' more times than I can count."

"I've seen this one," countered Ibrahim. "She's very pretty."

"Really? Mmm. What's her name again, Kat?"

"Michelle."

"You say she's from France, right?"

"Mais, oui."

"She speaks English?"

"Of course," laughed Katrina.

"Well, then," I drew the word out in mock emphasis, "maybe I will check her out when I show up. I'm between girls right now anyway."

"You are? What happened to this 'Carole' person you wrote about? Is she no longer on the current 'Lauring List of Loves'?"

"When we have the time, I'll review my love life with you and bring you up to date. Try to reserve the entire day, though. You'll need it. However, right now we should press on with more important things."

"Oh, I don't know. Your love life sounds very interesting," said Ibrahim, a twinkle in his eye.

"Get out," I grunted. "All of you, get out. Back to the reason for our being here. Let's go see what this heretofore unexplored tunnel has to offer."

"Maybe it will turn out to be the Tunnel of Love," Katrina whispered, her voice low and breathless as she pulled me closer. "Perhaps there's a beautiful young maiden waiting for you at the other end."

"I can see this is going to be a long afternoon," I responded dryly, looking despairingly at the others. "I've spent a lifetime trying unsuccessfully to get my little sister under control, and I see the time she's spent in Turkey hasn't brought about any improvement."

Ibrahim and the two cameramen laughed.

Katrina tossed her hair, her face wreathed in the glow of sweet innocence.

We were all having such a good time. How could we have possibly anticipated what was ahead?

We hadn't gone far before I made my first discovery about exploring uncharted territory. There are no lights hanging from the sides of the tunnel to make your steps more certain. And in some spots, walking gets to be a real challenge.

Fortunately, Ibrahim had anticipated this. With his free hand, he retrieved a flashlight for each of us from his backpack. Then we sipped some water from small canteens attached to our belts. After a short rest, we continued on.

The lack of even modest lighting also made filming extremely marginal. After some initial footage I suggested to the guys that they go back. They declined. They weren't about to do that. Both K.C. and Jack were as hooked as I was on the thrill of walking where no other person had been for hundreds of years. They insisted on coming with us, assuring me that there would be something they could redeem from tagging along.

The passage was narrow for the most part; in one place, we had to remove a good bit of debris in order to squeeze through. After what must have been sixty meters, the tunnel widened and two could walk side by side. This lasted only a short distance, however, and soon we were forced to go single file again.

"This is interesting," Ibrahim commented at last, to no one in particular.

"It is?" Katrina responded. "Maybe for a good case of claustrophobia, but not much else. Why aren't there any rooms or anything? You know, like in the other part of the city."

"That's exactly the question that is so interesting. This passage seems to be a long tunnel with a few sharp defensive turns thrown in. Nothing more. People didn't live along here. I think instead that this is taking us somewhere. My guess is that it's a secret escape route opening up to the outside. We seem to be moving on a fairly level course. I don't think we're headed down at all."

"If this is only an escape tunnel, why did it lead down to the crypt?" I asked. No one responded. It was obviously the question we were all asking ourselves.

Then suddenly Ibrahim spoke up. "Here's our answer."

He shined his light along the left side of the tunnel into an opening.

"I'll bet my lira against your dollar that this connects with what we call the West Tunnel Road. We're at about the same elevation."

"How about splitting up?" Jack suggested. "Some go to the left and the rest stay on in this direction?"

"No," said Ibrahim. "We'll check this side tunnel out another time. I don't want anyone to get lost. We'll stay together and keep moving ahead as we were."

We walked in silence for what seemed quite a distance. At times the tunnel ceiling was so low we had to crouch down to avoid scraping our heads. I'll have to admit to a few heavy-duty moments of claustrophobia. How much farther could this go?

Ibrahim stopped so suddenly that Katrina ran into him. "Sorry," she apologized.

"Shh." Ibrahim waved his hand behind him for silence. We stood still. The only thing I could hear was our breathing.

"What is it?" I asked.

"Shh," he ordered again, this time more intently. We held our breath, straining to hear whatever it was that Ibrahim thought he had heard.

"It was a voice," he said at last, twisting around in the narrow passage to look at us. "Maybe two, I can't be sure."

"A voice?" Katrina asked incredulously. "Are you sure?"

"Positive. At first I wasn't but then I heard it again."

"But who could be in here?" I asked in disbelief, staring ahead at the inky darkness.

"I don't know," Ibrahim replied. "It could be that we're near the end of the tunnel and that the voices are coming in from outside. Yes. That's probably what it is . . . listen!"

We stood absolutely still. K.C. scraped his flashlight across a rock as he balanced himself against the wall. Then I heard them.

"You're right, Ibrahim! There are two voices. Wait. Do you hear that?" We looked at each other in disbelief.

It sounded like a motor!

"Let's go find out where we are," I urged excitedly as the others nodded. "Maybe we can catch a ride back on the top rather than walking through the tunnel again."

"One moment, please," Ibrahim cautioned. "When we move forward I must ask you to be very quiet and remain behind me."

"Why, Ibrahim?" asked Katrina. "What's the matter?"

"Ah, lass, ye should 'ave to live a wee bit in me homeland to appreciate what the good doctor is sayin'." K.C.'s voice was quiet, yet his deep Irish brogue filled the underground cavity in which the five of us huddled shoulder to shoulder. We looked at him curiously.

"What he's tellin' ye is that yer not at home in America, lass," K.C. continued. "This is Turkey. He wants to be sure about what and who's ahead before tippin' our hats and bringin' 'em greetin's from the underground."

"Right you are, K.C.," Ibrahim responded. "The fact is that our team has covered most of the terrain above ground at some point during these past months. It seems to me that I should know who is out there. The problem is, I don't. I've been checking my compass regularly since we started. I don't think that we can be at Güzelyurt. We're too far north and east. Of course, it's hard to be certain, but I want us to proceed slowly and with caution. Just to be sure."

"What could there possibly be to be afraid of?" Katrina asked.

"I'm not afraid, Kat, just prudent," he smiled sincerely. "Now, please do as I say. You take up the rear position. Kris, follow me. Next is Jack. Then K.C. All right?"

Heads nodded, and a new feeling of excitement mixed with apprehension caused breathing to come in shorter, more shallow breaths. I knew what we were all thinking—*This is silly! Let's just get on with it.* But K.C. was probably right. And besides, we were too polite to criticize our leader.

"Let's go."

We moved forward more deliberately, following Ibrahim's slightly bent form as we made our way through a low, narrow section of the tunnel. All I could see was his backside until suddenly his flashlight was waving in my face.

"Turn out your lights!" he whispered. Reluctantly I pushed the switch, as did the others. The absolute darkness inside a cave is overwhelming. I don't think I could make it in here week after week like the ancients used to do.

"Someone has been in here, at least this far."

"How can you tell?"

"I just saw a footprint! Look."

We crowded in as Ibrahim turned on his flashlight and stared at what appeared to be a partial bootprint in a brief span of soft earth. Then he flipped the light off.

"Put your hand on the person in front of you. Then, come."

I felt for Ibrahim, running my hand over his back until my fingers were secured in his belt. I could feel Jack doing the same. We started forward again, this time with stutter-steps so as not to crush the heel of the person in front. When I felt Ibrahim's body straighten, I did the same.

Then I saw it . . . a pinpoint of light. I guessed the distance to be at least the length of a football field. Maybe more.

"Shh," Ibrahim repeated once again, his voice a whisper now. "Come closer. Be careful."

All at once a shadow blotted out the pinpoint of light. Then another. And another. I watched as at least five vehicles broke the prism of light while entering the huge chamber.

Voices could be clearly heard. I sensed Ibrahim's tenseness as he concentrated on listening.

Lights came on abruptly at the far end of the cavern. Their glow didn't reach to where we were standing, but we shrunk back anyway. A number of men were milling about, working with stacks of boxes piled along one of the walls. They were loading something into the vehicles. But what?

"This place is big enough to hanger a 747!" Jack exclaimed in a loud whisper.

"Stay quiet. I'm going to move closer," said Ibrahim.

"Who are these people?" I whispered.

"I'm not sure. They don't look like military, and I know of no official units in this area other than the ones who've brought supplies to *Kilçilar.*"

"Can ye tell what they're sayin'?" asked K.C.

"Not for certain. That's why I need to get closer."

"Wait," I protested. "Why not go back and get the soldiers at the camp to come over and check this out?"

I thought my idea was the more prudent of the two presently under discussion.

"Because they're preparing to leave soon. That much I could hear when one of them raised his voice. They're loading equipment. Stay here. I'll be back shortly."

"I'll go with you," I said, my hand on his shoulder.

"No."

"I've been in the military, Ibrahim. I'm probably better at what you're about to do than you are. Besides, you've only got one good arm. I'm coming with you."

Ibrahim hesitated, then gave in. "Okay, let's go. But stay close. I have a feeling that these people are up to no good."

"Be careful!" Katrina whispered, her voice edged with concern.

Jack and K.C. stood by as we moved out into the dark open area.

Fifty-two. Katrina

1445 local time

Wearily, Katrina slid down until she was seated on the earthen floor where the tunnel opened into the large chamber. For a brief second, she closed her eyes.

Suddenly she froze!

A voice shouted out, followed by a stab of light. Its beam caught Ibrahim's and Kris' shadowy forms midway across the chamber.

Then another light.

"Durmak! Nereye gidiyorsunuz?" *Stop! Where are you going?*

A third powerful flashlight merged with the others to form an incandescent web in which the two now stood helplessly trapped.

A moment later a shot rang out!

"Get back!"

K.C.'s low growl set off an alarm inside Katrina. She recoiled and instinctively rolled sideways into the tunnel. She heard K.C. and Jack stumbling toward her in the darkness and tried to get out of the way, but the passage was too narrow. Both men tripped over her, Jack grunting audibly as K.C.'s full weight came down on top of him.

"Be quiet!" Katrina whispered, as the two struggled to untangle themselves.

She inched forward until she could see into the chamber again. To her horror, there were other lights now, all trained on Ibrahim and Kris. They were surrounded by dark figures shouting excitedly, pointing their weapons, but no more shots were fired.

She heard Ibrahim say something in Turkish, then choked back a cry as one of the men raised his gun and hit him across the side of his head. The blow sent him to the cavern floor. A moment later, Kris was thrown down beside him. She watched helplessly as their captors bound them and then yanked them to their feet.

"Katy, darlin'," K.C.'s calm voice startled her. Then she felt his heavy breathing only inches from her face. "Ye 'ave to go fer help."

"What do you mean?" Katrina's words came shakily as she tried pulling herself together.

"Have ye yer light?"

"It's here somewhere," she answered and began moving her hand back and forth across the tunnel floor. "I lost it when you . . . wait, here it is!"

"Good. Now, get yerself goin', lass!"

"But what about you . . . and them? What about Ibrahim and Kris?"

"Jack and I'll be stayin' here to help 'em. An' don' ye stop to rest along the way. They'll be comin' after ye."

"But what will you do? They'll find you if you stay here!"

"Ne'er ye mind, lass. Just be goin'. Ye 'ave but one job to do. Get back to the camp and send help. We'll be takin' care of ourselves, don' ye worry none. Jus' hurry!"

"Okay," she whispered, scrambling to her feet. "Do be careful. I'll send up an arrow prayer."

"We can use a lot of prayer," mumbled Jack in the darkness behind them, not at all sure what an arrow prayer might consist of. "And a couple of fast answers too! Now go!"

As Katrina turned, she glimpsed lights randomly probing the great cavern and knew that whoever they were, they had started searching for others. Without a word, she began feeling her way back into the darkness of the tunnel until she reached a small turn. Only after she rounded the turn did she switch on her light and begin to run as fast as the narrow passage would permit. Silently, her prayers shot upward. Swift. Brief. Pointed at the target of her faith.

Dear Lord Jesus, please help us. Don't let them hurt Ibrahim and Kris. And protect K.C. and Jack as well!

"WHAT DO YOU THINK, K.C.?"

"I think we're into somethin' pretty deep that I'd just as soon not know about," he whispered. "It's a sure thing that these are not the good guys."

"What shall we do?"

"They've got the guns. We've got nothin'. I'm thinkin' we'd do well to hide our buns behind a stone somewhere fer right now. They'll be comin' this way."

"What about Katy?"

"They'll be findin' the tunnel all right, soon enough. Like as not, they already know it's here. Anyway, there's nothin' can be done about it. She's got a head start. Best news? She'll be bringin' back some help. Worst news? I think she'll make it to the camp before these cave rats can catch up to 'er."

"That's really why you sent her back, isn't it? You're pretty cool in a crisis, pal."

"It comes sort o' natural when ye grow up in Ireland. Now, come on. Let's swing o'er to the right. This way."

The two men moved stealthily through the darkness, away from the tunnel, along the cavern wall. Jack saw the lights coming toward them and suddenly wished he had not taken this assignment. Right now, anywhere else would be wonderful. This sort of thing was not his bottle of bourbon.

"'ere we go, Jack. Quick. Inside!"

Jack felt himself being pushed down onto the cavern floor.

"There's a hole here. Inside. An' be quick about it!"

Jack couldn't see anything. He ran his hand around until he felt the small opening. How had K.C. found it? The guy is incredible!

Feet first, Jack slid inside on his belly. K.C. was hard behind him, sliding, pushing, scraping. There was barely enough space to sandwich themselves inside, pressed together, with Jack's chin shoved hard against the back of K.C.'s shoulder. Jack felt K.C. moving again and heard a scraping sound.

"A stone in the hole," K.C. whispered. "It's only 'alf the size, but maybe . . . shh!"

Jack froze as a beam of light swept across the hollow cavity in which they had hidden. For a split second it framed the outline of the rock K.C. had just pulled in front of them, then it was gone. Jack opened his mouth to say something when the light passed over their hiding place again.

He swallowed as he saw the back of a man's leg through the small opening above the rock. He was certain they were about to join Kris and Ibrahim. That is, if they didn't get shot first. But, as quickly as they had come, the voices and footfalls moved away. He let out a nervous sigh, suddenly realizing that he had been holding his breath.

Shouts off to their left brought more searchers running past their hiding place.

"I think they've found our cameras," K.C. grunted. "That means they'll be headin' down the tunnel after Katy."

"Some will stay behind," Jack whispered.

"Right ye are. But I'm feelin' it's better to be out there now and facin' 'em than squirreled away in this tiny hole, don' ye think?"

"I'm with you on that score."

The two men pushed the rock aside, careful not to make noise, and began sliding out, their hands and elbows pushing and scuffing along the dirt floor until there was room enough to stand erect.

"I've always wanted a close friend, but that was ridiculous!" Jack murmured, his voice hushed and his eyes darting about the huge cavern.

"Come," K.C. ordered, pointing off to the left. "I think Kris and Ibrahim are over there somewhere."

For the next five minutes they moved furtively along the cave wall, blending with the dark shadows, careful to remain out of sight. The cavern was huge. The ceiling looked to be six or eight meters high at the center, sloping gradually toward the sides until in places the two were forced to crouch down in order not to hit their heads.

As they came nearer to the midpoint of the cavern, several strings of bare lightbulbs dispelled the darkness. There was no generator sound. Jack figured the lights must be powered by batteries. Beyond them, the sun shone through an entrance just big enough to accommodate the four jeeps and small van parked inside.

Several wooden cases were stacked to one side along the wall. The men, about twenty in all, had gathered near the vehicles. The one who appeared to be their leader was addressing them, while another man next to him held a small chalkboard with markings on it. The leader spoke in clipped tones, gesturing authoritatively, first at the chart, then at the men.

"He's givin' 'em their marchin' orders."

"Can you tell what's on that chalkboard?" Jack asked.

"Too far away," muttered K.C., his attention turning to the boxes near the wall, about twenty meters away. "But, ye can be sure it's not game strategy fer a football team. Stay 'ere. I'll be seein' what's in the boxes."

"I think they're empty."

"How so?"

"I used to work in a grocery store. Look at the way they're stacked."

The men studied the boxes for a few seconds. They were thrown together in a disorderly way, not neatly stacked.

"Yer probably right. Whatever they 'ad in 'em is likely in the jeeps an' that van."

Jack started as the men who had been listening to their leader abruptly shouted something in unison, thrusting their closed right fists into the air. With a preassigned quickness and efficiency, they ran to each of the vehicles. Motors rumbled into action, echoing off the cavern walls. The leader paused to speak to two men who apparently had been ordered to guard Kris' and Ibrahim's inert forms. Then he strode to the lead vehicle, climbed in, and the caravan slowly turned about, heading toward the exit. One by one they rolled out of the cave opening and disappeared.

"The odds are gettin' better all the time," murmured K.C.

"How many do you think are in the tunnel?"

K.C. shrugged. "Two. Three at the most. It's too crowded in there fer any more. Besides, these boys 'ave got other things on their minds. Not to worry, lad. That tunnel was designed fer defensive purposes. Ye can fight only one at a time. If Katy had a gun she could hold 'em off by herself."

"But she doesn't."

"No," K.C. mused regretfully, "she doesn'. Probably makes no difference. She doesn' look like the shootin' type anyway. But as long as she keeps runnin' she'll be all right. Meanwhile, ye an' I 'ave a wee little job to do."

"Yeah?"

"Which one o' them cave rats do ye want?"

Jack swallowed whatever it was that kept coming up. "The one on the left, I guess."

"Ye made a fine choice, Jack."

Jack wondered how he could tell. But then he was beginning to wonder about a lot of things where this Irishman was concerned. Nothing seemed to phase him, his only outward sign of tension a thickening of his brogue.

"The trick to this sort o' thing is gettin' close without rousin' 'em. Then, when I give the signal, pounce on yer man. Keep 'im away from 'is gun. Don't stop hittin' 'til ye know 'e's out cold. Or 'til ye have 'is gun pointed up 'is nostrils. Got it?"

Jack nodded with as much conviction as he could muster.

"All right. 'Ere we go."

They moved through the darkness, slowly edging out from the wall and into the half light. There was no other way. The guards were talking and, fortunately, had turned toward the exit. Jack and K.C. were still about ten or twelve meters behind them when one of the outlaw soldiers glanced back in their direction. For a split second his mouth dropped open and he froze with surprise. That hesitation turned out to be the difference.

"Get 'im!" K.C. shouted, as he leaped forward across the remaining distance.

The man on the left was fumbling for the automatic handgun holstered at his waist when Jack ran into him with the force of a snowplow. The impact hurled them both backward and Jack almost slid over the top of the guard, while battering the man's head back against the floor. He lay stunned as Jack scrambled to pull his gun away and pointed it at the fellow who now lay cowering in fright, certain that he was about to be blown away.

Jack could hear scuffling behind him and turned just as a gun went off, the bullet zinging past his ear before it glanced off the far wall. K.C. pounded the man's face again and again with his hamlike fist until Jack saw the guard go limp.

"A tough bugger, he was," complained the Irishman, looking over at Jack to be sure he had his man under control. "I told ye that ye picked the best o' the lot."

"You guys were terrific!" exclaimed Kris from where he lay propped against a large stone. "Now cut us loose and let's get out of here!"

"Hold it," cautioned Ibrahim, a trickle of blood oozing from where he had been struck behind his ear. "We can't."

"What do you mean, 'we can't'?" As soon as Kris' hands were free, he tore at the tape around his legs while Jack worked to release Ibrahim.

"I didn't want to say anything to make you worry more," explained Ibrahim, gingerly feeling for the wound behind his ear, wincing as his fingers touched the swelling bruise. "Three soldiers are in the tunnel. They went to see if there were any more of us."

"Where's Kat?" asked Kris, looking around for his sister.

"In the tunnel," Jack answered.

"Then they've got her!" he cried.

"I don' think so," K.C. butted in. "She's 'ad too much of a head start. They'll not catch 'er."

"We can't just stay here. Maybe we can follow after and surprise them."

"Let me go outside first and see if I can tell where we are. If we're close to a house or village, then we need to hurry." Ibrahim said gravely. "I overheard them talking about a ceremony taking place this afternoon in Ankara in the Matlepe district. It's being held at Anit Kabir, in the Atatürk Mausoleum. Have any of you been there?"

They shook their heads.

"It's a much revered place, housing the tomb of our great president, Kemal Atatürk, located in the western part of the city. They spoke of an event where your American ambassador, our Prime Minister, and most of the members of our cabinet will be together. Several other party members as well. Apparently, the United States is erecting a memorial in Atatürk's honor and the groundbreaking ceremony is today. These outlaws already have some of their people planted there, intending to attack the hill and kill everyone, including the Minister and her cabinet!"

"But how can we stop them?" exclaimed Kris.

"If there's any civilization nearby, I'll get to a telephone and call ahead. The military must be alerted to the danger. I'll be back as quickly as I can. You check to see what weapons they may have hidden here and arm yourselves."

Ibrahim turned and ran toward the exit.

The others rushed to look through the boxes stacked along the wall. Most turned out to be empty as Jack had suspected. But not all. At the bottom of one pile, they found a case filled with Uzi submachine guns designed with folding metal stocks, weapons originally made in Israel. Two more empty boxes. Then some small boxes filled with 20-, 25-, and 32-round magazines made for the Uzi weapons.

"Where do they get all this stuff?" Jack asked in disbelief.

"Who knows? Iran. Libya. Wherever." K.C. scooped up several of the magazines and wiped off an Uzi with his shirt tail. "There's always them that'll sell their souls fer a few pounds."

Each of them loaded a weapon and were busy stuffing extra magazines in pockets or tucking them through their belts when they heard a shout. They looked up just in time to see Ibrahim's outline in the sunlit opening and then he was inside, running toward them.

"One of the jeeps is coming back," he yelled.

"Can we get out?" asked Kris.

"Güzelyurt is only a short distance. And there's a couple of houses that I can see. But there's no time. They're almost here."

"How many?"

"Four, I think. Maybe five."

"Plus these two that are presently down and three more in the tunnel!" exclaimed Jack. "The odds are deteriorating rapidly."

Kris stared at the others for a brief second. Then, without a word, he picked up the weapon he had just wiped clean and started running toward the tunnel and Katrina!

K.C. ran after him.

Ibrahim and Jack followed.

KATRINA CRIED OUT AS SHE STUMBLED. The flashlight flew from her hand as she tried to catch herself. Her pants tore as rocks scraped skin from her knees and the palms of her hands. But the light was still working. Seizing it, she scrambled to her feet and resumed her desperate race back through the cramped tunnel.

By the time she reached the opening that branched off to her right, she was completely out of breath. Pausing, she leaned forward and closed her eyes. Hands on her knees, she sucked air into her burning lungs. It tasted old and stale and dirty.

Suddenly, every nerve went on alert. She heard something. *Wait. Be still and listen. There it is again!*

Only the sound was *ahead* of her, not behind!

Someone is coming!

Katrina froze, trying to make her mind work. *Which way? What shall I do? Oh, dear God, help me! I'm trapped!*

Light and shadows from beyond the turn ahead.

Then a face appeared around the corner.

Katrina uttered a tiny cry!

Fifty-three. Katrina

"Ms. Lauring?"

The hand that held the flashlight shook with relief as the beam illuminated the man's face.

"Çali! O Çali, am I glad to see you!"

"What are you doing, Ms. Lauring?" he asked, as he reached out his hand to steady her.

"We need help. The others . . . are back there," she said breathlessly, pointing the flashlight in the opposite direction. "Ibrahim and Kris have been taken prisoner . . . by some men. We don't know who they are. I thought at first they were soldiers, but they must not be."

"Where are your other companions?" asked Çali, removing his cap to wipe at beads of perspiration. "The ones they call Jack and Mr. Murphy?"

"K.C. and Jack stayed behind . . . to see if they could do something . . . to free the others. I don't know anything else. But we have to hurry. How much farther is it to the camp?"

"It's still a good way back."

"Then let's go. We haven't any time to waste, Çali. Their lives are in danger."

"No. Let's go back the way you've come. It will take too long for us to try to reach the camp."

"But there are too many of them. I think some of them may be chasing after me right now. We need the soldiers. We have no weapons. These people have guns!"

"It'll be all right. Let's go back and find your friends."

"Çali . . ." Katrina started to protest again when suddenly he reached out and grabbed her arm, twisting it like steel in a vise until she cried out in pain.

"Stop. You're hurting me!"

"We are going that way," he ordered calmly. Katrina stared up into his face. His eyes were no longer laughing and friendly. They reminded her of tiny steel-tipped darts, hard and unyielding, as he pushed her roughly in the direction from which she had just come.

"What are you doing?" Katrina cried out in surprise as she stumbled forward. He reached behind his back. A second later he was holding a Beretta 9 mm automatic, pointed directly at her.

"Çali?" Katrina stared at him in horror. "What's happening? I don't understand."

"Move!" The tone in his voice was cold and uncompromising. He shoved her forward again. "Ms. Katrina Lauring, you're an expendable American meddler in affairs that do not concern you. Nothing more. You understand so little because you are stupid foreign trash!"

Katrina unsteadily began retracing her steps, trying as she did to grasp what was happening. *Çali? The happy-go-lucky van driver and camp gofer?*

"Are you one of them?" Katrina asked finally, glancing back over her shoulder.

"Shut up and keep moving," glowered Çali, prodding her with the barrel of his handgun. They went a short distance farther before he answered. "Your infidel lover got rid of one of us, but we anticipated that possibility when we joined Dr. Üzünal's *Kilçilar* staff. When the good doctor became ill and was replaced by your boyfriend, we thought our task would be made easier. Actually, he surprised us. He's been more of a challenge than even he could know. Especially after finding that jar with the letter from the Apostle Peter."

"Was it you who came to Ibrahim's tent and broke into his files?"

"Actually it was both Dr. El and me," Çali responded, his voice edged with boastfulness. "I happened to be up the night your boyfriend found them. I knew it was something important when he said nothing about it the next day. While he was away, I opened the file and took the pictures. Dr. El read the letters. I delivered his handwritten interpretation and the photos to a newspaper reporter who also happens to be one of us."

"And who exactly is 'us'?" Katrina queried.

"Dr. El is an important member of the Refah Party. I am a member of the IBDA-C."

"What's that?"

"You truly are a stupid American," Çali spat the words out with chilling hatred. "Why have they brought you to my land to teach young girls your godless, capitalistic ways? You should have died along with our illustrious project leader in the explosion."

"The explosion?" Katrina's mind was spinning. "You set the explosion? And Renée Patry? That was you as well?"

"Some of my best work, actually. We wanted to get rid of all of you and shut down the project. And we will. Today. This will further embarrass the government leaders who are funding this activity and approving of foreign devils like Valetti and Hurstein rummaging through our treasures. And you as well, for that matter. We intend to drive all of you corrupt Westerners and your defiling influences out of Turkey!"

Katrina did not try to respond.

"Refah is an important political party that is committed to eliminating our country's secular government. We will form a nation under Allah, one that is guided by the Koran, not a godless constitution.

"And the IBDA-C is the Turkish abbreviation for the Great Islamic Raiders of the East," he declared with pride. "We are linked with our brothers in Iran in a mission that will bring our country under the total influence of Islam. No more separation of mosque and state, another result of your atheistic Western influences. As our Iranian brothers drove out the Shah and his infidel followers, so we will overturn the present government in our land and return it to the God of our fathers!"

Çali's tone grew more impassioned as they trudged along the passageway. Katrina was shaken, still trying to grasp the change in the one man she had never given a second thought with regard to his loyalty to Ibrahim.

When they approached another twisting turn in the passageway, it all happened in an instant!

As Katrina rounded the turn ahead of Çali, she saw what looked like two or three handheld lights moving rapidly toward them, no more than ten meters distant. In the next split second, the sound of rapid gunfire reverberated in the narrow tunnel!

One of the lights in front of her disappeared.

She heard a clatter.

A voice shouted something unintelligible.

Two more shots rang out.

Another light gone!

The sole remaining light started toward her again.

"Help!" Katrina cried out, dropping to the ground and dousing her light.

More gunfire! The sharp sting of a rock chip cut into the back of her hand as a bullet smashed against the rock wall beside her! Then the bobbing light disappeared!

Çali cleared the corner as the first shot was being fired. He snapped his light off and now they were enveloped in total darkness. With the last shots, the tunnel became eerily quiet.

The gunfire in the narrow passage had left Katrina's ears ringing. She closed her eyes and swallowed.

What's happening?

Her head felt like a hollow chamber. She swallowed and one ear popped painfully. She stopped breathing in order to listen. *Nothing . . . wait.* A pebble crunched beneath a boot and the cave floor. *He's right here beside me! Another footstep!* His boot grazed against her shoulder. *It's a wonder he hasn't stepped on me.* Katrina was afraid to breathe!

Without warning, a light turned on. Not more than three meters away, in the direction of the gunfire moments before. Çali's handgun roared once, twice! He was standing directly over her. The light went out. In the same split second three shots rang out from well beneath and to the right of where the light had been, aimed at the flash of Çali's weapon. She heard him grunt heavily as the bullets slammed into his chest!

Katrina closed her ears to his pitiful groan, pressing her face in the dirt, as she took the full weight of his body slumping down over her. Katrina lay face down, too petrified to move, hearing only the crashing of her heart against the tunnel floor.

Then a light was on again. She was afraid to look up, to give any sign at all that she was still alive.

"Katy, darlin'?"

That voice!

Slowly, wearily, she lifted her head, unable to make herself move beyond that. The weight of the man she knew was dead had seemingly spent all her life force with his own.

"K.C.?"

She dropped her head down and began shaking all over.

"Oh, dear Lord, is it you? Thank God! Is it really you?"

"Ye know any other Irishman in this underground hell?" he answered, lifting Çali's inert body off of Katrina. "And ye, dear lady? Are ye all right?"

"I . . . I think so," she stammered, as K.C. helped her to a sitting position. Ibrahim, Kris, and Jack crowded around, relief written on their faces. "I just can't stop shaking."

K.C. shined his light on Çali's face.

"What the . . . why . . . it's . . ."

"Çali. I know. I met him in the tunnel. He drew a gun on me and made me come back in your direction. He's . . . he was one of them."

"Did he tell you that?" Ibrahim asked incredulously, staring at the still form of his one-time driver and camp gofer in disbelief.

"Yes. I'm sorry, Ibrahim. He . . . was a member of the Islamic Raiders or something like that. That's what he said anyway. And Dr. El was his partner in all of this. They killed Renée. At least they were in it together. I think Çali was actually the one who did it. And he planted the explosives that almost killed us."

K.C. shook his head. "It's gettin' harder to tell the good ones from the bad ones."

Without warning, more gunfire suddenly erupted from the far end of the tunnel.

"Get those lights out!"

Kris wheeled about, returning the fire with his confiscated

Uzi. Then, just as the light went out, Katrina saw him stagger and fall backward, amid the echoing shots.

"Back! Back!"

"There's a corner. Get around the corner!"

"Kris!"

"Katy. Get back!"

"Kris!" Katrina called out again in desperation.

More gunfire punctuated the scrambling of bodies that pushed and shoved the others back into the darkness, each one willing themselves around a corner they could not see.

"I think Kris is hurt!"

"I have him! Move! Move!"

"Call out yer name if yer around the turn!"

"Jack!"

"Ibrahim!"

"Katrina!"

"Okay." It was K.C.'s voice.

"Kris? Where's Kris?"

"I've got 'im," K.C. answered. "Listen, Ibrahim, turn on yer light but make sure it's pointed away from the turn. Then let's get out o' here."

Ibrahim snapped on his flashlight and grabbed Katrina's hand, half dragging her forward.

Jack took Kris from K.C., slipping his arm around him. Blood was dripping down into his face from just above his ear. His left leg hung limp. And an ugly, dark stain was seeping through the front of his sweater. Jack looked at K.C. who shook his head and motioned them forward. He would bring up the rear guard.

"Ibrahim, get us to that cross-tunnel as fast as ye can!" K.C. called out.

"It shouldn't be much farther," came the answer.

Ten minutes, several slight bends, one major turn, and they were at the side tunnel opening.

"Thank God fer whoever designed this place," muttered K.C. "Otherwise we'd o' been dead meat long ago."

While they paused to catch their breath, Katrina pushed her way past the others to Kris. "How is he?"

"*He* has felt better, but he's going to make it," Kris mumbled.

"Listen carefully now," ordered K.C., having instinctively

appointed himself the officer-in-charge. "The rest of ye get out o' here as quickly as ye can. Get to the surface, an' send back the entire Turkish army, if it's available. While yer at it, if they can find the exit those cave rats 'ave been usin', so much the better. But send some help back down the tunnel. An' 'ave 'em bring a stretcher too."

"I can't leave my brother here," she exclaimed.

Katrina knelt beside Kris, her face pale with worry.

"He's stayin' but yer not, Katy. So get movin'. The quicker yer out and sendin' in some help, the less time Kris and I 'ave to hold these buggers at bay! Now, git!"

Katrina bent forward and kissed Kris on his cheek.

"Okay," said Ibrahim, "we're on our way."

"Wait. Leave us them weapons an' any ammo ye've got. We'll be needin' it more than ye will."

Each Uzi was laid in the side tunnel entrance together with the remaining magazines of ammunition.

"Thanks, lads," K.C. gave a crooked smile. "All donations are gladly accepted. Ibrahim, take care of our little lady. See she gets out safely. An' don't ferget to call home, ye hear? Remind them politicians in Ankara to keep their heads down."

Ibrahim smiled. "I will."

He turned and led the way along the tunnel, with Katrina close behind and Jack bringing up the rear this time. As they moved out of sight of the cross-tunnel, an ominous rattle of gunfire erupted behind them.

"Don't stop!" Ibrahim shouted to the others. He was in charge again. "We have to keep going. It's their only chance."

Katrina glanced over her shoulder, torn by her brother's bloody wounds and a terrible feeling that somehow it was all her fault and now she was deserting him.

With a wrenching sense of guilt and helplessness, she pushed on between the two men.

Fifty-four. Ibrahim

1620 local time

It was four-twenty when the beleaguered trio finally reached the landing and emerged from the new tunnel into the West Tunnel Road. The way was lit now and easier to traverse as they ran. At Level 5, Ibrahim stopped to ask one of the digging teams where Rocco could be found. The men thought he was on top.

After sending one of their number off to warn workers who might be on the lower levels, he ordered the rest to follow them out for their own safety's sake, assuming that if the enemy radicals managed to overcome K.C.'s position, it was possible they might pursue them all the way into the main underground city.

Ibrahim looked at Katrina. She was obviously spent, emotionally as well as physically. Her blouse was soiled and one of her pantlegs hung in tatters at the knee. Her face and hands were streaked with dirt, sweat, and dried blood. Her own? Kris'? Cali's? He couldn't tell.

Her eyes were dull, and vacant, as though her mind were somewhere else. He worried about her, but other things needed to be attended to first.

They hurried up through Levels 4 and 3, shouting for the

377

other work crews to follow them. At Level 2 they ran across Rocco walking down the tunnel path toward them. Ibrahim quickly filled him in as they continued their race to the surface.

The day's designated media pool film team had emerged from filming the underground church only minutes before Ibrahim and the others began spilling out of the entrance to *Kilçilar.* Ben Hur was with them and their number grew rapidly as Ibrahim explained the situation. Rocco ran to where several members of the Turkish military unit sat resting near the supply trucks, having just finished unloading additional food, tents, and bedding.

The military helicopter that had landed a half hour before with the officer-in-charge was nearby, rotor blades turning slowly as the pilot ran through his return flight checklist. Rocco rushed up to the OIC and explained what was happening. The pilot was ordered to stand down and prepare to evacuate at least one wounded person.

In a matter of minutes, the soldiers were transformed from truck drivers and workers into a well-trained, well-armed fighting unit. A small contingent ran to the cave entrance and disappeared inside, with Rocco and Jack in front to guide them to the new tunnel. Another company spread out across the mound in a west-northwesterly direction in search of the hidden cave that had been described by Ibrahim.

Meanwhile, Ibrahim and the OIC were busy conversing on the radio with his unit's command post. A warning message was relayed to Security Headquarters in Ankara, alerting officials there of an impending attack on the ceremony participants at Anit Kabir.

Ibrahim shook hands with the OIC and smiled his appreciation. Then he glanced at his wristwatch and frowned. It was now four-fifty. The ceremony in Ankara was scheduled to begin in ten minutes.

He spotted Katrina sitting alone on a bench at the edge of the dining tent, a cup of hot tea in her hands. Her eyes were closed. At first, he thought she was simply exhausted. But a closer look told him that she was still very much in the thick of the battle. He nodded his head. She would be okay.

Her lips moved silently. He knew she was praying for Kris and K.C.

Ward Tanneberg

1700 local time
Anit Kabir, Ankara

Truckloads of military personnel roared along Gazi Mustafa Kemal Bulvari, forcing traffic aside on one of Ankara's busiest streets. Citizens were left wondering what new crisis had developed in their capital city, as they watched the vehicles turn away from the boulevard and head up the hill.

At the end of Anit Kabir stood the familiar colonnaded temple, one of the nation's finest examples of modern architecture, completed in 1953. Formed out of yellow limestone, the huge and austere Atatürk Mausoleum housed the tomb of the revered late president, Kemal Atatürk. Poised on its high hill, it served as a prominent reminder of all that this man had accomplished for his people.

To the left of the mausoleum was the museum containing artifacts, photos, and even Atatürk's fleet of cars. He had been a controversial man, with a legendary reputation as a war hero, a political giant, a womanizer, and a heavy drinker. Before his death of cirrhosis at age fifty-seven, Atatürk had managed the difficult task of bringing Turkey into the modern world.

The charge forward into the twentieth century encompassed the influencing and initiating of numerous social and economic actions benefiting the people, including the abolishment of the 641-year-old sultanate; replacing the Arabic alphabet with the Roman alphabet; the near total abolishment of illiteracy among the Turkish people; the cessation of Islam as the state religion; the abolition of polygamy, along with equal rights for women; replacing Koranic law with the Swiss Legal Code in the civil justice system; and the rapid and very expensive modernization of agriculture, industry, and communication.

On the esplanade at the foot of the steps leading to the monument itself, a small crowd of onlookers, most of whom wore heavy jackets or overcoats to fend off the chill of the late afternoon breeze, along with several members of the press corps, strained to see the proceedings taking place above them.

Military honor guards, representing the Turkish Army and Navy, stood at attention on either side of the monument's entrance. A small security contingent was on duty as well, but its members were relaxed; this day was almost over for them. In another hour, they would be sitting down to dinner with their families.

Inside, one hundred fifty folding chairs were arranged for the honored guests, participating government personnel, and several business and professional people who had been invited from the local community.

The Prime Minister stood near the front, greeting friends and fellow power-figures in the Turkish governmental hierarchy as they strolled past to their assigned seats. American Ambassador Walter Joseph Logan and his wife, Dorothy, stood beside her, shaking hands and smiling, Mrs. Logan impressing her admirers with her proficiency in the Turkish language.

That an American without Turkish heritage was fluent in their language had been a major factor in her husband's popularity as ambassador in this Euro-Asian community. The fact that Mrs. Logan was also linguistically fluent in five other languages was inconsequential to them. This nation openly admired her and had adopted her as one of their own.

The mausoleum was enclosed on three sides by thick walls inscribed with excerpts from Atatürk's writings and speeches. Its simplicity was its crowning architectural achievement. There was nothing to distract attention from the huge marble sarcophagus containing the remains of Atatürk himself. Not far away was the sarcophagus of Atatürk's loyal friend and successor as president, Ismet Inönü. There was a feeling in the crowd today of peacefulness, contentment, and joy at the privilege of being in this place at this time.

The last of the guests had just been seated and the man designated to introduce the first speaker was stepping to the microphone when the first military truck loaded with troops ground its way onto the hill and roared across the parking lot. Out of the corner of his eye, the master of ceremonies saw the head of today's security team standing at the far left wall, talking to someone on his handheld radio.

He opened his mouth to welcome the guests, then paused, casting a glance of growing concern as more troop vehicles roared onto the hill and began fanning out across the parking area. The look became one of dismay as fully armed men in battle dress poured from the trucks and ran toward the monument.

The OIC of security was hand-signaling to other members of his team who were on their feet at once, scanning the guests and the surrounding area.

The crowd, whose backs were turned to the unfolding scene, began to detect that something unplanned was taking place and some turned to see what was happening.

Suddenly a man jumped to his feet, shouted something, snapped an Uzi submachine gun from under his coat, and began firing!

He was not alone. Others scattered through the crowd followed suit. A total of eight in all.

Pandemonium reigned!

People fell to the floor in a hail of bullets.

Others began running haphazardly, stumbling against overturned chairs and tripping over fallen companions.

Guns rattled.

Bullets thudded randomly in the ceiling, in the walls, in the flesh of human bodies. Panic ruled the moment. Cries of pain and sounds of dying filled the air. The tranquil afternoon ceremony had become a ritual of consummate horror!

A woman tried vainly to shield her child. Both lay twisted and dying in pools of mother-daughter blood.

Two security agents threw themselves on top of the Prime Minister. Both died instantly, their bodies riddled with bullets. She lived, with only superficial bruises suffered as she fell beneath them.

Three cabinet ministers were cut down. Two died instantly. The third lived until midnight.

Four more government workers, thirteen prominent civilians, and five soldiers were unmercifully slaughtered.

Twenty-seven others were wounded and subsequently hospitalized.

Six of the eight shooters were killed. The remaining two were wounded, one critically, and taken prisoner.

Three additional terrorists were captured during the confusion, while hurriedly planting explosives in the museum.

It was believed that two more had escaped on foot, and security police, together with their military units, searched the area surrounding Anit Kabir and the Maltepe district for the rest of the night, but turned up no one.

The tragedy would have been much worse, had Ibrahim's

warning gone unheeded. Still, it was a terrible scene as soldiers and security personnel brandished weapons and raced about, searching for their outlaw countrymen. Turkish citizens stood weeping, while others wandered in a daze, hardly believing they were still alive, shocked to see the beloved fruit of a nation lying wasted on the ground, torn viciously and recklessly from the tree of life.

The first to fall victim to this venomous terrorist attack had been the master of ceremonies, cut down before uttering a word of introduction.

The second was Mrs. Walter Joseph Logan.

Fifty-five. Katrina

2115 local time
Kilçilar

It was not until well after dark that soldiers began emerging from the underground city. Katrina stood beside Ibrahim at the cave entrance, anxious for some sign of Kris and K.C. Ben Hur and Tahsin Cem were nearby, talking in low tones. The soldiers walked past looking grim and fatigued.

Ibrahim spoke to the squad leader. He nodded without smiling and pointed back to the cave. Then something else was said and the soldier moved on. Katrina's eyes were on Ibrahim now, waiting for some signal. There was none. Her attention was drawn back to the cave entrance as more movement could be seen in the tunnel. Soldiers were carrying a stretcher.

Kris!

K.C. trudged behind the stretcher-bearers, an Uzi still in his hand, looking haggard and spent. Jack was at his side. K.C. tried to smile when he saw them, but it was halfhearted. Katrina ran forward to meet the soldiers carrying Kris' still form. His eyes were closed, his face pale and drawn.

"Kris?"

There was no response.

Katrina looked up at K.C. He shook his head.

"I don' know, Katy darlin'," he said sadly. "He's lost a lot o' blood. He stayed conscious 'til about an hour ago. Helped t' load the weapons, 'e did. It was pretty fierce down there fer a while. Them Turk soldiers are fightin' machines. They took no prisoners."

Katrina walked beside the stretcher as they made their way to the waiting helicopter. "What will happen now? Where are they taking him?"

"He's being transported by air to the hospital in Nigde," answered Ibrahim. "It's not that far by air and much better equipped for this than the clinic in Güzelyurt. They've called doctors in already to help deal with Kris' wounds. He's going to need blood."

"Can we go with them?"

Ibrahim turned to the OIC and inquired.

"He says they can take two. Do you happen to know his blood type?"

"It's the same as mine. A-Positive."

"I'm A-Positive too," said Ben Hur.

"Then that makes three of us. So am I. All right, you two go with the helicopter," ordered Ibrahim. "Rocco, you're staying here and you're in complete charge of the operation until I get back. Including the media. Kat, I'll work out some cleanup details with the OIC and the others and then join you as quickly as I can. They'll have his blood type on hand to start. We should have enough blood between us to see him through for the next few days. Hurry and get in!"

Katrina and Ben Hur were no sooner aboard the helicopter than it rose a bit unsteadily from the dirt parking lot, pitched left, and took off into the night sky.

KATRINA MOVED HER SCRAPED KNEE to a more comfortable position as she stretched out on the makeshift table, watching the plastic pouch fill with the color of burgundy. She thought the bag looked so impersonal, yet what could be more personal than taking blood from one body and giving it to another?

The nurse did not speak English and communication had so far been limited to hand signals and the translation efforts of Ben

Hur who sat patiently on a wooden stool in the corner, awaiting his turn on the small hospital table.

"Do you think he'll be all right?"

"With your blood and mine together, how can he miss?" Ben Hur answered, in an effort to lighten a depressing situation. He glanced at his watch. Ten-thirty.

"You are Mrs. Lauring?"

The voice came from the doorway. Katrina turned her head to the right and saw a youngish man in a blood-spattered white smock over an open-collar shirt and dark trousers. His brown shoes were worn and scuffed, obviously having seen better days.

"I'm Katrina Lauring," she answered. "Are you Kris' doctor?"

He nodded.

"How is he?"

"We've started him on a pint of blood already," he answered somberly, "but he's lost a good deal of blood and his type is in short supply. We'll have to fly some in from Ankara or Istanbul. We're going to need more before we're done."

Ben Hur spoke up. "I'm next on the table. And Ibrahim Sevali is on his way from the underground city. He'll be here shortly."

"You are all his blood type?"

"Yes."

"Good. I'll call our technicians and have them start preparing your units." His English was broken and halting, but understandable. He looked at Katrina. "Your husband's condition, it is serious, Mrs. Lauring. I am obliged to inform you of this."

Katrina did not try to correct him. That was unimportant now.

"We'll know more once we operate. A bullet went through his leg—here." He demonstrated by pointing to an area about six inches above his left knee. "The head wound is superficial and surgery for the injury to his leg must come later. For now, we close areas that lose blood. The second bullet is lodged here . . . above heart. That is our great concern."

"Is he . . . will he . . . " Katrina's voice faltered as her eyes filled with tears.

"He is young and strong," assured the doctor, as he stepped back into the hall. "I do my best."

"Thank you, doctor," Katrina responded to the empty doorway. The nurse removed the needle from her arm and helped her down from the table. The physician had disappeared from sight, but Katrina could hear his footsteps on the tile floor as he hurried down the hallway.

"My turn," grunted Ben Hur, brushing past Katrina and heaving himself onto the table. The room grew silent again, the only noise the swish of the nurse's uniform as she attended to her next donor.

Twenty minutes later Katrina was dialing a hospital phone. The nurses were extremely helpful, inviting her behind their station to use one of their phones.

What time is it back home? she wondered. It seemed only hours, not days, since her call to Kris, asking him to come.

Guilt twisted itself around her thoughts. Guilt at having involved Kris in this mess in the first place. *Yet, how could I have known? I wouldn't have asked him to come, if I had known.* She dropped her head into her hand as the phone began ringing in her ear.

A small voice inside said accusingly, *It's your fault! He came because of you.* It seemed as though a lifetime slipped past as another wave of exhaustion swept over her.

It's your fault!

She suddenly felt old. Very, very old.

It's your . . .

"Hello?" The voice startled her. It sounded distant this time. There was static interference. A bad connection.

"Hello, mom," she spoke up, trying to control the waiver in her voice. She was *not* going to cry. "It's Katrina."

"O Katrina! Oh, my, this is a surprise! It's so good to hear your voice. Are you all right, dear? Is everything okay?"

"I'm fine," Katrina answered, hesitating momentarily, "but Kris has been hurt. That's why I am calling."

"Kris hurt?" Her mother's voice became apprehensive. "What happened, dear? Where is he?"

Katrina took a deep breath. There was no way to soften this blow. "He's been . . . wounded, mother."

"Hello, Katrina?" Her father's voice boomed out over the extension phone in the bedroom. "What's this about Kris being hurt?"

"Katrina says Kris has been wounded," she heard her mother explain before she could answer.

"Wounded? What's going on over there?"

"Listen, please! Kris was shot by terrorists. It's too long a story. He was helping me ... us ... and ..." her voice broke, "and I feel so terrible."

"Is he alive?" asked Pedar Lauring, his voice at once low and apprehensive.

"Yes. They're operating right now. He was shot twice. Once in the leg and also in the chest, above the heart." She didn't bother mentioning the more superficial head wound.

A long silence followed.

"All right. Your mother and I are coming just as soon as we can."

"No, daddy. I mean ... I didn't ... oh, I don't know what I mean."

"Where are you now?"

For the next few minutes Katrina rehearsed the information they would need. Then she asked, "What will you do for passports?"

"We'll start to work on it now," her father answered, his tone surprisingly soft and deferential. "Don't worry about us. We have the numbers where you can be reached, and we'll stay in touch to let you know where we are. Just take care of yourself and Kris. All right?"

"All right."

"We love you."

"I love you both too."

Katrina hung up the phone and stood for a moment, dazed at what she had heard. Could she have been mistaken? No, it was her father's voice all right. No doubt about that. Saying the words that she doubted. How long had it been since she had heard her father say "We love you"?

She couldn't remember.

Fifty-six. Kristian

Sunday, 21 September,
0205 local time
Antalya

. . . floating . . . I hear voices . . . no control. Is that Katrina calling . . . can't be sure . . . a man's voice too . . .

And a woman . . . the same one . . . she's back again! Long hair like a golden waterfall cascading over bare shoulders . . . skin like pale ivory. Her eyes . . . blue . . . she looks at me . . . her lips move. What are you saying? Hands . . . reaching . . . so gentle . . .

In her arms now . . . her lips touch my cheek . . . hair brushing across my face . . . laughing . . . crying . . . perfume . . . no . . . antiseptic . . . where am I? Wait . . . don't go. I still don't know your name . . . or why you keep coming. WHO ARE YOU?

It was dark. At least, so it seemed when I opened my eyes. At first I thought K.C. and I were still in the cave. I felt for a weapon to load, waited for more gunfire. Nothing. Everything is still. And different. I'm not in the cave. I'm in a room. A bed. How did I get here? I turned my head. At the far wall, a light shown from behind a door. Then someone stirred in the darkness.

"Kristian?"

That voice. It sounds like . . .

"Are you awake, Kristian? It's me. Your father."

I knew I must be dreaming now as I stared up at the face peering down at me.

"What . . . how? Dad?"

"Yes, it's me. Your mother went to Katrina's apartment to rest. Katrina is outside in the waiting room. I'll get her."

"Wait . . . thirsty. Mouth is so dry."

"Here's some water," Pedar held the glass. "Put the straw in your mouth. That's it. Okay? Have you got it?"

I drew the water across my tongue. Cool and clean. I ran my tongue over cracked lips.

"You've been drinking through a needle the last few days, son. We've been waiting for you. And praying too. Now I'll get Katrina."

"Wait," I said again, my mind whirling. "Mother is here? You are here? Where is here? Where am I?"

"You're in a hospital in Antalya."

"How did I get here?"

"Katrina can fill in the details better than I," answered Pedar. "She's been with you all along—won't leave your bedside to go any farther than the couch in the waiting room. I'm not sure of the details, but they tell me you were flown here from another hospital where they patched you up. Let me go find Katrina and she can tell you exactly."

"When did you get here?"

"Yesterday morning, about ten o'clock."

My mind continued to race and my head hurt.

"What day is it?"

"Sunday. It's about two in the morning."

"Sunday," I repeated, hardly able to believe that I'd lost three days. "How did you get here so quickly? You guys don't even own a passport, do you?"

"We do now. An old friend of mine, actually the man who led me to Jesus when I was in college, is with the State Department. He not only got us passports overnight, but booked us with an airline that gave us a special emergency fare and, because they had two open seats, let us fly in business class. Actually, if we had not been so concerned over you, it would have been very pleasurable. We've talked about doing it again someday."

This was my dad talking. I stared at him again. I couldn't believe he actually had come all this way to be at my bedside. It was too much.

"Okay, dad, go get Katrina."

Alone in the semidarkness, I lay very still, gathering my thoughts and emotions as best I could, reaching back over three missing days. Back to the tunnel . . .

The door swung open and suddenly Katrina was there.

"Kris? How do you feel? Oh, big brother, you don't know how happy I am that you're awake. I've been so worried." As she leaned over to kiss me, a tear fell on my nose. I hate it when people I love start to cry.

"Hey, knock off the tears, Kat. You'll get my face all salty!"

She laughed as she held my face. Her hands were warm.

"You feel good, sis," I whispered, "really good."

"So do you! I've felt so terrible since all this happened. I got you into this, Kris. I'm so sorry. Will you forgive me?"

"Are you kidding? I wouldn't have missed it for a million dollars. For two million? And a ratings bonus? Maybe."

We laughed, though I tried not to. It hurt too much.

"Actually, this is turning out really great," I said finally.

"How so?"

"First, I'm still alive, though I hurt like the dickens. Second, you somehow manage to get Dad and Mom out of the country and over here for a visit. Although, next time use your own chest for the bullet that brings them, okay? Third, just think how all of this will play back home on my new show. I'll be The Wounded Hero. The fact that I don't remember much and somebody else had to carry me out of that place won't even figure in. Kat, I need to know, did everybody get out all right?"

"Everyone else is fine. You're too much, big brother," laughed Katrina. "Just count yourself lucky you were hit only three times. Once more and you might have been hurt!"

"Well said, as always," I chuckled. "Where are you going, dad?"

Pedar was backing away and turning toward the door.

"To call your mother. Katrina showed me how to use the telephone and gave me the number to her apartment, so I'm going to wake your mother up with the good news."

"Let her sleep. She's probably exhausted."

"No. If I let her sleep another minute now that you're awake, I'd have to fly home by myself. If I lived to make it to the airport."

Pedar disappeared through the door.

"What's with him?" I asked, as Katrina settled herself on the edge of my bed. "Does he seem different to you? Or did I take a bullet somewhere that's affected my perception?"

"I'm not sure, Kris. I thought I noticed it when I first talked to them on the phone, after all this happened. I called them from the hospital in Nigde. He sounded different even then. And since they arrived yesterday, well, I'm with you. I really don't know. I asked Mother how they were and she just smiled and gave me a hug. In spite of all this mess, they look . . . happier, I guess. That's the only word I can think of."

"How did I get here?" I asked, changing the subject.

"The doctor at Nigde did all that he knew to do for you there. He was fearful of removing the bullet from your chest, however. It missed your heart by a couple of inches.

"At first they were going to take you to the University Hospital in Ankara. But after consulting with some other physicians, they came up with two young doctors here in Antalya who are highly respected. One of them even spent a year working in Los Angeles in a trauma center. Ibrahim knew the other one from the University in Istanbul. It also made it convenient to have you here in my town. So, Ibrahim and I made the decision. And here you are."

"Thanks for taking care of me, sis."

"You'd lost a lot of blood by the time they got you out of the tunnel and to the hospital. For a while you continued bleeding internally. The doctor in Nigde finally managed to bring it under control, but you required several units to bring you back. It was touch and go for a few hours. You were such a pasty white when they first carried you out of that tunnel, Kris. I was so afraid . . . "

"Where did they get the blood? Do they have a good system over here or should I start to worry?"

"I don't honestly know. Everything seemed clean enough. Ibrahim assured me that the Nigde hospital was an okay place. And this one is quite modern. I watched to make sure they were using disposable needles and all that sort of thing when they took our blood. They started you on a pint of 'generic Turkish.' Before they were through, I gave you a pint. So did Ibrahim and Ben Hur. We're all your blood type. Can you believe that?"

"As Dad would say, 'There are no surprises with God,'" I answered back in my most prophetic voice. "So now I've got a pint of Jewish, a couple of pints of Turkish, and a pint of Danish sister in me, mixing it up with all my regular stuff. Good grief! No wonder I'm tired. My blood is in shock!"

Katrina squeezed my hand.

"Your blood has never had it this good!" she retorted. "Now get some rest. Don't overdo your first waking moments in three days."

"Fluff my pillow, will you? Turn it over."

"Why?"

"The cool side is on the bottom. It always feels fresh when you turn it over. Didn't you know that?"

"Whatever works, big brother," she responded, reaching for the pillow. "I know you're back now. You're starting to be a pain already."

I smiled and closed my eyes.

When I opened them again, it felt as though no time had passed at all. But the room was bright and early morning sunshine was pouring through the window. Mother was there. We hugged and kissed as best I could. Then Katrina brought someone else forward who had been standing just out of my line of vision.

"Kris, I'd like you to meet Michelle."

"Your roomie," I said, reaching out to take her hand.

"Her rummy roomie," came the response in the most delightful French accent. Her voice was clear and light. Her dark eyes twinkled. She was dressed in a simple white blouse under a jacket, and a pair of jeans.

"Your father told us you had awakened. I drove your mother over in their rental car and was going to stay outside. You should be with your family before having to meet strangers. But Katy insisted. She's told me a great deal about her big brother."

"Don't believe her, Michelle," I answered, unable to take my eyes off of her. "I'm really a nice guy."

"I'm sure you are," she answered back, an amused look on her incredible face. "And now, Mr. Nice Guy, I have to run home and change for school, so may I please have my hand back?"

I dropped it like a hot coal. It was my turn to be embarrassed and hearty gales of laughter filled the room at my expense.

Fifty-seven. Kristian

I slept off and on through the rest of the day. The painkillers were working overtime. Early that evening, the nurse brought me some food from what I assumed was the hospital cafeteria. Let's just say that food in Turkey's hospitals wasn't up to my taste.

Mom stayed with me during the afternoon. It was pleasant to wake up and find her there, just like I used to when I was sick as a kid. Talk came easily, "catching up" sorts of things, and her head nodded once in a while too, still feeling the effects of jet lag.

It was about six-thirty when Katrina and Dad walked into the room, along with two pleasant-faced people I did not know. Kat was all smiles. She'd had a good day in the classroom and was enjoying being back in what she had come to Turkey to do.

She introduced me to Ian Hedley, the principal of her school, and his wife, Dorothy. They were a cheery, lighthearted pair and I could see why Kat thought so highly of them. The thought occurred in passing that they were the exact opposite of what we had grown up with. Well, at least Kat had found an enjoyable place to use her skills and her brilliance in a way that was fulfilling to her. That's worth a lot in anybody's book.

After about twenty minutes, the Hedleys invited me to visit their school when I was released from the hospital and then excused themselves, saying that they still had an evening's worth of work before they could call it a day.

When they had gone, Kat and Mother fell into the usual small talk that women find so easy to engage in. I listened, not so much to what they were saying as to the sounds of their voices. Since waking up in the hospital after my brush with death, almost any human voice was soothing, but particularly my mother's and Kat's.

I guess I closed my eyes for a few minutes. When I opened them, Dad was sitting close to my bedside. I wondered what was going through his mind. He had a strangely unsettled look about him, as though he were nervous or concerned about something. As it turned out, I didn't have long to wait before I knew why.

"Everyone," Pedar began, his voice low and showing a trace of guarded emotion, "I need to say something. It's important to me that you all hear what I'm about to tell you. Especially you, Kris. It's also with a deep sense of sorrow and regret that I have waited to share this with you until now. You deserved better from me."

I stared at him, then glanced over at Mom and Kat for some indication of what was coming next. Their gaze was steady as they sat waiting. Mother appeared to be the more relaxed of the two, while Kat seemed as perplexed as I was. Wild things flashed through my mind. . . . *Are they getting a divorce? No, that's crazy. He must be seriously ill. What else could it be?*

"Your mother and I have talked about this at length many times recently, and prayed a great deal too," he continued. "Our family's emotional distancing is no secret to any of us and, as it has continued to increase, positions have been taken that only serve to further alienate us. Deep down inside I've known that I was the primary source of this conflict, but I couldn't seem to do anything about it. It was just there, like some insurmountable mountain.

"I know what the Scriptures tell us to do. James wrote, 'Confess your sins to each other and pray for each other so that you may be healed.' I know it's a very humbling thing when children must confess wrongdoing to their parents. Well, it's even

394

more so when the parent must confess to his children."

"Dad," I started to interrupt, not even sure why, or what I wanted to say.

"Please." Dad raised his hand for silence. "Let me finish. Then you can all say whatever you wish and I'll listen. This began years ago, before either of you children were born, even before I met your mother. I was in college, studying to be an accountant. Sarah told me that she shared that with you, Katrina. When I became angry and protested, she said that you deserved to know."

Katrina nodded, her countenance taking on a look of uncertainty.

"Well, Sarah was right, as she is a good deal of the time. You deserve to know that, and a lot more besides. Anyway, in those days I was living a godless, careless life. My parents were not churchgoing people. Dad was an alcoholic and drove my mother to an early grave. Soon after she was gone, he was killed in a barroom, beaten to death by a drunk who hit him across the head repeatedly with the butt-end of a pool cue over some foolish argument.

"We've told you that your grandparents died before you were born, and that is true. But I could never bring myself to tell you how my parents died. Until now I was always too ashamed."

Dad looked across at Mother, as if seeking her support. She smiled and nodded almost imperceptibly. He took a deep breath and turned back to me again.

"While in college, I met a young female student. We thought we were in love. Actually, it was more serious than that. We became lovers. Then, one day, she came to me and told me that she was pregnant and that I was the father."

I closed my eyes and then opened them again. I could not believe what I was hearing. This was my father talking. I was stunned!

"She and I went home to tell her parents. Her father was a wealthy businessman in Tacoma, and her mother was well known in society circles there. They were furious, of course, and threw me out of the house. Worse yet, they disowned their daughter who had become an embarrassment to them.

"We returned to WSU and finished out the quarter together. Eventually, she had the baby. I was in the waiting room when it came—in those days the father wasn't permitted in delivery. I took the two of them home and we lived together for just over two years while I worked and continued my studies part-time.

"We rented a tiny apartment and tried to make a go of it, but it was very hard. She missed her friends, her family. Even her brother and sister turned their backs on her. I worked and studied. That took up most of the time we might have spent with each other, had things been different.

"It didn't take us long to realize we did not love each other. We both knew it, but our wrong choices had trapped us. The only thing we really had in common was the baby we'd created. Her unhappiness grew, causing her to withdraw more and more into her own private world. She became depressed. And very lonely. I confess that I didn't see it coming. I was too wound up in myself to understand the depth of her hurting.

"Then one day I came home . . . and found her. The note said simply that she was sorry and that she had locked our child in the bedroom. Ingé . . . that was her name . . . had put him there so that he would not come out and find her before I returned home. When I opened the bedroom door there he was, sitting in the middle of the room on the floor, hungry and crying."

He paused for a long moment, looking at me, and his eyes grew moist. My stomach began tying itself in little knots as I watched him fight to control his emotions.

"I'm sorry," he said at last, clearing his throat. "The memory of that afternoon is still very hard for me. I've carried so much guilt for so many years. Ingé and I had both been irresponsible. I knew that I had not taken her life. At least, not overtly. Yet there I was, spiraling downward, so full of guilt that I seriously thought about suicide myself. The only thing that stopped me was the child."

He hesitated again, then spoke.

"You are that child, Kristian."

There was only a stunned silence.

I felt like a huge fist had hit me in the stomach! For a moment I couldn't even breathe. I closed my eyes . . . and there she was.

The woman with the long blond hair . . . her name is Ingé. . . . She's my mother!

Dad's voice drew me back as he continued.

"I finished school. An aunt took you for a while. I went into a deep depression and started drinking heavily. One day a young man from the opposite end of the dorm hall . . . my friend in the State Department I mentioned to you . . . came to my room and confronted me with what I was doing and where I was headed if I kept it up.

"Most of all, he talked about what a difference Jesus Christ can make in a surrendered life. I remember going to my knees there in the room with my friend. He prayed. I prayed. It was the first time for me. I had never prayed about anything before. Not for my parents. Not for anything. Not even a blessing on a meal. But that day, I asked for Christ's forgiveness of my sins and for the terrible hurt and anger I was carrying inside. That was the day I became a Christian.

"After graduation, I went to Bible college. Sarah and I met there. We fell in love. Before I asked her to marry me, I told her everything about my past. She loved me anyway, for which I shall ever be grateful. I brought her to visit you. It was love at first sight where you were concerned too. Though we were not married for several more months, that day Sarah became your mother in her heart. I knew it and so did she. There was never any doubt about it. Sarah fell in love with you as if you had issued from her own womb."

I looked over at Katrina. Tears had begun tracing a path down her cheeks. Dad saw me glance her way.

"Katrina is your half sister, Kristian."

I turned back to stare at him again.

"I've always carried the guilt of my past," he said, wiping at his eyes with his hand, "like a heavy weight on my heart. It's one thing to be forgiven by God. Quite another to forgive oneself. They go hand in hand, but they are different.

"God's forgiveness came freely and easily to me. But I've still not fully accomplished the act of forgiving myself. At least not until now. I loved you, Kristian. It was myself that I hated, what I had done, the life that I felt responsible for ruining. Even after we entered the ministry, my past continued to haunt me.

"I'm afraid as I saw society changing, morals in decline, I imprinted my own weaknesses and fears on my family. I was overly strict and harsh with you both because of my own failures. I know a parent sometimes has to be a dictator where the welfare of his children is concerned, but I overdid it with the two of you. I secretly feared that you might go out from us and fail as I had done.

"Thank God for the softening influence of your dear mother, or it would have been much worse.

"I even hid the facts of my earlier life from my denominational officials. It's only recently that Sarah and I went to them so that I might confess my deceitfulness. Thank God they've responded with love and gracious forgiveness.

"Your mother has stood with me and loved me all this time, even when I couldn't love myself. Were it not for her . . . well, I can't imagine what I might have become. But the truth is that I've lived with this terrible lie these many years.

"There are sins of commission and sins of omission. I've been guilty of them both where you dear children are concerned. I know there's nothing I can do to rectify the harm I've caused. I'm sure I'll regret it for the rest of my life. I am so very sorry. I can only ask you to forgive me and, if you have it in your hearts, to begin anew . . . "

"O daddy!" I heard Katrina's sob as she hurried around the bed and threw her arms around his neck. "Daddy, I love you so!"

I couldn't stop staring as they hugged. This man, whom I felt had kept me at arm's length for twenty-eight years, suddenly wrapped those arms around his daughter for the first time that I could remember since she was in elementary school. His tears ran freely down onto Kat's shoulder. After a while, she pulled herself away and went to hug Mom, who had sat very still through it all, watching everything intently. Dad was left to wipe his face with a handkerchief he pulled from his pocket.

Finally, we mustered up enough courage to look at each other again. A parade of jumbled emotions had climbed into bed with me. My lips were dry. I tried unsuccessfully to lick them. Without a word, Dad reached over and handed me a glass of water from my nightstand. I sipped and then handed it back.

"Wow," I said at last, heaving a deep sigh. "That's heavy! I have no idea what to say."

I lay motionless, drained by what I had just seen and heard. Then I sighed again.

"No, that's not true. On second thought, maybe I do."

I reached out my hand to my father. The same one he'd rejected the last time. He took it in his.

I struggled to find the right words. I wanted to let go and cry, to rid myself of all the pent-up anger and hostility that I had "stuffed" for so many years. But, that could come later.

"I guess I'm in need of forgiveness too," I said at last, "for stuff that I've carried around so long I can't even remember. And for things I've said that have made the hurts between us even worse. I didn't make it any easier for you, I'm certain of that, but I really do love you. I guess that's why I was so angry. I just couldn't find a way to get through to you. Now that I know, I'm sorry for what you went through. Of course, I forgive you, dad, and I'm asking you for the same. I love you very much. And, hey . . . I'm proud to be your son!"

He looked as though he would break apart at any moment. He squeezed my hand until it hurt and then he leaned over the bed and hugged me. That hurt too. Like crazy. And felt sensational at the same time!

"She had long blond hair, didn't she?"

Dad stared disbelievingly. He started to speak, then stopped short.

"It came down past her shoulders. Her eyes were blue. She was a very pretty woman."

"But how . . . ?"

"In the night sometimes. She's come to me in the night. In my dreams. Almost like a vision. At first, I saw only her outline. Later she was clearer, like a fuzzy photograph that comes into focus. I've had no idea who she was. I even thought it might be some sort of premonition about the person I'd fall in love with one day. But it was her, wasn't it? I was remembering . . . my mother."

Dad nodded silently, his lips trembling.

"Her hands. I remember her hands and times when she held me close to her. Her fingers were long and graceful. How old was I?"

"Two years and two months on the day she died," he whispered, as tears spilled down his cheeks. He made no attempt to wipe them.

The room filled with silence as we looked from one person to another. I took another deep breath and let it go.

"What a relief."

"A relief?"

"Yes. You just broke a huge hole through the wall that's been between us our entire lives, dad. That took a ton of courage! Thanks for being humble . . . and courageous . . . and honest with me. With us all."

Mother was standing at the foot of the bed, teary-eyed like the rest of us, looking a little unsure as to what to expect next. I could almost read the thoughts running through her mind. Where did all of this leave her?

"Mom, now that I know who she was, my birth mother is still only a dream to me. You're the one who's really my mother. She gave life to me, but you made a life for me. You've loved me as your very own and that's the way I'll *always* love you!"

Mother moved to join the rest of us as hugs and kisses and tears and laughter started all over again.

Family.

My mind flashed back to the underground city, down the ancient stone steps and into the house of death. To The Writer. Pulcheria. Theodora. We were from different worlds, and yet so very much alike. "For us and for our salvation He came down from heaven," he wrote. Words of faith and hope and courage. But, more than that, words of truth.

Family.

Like The Writer's family, we really are one after all.

But truth is what it has taken for us to find that out.

• • •

ASSOCIATED PRESS. October 04
Following a major crackdown on terrorism in Istanbul,
Ankara, and other major Turkish cities, seventeen days
have come and gone without a single act of violence. The
Prime Minister has applauded the work being done by
police and military personnel. A sweep of known terrorist
hideaways has resulted in numerous arrests. The mayors of
Istanbul, Ankara, Izmir, and Kusadasi have indicated their
support of the Minister's handling of the crisis and have
formally declared their backing of a coalition between
ANAP and the Minister's own True Path Party [DYP]. The
leader of ANAP remains resolute in his opposition to such
a move.

• • •

Fifty-eight. The Commission

Kris stayed in touch with the studio by telephone and fax for the next several days. The *Kilçilar* story had heated up considerably with its connection to the Ankara terrorist massacre. At the heart of it all were various groups of young terrorist radicals, such as Çali's Great Islamic Raiders of the East.

Side chambers in the secret cavern had turned out to be a repository for guns, grenades, plastic explosives, even SAMs smuggled into the country, primarily from Iran. Word came that this discovery, along with subsequent arrests, had resulted in defusing a major terrorist assault planned for Ankara and Istanbul. One source of illegal weapons had reportedly been cut, due to the help of a lone shepherd somewhere in eastern Turkey, near Mt. Ararat. Security was being beefed up in the southeastern section of Turkey as a result, and a strong protest had been formally lodged with the Iranian government and the United Nations.

The war against terrorism was far from over, but many Turks were beginning to stand up now for the preservation of their Republic. There was renewed hope!

Well before Kris was released from the hospital, Tom Knight and Carole Upton were busily working on a prime time special that would tell the entire story from the "inside." It was tentatively scheduled for the Sunday night following Christmas.

Three days after waking up in Antalya, Kris had been given the green light by his physicians for surgery on his leg. Where the thigh bone had been splintered by the bullet, a six-inch rod was inserted to compensate for its weakened structure. During the following weeks, Kris slowly began engaging in daily physical therapy sessions under the watchful eye of his doctors and an excellent physical therapist who had been trained in Paris.

They praised his progress in the rehabilitation of his leg. Kris congratulated himself on having made the decision to have the surgery in Antalya, rather than attempting the long journey back to America. Both doctors, trained in Istanbul, London, and Chicago, had proven their expertise and skills, overcoming all of Kris' initial apprehensions.

On the day of his release, Kris carried his crutches across his lap as the therapist wheeled him out the hospital's main entrance and to a waiting car. He was trailed by watchful parents and a sister on whose face was a smile that wouldn't quit. The three of them crowded into the backseat while Michelle de Mené stood by, holding open the passenger door. She watched as the therapist helped Kris squirm into the front passenger seat. Carefully closing the door, she paused to thank the man for his help and then skipped happily around to the driver's side.

Michelle had visited Kris every afternoon after school. At first her visits were short, but they grew in length as the days passed. What had seemed at first only polite concern for her roommate's brother soon deepened into warm friendship and mutual admiration. The three backseat passengers nudged one another and grinned as Michelle started the car, then paused before pulling out into the traffic, checking to be sure Kris was as comfortable as possible and reaching over to see that his seat belt was securely fastened.

"You didn't bother to ask if we were okay back here or if our seat belts were fastened," chided Katrina, slapping gently at Michelle's shoulder. This time it was Michelle's turn to blush.

In between continued daily physical therapy, Kris managed to visit Katrina's and Michelle's classrooms. His picture had been in the country's newspapers and on television along with Ibrahim, Katrina, Jack, and K.C. To the students he was the personification of the American hero—the handsome, dashing, television star and brother of one of their very own teachers. He spoke briefly to the *ortaokul* and *lise* sections of the AGS student body, answering questions and signing autographs.

When Michelle told him that her students saw him as some sort of valiant, courageous champion, he felt embarrassed and was quick to encourage them to study and emulate the lives of great men and women who had made outstanding contributions to mankind in their own country. During one such classroom discussion, one student raised her hand and asked who Kris saw as his own personal hero.

Later at the apartment, while Kris napped on the couch and Katrina had gone to the kitchen to begin preparing dinner, Michelle found herself alone with Pedar and Sarah on the veranda. She described the classroom scene and told them what Kris had answered.

"I think the question caught him off guard at first," she said, "because he hesitated before responding. I could tell he was thinking seriously about his answer. The whole room was so quiet as my girls waited. I wish you could have been there. Kris said, 'Several people come to mind, but three stand out to me right now. First is Jesus Christ, whom I am beginning to realize has done for me more than I will ever be able to tell. And next on my list of heroes are my dad and mom!'"

Pedar's chin trembled. Sarah dabbed at her eyes with a kerchief. Michelle gave them each a kiss on the cheek and stepped back. "I think his heroes are the best ones he could have shared with my class, don't you?"

Not waiting for an answer, she left them and went inside to help Katrina with dinner. As she passed by the window that looked out onto the verandah, Pedar and Sarah were in each other's arms.

The end of Kris' third week of recovery was also his first night out in Antalya. On Katrina's recommendation, he took Michelle to dinner at Françesco's. The next morning, he prepared to board a plane for his return trip to America. Pedar and Sarah said good-bye to the Hedleys, who had come to the airport as a farewell gesture.

Katrina stood by listening to the two older couples talk, while watching Kris and Michelle who stood apart from the others, their heads close together in private conversation. Her arm was around his waist.

When the announcement for boarding the flight to Istanbul came over the public-address system, Kris leaned on one crutch and put his other arm around Michelle. Drawing her to him, he kissed her.

As the Laurings and Hedleys continued to converse, Katrina's thoughts were on her brother and her roommate. What had that kiss really meant? Was it a polite way for two new friends to express fondness for each other? Perhaps, but she sensed something more than that.

What was going through their minds just now? The sadness of separation after only recently having found each other? Uncertainty over what their new relationship might mean and whether or not it would become something lasting? Would absence truly make the heart grow fonder?

Perhaps these were just her own thoughts, as she considered her relationship with Dr. Ibrahim Mustapha Sevali, son of Mustapha and Sevei, youngest of ten brothers and sisters, all of whom she had yet to meet. What had happened thus far between them was extraordinary. And frightening.

A farm boy from Turkey's rural countryside who grew up near a dot on the map called Lisla, the son of simple, hardworking parents, had become the gentle, brave, and brilliant archaeologist professor from the University of Istanbul. And of this much she was certain. . . . This contradiction to all of her life fantasies and dreams had successfully stolen her heart!

She thought back to the moment of their first meeting.

"Hello," he had said, looking up at her on the paint ladder while he stood in the doorway.

"Oh! You startled me. I didn't know anyone was there," were my first words to you, Ibrahim. How very true they were. I had no idea that anyone was there in my life. Especially anyone like you!

Hugs and kisses all around. A few "mother" tears when Sarah told Katrina how proud she was of her; and promises by everyone to write or call.

A pledge from Pedar to send the girls a modem and computer for Christmas so that they could e-mail their parents.

Katrina and Michelle waving from the concourse window as

the attendant wheeled Kris out to the airplane, with Pedar and Sarah close behind.

The empty feeling that parting brings as they walked back through the passenger terminal to the auto parking lot where the Hedleys had left their car.

Quiet voices.

Little conversation.

Thoughtful looks.

A sigh.

The first signs of love's early feelings about separation and loneliness.

Wednesday, 17 December

ON December 17, the "Letters Commission," as it had been dubbed by the media, completed its work behind closed doors. In an unprecedented move, the chairman of the Commission, Rabbi Mordechai Nowitzky, announced to a waiting media that he had sworn the Commission to secrecy until he and the discoverer of the letters in question, Dr. Ibrahim Sevali, could hold a joint news conference. Though questions were shouted loud and long and on top of one another, Rabbi Nowitzky refused them all, other than to state that the purpose of the delayed news conference, tentatively set for ten o'clock on the morning of December 20, was to make it possible for interested people everywhere to hear the results of their findings at the same time.

"In other words," one reporter said to his colleague, "the wily old fox has managed to turn the tables. Now he is using us for his purposes!"

As the day of the news conference drew near, the approaching Christmas holiday served only to heighten worldwide interest in the matter of "the letters."

It was learned that the Commission had chosen Dr. Cemil Kutlu, Professor of Islamic History and Theology at the University of Istanbul, and Dr. Robert Culpepper, Professor of Archaeology at Eastern Theological Seminary in Philadelphia, to join Rabbi Nowitzky in representing the Interfaith Commission's three major belief systems: Islam, Christianity, and Judaism.

Together with Dr. Bülent Üzünal and Dr. Ibrahim Sevali, they would respond to the press and media corps in attendance. Between December 17 and 20, the Commission's confidentiality remained intact. This served to further heighten world interest in the news conference. The "wily old fox" had clearly pulled one off.

Saturday, 20 December
Ankara

On the morning of December 20, Ankara awakened to a gray-blue dawn as a hard rain fell on the city. A major storm had moved in from the north during the night.

As the ten o'clock hour approached, nature's cold assault was pelting the Atpazari district's streets with enough rain to cause little "runoff" rivers to zigzag crazily along the curbs and gutters. Reporters, camera crews, and invited guests covered their heads as they ran from parking areas to Ankara's Anatolian Civilizations Museum.

The Atpazari, or "horse market" district, is located to the south of Ankara Castle and occupies two renovated Ottoman buildings. The Mahmut Pasha Bedesteni had been built in the fifteenth century and Ankara *sof,* a cloth made from goat or camel hair, was sold here. The Kurshunlu Han wing was originally erected by Mehmet Pasha to provide revenue for his soup kitchen serving the poor and needy in the Üsküdar district of Istanbul. A fire caused the buildings to fall out of use in 1881, and they remained in disrepair until early in the twentieth century when the Museum was established.

The meeting site, originally set for the Museum conference hall, at the last minute had been moved out into the public display area to better accommodate participants and to offer the public a "first presentation" of several articles recently removed from *Kilçilar.*

Rabbi Nowitzky, a portly man whose fleshy face was partially covered with a long gray beard, wore a dark suit that looked shiny in the bright lights of television, making him appear even more uncomfortable than he was.

A reporter from the influential *Yediot Ahronot,* Israel's largest afternoon journal, noted that "as usual, the rabbi's shoes were scuffed and dull and revealed absolutely no propensity toward fashion or good taste whatsoever."

The man's brilliance had earned him the appellation of the "Einstein of Judaism." And like the great mathematician, his shoes were among the least of his concerns.

Lights were turned on, cameras began their incessant whir, pencils and pens raced crazily across notepads as the rabbi walked to a phalanx of microphones at the speaker's podium. As he stepped to center stage, his countenance underwent a subtle change from otherworldliness to that of the benevolent patrician. His eyes twinkled and he smiled, waiting for the crowd to come to some semblance of order.

It reminded Ibrahim of the familiar line drawing of a face that, when held one way looks dour and morose, but when turned upside down appears happy and jovial.

In Katrina's homeroom at the Antalya Girls School, as in classrooms, living rooms, bars, fitness centers, and a hundred other venues around the world, her students watched the conference on television. The rabbi's discourse began in thickly accented English and was translated into scores of other languages, including Turkish.

After a somewhat rambling recounting of the *Kılçilar* project and events leading up to the discovery of the letters, Rabbi Nowitzky introduced Dr. Ibrahim Sevali.

Katrina tried to suppress the smile on her face, but she could not keep back the look in her eyes, as her oldest girls giggled knowingly and nudged one another, while watching the screen's image with one eye and their teacher with the other.

When Dr. Sevali finished his modestly brief comments, he was afforded a standing ovation by the news-hardened media with whom he had rapidly become a favorite, in spite of his firm regulation of their access to *Kılçilar.* Although firm, he had been uncompromisingly fair.

Rabbi Nowitzky waited, seemingly unmoved, his gaze fixed on an invisible dot somewhere above the heads of today's constituents, as quiet once again settled on the scene.

"And now," he announced, with a dramatic flourish of his hand, "what you have all been waiting for. The report of the

Interfaith Commission on the *Kilçilar* Letters. Printed copies of what I will be referring to are being passed among you at this moment. Please, one only per person. When I am finished, time will be given for questions that may be directed to me or to my two respected Commission colleagues, Dr. Kutlu and Dr. Culpepper, as well as to Dr. Üzünal and Dr. Sevali, for whom we all hold the deepest and the highest respect as colleagues and professional gentlemen.

"Permit me to dispense with some of the initial paragraphs that name the Commission's members and their qualifications. I would simply remind you that this was a nine-member Commission, made up of three Muslim, three Jewish, and three Christian representatives whose religious background and professional expertise acquitted them as worthy to serve mankind in discerning the truth about the *Kilçilar* letters. I will begin reading at page four, paragraph two."

Rabbi Nowitzky paused until the rustle of pages had subsided before proceeding to read the text of the letters themselves, explaining as he did some of the controversial nuances and their potential impact on Christian church doctrine and on traditionally accepted biblical teachings related to the divinity of Jesus Christ.

As she watched, Katrina could not fail to see the humor in a Jewish rabbi taking pains to give a clear presentation of a Christian doctrine. He paused on one occasion to wipe his brow under the hot lights, wink at Dr. Culpepper, and say to his audience that he wished his Christian friend had volunteered for what he had been nominated to do.

"As a Commission, our ultimate purpose has not been to prove or disprove Christianity's long-held views concerning the deity of Jesus Christ, but rather to deal with the problem of authenticating these particular documents by answering questions of dating, style, and content.

"In cases such as this, the problem of dating is basically fourfold in nature. It has to do with accurately establishing the date of the composition of the work in question; the period when any presently available copies were made; the date to be given to the linen in which manuscripts are often wrapped; and, in this case, the actual time when the jar was deposited in the church at the underground city known as *Kilçilar.*

"Stylistic issues and matters of similarity or dissimilarity come into play when other known writings are attributed to the same person. In this case, there are two such letters that for centuries have been widely attributed to the Apostle Peter.

"In light of all this, the Commission wishes to make known its unanimous verdict regarding the veracity of the two specific letters in question:

"It is our *unanimous* conclusion that the letter purported to be written by the Apostle Peter, the same man credited with writing two New Testament letters in the Christian Bible, *is a complete forgery!*"

An explosion of excited voices overwhelmed the rabbi, causing him to pause once more until order had been restored. He smiled congenially and without reprimanding their interruption before continuing:

"I will now call to your attention the main points undergirding the Commission's reasoning leading to this finding. Dr. Culpepper is an expert in the field of carbon-14 dating and can answer any technical questions you may have regarding this first point.

"1. Various tests were scientifically administered by the independent Keitzel Institut in Frankfurt, Germany, using portions of the linen material which Dr. Sevali found wrapped around the letters, and portions of the parchment on which the letters were written, as well as portions of the ink itself.

"The pieces of linen removed from the letters proved to be of local manufacture, and were dated by means of the radiocarbon method of computation. Simply stated, carbon-14 is based on the idea that every living organism contains some amount of this radioactive material. The material degenerates when the species dies. It is a reasonably accurate science, though there is a small margin of error, and the scientific community has declared that the present range of measurement does not exceed 30,000 years.

"Dr. F.R. Hittleman who tested the *Kilçilar* linen and parchment at the Institute, announced that it ceased to absorb carbon-14 in A.D. 323, with a plus or minus range of 200 years, furnishing a range from 123 to 523. The traditionally accepted date for Peter's death is A.D. 64, during the Neronic persecutions. Given that date, or any other that could be considered as even remotely attached to his death, it would have been impossible for

410

him to write the *Kilçilar* letter on parchment that was not made before 123, and probably much later.

"2. The actual time of placing the letters into the jar and the jar in the cave church is less easy to establish. The second letter identifies its author as one 'Auderius of Antioch' and establishes the time of its composition as sometime prior to the Council of Nicea in 325. Yet the church in which these letters were found was not established before the sixth century, at the earliest, and perhaps as late as the seventh century.

"If I might digress for a moment from the report, Dr. Sevali has put forth an interesting theory to the Commission that seeks to answer this question by suggesting that the cave in which the church exists was likely to have been at one time a shelter for shepherds or perhaps even a hideaway for robber bands known to have plagued the Silk Road trade route during this era.

"When the Commission visited the site, Dr. Sevali pointed out several pegs in the wall near the doorway of the church. He knew of no Christian ritual that would place them there, a fact corroborated by the Christian members of the Commission.

"Dr. Sevali suggests that those pegs predated the use of the room as a church to a period in which animals were tethered by earlier inhabitants, a theory which, if true, lends further credence to his thesis that some follower of Christ may have found the jar, discovered its contents, and for fear of the impact such a letter would have on the Church Council or on the belief system of succeeding generations of Christians, hid it in the cave. Or, possibly it was taken in a raid and left behind as worthless by outlaw bandits who used the cave as their hideaway.

"Dr. Sevali further theorizes that the unfinished wall behind the altar was left this way because the jar had been rediscovered at a later time by the Christian inhabitants, its contents read and returned to its hiding place. When members of the Commission asked Dr. Sevali why it was not destroyed, he suggested that it might have been for the same reason that pre-Christian idols, figurines, and other artifacts were stored instead of being destroyed. Not everyone in that era was primitive and superstitious. Some of those living then appear to have had the same sense of history that we possess today!

"Dr. Sevali's thesis regarding these matters does seem to have some verification from a parchment diary discovered in the sepulcher, about which you men and women have been writing much in recent days. The author's name remains forever lost to antiquity.

"The parchment on which he inscribed his diary of events lived out in this underground city, and the linen wrap in which it was preserved, ceased to absorb carbon-14 in A.D. 758 with the usual plus or minus range of two hundred years. In this diary, his mention of 'the letters' may possibly be attributed to the ones that are before us, though that cannot be definitely confirmed.

"While we are the first to admit that Dr. Sevali's theories are still just that, only theories, we accept them as plausible explanations until evidence of another kind dislodges this logic."

"3. There are numerous stylistic differences, as well as significant content contradictions between the two letters currently recognized as having been written by Peter, and the letters examined by this Commission. Dr. Culpepper can fill you in on those after I have finished. Perhaps Dr. Kutlu will have some things to add in this regard as well.

"The final and most incontrovertible evidence, however, has been determined by a careful analysis of the handwriting on both letters. In the report before you, it is listed as Item 4, and concludes as follows:

"We are unable to compare the handwriting or signature on the *Kilçilar* letter with historically verifiable evidence of Peter's own handwriting. We did, however, compare the first letter discovered by Dr. Sevali with the second. The experts in this field whom we called upon are listed at the bottom of this page. They have concluded that there is more than sufficient evidence to indicate that both letters were authored by the same hand. Since 'Auderius of Antioch' claims to have written the second letter to his friend 'Eusebius, Bishop of Nicomedia,' we may now assume that it was he himself who forged the first letter.

"We may also assume that it was his intent to sway delegates present at the 325 Council in Nicea with a falsified document, in hope of undermining opposition to his friend Arius, as well as to his teachings.

"These facts are verified to be the true and accurate findings and expression of the Commission, and represent the unanimous consensus of its members."

Ward Tanneberg

Rabbi Nowitzky wiped his brow with a handkerchief and shuffled the papers from which he had been reading. Looking up, he added, "You see the date of the Commission's findings, together with the signatures of all nine representatives, three Muslim, three Christian, and three Jewish. That these letters are ancient forgeries is categorically undeniable.

"With an integrity and professional expertise that sets him among the leading archaeologists of this modern era, Dr Sevali has done us all a service. He could have hidden or destroyed these documents. He could have turned them over to one or the other of the Christian, Jewish, or Muslim communities, and taken the chance that we might twist them to our own respective likings."

He looked around with eyes crinkled in amusement. "Not that any of us would ever stoop to such a mendacious act!"

Laughter filled the room.

"Thank you, Dr. Sevali. It was at your insistence that the Anatolian Civilizations Museum, together with the generous assistance of the Turkish government, established this historic Interfaith Commission. And thanks to those who worked with you in bringing the truth to light.

"It goes without saying, but I will say it anyway. We need never fear the truth and we must always pursue it no matter where it leads! Truth is not something that substitutes one person's view for that of another. Truth cannot be one thing to the scientist and something other to the philosopher. Truth is not that which makes the Christians right and others wrong. Nor can it be separated from man's innate moral judgment.

"Truth is truth! In its purest and most unadulterated form, true truth transcends the scientist's theories and the philosopher's postulates and the religionist's theologies. Truth simply is!

"Unfortunately, our society today has become the victim of 'truthettes.' [Laughter] We say to each other, 'If it is truth to you, then it is true.' Ladies and gentlemen of the world, truth does not begin or end in you and me. Truth does not float through the air like pollen. It must be rooted and grounded in something or someone or it cannot be truth. This is so in science. In history. In religion. Or, as in our case today, in the findings of archaeology. I say again, truth is that essential something in life we need never fear and that we must always pursue. No matter where it leads us.

"Truth forever and always!" The rabbi's fist shot into the air suddenly, like a punctuation mark. "This concludes my remarks. I now turn our meeting over to Dr. Kutlu."

With that he stepped away from the podium.

His audience sat in stunned silence, completely absorbed in the old rabbi's words and the emotion and power with which he delivered them.

In the third row of reporters, a man laid his pen and notepad in his lap and put his hands together in a slow, thoughtful applause.

A woman two rows over joined in.

A man in the second row, left side, wearing a beard and a Jewish yarmulke on his head, stood to his feet and began applauding vigorously.

The short, heavyset woman seated next to him, wearing thick glasses and a raincoat she had not removed during the entire session, stood as well. And so it went, like dominoes . . . until the room was filled with applause.

Some cameras followed Rabbi Nowitzky while he shook hands with Kutlu, Culpepper, Üzünal, and Ibrahim. Others panned across an audience now standing on its feet.

"There is no shouting, stomping, hooting, or yelling," said one news commentator, as he tried to describe the moment. "The mood here can only be described as respectful. Admiring. There is almost a sense of awe in this place, if you will. Everyone seems to have been caught up by the rabbi's simple profundity.

"It's amazing, isn't it, that in life's constant hustle, in jockeying for the best positions, in making certain our viewpoints are heard and believed by those who have none better, we find ourselves brought to a halt in the rain-drenched city of Ankara, Turkey by an old, gray-bearded Jew in a suit that shines, wearing shoes that don't.

"'Truth is truth,' the rabbi said. 'Truth simply *is.*' And as we consider his words, the question that must surely trouble the conscience of every member in the human family is, 'How could we ever have forgotten this?'"

At last the applause died away. People returned to their seats. The room became silent once again, but not for long. Photographers began snapping pictures. Reporters scribbled notes. Dr.

Kutlu assumed the podium and opened the question/answer session. Hands were up now as questions were shouted and each reporter tried to be heard above the others.

Ibrahim was not sure that anyone else saw it.

The heavyset woman had been looking at the Jewish man next to her for several seconds. All at once, she reached out and took his hand. He glanced at her in surprise and started to pull away. It was the look on her face that stopped him. He obviously felt something in the way she was smiling at him. He responded with a smile of his own and let his hand remain with hers.

Then, the Jew looked to his left where a man in a dark suit and clerical collar was busy placing his thoughts on paper before they were forgotten. The badge he wore identified him as a member of the Vatican press. The Jew reached over and tapped the priest, then extended his hand, palm up.

He was greeted by the same look of surprise that he had given the woman whose hand he was holding. Then the priest grinned, put down his pen, and grasped the Jew's hand tightly. For several seconds they sat this way, looking at each other, smiling, holding hands, bridging centuries of mistrust, animosity, and separation, before releasing their handholds and turning attention back to the podium and the real reason they were there.

Was it the real reason? Ibrahim thought.

Or had the real reason for this day just occurred in front of him as reporters from Vatican City and from Israel's *Ha'aretz* daily and from Istanbul's *Hürriyet* held one another's hand, looked into each other's eyes, smiled and, for a brief moment, forgot their prejudices and differences and remembered they were children of the Creator?

If only the moment could last long enough for them, for us all, to honestly seek the truth together, mused Ibrahim.

True truth. Truth that simply is!

Fifty-nine. Katrina

Tuesday, 23 December
Antalya—Los Angeles

She knew it was in her carryon, but she reached in front of her to double-check anyway. She smiled as she saw it there, inside the zippered section. It was only a letter, but it was from one important person in her life to another, and she felt like a courier who had been entrusted with a secret message.

The early morning THY flight from Antalya to Istanbul had gone off without a hitch. The airplane on which she had been a passenger was only half full and on time.

When Michelle and Katrina said good-bye at the Antalya airport, Michelle handed her the envelope with "Kris Lauring— personal" attractively scrolled in calligraphy.

"I'll see that he gets it as soon as we arrive in L.A.," Katrina promised.

Michelle hugged her.

"You won't forget?"

"I won't forget."

"Thanks. Tell him . . ." she hesitated, "that I enjoyed the time we had together. Very much!"

"I will."

"And tell him . . . just say that I hope we can do it again sometime."

Katrina smiled and hugged her again.

"I wish you were going with us, Michelle."

"I know. But for me, it would be only for pleasure, and right now I cannot afford that much pleasure. For you, it's a necessary trip. You're going to be a big TV star!"

"And you'll be the first woman president of France!" Katrina retorted. "Anyway, Ibrahim will be the one Kris talks to the most on this network special of his. I'll bring back a tape of the show so you can see it. Thank goodness the holiday means I'll not be missing more class time doing this. I wonder now and then if the Hedleys wish they had asked someone else to teach this year instead of me."

"The Hedleys love you, Katy, and they are so proud of you," Michelle responded enthusiastically. "And besides, a member of the Antalya Girls School faculty is about to be on national TV. Talk about publicity. The whole world will know about us after this!"

"That's probably true and it's one reason I said I would do it."

"And the other reason is waiting for you in Istanbul, oui?"

Katrina smiled and felt her face grow warm.

"Are you blushing, mon amie?" teased Michelle. "Mais oui, you are in love and you are blushing!"

"Be serious," Katrina said with an embarrassed laugh, as she glanced at her watch. A moment later, her flight was called.

"I've got to go. I love you," she said, kissing Michelle on the cheek. "I'll see you on New Year's Eve. Bye."

In Istanbul, Katrina transferred from Yesilköy to Atatürk International where Ibrahim was waiting at the Alitalia ticket counter. Ninety minutes, and two cups of hot tea later, they were in the air and on their way to Rome, New York, and Los Angeles.

"An important letter, Kat?" Ibrahim had been watching as she looked into the carryon.

"Not as important as some letters we know about," Katrina replied, "but important to at least two people."

"Yes, I understand. And I think one of those people will be very happy to hear from the other."

"I think you're right. Anyway, I don't want to lose it. I may be delivering mail from my future sister-in-law."

Ibrahim chuckled and shifted toward her in the seat.

"We have written many important letters as well these last weeks, would you agree?" he asked, reaching for her hand.

"Actually, yes," Katrina smiled warmly. "I would agree. And they have been very nice. Especially your last one."

Ibrahim glanced away, smiling, a bit embarrassed as he remembered.

"I didn't write you a letter for this day, Kat, but there *is* something I'd like for you to know."

At that moment, the flight attendant appeared and began removing their meal trays. Katrina leaned back in her seat and peeled the wrapper from a dinner mint. Ibrahim waited until she had placed the mint in her mouth. Then he took her hand again.

"I'm used to giving speeches to large groups and standing before my classes at the University, but I find myself at this moment feeling very awkward and incompetent. There's much that I wish to say, yet the right words are difficult to find."

Katrina shifted so that she could look directly into his face.

"We've known each other now for only a few months," Ibrahim continued, "but you must admit that we've been through a lot together. In fact, it's hard for me to comprehend sometimes just how much. I lie on my bed and remember your face in the matchlight, as we sat waiting to be rescued. It's like a portrait in my mind. I'll never forget the way you looked. So weary and dirty and scruffy . . . and so beautiful."

Katrina smiled, recalling her own matchlight thoughts, but did not interrupt.

"I've grown to admire you so very much. No, that is not exactly true. At least, it's not all of it. What I'm trying to say, my dearest Kat, is that I have fallen in love with you."

The plane suddenly grew silent. There were no other voices competing to be heard. The drone of engines thrusting them through the night sky was gone from their hearing. They were two people, suddenly alone in the universe, floating on a magic carpet!

Or so it seemed to Katrina. Ibrahim's dark eyes were tender in their gaze, like pools of deep water, drawing her until she felt completely lost somewhere inside of him. She moved her other hand across the armrest and placed it in his. Her gaze did not waiver from his own as she whispered her answer.

"And I have fallen in love with you."

To her surprise, Ibrahim dropped back in his seat and let out a sigh of relief. "I was not certain. I thought perhaps . . . that is, I hoped . . . "

"That I'd tell you I love you?" she finished. "Ibrahim, I've been attracted to you since the day we first met."

"But when did you know, really?" he asked, leaning toward her again. "Was there a moment? A lightning bolt in the night? Or has it been a gradual awareness?"

. "Some of each of those things," Katrina replied, her eyes shining with happiness at having just declared her love. "Your touch. Our first kiss beneath that beautiful mosaic of Jesus. Times I've had alone to think about what I see in you. Your courage, your integrity, your passion for what you do.

"But, I think that I first knew I loved you when we were trapped underground in that little space, after the explosion. I was so afraid that you were dead, or that you soon might be. And I knew then how much that frightened me. Not just the thought of being alone, buried alive beneath more than a hundred meters of dirt and stone. It was the thought of you no longer being a part of my life.

"Then, after we got out safely, I began having second thoughts. I was uneasy. It's a big thing, Ibrahim, and I still wasn't absolutely sure."

"When did that happen?" Ibrahim asked, leaning toward her.

"This morning. On the flight to Istanbul. My initial fear was that I had experienced what soldiers used to call 'foxhole religion.' I kept asking myself whether our trauma simply pointed up my need to be loved by someone. Was it a 'dying wish' sort of thing that would fade when life returned to normalcy? But this morning, it all seemed to click into place.

"And when I saw you in the airport, I couldn't believe the feeling I had. My heart began beating faster. Honestly! It did! Like one of my high school girls. And I thought then that we might be having this conversation."

"You're not only beautiful and brilliant," Ibrahim smiled as he lifted her hands to his lips, "but you are psychic as well."

"No," Katrina responded, leaning her head back against the

cushion, "not psychic. Just in love. So very deeply in love!"

Their voices were low. There was no wish to disturb the other passengers with a conversation meant only for two. Now a delicate silence covered the space between them as what had just been declared was folded into their hearts.

Ibrahim reached out to draw her closer when she placed a hand on his shoulder. A resisting hand. He stopped short.

"This is why you must hear me out, my dearest. I've never felt for anyone the feelings I have for you. I've never before made such a declaration of my heart to another. I've never loved a man before. Not emotionally . . . or physically. It's important to me that you know this."

Ibrahim did not move as Katrina went on.

"It's also important for you to know that I have spoken to God about this as well. For years, I've told Him that He must be the one to introduce me to His choice for my life, if it is His will that I should someday fall in love and marry. My only request was for that person to be someone I could love and respect without any hesitation. Someone I could admire and serve as one equal serves another."

Katrina turned now so that she faced Ibrahim directly. She lifted the armrest back into the seat and curled her knees against him.

"All of this and so much more I have found in you, my love, except . . . "

She paused.

"Except?" Ibrahim's face was that of a man who has been thrown a life preserver only to have it suddenly deflate in front of him.

"I love you deeply and respect and admire you more than I ever thought possible for anyone to do. You're everything I've asked God for—except for the 'hesitation' part in me that acknowledges that you are a Muslim and I am a Christian."

Katrina paused again, her eyes never leaving Ibrahim's.

"That's it?" he asked. "That is your hesitation? That I am Muslim and you are Christian?"

"Yes," she answered softly.

"But this is not a problem, Kat. A Muslim can marry a Christian."

"Was that a proposal?" she smiled coyly.

Ibrahim laughed nervously.

"No, it was not deserving of such a name. But there is one in my heart for you."

"O Ibrahim," she sighed. "I want so much to say yes to all you are leading up to. I want to, but I can't. At least, not yet."

"Why? What could possibly be wrong with our being in love?"

"You said a moment ago that it was all right for a Muslim to marry a Christian."

"Yes. Of course."

"Didn't you mean that it's all right for a Muslim *man* to marry a Christian *woman?*"

Ibrahim was suddenly silent as he sat back in his seat.

"Would it be acceptable in your family and in your religion for one of your sisters to marry a Christian man?"

Ibrahim did not answer immediately. Instead, he stared at Katrina with uncertainty. There was an ever-so-slight hint of hurt and anger in his voice when he finally asked, "What are you driving at, Kat? Where is this going?"

"Let me try to explain," she answered. "The Christian Bible offers a very important question. It asks, 'Can two walk together except they be agreed?' I know that we can easily agree on many things, perhaps most things. But there is one so major that we dare not overlook it or just assume it'll work itself out. Already, just admitting its existence is causing tension between us.

"You see, Ibrahim, it may be all right for a Muslim man to marry a Christian woman. But, according to the teachings of Scripture, it's not all right for a Christian woman to marry a Muslim man. Or anyone, in fact, except another follower of Jesus. The Bible says that a man or a woman should not be 'unequally yoked' with an unbeliever. How much more 'yoked' together can two people be than in a marriage?

"It's true that often after a marriage is consummated, one person becomes a believer while the other is not. In that case, the Bible says that if the unbelieving partner is willing, the believer is to remain true to the marriage bond. But it's not wisdom for a believer to knowingly marry an unbeliever and, in all likelihood, be the central cause for emotional pain and spiritual dissension as they attempt to go through life together, marching to different drumbeats. Do you understand?"

"But I am a believer," Ibrahim insisted.

"Yes, you are, and one whom I thoroughly respect. But consider Jesus with me for a minute. You see Him as one of the prophets. I see Him as the Son of God. You view Jesus as a man only, one who did not really die on the cross for man's sin. I see His death on the cross as both an historical fact and as the divine sacrifice for the sins of the world. Your sins, Ibrahim, and mine too."

"But you are not a sinner, Kat! You are a good person. The finest person I've ever known."

"Ah, but I am a sinner. Here's another one of those tension-producing issues. The theologians refer to it as 'original sin,' the idea being that we're all born into the world with a 'sin nature' and a propensity toward sinning. As a Muslim, perhaps you do not believe in this sin that requires a divine Savior, but I do.

"I need a Savior, one who can forgive me my sins and admit me into the family of my Heavenly Father. Jesus did that for me. I've come to respect much that Mohammed and the Koran has taught you. In some ways it's very much the same as I've been taught. But when it comes to Jesus, there is this huge gulf between us.

"There's something else too. While it's permissible for a Muslim man to marry a Christian woman, how are the children to be reared in matters of faith? As Muslims or as Christians?"

"I would permit you to do as you saw best," answered Ibrahim.

"Still, if your children were raised as Christians by your Christian wife, how would that be viewed in your Muslim world? By your family? Your friends? The people with whom you work professionally? I think it would not be looked upon with great favor. Am I right?"

Ibrahim did not answer.

"You believe God has called you to be an archaeologist. I believe that too. You have all the gifts and skills that God could ever give to one man for such a calling. And, as we have recently seen, your calling is important to those pursuing truth, to those who would follow after our God.

"But I believe that He's called me to teach His Word. I mean by that, the message found in the Old and New Testaments of the Christian Bible, Ibrahim. Would you expect me to give up my calling?"

He shook his head slowly.

"And I certainly don't expect you to give up archaeology to

follow me wherever I choose to go. So where does this leave us?"

"I'm closer to being a Christian than when we first met," Ibrahim responded lamely.

"And I'm more deeply appreciative of the Koranic teachings since knowing you," Katrina answered. "But does that make me a Muslim? It's a little like the Roman king in the Bible whose name was Agrippa. One minute he was shouting at the Apostle Paul, 'Your great learning is driving you insane.' He argued with Paul and finally said, 'Do you think that in such a short time you can persuade me to be a Christian?' And do you want to know what Paul answered?"

Ibrahim nodded weakly, not at all sure that he really did.

"Paul said, 'Short time or long—I pray God that not only you but all who are listening to me today may become what I am, except for these chains.'"

Ibrahim sat silent, reflective for a long moment. Finally he said, "I'm not ready to say that Jesus is divine—that He is God and not simply one of the great prophets."

"I know," Katrina said softly, her eyes filling with tears. "And I cannot say anything other."

"And for this you would turn our love away?"

"I would lay down my life for you, my dearest," said Katrina, as tears spilled on her cheeks. "I love you that much. I would follow you anywhere and do anything you asked . . . except disobey my Lord Jesus Christ or throw away His truth. Ibrahim, if you truly love me, you cannot ask me to do that."

She lowered her head and snuggled down against Ibrahim, her arm over his chest, and hid her tears in the folds of his sweater. The plane droned on now, the sound of its powerful engines unvarying and steady in her ears. Voices filtered across the aisle and into the seats that had moments before been their own private world. They did not speak for a long time. Katrina wondered if Ibrahim had fallen asleep, but didn't move to look.

"I'm not ready to say He's not either."

"What?" Katrina lifted her head and looked at Ibrahim.

"I said that I'm not ready to say He is not the divine Son of God."

Katrina remained silent.

"I'm thinking about what you've said. I am also reminded of

something Dr. Üzünal told me before his surgery. There's much to think about. But, if I were to acknowledge that He is the divine Son of God, as you say, I can assure you of this—it would be because I knew it was true. I will never 'convert' just to trick you into a marriage. Do you believe me?"

"I do," she answered. Then thinking how much that sounded like the wedding vow she held in reserve in her heart, she quickly added, "I do believe you."

Katrina took his hand in hers.

"We understand each other then? I've not hurt you with my honesty about my love for Jesus being greater than my love of parents . . . or my brother, Kris . . . or even my love for you?"

Ibrahim smiled and kissed her forehead.

"We understand each other," he replied. "In the days that are before us, we will search our hearts and our faith in the God of our fathers. You seem much stronger in your beliefs than I am in mine. But, I will not easily abandon them. I will, instead, sincerely seek the truth . . . not in the name of Islam or Christianity or Judaism or any other religion. Just true truth. And since it's you who have made this a necessity, I'll begin with the things you believe. Are you willing to join me in this search? Or are you afraid?"

Katrina laughed and sat upright.

"In the words of the great Rabbi Nowitzky, 'We need never fear the truth. And we must always pursue it no matter where it leads. Truth forever and always!'" Katrina's fist punched the air as she mimicked the good rabbi's Ankara performance.

Ibrahim leaned forward until his lips touched first one eye, then the other.

"Kissing the iris of your eye," he said softly, "is an ancient Turkish custom between lovers."

"Is it now?" Katrina said demurely, her eyebrow arching suspiciously. "And does this custom date back to the Ionians or the Hittites? Or does it go all the way back to the Stone Age when your men dragged their women home by their hair?"

"We're still unclear on the dating of this custom," he said, repeating the tender act once more. "It has been difficult to measure with any degree of accuracy through the carbon-14 process. I'm personally convinced that it will require a good deal more research."

He ran his fingers through her hair.

"It is like hay," he said, "and you have sky eyes."

"Is this more of your ancient Turkish seductiveness?"

"In my country, most of us have dark skin and dark hair. When someone has blond hair like yours, we say that it is like the stacks of hay in the field. And blue eyes are the color of the sky."

"Mmm. I like that. It's very romantic. I should learn more of your sayings. Are you willing to teach me?"

He leaned toward her. "It is my duty and honor," he said with mock seriousness.

"Good. Then there's something you will need to learn as well," she said, her head resting against his shoulder.

"More? There's more already? What is it now?"

"I understand that, in certain circumstances, a Muslim is permitted to have as many as four wives at one time. Unfortunately for you, if some evening you decided to bring home even one other woman, you would not live to see the dawn!"

"That doesn't sound like a very Christian attitude," Ibrahim chuckled, and looked up to see the flight attendant standing at his shoulder with a tray of complimentary soft drinks.

"What would you like?" she asked.

"Someone brave enough to make truth the standard for her love," he answered.

The startled attendant glanced over at Katrina.

"I'll have a Coke," she replied.

Epilogue

"Are you ready, sis?"

"Are you serious, Kris? I don't know how you do this!"

"It's just a matter of lining up your butterflies and then keeping them in formation."

"Easy for you to say. Where's Jack? Why isn't he with us?"

"Stand over here and look. Here, let me part this curtain a bit. See? Beyond the stage to the audience? First row, left hand side. He's standing by Camera 4, looking up into the balcony and talking to someone on his headset, probably one of the other cameramen."

"Yes, I see. But why isn't he with us?"

"He normally doesn't work the studio floor. His specialty is outside news and field projects. I asked him to join us, but he wouldn't. He said this was as close as he was getting, and no amount of prodding or threats would make him do what you guys are about to do."

"Thanks for telling us that now!"

"I guess the only place he feels really at home is behind a camera. Like I said, he doesn't usually come inside, but he signed on for tonight's special as soon as he arrived back in the country."

"Isn't that the man you introduced us to this afternoon? Tom Knight? Standing over there by the woman with her back to us. He's certainly . . . an interesting character."

"You could say that. He and Carole are making sure everything is ready. She's our assistant producer-director."

"Wait a minute. Did you say, 'Carole?' Is she . . . "

"Right. One and the same. Were those two made for Hollywood or what? Whatever else though, they're professionals. And a lot is riding on tonight."

"What do you mean?"

"You can sum those two up in one word, Kat. Ratings. That's what this is all about, as far as they're concerned. And tonight should be a good test for the ratings geeks. But don't put them down as totally shallow. A month ago, I thought the same way. What a difference a few weeks can make."

"Two minutes, Kris."

"Thanks, Jill."

"She certainly seems nice."

"Did I introduce you? I can't remember, it's been so hectic with all the last-minute stuff. She's my new assistant. Very sharp. A third-year UCLA drama major. The network hired her as a temp to begin with, and I signed her on permanently last week. She's really good."

Just then a young woman with a hand mirror and a makeup tray tapped Kris on the shoulder.

"What's this? Another mirror check? Go away, Sherri. What you see is what they get. I just have to go out and do my stuff, that's all. They don't really care how I look anyway. Except maybe for Tom and Carole. No, forget the 'maybe' part. As far as those two are concerned, image really is everything! Hey, I'm sorry, guys. Don't mind me. I know I'm running off at the mouth, but it settles me into a groove. Okay?"

"No problem," Kat and Ibrahim answered simultaneously.

"Good, because, to tell you the truth, I am a little nervous. Actually, I'm a *lot* nervous! This live-to-tape one-hour special during what's normally television's deadest week is a really big gamble, as far as the network execs are concerned. Even if it is Sunday night.

"So I tell them, 'Look, after Christmas it's mostly old movie reruns and holiday bowl games, so don't worry. Be happy. Besides,' I say, 'this is not going to be your average throwaway special. It's got all the elements for a genuine blockbuster.'

"It does too, if we don't mess it up. I used to think God probably never watched TV, but I'll bet He's tuned in tonight. Talk about your Producer-Director! It feels like He's been orchestrating this whole thing right from the beginning, you know? Well, maybe He has. I'll tell you this much—if media hype is any indication, then the channel surfers are stopping here tonight to spend sixty minutes with us!

"I guess you know, Ibrahim, having your face on the covers of both *Time* and *Newsweek* with you as their lead story hasn't exactly hurt us. That's exciting stuff! And you and Kat looked great together in that *Newsweek* photo in front of the cave. Our show featured on the entertainment page of both magazines isn't the worst free publicity we could have come up with, either. This is a crazy business, isn't it? But then this is a crazy world!"

"Can you see the others from where you're standing, Kris?"

"Sure. They're in the front row, waiting for the show to begin. K.C. got in this afternoon from Belfast. You'll get to talk with him after the show. We're all going out to dinner. And my other guests that I thought I'd *never* get? You should have seen them. They were having the greatest time when I went out a few minutes ago to kibitz with the audience."

"How did it feel out there?"

"Really good, Ibrahim. I think it helps people get into the show by meeting with them in advance. I always did it in San Francisco, but this is my first opportunity here in L.A. I was worried a little about this scar being a distraction, but you can't even see it unless you're up close. It's healed pretty well and my hair has almost grown all the way back. And Sherri did a good job on it in Makeup. It's still tender to the touch, though, believe me."

"You're navigating quite well."

"Thanks. I'm pleased with the way it's going so far. In fact, tonight I'm actually walking on stage with the help of a cane. Can you believe it? At least I've tossed the crutches, but it's still not exactly what I had envisioned for my first go on national TV."

"One minute, Kris!"

"Gotcha. I'm ready. Okay. It's 'arrow prayer' time, guys. Here, let's hold hands. We are ready, aren't we, God? This seems like it's been slammed together really fast, though I suppose You don't think so. You've been sitting on this one for a long time, haven't You? I know it's all a part of Your 'bigger story,' so help us do You justice in the telling tonight. Okay? Amen."

"Fifteen seconds!"

"Would you listen to that music? This new band leader is really good. He's not exactly playing from the hymnbook, but, wow . . . "

"And now, here he is . . . "

"There's Carole starting my intro."

"Here, Kris. Let me straighten your tie."

" . . . having only recently arrived home in Los Angeles from the mystical and mysterious heartland of the Republic of Turkey . . . "

"Thanks, sis. Well, who'd ever have thought I'd be doing my first special about a homely little hill half a world away, that nobody ever heard of until a few weeks ago?"

" . . . our host for tonight's network special and the star of our new early evening show . . . "

"All right, everybody. Here I go! See you in a couple of minutes."

"I'd tell you to 'break a leg,'" exclaimed Jill, pulling the curtain just far enough back to let me through, "but I guess you've already done that!"

I couldn't help but laugh. It's exactly what I needed. My butterflies suddenly shaped up and looked like geese heading south for the winter. I was still laughing as I made my way around the curtain and waved to an audience already on its feet, yelling and clapping and stomping as I came onto the stage.

They were great. They did it every bit as well as when Carole rehearsed them through this "spontaneity" ten minutes earlier!

"Hi, everybody! It's great to be with you tonight on this first special edition of *Pursuit* . . . a show we've designed for children, parents and grandparents alike. Starting the first week of January, we'll be with you for one hour, every evening, Monday through Friday. It's part of a giant media plot. [laughter]

"One of the hardest things we had to do, which tells you just

Pursuit

how easy it is to be in this business, was coming up with a name for this show. I wanted to call it the "KL Show," like where I came from in San Francisco. Hey, all you guys up north. How's it going in the City by the Bay?

"Well, anyway, after weeks of arguing, discussing and just plain cussing [laughter] the best network minds came up with "Kris!" Now, how's that for creative genius? [laughter/hoots]

"Finally, as you can see, we managed to find a name that I think really says what we're about here. In fact, I think it says what *all* of us are about every single day of our lives.

"So . . . welcome to 'Pursuit!' [loud applause]

"We've decided that if we can't get the family together in front of the fireplace anymore, we'll try the tube instead. We'll give you something to laugh at that's clean, something to think about that stirs your brain cells up a little, and something besides sitcoms and old movies to talk about around the office cooler in the morning. [cheers and applause]

"'Pursuit' will give us the opportunity to become acquainted with men, women and young people the world over who are in pursuit of truth. We'll talk to the scientist and the philosopher as well as the actor and singer. We'll meet business people and professionals from all walks of life. We'll talk to theologians and comedians . . . some of whom may be one and the same, I don't know. [laughter] We'll meet some fascinating young people and some super seniors along the way too, all coming at life from their own unique vantage points. We'll take a look at what's happening in the news each day and roll it up in a little different wrapper.

"Will Rogers used to do this all the time. We still laugh at dinner shows and stage presentations of that Oklahoma cowboy's insightfully witty and humorous way of looking at his world. I know, I know. Some of you seniors out there are already saying, [southwestern drawl] 'I knew Will Rogers, young fella, and you're no Will Rogers!' [laughter and applause] Yes, yes, I know. But you get the idea. Anyway, enough for now about what we're going to do. Let's turn our attention to why we wanted to get together with you tonight.

"We decided to do a special edition of 'Pursuit' in order to introduce you to some people who've recently been pursuing truth, in spite of great personal danger. You've been reading about them in the newspapers and magazines and you've followed this story on the network news shows. Last week the results of their pursuit were announced in Ankara, the capital city of Turkey.

"And tonight you're going to meet the man who found the famous Letter from the Apostle Peter that everyone has been talking about . . . Dr. Ibrahim Sevali! [thunderous applause] You're also going to meet the young lady who helped rescue them both from a terrorist-inspired cave-in, one hundred ten meters below the earth's surface . . . my own kid sister, Katrina Lauring. [more loud applause]

"And, we have with us tonight an Irishman who means more than life to me personally. This is the guy who barely knew me at the time, but risked his life to save my own skin, and he's here tonight all the way from Belfast, Ireland, Mr. K.C. Murphy! [cheers and applause as the band plays a couple of bars of "Molly Malone"]

"And on Camera 4 is our own Jack Millerton, who made the journey with me and was right there in the thick of it all, from beginning to end. Wave to everybody, Jack! [cheers/applause]

"All right. Well, the incredible underground city of *Kilçilar* is just ahead of us, so let's get started, what do you say? [more applause] But, wait a minute. This is *my* show, so, I can do whatever I want to, right? [cheers and yells] Okay, then. Let me start out by introducing to you two people I once thought I might never be able to do this with . . . but that's a whole other story.

"Hey, everybody, please welcome Sarah and Pedar Lauring, my mom and dad!"

Afterword

Pursuit is a novel that brings together the past and present and reminds us that we are never finished with either one. While the story is set in a real time and place, in certain instances I have taken small liberties with history, but not in such a way as to distort essential historical truth.

The region of Cappadocia has no official existence, yet any Turk knows exactly where it is. Its most interesting inhabitants were not the Seljuks or the Ottomans, but the Christians. The Apostle Paul introduced the Christian message there. It lasted for a thousand years after.

Nature also has had a hand in Cappadocia, making it the incredible landscape that it is today. Ancient volcanic activity spewed lava onto the area, supplying its distinctive topography of soft, porous stone. Wind and rain further shaped the strange conical towers and the "fairy chimneys" one can only marvel at today.

While researching in this region, I visited several Turkish families in their homes, and a Bedouin "black tent" family whom I shall never forget. I saw much of myself in each one of them.

I spent hours in numerous cave churches and a major underground city believed to have served as many as twenty to thirty thousand inhabitants at a time. Originally, only a few buried settlements were thought to exist. Now it is believed there are as many as four hundred such villages, towns, and cities. These things are all true.

There is no real *Kilçilar*, though I have located it in the real Cappadocian triangle of Kayseri, Aksaray, and Nigde. It is a figment of my imagination, but the telling of its story depicts all of these underground memorials that testify to ultimate courage in the pursuit of truth. It reminds us of our brothers and sisters in the human family who never gave up, in spite of incredible obstacles and the most terrible persecutions.

The Council of Nicea did take place in A.D. 325. The man, Arius, and "Arianism" were at centerpoint in the controversy that caused Emperor Constantine to call the council. Lucian of Antioch and Eusebius, Bishop of Nicomedia, were also the real friends of Arius. Auderius is fictional, as are the letters.

In fact, most of the characters in this book are not real, though bits and pieces of people I know are scattered throughout, proving again that to befriend a writer is a dangerous thing.

I would remind young readers that all of us owe so much to people we will never know. In an age more focused on computer games than historical chronicles, it's important to remember that people everywhere have the same desires and dreams as we do. They want to believe life is meaningful; they want a sense of community and deepening relationships; they wish to be appreciated and respected, to be heard, to feel that they are growing in their faith, and to experience the help of someone else in developing that faith.

Never lose sight of that truth.

And never, never give up the *pursuit!*

WT

DID YOU ENJOY THIS BOOK?

To comment on
• Pursuit •
write to:
Ward Tanneberg
P.O. Box 11952
Palm Desert, CA 92255-1952

*

The author of *Pursuit* and other novels
enjoys hearing from readers
throughout America and the world.
Ward Tanneberg has served over thirty-six years in
pastoral ministries.
In addition to his writing activities,
he accepts a limited number of
local church/conference or retreat
engagements each year.

Please use the above address to inquire.

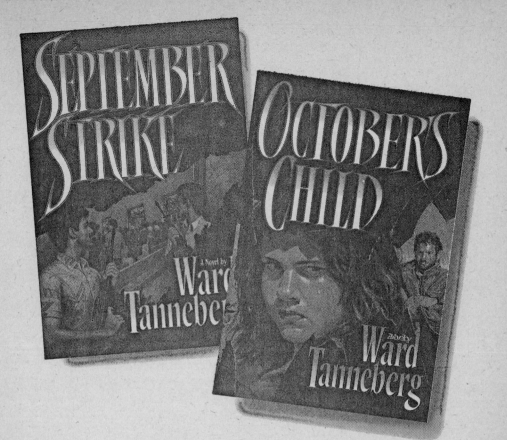

A ruthless world of terrorism threatens to tear the Cain family apart!

Life will never be the same for American pastor John Cain and his family. Unwittingly caught up in the high stakes game of international terrorism, the Cain family struggles for survival.

Look for *September Strike* and its sequel, *October's Child*, in your local Christian bookstore.

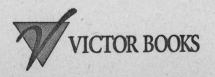

VICTOR BOOKS

What does the future hold for Sgt. Reagan Cole and Beth Scibelli?

The spellbinding adventure and intrigue that surrounds Reagan and Beth will have you racing through the pages of *Millennium's Eve*, *Millennium's Dawn*, and *Doomsday Flight*. Don't miss a single twist or turn as bestselling author, Ed Stewart, weaves his captivating stories.

Look for them at your local Christian bookstore.

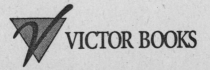

VICTOR BOOKS